Also by Katrina Kittle

Two Truths and a Lie
The Kindness of Strangers

HARPER ◉ PERENNIAL

A hardcover edition of this book was published in 2000 by Warner Books, Inc.

P.S.™ is a trademark of HarperCollins Publishers.

HarperCollins books may be purchased for educational, business, or sales promotional use. For information please write: Special Markets Department, HarperCollins Publishers, 10 East 53rd Street, New York, NY 10022.

FIRST HARPER PERENNIAL EDITION PUBLISHED 2008.

The Library of Congress has catalogued the hardcover edition as follows:
Kittle, Katrina.
    Traveling light / Katrina Kittle.
        p. cm.
    ISBN 0-446-52480-8
    I. Title.
PS3561.I864T73 2000
813'.54—dc21   99-41377

ISBN 978-0-06-145137-9 (Harper Perennial edition)

12 RRD 10 9 8 7 6 5 4

TRAVELING LIGHT

KATRINA KITTLE

HARPER PERENNIAL

NEW YORK • LONDON • TORONTO • SYDNEY • NEW DELHI • AUCKLAND

For my parents,
Butch and Beverly Kittle

Heartfelt thanks
to the following people:

Lisa Bankoff and Claire Wachtel for their faith in me, for their extraordinary efforts on my behalf, and for their shared wisdom on shoes, Italian men, and life in general over strawberry-ricotta pancakes.

The Antioch Writers' Workshop, where this story began in a class taught by the beautiful poet Terry Hermsen and where I learned from many talented writers too numerous to name.

Liz Trupin-Pulli and Diana Baroni, who first gave this book a life.

My two writers' groups, in Yellow Springs and Oakwood—talented, giving people who invested more time and energy in this novel than I can ever repay. You all inspire me.

The brave people who are the staff, volunteers, and clients of the AIDS Resource Center (formerly AFMV), with special love and thanks to Dave Foor and Anne Henry, and to the dedicated case managers I was privileged to work with while writing this novel: Rachael Richter-Hauk, Amanda Malko, Lori Dangler, and Amy Susong.

Dr. Robert L. Brandt Jr. for his commitment and generosity, not only in assisting my research but in his daily work for people living with HIV and AIDS.

Eddie for the gift of the poem "12:01 AM."

The Keilys for my haven of an office during the writing of this novel; everyone who hired me to clean their houses when I left teaching high school; my friends—human and otherwise—at Rocky Point Farm and Hide-Away Stable; Montgomery for the welcome distractions during the long writing hours; Scott Rogers, a one-time intrepid traveling companion, for his support during this process.

Every reader who has ever written me a note and every book club who has ever discussed one of my novels. I'm eternally grateful!

Tina Wexler at ICM, a fellow chocolate lover.

Gregory Kulick for the beautiful cover design, and to Kevin Callahan, Mick Castagna, Samantha Hagerbaumer, Beth Harper, Julia Novitch, and all the amazing people at HarperCollins. I am so fortunate to have their expertise at my back.

My dear friend Michael Kenwood Lippert for the gift of Patience (both big and small).

Monica and Rick Schifflerp for being nothing like the sister and brother-in-law in this book and for acting as my hockey information source.

Mom and Dad (Dad read every single draft) for their unwavering belief in me.

Chapter One

∽

I woke and wondered if my brother was dead; gone before I could keep my promise. He'd been fine last night and was probably fine now, but so many mornings began with new crises, trips to the emergency room, frantic calls to doctors' homes and the pharmacy, that my dread wouldn't release its grip until I saw him and knew for sure.

I sat up and shut off my alarm seconds before it whined, careful not to wake Nicholas beside me. As the percussion of my pulse lessened in my ears, I strained to listen for a clue. I heard only silence outside my bedroom; the silence that had become the sound of Todd's slow death. As my eyes grew accustomed to the dark, I tried to slow my breathing. It was cold—in that lingering, high-ceilinged way of old houses. All this expensive, antique beauty was at the cost of some comfort, but it was my brother's house, not my own, so I didn't complain.

A tentative knocking began along the floorboards, growing slowly bolder, until the radiator groaned, rising to a mournful wail, like lost souls trapped in the walls and floors. When my breathing matched the slow, slumbering rhythm of my lover's beside me, I pushed back the heavy quilt and slid out of bed. I was prepared for the shock of the cold hardwood floor on my bare feet but surprised yet again by the shock of my stiff, injured ankle bearing weight and grabbed a mahogany bedpost to keep from crumpling. I cursed and held the foot off the floor, feeling the throb of it all the way to my shoulder. Balancing on one leg, I reached for the lamp and examined the old surgical scars, vivid blue in the chilly morning air.

I'd lived here only four months, but I'd never woken up and not known where I was. So why was it that I hadn't danced for over three years and still woke up every morning forgetting the reason why?

"You okay, love?" Nicholas asked, sitting. He was used to this morning routine.

I nodded, still frozen, waiting for the throb to subside before trying again.

"Is it my imagination, or is it getting worse?"

"It's this bed," I said, "it's too high. I miss our little mattress on the floor."

"You've got to be kidding. I love this bed." He lay back, stretching out spread-eagle. "I look forward to weekends just so I can be in this bed."

"Hmm. I bet you do." I grinned. I looked forward to weekends, too, but especially so I could sleep. The deep, safe sleep that came to me only when he was here. I rotated my ankle.

"Get back in bed and I'll massage it," he offered, propping himself up on one elbow, his thick-lashed eyes, the chambray blue of old denim, playful and teasing.

"That's so sweet," I said, "but I don't trust you to stop there."

"Well, of course not." We both laughed, and he ran a hand through his soft mess of black curls. "Seriously," he said with a yawn. "You need me to massage it?"

"I think I'm okay." I set my foot down. A couple of *pliés,* a few *tendus,* a cautious *relevé,* and I could walk normally. I tested this by going to the closet.

"Don't get dressed," Nicholas said, but I pulled on Todd's old film school sweatshirt that reached my knees and a pair of his black sweats discarded after his latest weight loss. I'd always been the skinny one of the family, even before I danced, but these sweats fit perfectly, except that I had to roll them twice to cuff their length.

Nicholas watched me dress with such disappointment that I lifted my sweatshirt to give him one last look. The cold air helped make the most of my small breasts, goose-pimpling my flesh, drawing it tight in an appearance of fullness. He laughed.

"I'll be right back," I said. "I just need to check on Todd."

He nodded. "I love you, Summer."

Something swelled within my rib cage, slow and warm, like bread dough rising. "I love you, too." I went back to the bed and kissed him. I left the room, my face tingling from the cat-tongue rasp of his unshaven chin.

In the hall, the winding stairs creaked under my still stiff, uneven gait as I followed the reassuring aroma of hazelnut coffee to the brass-fixtured kitchen. I found Todd working a crossword puzzle at the kitchen table and knew it would be a rare, calm morning. He was wearing jeans and a thick sweater in a shade of gray that made his skin appear transparent. Arnicia, the nursing student who lived with us and took care of Todd in the mornings, sipped coffee beside him, tapping her manicured red nails on the table in a delicate tune.

The door to the master bedroom stood open, and the shower blasted on in the adjoining bathroom. Just above the water rushing came the humming of a familiar movie theme I couldn't quite place.

When Todd looked up from the puzzle, the one eye that could still see sparkled as he flashed me his Auschwitz grin.

"Morning," I said. "Just wanted to see if you were still breathing."

"Sure am, little sister," he said in that voice I hardly recognized since the throat tumor, a deeper, aged distortion of his original voice. I sat down at the table.

"Chemo today?" I asked.

He made a face and nodded. "If I'm allowed. It's up to my white blood cells." Last month, when the oncology staff held his treatment because of low white count, Todd took it as a personal rejection.

"You'll make it," Arnicia assured him, going to the stove to prepare his Cream of Wheat.

I looked at the pale dry skin, the almost bald head, the lifeless eye, and leaned my head on his shoulder, sharp under the camouflaging sweater. "I wish I were seven and you were ten again and we were going to make a blanket tent today."

He laughed, a rattle echoing just beneath it. "Oh, God. Not me. All that teenage angst? I'd have to come out again. No way."

"Maybe this time you could do it a little less dramatically."

Color snuck into his gaunt cheeks, even after all these years. "Thanks, but no thanks. But we can make a blanket tent any time you want, little sister," he said, patting my knee.

"I just meant—"

He snatched my hand and squeezed it. There was a hint of fear in the motion, but his voice was calm. "I know." He smiled. "I know."

The shower stopped, but the humming did not. The humming changed to a theme we recognized, and we laughed. Arnicia's laughter was musical and her mouth hypnotizing to watch. I envied her smooth, cocoa skin and impeccable nails. No matter how little sleep she ran on, or what horrors unfolded, she looked glamorous and serene.

I ran a hand through my still sleep-tangled hair and wondered what I looked like.

The phone rang, and Jacob answered it in the master bedroom. He came into the kitchen, an imposing figure even in his bathrobe, toweling his spiky black hair. He held out the cordless phone to Todd. "It's your grandma Anna, babe."

Todd mouthed the words "Did you talk to her?"

"I said hello." Jacob refused to whisper.

"Say something nice to her," Todd pleaded. "I'll be there in a minute."

Jacob pressed the phone against his chest, muffling the receiver. "I can't think of anything nice to say to her. And my mother taught me that if you can't say anything nice . . . Here." He held the phone out again.

"I'll take it in the bedroom," Todd said. He refused the cordless with a sulk but still paused to kiss Jacob before making his slow, measured way into the bedroom.

Jacob listened on the cordless until Todd picked up in the other room. I watched him, his sharp, chiseled features, the tan Mediterranean look of his skin, the hint of a tattoo peeking from under one sleeve of his robe. Although he was tall and thin, almost comically so, there was a hard, severe edge to his appearance. He scowled as he hung up.

"What did she want?" I asked him.

"I don't know, but it sure wasn't to talk to me."

"I don't get it," I said. "Why is he so nice to her?"

Jacob shrugged. "That's who he is." He paused a moment. "But it doesn't mean that we have to be."

Arnicia hummed her disapproval, still stirring at the stove. "Mmm. That is some mighty bad karma, you all."

Jacob smiled and gave Arnicia a peck on the cheek and a quick grab of the butt. She smacked him with her wooden spoon. He fled from her, laughing, and kissed me on the cheek as well. He was usually gone by this time, off teaching stage combat to the acting majors at the local university, but on chemo days he left his students watching filmed fights and accompanied Todd to the hospital. "Ready to save the youth of America?" he asked me, pouring himself some coffee.

I groaned. "I don't think I'm cut out to be a teacher."

He sat across from me at the table. "If you don't like it, quit. We've got plenty of money, Summer. You know that. It would be great to have you on call for us all the time."

I didn't answer. It was tempting at times, but I couldn't do it. It was bad enough to be the family member described most frequently by "used to," as in "Summer used to be a ballerina," "Summer used to get fan mail," "Summer once got reviewed in *The New York Times*," as though I was already, at twenty-six, a washed-up old eccentric, a novelty to all the young cousins. But to be kept and sheltered seemed even worse. I could just hear Aunt Marnee saying, "Summer used to be a functioning member of society." Besides, I should be able to tackle this. I'd breezed through the teacher certification—my ballet years giving me an edge over the typically distracted, undisciplined college student—and had landed a job within weeks of applying, teaching English at my own old high school, an easy commute from Dayton, where I'd returned to help care for my brother.

But none of that classwork, including student teaching, prepared me for the grueling reality. I'd been shoved onstage to perform a role I'd never rehearsed full out.

"Summer?" Jacob prodded me.

"No thanks," I said. "I want to work." I flexed my ankle under the table. "But I wish I could do something . . . special again, something people notice, not just behind a closed door where nobody knows or cares because I'm just doing what every adult in the building can do better than I can." Jacob leaned back in his chair, putting his bare feet on the edge of the table. I reached across and squeezed his toes, seeking some playful comfort. Looking only at his toes, I said, "I used to define myself by what I did. I could say, 'I'm a dancer.' But I never say, 'I'm a teacher.' I always say, 'I teach high school right now,' like it's some sort of temporary job."

"Well, it is, isn't it?"

I stared at his toes.

"Look," he said, "you think I defined myself as a bartender all those years in L.A?"

I let go of his feet. "That's not the same. You knew you wanted to act. And you were an actor, even if you paid the rent some other way for a while. I just wish I could get my life together like Todd did, you know?"

Jacob laughed. "That was survival, baby. If he was going to keep you all from getting shipped off to foster homes, he had to get his shit together."

I blinked. I didn't know Jacob knew that story. But, of course, Todd would have told him. "We were never really in danger of foster homes," I said. "Not with Grandma Anna there."

"Thanks to Todd," Jacob insisted.

I thought about that. "It shouldn't have been that way. Abby was the oldest."

He snorted. "And? What's your point? Oldest or not, your sister didn't get her shit together."

No. She hadn't. When Mom and Dad took off, Abby opted to go on her overnight cheerleading trip as planned, rather than draw attention to trouble at home.

Todd, only in seventh grade at the time, skipped a hockey tournament so I wouldn't be left on the farm alone. Grandma Anna was off feeding the homeless in Cleveland with her church group that weekend. Todd kept me and the horses fed, and the people who boarded horses at our farm from knowing anything was amiss. Our electricity was shut off; money, as usual, being the root of Mom and Dad's argument in the first place. The darkness slapped the two of us like a sodden horse blanket during our peanut-butter-and-jelly sandwich dinner, and for two nights I followed Todd stall to stall with a flashlight as he double-checked latches and refilled water buckets. We read stories together by candlelight and slept in a blanket tent in the living room to combat the creepiness of the empty farmhouse.

Back then, one of our parents just up and leaving was no big deal. It was usually Mom. Dad was always sort of gone, even when he was home. But they'd never both left us before. We found out later that neither realized the other had left as well. They insisted that they'd never meant to abandon us, only each other. Mom never left again after that, although I sometimes wished she had.

Jacob leaned toward me across the table. "Hello? You in there?"

I shook myself back to the here and now. "Yeah. I just wish I knew what I wanted."

Jacob sipped his coffee and studied me. "What you want," he said, "is to prove something. I just can't figure out what or why."

"I'm not trying to prove anything. It's just—I feel like I had this great example, this role model, but I still can't get it myself. I mean, I always thought Todd knew so much and was so strong because he was older, but here I am, way past the age he got his life together, and I don't know shit."

Jacob pulled his feet back, stood, and dumped his coffee in the sink. He turned and squinted at me. "I really hate it when you talk about him in the past tense."

Arnicia set Todd's cereal aside and poured herself more coffee, clucking her tongue.

"I'm going outside to smoke," Jacob said, leaving in his bare feet and robe. He let the back door slam. No one smoked in the house anymore.

Todd came out of his bedroom, grinning, but it faded as he looked at us. "Whoa. Bad vibes. What's going on?"

Arnicia handed him his bowl and said, "Just Summer and Jake doing that love-hate dance again." Todd rolled his eyes and sat down. Arnicia popped the tab on a can of vanilla Ensure and poured the thick cream in the pattern of a smiling face onto the hot cereal. Todd shook his head, chuckling.

"I can't stand this stuff," he said.

"Really?" Arnicia asked. She took a sip from the can. "Mmm. I like it." She patted her hips. "Not that I need it."

"So, what did Grandma want?" I asked.

Todd smiled and said, "Get this," making sure Arnicia was listening as well. "There's some talk show on this afternoon, where the guest is going to be this woman who's been 'cured' of her homosexuality and she's on a rescue mission to save the rest of us from hell." He cleared his throat and added, "Grandma wanted me to know the time and station."

Arnicia laughed, a lovely melody that I couldn't join.

"God, I hate when she does this shit to you," I said.

"Summer," Todd said. "She's old and . . ." He searched for a tactful word.

"Evil?" I offered.

He sighed and shook his head.

"So, what'd you say to her?" I asked.

"I thanked her for letting me know but told her that wasn't the cure I was interested in."

"I don't know how you do it," I said. Todd shrugged and began to eat.

Arnicia sat back down at the table, looked at her watch, and asked me, "Where's that man of yours?"

"Still in bed."

"Then what are you doing down here? If I had a man like that, I'd never get out of bed."

"Amen," Todd agreed.

"We can't stay in bed all the time," I said, grinning.

"But I noticed," Todd said, "that you did manage to spend most of the weekend there."

"Hey, I only get two days a week until Christmas, so I'm making the most of them." Nicholas was stage-managing a show at the Cincinnati Playhouse-in-the-Park that had turned into a technical nightmare. "Rehearsals are really kicking in, so he can't get away as much." It had been difficult for him to get here at all this week. He'd been paged from the theater twelve times yesterday alone.

I stood and kissed the top of Todd's head. "I've gotta get ready for work. I'll see you later."

He paused and looked over his thin, wasted body, as if taking inventory. "Yes," he said finally, "today, I think you will."

Laughing, I left the kitchen. I climbed the stairs to my room, eager to return to Nicholas. He was up, wearing the dark blue silk robe I'd given him for his birthday, just leaving the bedroom as I was coming in. I was literally swept off my feet as he pulled and I pushed the door, both of us with hands on the doorknob at the same time. I stumbled forward, and he caught me. We kissed.

"How's Todd?" he asked, pressing his forehead to mine.

"He's good today."

"And how are you?"

"Wonderful, now," I said, kissing him again. Strands of my long, red blond hair stood out like embroidery on his robe. He picked me up and carried me to the bed. I waited until he was lying across me to say, "I'll be late to school. . . ."

I began, as usual, with too much urgency, desperate in my attempt to store the heat his lips sparked on my skin, the rich, morning musk rising from us both, the safe haven of our familiar rhythm, trying to hoard every detail to get me through the days without him. And, as usual, he was so generous, so delighted and present, that I forgot myself. I forgot everything except our bodies and how deliciously they fit together. I forgot everything but the look in his eyes as he loved me. I held his face in my hands and pulled it down to my own.

It was nearly half an hour later before I hit the shower, reveling in the hot water that finally brought my ankle fully to life. I dressed quickly in clothes that I loathed. I always thought of myself as costumed to teach school; cast in a role for which I was ill suited. In the mirror, my long navy skirt and ivory sweater set reflected dull good taste and a hint of dowdiness. I twisted my hair into a bun and became a caricature of an old maid librarian, but Mr. Vortee, the principal, would be pleased. He'd said my jeans and black cowboy boots were not professional enough attire. Neither, he'd said, were the men's shirts and ties I'd borrowed from the closet here at home. And when I'd bought dresses, they were too short, and he'd pointed out that I must wear hose. I questioned why he was looking at my legs in the first place.

Of course, Nicholas claimed they all did. "All those poor boys in your classes," he said, watching me dress, "looking at your dancer legs."

"Ex-dancer," I said, but the truth was I prided myself on the lean, snatched dancer's body I'd maintained with fierce diligence since the injury.

"Whatever. You know they're all in love with you. But none as much as me."

I kissed him good-bye, hating to leave the warm cocoon of the house. Yesterday we had all laughed together with our rented movies and take-out Chinese. The sickness had felt outside the house, looking in. It had held no power over our joy except to make it more precious. Leaving felt wrong; it fractured our strength, left holes in it, room for things to go bad. But I zipped up my parka, scraped the frost off my car windows, and drove to school.

Ohio's brilliant autumn was almost over, many trees stripped bleak and bare. I felt just as naked the farther I got from the house and the closer I got to Old Mill, the rural town I'd grown up in, and to the high school I'd never expected to think of again. I'd left as one of its most promising graduates, on my way to New York City on a full scholarship to the School of American Ballet. I tried to steel myself for the day, tried to prepare for the glances of pity from my former favorite teachers and the pursed lips of smug glee from some others. I tried to release the resentment I felt at the students who looked through me, past me, who saw me as a nobody, a minor obstacle on their own paths to greatness and glory. I had to find the way to be more again; I had to find my calling somewhere. I'd promised Todd he'd see my other gifts, once I found them. Only then, I hadn't known there'd be a deadline.

Todd had. He hadn't told us for two years. For two years he'd swallowed that secret, after his own body had withheld the information for eight. When he'd confessed, he'd admitted to not wanting to worry Mom, already so busy with Grandma's illness. Our grandma Anna had a brain tumor; now she and Todd were locked in a grim competition to collect a host of bodily horrors.

Nicholas was there the night Todd told us, and I credited him with my surviving the news. A week seemed such an impossibly long time to be without him, just as a school day seemed an impossibly long time to be without Todd. I spent half my waking hours these days watching clocks and calendars.

I wasn't late to school, but I was running behind enough that all the parking places were taken in the teachers' lot, and I had to search for a spot way out in the graveled student lot. I parked and picked my way in the rough footing toward the squat, tan brick building.

"Hey, Ms. Zwolenick." A young man materialized at my elbow. "You need a hand?"

I wasn't carrying anything but a briefcase. "I'm fine, Zack, but thanks." Ever since I'd choreographed the fall play—an abysmal production of *A Midsummer Night's Dream* in which he'd worked on set crew—Zackery Hauser had been lingering after my class. Last week I'd received anonymous flowers I suspected were from him. He was nice and attractive—in a hungry, gypsy boy sort of way—and his crush amused and even flattered me. I felt sorry for him for having it, but I tried not to be too nice. I'd been through this last spring when I student taught at Cincinnati's High School for the Arts and it had snowballed into an embarrassing ordeal I was determined never to repeat.

He walked by my side in silence, speaking in a sudden rush as we reached the back door. "Um, Ms. Zwolenick, I was wondering, if I could, you know, talk to you about something?"

"Sure," I said as he opened the door for me and the clamor of the pre-homeroom hallways surrounded us. Lockers slammed, the school radio station blared through the intercom, and students called down the crowded hallways to each other. At this time of morning, the halls reminded me of New York. I felt the same agitated claustrophobia that used to accompany my walk from apartment to rehearsal.

Zackery hovered while I signed in, checked my mailbox, and

headed upstairs to my room. "So, when do you want to meet?" I asked him. "It's almost time for homeroom. Will it take long? You wanna talk now?"

He blushed and opened his mouth to speak, when a girl with an unnaturally orange, salon tan stepped forward. She'd been waiting outside my classroom. "Ms. Zwolenick," she said, "I want to talk to you about that pop quiz Friday?"

"Hang on, Amber," I said. "Zack wanted to talk to me first."

He smiled graciously, backing away. "No, that's okay. We can set up some other time." Before I could answer, he turned and trotted back down the stairs.

Amber stood in my doorway, blocking my path. "I don't think I should've had to take the quiz, since I'd been on vacation—"

"Amber, I told you to have the book read by the time you came back."

"That's not fair," she said, pouting away.

Later, another girl cried at her C+ when I passed back some tests, her tears offending the generosity I'd extended. "It's just not fair," she sobbed in the hallway after the bell rang. I'd been heading for the phone in the lounge to find out if Todd had been permitted to proceed with chemotherapy and found myself confronted by her streaked makeup.

Oh, for the days when a C+ had the power to break me. I wanted to shake her, to warn her, to prepare her for some sorrow that required real tears. She was escorted away by comforting friends.

During lunch, before I could even leave my room for the phone, a cocky sophomore announced, "I need to take the makeup test."

"You only get to make up work if you have an excused absence."

"I was sick." It was hard not to haul off and break his jaw for that one.

When I wouldn't budge, he kicked my trash can on his way out the door, muttering, "That's real fair."

I had put up a quote that day that I knew they didn't understand. I always wrote a quote of the day on my chalkboard. The quotes were mostly given to me by my brother, who had collected and written them on the memo board in our parents' kitchen when we were kids. I kept a big notebook in my file cabinet crammed with little pieces of paper, postcards, and letters he'd sent to me from college, his travels, and his former home in Los Angeles.

Today I picked a postcard from Grenoble, France, and wrote, *"Travel light and you can sing in the robber's face."*—*Juvenal.*

Travel light. My father had told us that was the secret to life. I hadn't understood it. At one time I thought he said it to mock me as I piled our horse trailer high with my belongings to move to New York. And I hadn't always realized who the robber was. I did now.

My students didn't, and I despised them for that. That was what wasn't fair, though. How could they know?

I wished there was a way, a shortcut, to teach them. Some way besides the one that drowned a person in grief, bloated with sorrow, because I couldn't bring myself to wish that lesson on anyone else. Where were the Cliff Notes for impending loss?

In the lounge, when I finally dialed the hospital—a number I now knew as well as my own—the receptionist was new and confused and couldn't connect me to the right oncology desk. I gave up and called home. No answer. That was a good sign; at least he hadn't been sent home right away. I called my parents' house.

No answer there, either. My grandmother rarely left the house anymore. Had something happened to her? Or . . . had something gone wrong with Todd? I couldn't find anyone anywhere and left a series of desperate messages on every answering machine.

The bell rang, and I hadn't eaten any of my lunch, much less made it to the bathroom. I headed for my afternoon class, and there stood Zackery Hauser outside my door. When he saw me approaching, red splotches broke out on his neck.

"Ms. Zwolenick, I really have to talk to you."

The tardy bell rang. "Can it wait until after class?"

"Well, it's actually about class. How we're reading the poems today, and, well, I don't want to read mine." Sweat beaded on his upper lip. He cleared his throat. "It's, um, really personal, and I don't . . . want anyone to read it but you."

Oh, brother. I couldn't wait to tell Nicholas that his theories about my boys in class were right. "Sure, no problem," I said.

"And," Zack went on, "I wanted to tell you, you know, before you maybe called on me, and I'd have to say in front of the class, that, you know, I couldn't read it."

"Okay." This sweating, stammering wreck before me was the school's top debater, normally an articulate asset to any class discussion.

"And I want to talk to you . . . about my poem. I—I'd like to know what you . . . how you . . . you know, feel about it." The splotches deepened to a miserable shade of burgundy.

"Sure, of course. Tomorrow before homeroom?" His brown eyes widened, grateful.

"Thanks, Ms. Zwolenick." He handed me the manila envelope, and we both went in to class. It was difficult to concentrate as a few volunteers read poems with Zackery blushing every time we made eye contact, and Denny Robillard, a kid I swear belonged in the Hitler Youth, snickering in the back of the room. Policing Denny exhausted me. I'd long sensed his antagonism but had never understood it until the day I'd seen the word *Faggot*—spelled F-a-g-i-t; the cretin couldn't even spell the object of his hatred correctly—penned into his desk. Old Mill was a small town after all, and I couldn't expect that no one knew about Todd.

I ran for the phone at the end of the day. The same confused receptionist picked up at the hospital. "Can you at least tell me if he had chemotherapy today?" I asked her.

"Well . . . just a minute . . ." She didn't put me on hold, and I could hear her ask someone. She mispronounced our name.

"Oh!" she said, sounding pleased with herself. "His treatment was delayed."

"Why? What was wrong?"

This time I had to listen to Christmas carols on the line. It wasn't even Thanksgiving yet. After a carol and a half, while the school halls quieted and the parking lot slowly emptied, she said, less brightly this time, "Okay. He had to go to X-ray."

I took a deep breath. "Why? What are they x-raying? Is it his lungs like last time?"

She sighed. The carols started again, then stopped. I'd been cut off. Rather than dial again, I hung up, imagining myself slamming the receiver into the receptionist's head.

I was sick of waiting. Waiting for this conniving virus to marinate itself in Todd's cells, waiting for those first signs, the first infections, waiting for the official day the numbers dropped low enough to call it AIDS, and of course, now, waiting for the inevitable.

I had to wait for a lot of things, but I wasn't about to wait for her.

I ran to my lone car in the parking lot, head bent against the bitter wind.

Chapter Two

Trying to squeeze information from the hospital staff in person infuriated me more than begging for it on the phone. Todd had had x-rays that morning upon arrival, but the shifts had changed and confusion reigned. Nurses sent me on a goose chase from X-ray to the lab to Infectious Diseases to Oncology, all of them appearing wary of my desperation and I wary of their reserved, careful answers.

The new receptionist's eyes widened when I introduced myself. She pushed her chair back from the counter as if she feared I would strike her. "All I want to know is if he's still here," I said to her. "Can you at least tell me that?"

She could. He wasn't. He'd been released. An hour ago.

But still no one picked up at either house. I drove again.

I reached the whitewashed fence of my parents' farm and turned into the gravel driveway, which sucked my wheels into its deepening potholes. The station wagon was there, but the red pickup was gone. That meant Mom was inside with Grandma Anna, and Dad was who knew where.

The dogs came tearing from all corners of the farm, announcing my presence and continuing to bark until I gave them each a cursory scratch behind the ears, speaking to each one by name—Pip, the stout red dog, Mario, the old, stiff border collie, and Shoe Button, a ferocious terrier of some sort.

"Hey!" My mother called from the back kitchen door of our two-story, peeling, yellow farmhouse. She appeared relaxed and smiling. My heart slowed to a normal pace. "We just got back. I was trying to call you. You sounded so worried on the machine."

Rather than try to yell through the wind, I cut across the yard, my shoes sinking deep into leaves the color and consistency of soggy breakfast cereal before hitting frozen earth beneath them. If the yard wasn't raked soon, no new grass would grow come spring. The job would take a whole afternoon. For every item accomplished on the list of work the farm demanded, three more would arise—some hussy of a mare would kick a board off a fence torturing a simple-minded gelding, some wind would knock a branch into the riding arena, some old, battered dresser discarded miles upstream would float untroubled to our property, then get stuck and make a swamp of the mares' pasture. There was never a day my father could say, "I'm done. The work is finished." And never a day my mother didn't ask when it would be.

She hugged me when I reached the back door. "What's going on?" I asked. "Why did Todd need x-rays?" I stepped into the warmth of the cluttered kitchen and the cheer of its red gingham curtains. The tartness of apples and cinnamon hung in the air, palpable enough to taste.

"He fell in the parking lot and they just wanted to play it safe."

"He fell?"

She tucked a red curl behind an ear. It immediately sprang forward again. "You know how he just . . . melts every now and then?"

I nodded. He'd be fine one second, and in the time it took to blink he'd be on the ground, without a clue as to what had happened for the last ten minutes.

"Jacob said he hit the curb pretty hard, but nothing broken."

"Did he get chemo?"

"Yes, but he had a blood transfusion first, though, so it was later. He had a low red blood cell count, not white. He was anemic." She sighed. This was all so hard to keep up with. "He was pestering everybody about getting his chemo in. They kept teasing him, telling him how most people try to get out of it."

Today was his fourth time. I thought of Todd, lying there with the cold poison dripping into his arm. I thought of him accepting it, welcoming it into his body, probably flirting with his nurse, all the while knowing that within twenty-four hours he'd be lying on the bathroom floor for the next forty-eight, shivering between the rounds of vomiting and diarrhea.

"So, everything's fine, Summer. Anna and I had lunch with them. He and Jake were talking about going out for a while before they headed home."

"It would be nice for someone to tell me."

"How about some hot cider?" She poured it without waiting for my answer and set the pan on the stove. "How's Nicholas? I'm sorry I didn't get to see him this time."

I smiled and sat at the table, still in my coat. "Wonderful."

I watched her slice an apple and drop it in the cider. Her face was weathered and lined, her body stray-dog thin. She'd never lost that scrappy look of a youth spent in poverty. She was the one, not her mother-in-law, who looked as though she'd spent time in a concentration camp. My grandma Anna, in spite of three years of beatings and hard labor in camps in Poland—for hiding three Jewish teenagers in the loft of the dairy farm she ran with the grandfather I had never met—had been round and vibrant all the time I'd known her.

"Did he get that job in D.C.?" she asked, stirring the cider.

"He should find out this week."

She turned to me, her eyes hungry. Mom always looked this way at the prospect of someone "getting out," going away, moving on. Ever since Nicholas had interviewed for a stage-managing job at the Arena, she'd been poring over maps of the capital city, descriptions of its museums and sites, the way she had the year Todd had traveled abroad alone, the only one of us who'd supported him, even encouraged him to go. "Would you move there with him?" she asked me.

"I don't know. It's not until July. I don't know if I'd be . . ." I trailed off, not sure what to call it. I didn't know if I'd be done here. I didn't know if Todd would be dead in July. July might as well be a decade from now.

She sat beside me, smoothing my hair with her fingers. I'm not sure she even realized she did it. "Are you any closer to setting a wedding date?"

"No, Mom."

"Has he given you a ring?"

"Would you stop it? You're as bad as Aunt Marnee."

She clamped her mouth shut and scowled as best she could without laughing. Being compared with Mom's oldest, bossy sister was the worst insult in the family. "Fine," she said, smiling. "It's none of my business. I won't pry into the private lives of my children."

My laughter rang too bitterly and echoed against the kitchen walls. The playfulness fell away; she seemed hurt and more than a little angry. I knew she thought I accused her of not prying enough. She got up and poured the cider with a fierce, focused energy.

Mom had worked at a feed store in the evenings when the farm buckled under its bills and spent most weekends selling produce from our garden at the farmer's markets. Todd was the one who'd helped me with my homework, asked about my grade cards, and quizzed me on my boyfriends.

I watched her now and knew that she was thinking these things. "I'm sorry, Mom," I said. She pursed her mouth into a small, tight smile. I tried to joke. "What you don't know won't hurt you."

But a cloud crossed her face, her eyes darkened, and she looked ten years older. "Yes, it did," she whispered.

"Oh, Mom." I stood and put my arms around her, and we rocked there together while the cider cooled.

We separated, and she handed me a cinnamon stick for my mug. We stirred and drank in silence.

I looked at the clock. "It's feeding time."

Her shoulders slumped. "Your father! He's helping those idiot Webers load their new colt. He's been there two hours already, and you can bet he won't even think to charge them a dime. God forbid this farm should ever make us one red cent." Mom had never stopped being angry at finding herself back on a farm. "You wouldn't want to feed?" she asked me. "Or, since you're in your school clothes, you could stay in the house in case Anna needs anything while I do it."

"I bet there's clothes and boots here I could borrow," I said. "I'll feed."

She shook her head. "You don't even try to hide it."

I shrugged.

"I don't understand how you can hate an old woman so much."

"I don't understand how you can not hate her," I said, regretting it the instant the words left my mouth.

"Oh, Summer. Feed, then. But at least say hello to her."

I concentrated on the bottom of my mug of cider.

"Whether you care to know or not," Mom said, "your grandma's not going to live much beyond the New Year."

So, Grandma, too. I thought of all the time lines and deadlines and punctuation marks we'd been given lately.

"Go," Mom said, nodding her head toward Grandma's room. I looked at her sad, haggard face. It was only to make up for hurting her feelings that I took off my coat and went to the little room that had been my grandma Anna's since I was born.

Inside, she was lying in her twin bed, holding her Bible and looking out the window at the horses standing huddled together, tails to the wind, heads down. The room choked me with the claustrophobic, powdery air of long illness. She seemed smaller every time I saw her—a little more frail, a little more pained. Although I didn't rejoice in her suffering, I'm ashamed to admit I didn't mourn it too much, either.

"Little One," she said, smiling.

"Hi, Grandma." I bent and kissed her. The only place to sit was in an old rocking chair at the head of the bed, currently occupied by a stack of library books the church youth group delivered to her. I picked up the books and cleared a space for them among the religious icons littering the dresser, the only other piece of furniture in the room. As a child, I'd been fascinated by her lineup of three-dimensional, biblical postcards. One was of some gruesome, bleeding saint whose wounds disappeared if I moved my head just so. The card of Jesus praying was even creepier, since he'd open his eyes and look right at me, no matter where I stood in the room. I cocked my head when I set down the books, and sure enough, he opened his eyes as if I'd woken him from deep sleep.

"Why aren't you home looking after your brother?" Grandma asked me.

"He's not at home. He felt good enough to go out, I guess." I sat in the rocking chair.

"Is someone with him?"

"Yes, 'someone' is with him." She never said Jacob's name. I shook my head, picturing the awkward lunch they must've had today in the hospital cafeteria. Poor Jacob.

"Ack. Not for me, that poison he takes. It is time for nature to take her course. I am not afraid to die."

"Todd's not afraid to die," I said. I clamped my teeth together before I said more.

She turned to me. "No, no. Me. I just want to die in peace, with my family." She touched her head, where the tumor lay beneath her white hair and skull. "Nothing to be done. No operation will work." She sighed. "My heart, it hurts to think of my Angel so miserable, so sick from the poison."

Her Angel. I thought of how they used to sit for hours, talking on the porch swing. How they'd pore over the Sunday *New York Times* he'd buy for her, drinking pot after pot of coffee, talking about art and politics and religion. How his letters home from college to her were always longer than his letters to anyone else. How he'd listened spellbound to her impassioned speeches about prejudice and the dignity of all human beings, her experience in the camps having strengthened her beliefs rather than killing them. Todd had been more receptive than any of us to her tales.

Todd was Grandma's favorite. Mom said it was because Grandma had brought him into the world with her own hands during a freak March blizzard. The ambulance took over two hours in that weather, and Dad, in those days before cell phones and pagers, had stopped at a diner to wait out the storm on the way home from the office building where he polished floors at night. Grandma felt that delivery was her greatest accomplishment. In her eyes, Todd could do no wrong. Well, no wrong save the big one . . . but that would come much later.

As usual, I had no idea what to say to her and was somewhat relieved when she asked, "And the Beauty? How is she?" We were the Beauty, the Angel, and the Little One. Why did I feel gypped?

"I haven't heard from Abby in a while," I said.

Grandma frowned. "She doesn't visit enough."

"Things are a little hard for her right now."

Grandma frowned again, troubled. "When are they not?" she asked.

She grimaced and touched her forehead. When the pain had passed, she said, "I thought I didn't have to worry about her. I had to worry about your brother. And you, so wild. I thought she'd be fine."

We all had. The traditional silence fell between us. "Look at you," she said. "I always knew you'd be a teacher. You look so professional. So like a lady. At last."

I was still in my school clothes, longing for my jeans and sweatshirt. "I clean up all right, don't I? When I shake the hay-seeds out of my hair?" We both got caught on that image, though. Those hayseeds. It took us both to a night that had changed this family forever. She set down her Bible and turned to look out the window again.

I picked it up and idly opened it to where she'd been reading. Her bookmark was an old postcard Todd had mailed to her the year he'd traveled abroad. He'd sent only quotes to us from the many places he wandered alone, never letters and never an account of where he'd been or where he was going. Todd had gone all over Poland at one point and taken pictures of where Grandma and Grandpa Zwolenick used to live. He found their dairy farm. He took rolls and rolls of the town of Lodz. He went to the camps and took photos of the memorials that are there now. He went through lots of trouble for her. Grandma wept when she saw them. She had lost all her pictures, of course. She pointed to buildings in the photos and showed us where she went to school, where she used to buy groceries, and where she went on her first date.

He sent her a postcard of Lodz, too, this postcard, marking her Bible—an aerial view of the whole town. And on her postcard he wrote a quote from the Gnostic Gospels:

"If you bring forth what is within you, what is within you will save you. If you do not bring forth what is within you, what is within you will destroy you."—Jesus Christ.

She'd tucked all the other postcards from Todd into the side of her cloudy, beveled mirror, but not that one. I had thought all these years that it had angered her so much, she'd thrown it away. But here it was. Marking a place in Leviticus, of course.

My blood rushed in my ears. I bit my lip. "I gotta go find some clothes, Grandma. I'm feeding for Mom. I'll see you later." I handed the Bible back to her and left the room before she could speak.

I went upstairs, to our old bedrooms. The dressers and closets were filled with Mom's and Dad's clothes now, but the rooms themselves were still as we'd left them, years ago. The room Abby and I had shared was a sickening haze of pastels and was crowded with Abby's table favors from all the homecomings and proms, collages of her stunning photography, and the garden of trophies she won at the end of every year for being Outstanding Freshman, Outstanding Sophomore, and on and on. There were no such awards for Todd or me—he'd been suspended too often for fighting, and I'd been prone to skipping. Instead I had battered, bloodstained toe shoes hanging from my bed frame and ballet posters thumbtacked to the wall, many with cast signatures scribbled across them. The room looked oddly tidy now. Neither of us had ever made our beds or hung up clothes. Our door had mostly been kept shut because Grandma Anna said she didn't want to look at our mess. Todd's door was always open, unless he was in there.

I leaned in his door frame. A poster of Mario Lemieux and another of Wayne Gretzky were evenly spaced and secured to the wall over his bed. A world map was expensively matted and framed. His *National Geographic* and *Hockey News* magazines were stacked neatly in a corner, bindings out. Even the hockey awards and varsity letters on his desk were arranged in careful rows, although coated now with dust. There was one photograph—his senior prom picture.

Todd had been the first non–football player in Old Mill to be prom king, which had been a rather big deal, especially since his queen was the football captain's ex-girlfriend. I looked at the yellowing photograph. Todd looked slightly goofy, like the stereotypical country boy, with his sunburned nose and sandy blond hair in his eyes. A raw-looking cut outlined half of his upper lip, making his smile lopsided. I couldn't remember if the cut was from a hockey game or, more likely, that late in the spring, a fight. Todd had asked the doctor to remove the stitches—marching like black ants above his lip—too early, for prom. I remembered telling him the unhealed cut looked worse than the stitches had. He looked so out of place next to Becka, flashing her frosty pink Miss America smile, her tiara sparkling atop the salon coif she'd spent two hours and fifty dollars to achieve. She looked like a supermodel; the representative of everything he'd tried so hard to want. I'd tried hard to hate her, then and later. But something about her dark, ancient eyes, or maybe the exposed hollow at the base of her throat, made it impossible. I was struck by how vulnerable they both looked. How already wounded. I blinked hard and turned away.

I found some long underwear, two sweatshirts, and some thick work overalls of Dad's. My mother's Wellingtons fit well enough. Awkward and lumbering under my layers, I headed to the barn to do the evening feed.

For as long as we'd lived at home, Todd and I had done morning feed. Abby despised it, as she did most everything about the farm, and took on the entire family's laundry—and ironing—to be exempt. Every morning Todd and I got up at 6:00 A.M. and by 6:10 walked, bleary-eyed, together down to the barn. In the summer it was magical, being outside before the sun really rose, the morning a secret that only we'd discovered. But in the winter, as now, it was hard, cruel work—hammering frozen water buckets and breathing on door latches to melt the ice.

I measured grain and dumped each meal in the feed box of the appropriate stall, loneliness hanging heavy in the empty barn. When we'd fed together, it was fun; alone it was a chore. I'd done it by myself for two hockey seasons so Todd could go to practice at the obscene hour of 5:00 A.M., the only time Old Mill High School could use the rink at the local recreation center. In exchange for this favor, he helped pay for my ballet lessons. He worked a construction job with some other hockey players in the off season, saving up for college. It took me a year to realize how unbalanced this deal was; it took me opening my tuition bill and seeing that my ballet lessons equaled nearly a month of his back-breaking work. Work that cooked him dark as saddle leather and speckled his calves with scars from splashes of cement. When I tearfully confronted him about it, he said I was making it possible for him to do something that he wanted, just as he was doing for me.

And that's how we got by, all three of us, bartering chores and allowances and turns driving the pickup. We rarely consulted our parents or asked permission. There was no need; if we could find a way to make things happen, Mom gave her blessing, and if it meant no extra trouble for him, Dad had no opinions or attitudes. We joked that with Dad, we were no different from the horses. He took care of us. He never abused us, made sure we had food, water, clean beds. Kept us healthy. But he had no sentimentality attached to us whatsoever. No syrupy voices. No sugar cubes or store-bought treats. No praise for doing what was expected. It wasn't his way. But, it struck me now, it was love as he knew it.

I'd lost the speed and efficiency I'd once had doing this job, and by the time I was done measuring grain, the horses whinnied and rattled the gates. I started with the geldings—simply propping open their gate and standing back as they went trotting and nipping at one another to their own stalls. I followed, latching their stall doors behind them.

Next I had to lead the three ponies, all boys, individually, because they would not follow the honor code and go where they belonged.

And last came the mares. This evening they were solemn and shuffled past me one by one. Standing at the mares' gate, I had a vision of Todd and myself as children, at ten and thirteen.

In the summer the humidity of the Miami Valley made a clinging haze hover in the mares' hollow, until the late morning sun burned it off. This aluminum gate used to be wooden, and it sagged. Todd would have to prop it open with a broken-handled shovel, and on summer mornings we'd look out toward that fog and wait.

Without a word, we'd wait.

A stomp . . . a snort . . . a clink of iron on stone . . .

Sensing its strength, the presence of its flesh, one giant beast obscured behind a shroud, a dragon hidden by its own breath . . . it approached. We stood side by side, poised and waiting.

"There!" Todd whispered at the exact moment—the exact moment the mares emerged from mist and took on shape, lumbering in to breakfast, with sleepy eyes.

I wanted to touch that thirteen-year-old. To save him. To reach him in time that his life didn't alter, go off course.

I looked out toward the pond. It was there I should have known.

I glanced at my watch; I still had time. Once I'd latched the mares' doors, I ducked under the gate and hobbled across the frozen, uneven terrain of the pasture. The dogs followed me from the barn, Pip and Shoe Button snuffling and snorting, on serious business, but old Mario just limping along beside me, butting my knee with his head every few steps.

I pushed my way through the now overgrown, mere suggestion of a path sneaking down the hill toward the water. Past the old oaks worthy of fairy tales, full of twisted roots and branches, holes and hollows. I hadn't been down here in years.

I looked at the pond, crusty with ice, and a bit of despair hammered at me. If only I had caught on, paid better attention, picked up on his secret way back then. I stepped out onto one of the flat rocks surrounding the pond, this one the size of our family's dinner table. These rocks were perfect for sunbathing, or for diving into the water, which fell away from the banks into dark, mysterious depths.

Todd and I used to skinny-dip in this pond. At one time all three of us had swum naked down here, but Abby grew out of it. Todd and I never stopped until our lives took us away from our parents' home, and in spite of our differences in age and sex, it was never awkward. As I developed hints of breasts and pubic hair, Todd never commented one way or the other. We stretched out on our bellies beside each other, both of us hugging the hot rock, feeling the warmth absorb into our bodies, the sun drying our hair, and had long, unhurried talks. He offered condolences on the arrival of my period, and we kept a running competition going of who had worse design flaws—men or women. He taught me everything I needed to know about sex in a candid, no-nonsense manner I could not fathom Abby or my mother ever managing. When I finally studied sex education in school, it amazed me what was left out, skimmed over. I was thankful that I'd had Todd, who answered every question of mine with blushing, exasperated honesty.

Until the summer he was fourteen, that was, and I asked him if he was a virgin. He'd said, "Technically," and refused to elaborate no matter how I pestered him. I'd told him I was going to wait until I was "madly in love" with someone I wanted to marry.

"Hmm," was all Todd said at first. After a pause, where the neighbors' voices carried to us on the heavy breeze and the cicadas screamed away in the trees, he added, "What if you never get married? Not all people do, you know."

"What did you mean, 'technically'?" I tried again. "Tell me. Please?"

"Summer!" Todd said. "I hate it when you get this way! That's all the sex ed for one day, little sister!" He rolled over and sat up, his sun-dried hair standing on end. He slicked it back with both hands, then stood and put on his discarded clothes, tossing mine to me. I dressed, too.

We promised to tell each other when the time came and had done so. For me, it was early and none too romantic. I grew up fast in the world of ballet and lost my virginity as a sophomore in high school. He was a company member, too, a soloist, blond and pale. His name was Ricky and I'll never forget him, although our act was quite forgettable.

Todd was appalled. He thought I'd be sorry later and that the first time should have been a bigger deal.

"You're just jealous, 'cause I got there younger than you did," I said one evening at the pond. Todd had finally shed his own virginity on his prom night, and here I was, catching up to him only a few months later.

"You just better be careful, little sister," he said.

"We were. I'm not stupid. And look who's talking, anyway."

"That's what I mean. Be careful. Because it's really easy to screw things up."

"So, is Becka pregnant? What did the doctor say?"

"She's not." He shrugged. "She's back together with Chet, anyway."

"Good. They deserve each other." Todd hadn't been himself since his fling with Becka. Their much noted courtship at school had foundered with a broken condom and some fretful months of waiting.

Todd eyed me and opened his mouth, then shut it and looked away. "It's complicated, Summer. But, trust me, she deserves a lot better than she's getting."

We sat in silence on the rocks by the pond.

"It should be special," he said. "It should mean something."

"I like Ricky."

"But you're no ways near being in love. You're not in love with anything but ballet, so why did you do it?"

I thought a moment. I was honest. "I don't know. No reason."

The neighbor's dog barked. It was nearly dusk. The dog was insistent, and I pictured a raccoon up a tree.

"We need to have a reason," Todd had said. "We should always have a reason."

*   *   *

Shoe Button barked from the top of the hill. "I know. I'm coming," I answered him. Pip and Mario must have grown bored with me and moved on. The path was steeper than I remembered, and standing at the pond so long in the cold had stiffened my ankle. Just past the top of the path, I stumbled on a tree root and slammed into the ground. No time even to flail for balance; I hit the frozen earth with an unladylike grunt, almost smashing the dog. He scrambled away, then wheeled and growled at me. I ignored him and lay there on my belly, the cold seeping through my clothes, sharp in my throat as I panted to catch my breath.

A terrifying déjà vu seized me as I raised up on my elbows to assess the damage. Through the thick, rubber Wellington boot, my ankle felt fine. I pointed, flexed, rotated it; no problem. "Thank you," I whispered, overcome with relief. I remembered looking over my shoulder just like this, three years ago, and seeing the bone shining dully in the sun.

I'd known immediately, looking at the bone, that my dancing days were over. I'd shivered out in the mud for hours, unable to move the leg without passing out, until someone noticed the horse, Mocha Mocha, a Morgan too fat for one name, still in saddle and bridle, grazing up around the house. Dad found me, and after an ambulance got stuck in the soft, sucking mud of the pasture, and a paramedic fell down in the swollen creek between me and the road, Care-Flight finally came for me. Although I was certain I closed my eyes for only a moment, when I opened them, I was in recovery, with a pin in my ankle and a promising career over.

Over. Just like that. I'd come home from New York for the holidays, right after *The Nutcracker* closed. Recently promoted from the ranks of the corps, that year I led the "Waltz of the

Snowflakes" in act one and danced the "Arabian Coffee" pas de deux in act two. It was that sexy Arabian adagio—with my bare midriff and filmy harem pants—that got me noted in the *Times*, raised the volume noticeably at my appearance in the curtain call, and had patrons lined up for my autograph in their programs. Todd and Jacob came to the city to see me perform.

"You have arrived, little sister," Todd said, beaming and tear-streaked backstage. "You have arrived."

Jacob pressed a hand to my rippled, hard belly. "You are something fierce, baby."

We got tipsy on champagne flying home to Old Mill together for Christmas.

The accident was two days after Christmas, the day of my scheduled late-evening flight back to New York, back to rehearsal, back to my first full-length featured role as Myrta in *Giselle*. The weather was bizarrely warm, and I thought it would be fun to go for a ride. I was just out on a trail, nothing ambitious, on the oldest, most reliable horse on the farm. We were only trotting slowly along. But we startled some deer sleeping in the brush, and they crashed out of the dead, dry growth sounding like a forest fire. And the next thing I remembered was looking at my gloved hands in the mud in front of me, wondering, What happened?

I stayed at my parents' after surgery that wasted year. I became the queen of tantrums, melodrama, and drinking too early in the day. Remembering how childish and bitter I'd been in my disappointment shamed me, even now.

It was Todd who'd saved me.

"You're pathetic," he'd said to me. He'd come home, from L.A., with Jacob, to visit me shortly after my third surgery. Everyone else had abandoned me that afternoon; I wasn't much fun to be with. Jacob took Mom to a movie, Dad loaded hay, and Grandma worked a church bake sale. Only Todd stayed with me. He washed the dishes I left out after my one-thirty breakfast without comment. It wasn't until I poured a glass of wine that he asked, "How long, exactly, do you intend to milk this?" I swallowed wrong and choked, wine burning in my nose. He dried his hands and carefully folded the dish towel. "What's the point to all this bullshit, Summer? All this wallowing in self-pity—it's not going to bring your dancing back; it won't make your ankle better. Nothing can. So can we please move on?"

I hated him at that moment.

"What are you going to do now?" he asked. "Live here at Mom and Dad's forever?"

Dragging my cast behind me, I tried to walk away from him, out of the kitchen, but he blocked my path. I hit him once, tried to punch him, but he caught my arms and held them. I couldn't think of anything else to do but burst out crying. He let go of my arms, and I slid down to the kitchen floor. He just stood over me, watching, disgusted.

"I don't want to do anything but dance," I said.

His face was stone. "Well, you know, that's too bad. That's the one thing—do you hear me? the one and only thing out of millions of possibilities—that you can't do. And that's your fault, Summer. Mom tells me you stopped going to physical therapy."

I opened my mouth in protest but shut it. Todd sat on the floor beside me and poked me in the ribs. "What were you going to say? "

"Therapy was . . . too hard."

He shook his head. "See, if it was me, I'd be in physical therapy every day. I'd do every exercise they told me to—I'd do more than they told me to—"

"Well, excuse me for not living up to your high standards. Not everyone can be the perfect specimen of a human being you are."

Instead of being angry or walking away from me, he only looked sad, almost thoughtful. "I'm not perfect, Summer. What you think is perfection is nothing but overcompensation, that's all." He glanced at Grandma's bedroom door. "Not that it does me any good."

I said nothing.

After a moment he said, "God, I loved to watch you dance. You seemed somehow . . . not of this earth." He blushed pink at his own emotion. "I feel as though a gift has been taken back. It—it pains me, okay? I know that's corny, but it physically pains me to know I'll never see you dance again. But I know you've got other gifts to give. I can't wait to see what they are. The way you're wasting time, though, I'm starting to worry that I'll never see them."

In that way of ours, all of the anger lifted away. No grudges. No hesitation in admitting he was right. No foolish pride to hang on to. "You'll see them," I whispered.

"Promise?"

I nodded. And I started to cry again. He rocked me and pushed my hair back and kissed the top of my head over and over again.

Today, my tears flaked thick and salty in the cold. Shoe Button growled, a hint of a whine underneath it. When we made eye contact, he barked, demanding that I get up and return. I obliged stiffly, already feeling the soreness setting in, knowing that I'd be bruised tomorrow. Shoe Button escorted me back to the barn, where the horses ground at their grain with piano-key teeth. A comforting, contented sound. "Like one giant machine," Todd always said, as if he'd never said it before.

I checked my watch again. I should hay the horses and be on my way. I cut the twine on the thick, fragrant bales and carried flakes to each stall. When I finished, hayseeds and chaff covered the front of me. I tried to brush myself off, but the hay clung, tenacious as it had been that night long ago, the eve of Abby's wedding. I stared down at myself and wondered how I'd missed the truth about Todd. I'd had so many hints and clues, but the information, when it came, took me entirely by surprise.

Chapter Three

"Someone" was home. Jacob's car sat in the driveway.

Bach's *Cello Suites* poured from the house, straining the corners and windows. So loud, I felt I pushed through a force field when I opened the back door. A ringing hovered, pulsating in the air when the music stopped and Jacob came frowning through the doorway into the kitchen.

"Oh. It's you." He relaxed at once.

"Where's Todd?"

"He's with Dr. Sara. They went out."

I opened the refrigerator and looked past the rows of medicine bottles at my meager choices for dinner. Over the past year Todd's diet had evolved into a reminder of the most unpleasant aspect of my dance career, and the thought of one more bite of rice, applesauce, or tofu turned me mean-spirited.

Jacob, as if reading my thoughts, closed the refrigerator door and announced, "And we're going out, too. I'm taking you out for a big, fat, juicy steak. And a giant, oozy dessert. We'll eat like pigs and smoke like chimneys."

My mouth came alive, craving spice and greasy fat. "Sounds fabulous, Jake, but I can't. I have a whole stack of poems and tests to grade." I might as well strap them to my back, the way their very existence burdened my every step.

"Screw the grading. We haven't eaten out in months."

"I know. I want to, but I'm so behind. I'm only ever a step ahead of these kids as it is. I can't."

He stood, radiating energy, as if a tantrum boiled beneath the surface of his skin. Then it died, his shoulders slumped, and he looked at the clock with blank eyes. I saw that he would not go without me; he'd sulk all evening instead. And I saw that he needed to get out. And, in truth, so did I.

"Okay," I said. "But we can't stay out late."

He grabbed my face in his hands and kissed me on the lips. "Thank you, baby." He stepped back and really looked at me. "But you've got to change clothes." I was still in the layers I'd borrowed from my parents. "You can't go out in public like that."

I ran upstairs and changed into black velvet overalls and a tight, periwinkle turtleneck Jacob had bought me. He loved to buy me clothes, and since I hated to shop and had no money, I loved to let him. He bought me items I would never pick out for myself, but that garnered me compliments from strangers. When I returned to the kitchen, he nodded his approval, and without any discussion, he drove us out of the red-bricked streets of our historic neighborhood, through downtown, and onto Interstate 75. I smiled, knowing where he'd chosen. An exquisite Hispanic restaurant, our very favorite, expensive but worth it.

We got a table after only a five-minute wait, which still astounded me; I would have sat at a bar for at least an hour in New York for a place of this caliber. My nostalgia surprised me as I took in the steamy room, the air thick with olive oil and grilled beef, and the snatches of Spanish that floated to me over the tinkle of the fountain near our table.

"I'm also going to drink," Jacob announced, ordering us a pitcher of the signature blue agave margarita.

I watched the waitress take stock of him as he ordered, I saw her looking at his strong arms in his black polo shirt, saw her eyeing the tattoo. I saw her attraction. And I saw the double take I was used to encountering when I was somewhere with Jacob Kenwood. "Do . . . do I—? We've met. Haven't we? Don't I know you from somewhere?"

"Nope. Sorry. Don't think so." He wasn't unfriendly, but hardly gracious. She smiled anyway.

"You just—oh, well. You remind me of someone, I guess." She smiled again, blushing.

"Bet I know what soap opera she watches," I said when she'd taken our orders and flirted off.

"Hell, I haven't been on that for what, seven, eight months now? Maybe they were rerunning something else." When they'd moved back here from L.A., we knew why Todd was coming home. We also knew, but none of us discussed with each other, what this change meant for Jacob. Although everyone in "the industry" was sympathetic and supportive, this move could mean death to Jacob's career as well as a foreshadowing of death to his lover. He knew that, but the one time I'd approached the topic, all he'd said was, "For better or worse, baby."

Of course, he joked that his penchant for drunk driving violations had made it a prime time to leave L.A., but it was joking and nothing else. I wondered if I could do that. It was hard to imagine, not having anything glorious to give up at the present. But when I'd danced? No. There was no way anyone could have pulled me from New York City.

"How long do we have?" I asked.

He looked up, across the glass-enclosed candle, his eyes

wounded and betrayed, believing I was broaching the subject more taboo than any other.

"No, no," I assured him quickly. "How long do we have to eat? When will they be back?" Neither of us so much as smiled at the misunderstanding.

"I don't know. But it's not like Sara will just dump him out in the driveway, you know." Dr. Sara Grork had become our friend as well as Todd's doctor. Jacob leaned across the table and lit the cigarette I'd accepted from his pack. My margarita began to round the edges of the day. Even on this bleak November night, the sultry scent of lime and tequila conjured images of sex and humidity. I licked the salt from my lips.

"What are they doing?" I asked.

"I have no idea." He thought a moment. "I didn't even ask. To be honest, baby, I kind of jumped at the chance to be by myself."

"Hello? What am I?" I asked, laughing, but Jacob didn't join me.

"I didn't mean alone. I just meant—" He looked away. He fiddled with the heavy glass ashtray. "Does that make me a terrible person?"

I shook my head.

"I get . . . tired," he said, making a face. "I hate watching and feeling so goddamn helpless. Like tomorrow. I'm dreading tomorrow."

"Me too."

"It doesn't have to be that way. Dr. Sara was after him again today. He should stay in the hospital for his chemo, he could get meds around the clock, he could—"

"He hates the hospital, Jake, you know that."

He sighed and nodded.

The waitress served our calamari, leaning low over the table in her off-the-shoulder ruffled blouse; I almost laughed out loud.

The calamari was tender and juicy as steak fat, brushed with olive oil and grilled with garlic, parsley, and chili peppers.

Jacob closed his eyes, relishing the taste. When he opened them, he smiled at me, that damn smile that made my knees dissolve, even though I was sitting down. He reached across the table, palm up, for my hand. I gave it, and we stayed like that, looking like some lovestruck couple. "I don't know how I'd get through this without you," he said. "I'm so glad you said yes."

"You didn't think I would, did you," I accused him.

"Wasn't sure." He licked olive oil from the crook between the thumb and forefinger of his free hand. I swallowed. I tried to take my hand back, but he held on.

"I had to say yes," I said. "I wanted to say yes." I stopped pulling.

He smiled and released my hand. "I'm glad you're along. He knew what he was asking."

Our meals arrived. Jacob had the *solomillo,* a beautiful filet mignon, so tender a toothless person could eat it. It was served rare, on a sizzling, six-hundred-degree plate that cooked the meat according to how thick or thin he sliced it. I had a quesadilla of smoked salmon sandwiching a layer of creamy horseradish sauce on a crisp flour tortilla, dwarfed on the plate by the side dishes of bean salsas, perfectly ripe avocado slices, and fried plantains stuffed with exotic vegetables. We both made rather sexual moans over our meals, focusing only on eating for several minutes.

Jacob paused at one point. "Your brother says that you can tell what kind of lover someone will be by how they eat."

I thought about this. I raised my eyebrows. "Todd's a bottomless pit."

"I know," Jacob said, grinning broadly. "And so is Nicholas, I've noticed."

I blushed. "Yep." I looked at my own plate, which I had all but licked clean.

Jacob winked at me, then cleared his throat, changing the subject. "And how was school today, Ms. Zwolenick?"

"The usual. Only I think there's another kid in love with me."

He laughed. "Oh, baby, they're all in love with you. Don't sound so surprised."

"No, it's awful. He's written a poem he wants me to read. He says it's personal and he'll only show it to me. What am I supposed to say to him?"

"Tell him you're flattered, but you're already madly in love with someone else."

I grinned. My skin warmed. I felt the heat spread across my cheeks and down my throat. Jacob laughed at my reaction. "Speaking of . . . have you set the big day yet? When do we start shopping for your dress? I do get to help pick out your dress, right?"

"Of course. I was counting on it. And I want you to be my best man."

"Uh . . . honey, Nicholas gets to pick the best man."

I swirled my glass, the tequila unfurling in a silky dance through the melting ice. "No. He can pick his own best man. I want you to be mine."

"You're going to have a best man?"

"My best friend is a man, so I'm having a best man. Will you do it or not?"

He tilted his head. "Sure, babe," he said in a voice foreign to me, raspier than his own. He blushed and cleared his throat, then raised his glass, and we both drank. He cleared his throat again and said, "Hell, no other wedding at the farm has been too conventional. Your relatives should be used to it by now."

"And our wedding is not going to be the huge deal yours

was," I said. I helped myself to another cigarette from Jacob's pack.

"Oh, ours wasn't that big a deal."

"Excuse me? You had to rent a toilet!" What had started as a beach party in L.A. with beer, steamed crabs, and a few words of love had exploded into a $10,000 extravaganza on the farm.

"Well, we thought nothing should keep us from having the full heterosexual wedding experience."

"And you got it. The only thing you didn't do was register somewhere."

Jacob snorted, splashing his tequila. He wiped his chin. "Remember when your aunt Marnee asked us that? We could've, I guess, but, I mean, who would've been the bride?"

We laughed. "I want it low-key and fun. Like I picture the rehearsal dinner being a big bonfire and barbecue out in the mares' field. And the ceremony should be followed by skinny-dipping in the pond."

"Okay, maybe your relatives aren't used to this by now," Jacob said. "Will you have any bridesmaids?"

"Why? Would you rather be my maid of honor than my best man? I never knew you were into that."

He flipped me off, trying hard not to laugh. "Seriously, will you have any?"

"I don't know. Maybe Arnicia."

He peered at me a moment. "What about your sister?"

I shrugged. "I don't know if she'd even expect me to ask her."

"Well, you should."

"You don't even like her."

"But I asked her to be in our wedding, didn't I?"

"And the bitch didn't come, did she?" I asked, too loudly. A couple at the next table glanced over. I lowered my voice and mimicked Abby. "No. We'll be on a cruise in St. Barth's. We won't be able to make it."

Jacob leaned across the table, close to me. "Summer, get a clue. Todd picked the damn date knowing she'd be out of the country. He knew she couldn't come, so he made it easy for her, gave her an out." He stared at me, waiting for a reaction, but was distracted when the waitress came back and asked for our dessert orders. Todd gave Abby too many outs, in my opinion.

The waitress spoke only to Jacob, never so much as glancing at me. She laughed at everything he said and kept touching her necklace, fingering the base of her throat.

We both smoked in silence until the dessert arrived. Jacob stripped the fruit from the orange twist garnishing his caramel crepe and worked some orange into a bite of caramel. He chewed, nodded, then looked at me as if he couldn't stand the suspense any longer. "You never answered my question."

I, too, was eating caramel, but mine was on vanilla ice cream, with blackberries. I stopped sucking the caramel from my spoon. "What question?"

"When's the big day?"

"For God's sake. You're as bad as my mom. Would you all back off and leave us alone?"

"What are you waiting for?"

"What are you rushing for?"

"Last weekend you were coming up with names for the kids you two will have." He popped another bite of crepe into his mouth and chewed slowly, watching me.

My turtleneck began to itch. The crowded room had grown hot.

"Please don't make such a big deal out of this," I said. "We know we're getting married, but not tomorrow or anything. We're not ready yet."

"We?"

"Look—not everyone is under the time constraints you are."

I shouldn't have said it. Jacob looked stunned that I had. He shoved his plate to the edge of the table, and for a split second I thought it was going over the edge, to shatter on the floor. He lit another cigarette, putting his pack onto the seat beside him, not offering me one this time.

He smoked, brooding and silent, until the waitress brought the check. Jacob took it, counted money from his wallet, and shifted his weight to stand, when I touched his arm and asked, "Did you know for sure? That you were ready? That Todd was it?"

His face softened. He settled back into his seat and nodded. "Yeah, I knew. He was the one, baby. The one that's for life." He looked at me, but I could tell he was seeing something else. He was lost for a minute, but he came back. "I mean, I can't imagine life without him. It's gonna be like an amputation, Summer. You may as well hack off my goddamn legs." He stabbed out his cigarette and wiped his eyes. "I want to get home."

Dr. Sara's car was in the driveway and the house's windows poured out welcoming light. Laughter greeted us at the back door. They were in the living room watching a videotape and had a fire going. I heard Todd say, "There! There! That's him. Jake's the British soldier on the left. Watch, he's gonna blow this colonist's head off."

Jacob and I looked at each other and laughed. *One If by Land.*

Todd hit pause and turned to us. His skin was supple, his cheeks the color and texture of a sun-kissed peach, and his eyes sparkled with fluid instead of a dry, fevered glare. I'd seen him like this before when he'd had transfusions. As though he were a vampire freshly fed, you could look at him on these days and never know he was not among the normal living.

He and Jacob kissed with such a naked affection that Sara and I turned our eyes away and smiled at each other. She was in jeans and soccer shoes and a big, baggy T-shirt. Her black hair was down and touched her shoulders, making her appear years younger than she did at the clinic.

"I was showing Sara our movie," Todd said like a little boy. "Everybody ready?" He released the pause button, and the British soldier did indeed blow the colonist's head off.

"Okay. And here—do you see?—on the big, bay mare? That sexy soldier with the ripped coat— here he is! Watch! Ooh! Slices him across the throat and never looks back!" And the colonist's blood spattered across Jacob's white breeches. "But wait, there's more!" Todd controlled the remote with glee, stopping at just the right moment. "Watch this: Knocked from his horse by a hatchet thrown into his shoulder, this amazing soldier gets back up and—hatchet still entrenched—cuts the rebel across the face with his sword and then runs him through. What a man. Let's watch that again."

We watched the scene again, and Jacob said, "Whoa. Whoa. Rewind that. Now listen: Do you hear that hatchet hit and embed in flesh? Isn't that amazing?"

Todd fast-forwarded until the credits, stopping at a huge three-column list of stunt workers. "There he is! Jacob Matthew Kenwood!" We cheered.

Jacob fast-forwarded farther and stopped at assistant sound editor. "There he is! The one, the only, Todd Philip Zwolenick!" We applauded.

"Wow. I'm impressed," Sara said. "So, Jacob, do you know how to fall down stairs and get hit by cars and stuff?"

"Sure. Cars are easy. You could run me down in the driveway if you want. I'll show you."

She made a face. "There are days, you know. Don't tempt me."

She and Jacob were known for their shouting matches at the clinic, both of them desperate for, and often in disagreement about, what was best for Todd. "So, this is where you met each other?" She changed the subject.

"Well, kind of," Todd said. "We'd met each other once four years before this, at the Pride March in D.C., but this movie's where we met for real. The march doesn't really count."

"Yes, it does," I said. "That's the best part of the story—that you'd met before and you actually remembered each other."

"Oh, baby, of course I remembered him," Jacob said. "Who wouldn't?" They were gearing up for the story I'd heard a thousand times. They loved to tell it, and I never tired of listening.

"It started raining at the march," Todd said. "Heavy, torrential rain. Summer ended up entirely see-through in her T-shirt, no bra, of course. Mom was mortified."

"I didn't need one!" I said. "I still don't." Back then I considered myself blessed with my ballerina-flat chest.

Todd ignored me and continued. "We ran under a shop awning, and there, out of the hundreds of thousands of people in D.C. that day, was Jacob."

"So"—Jacob took over—"in the spirit of the day, we exchanged greetings and names. And this lucky little shit was there with his *mom and dad* and little sister. I told him, 'I hope you know how lucky you are.' "

Todd grinned. "I told him I knew."

"Your mom even gave me a hug," Jacob said. "But your dad didn't."

Todd and I laughed. "That day," Todd said, "was a tough one for old Dad. I think that about pushed his limits to the max."

"I still can't believe you got him to go," Jacob said.

"I didn't. I didn't even ask him; Mom did. I think she made it pretty damn clear that on this issue they would agree, or she might finally walk out for real. He tried to stay in the hotel room, and she made him march."

We pondered this a moment, and Todd said, "Anyway, eventually the rain let up, we shook hands, and Jacob disappeared into the parade. Four years later, I was working on my first film. We'd been working on that big fight you saw for the first time that day. All day. It ended up taking three weeks for what eventually became eight minutes of film. Anyway, the actors had been excused for the day, and I was looking at footage. There was a knock on the trailer door, and when I opened it, there stood—"

"The most beautiful man you'd ever seen," Jacob interrupted.

"Only I'd seen him once before. It took a second, but only a second."

"That's true. He even remembered my name."

"And you remembered mine. You even pronounced it right."

"It was wild," Jacob said. "He even remembered Vince's name, who'd been with me at the march. He asked about him right away."

"Well, of course I did. There was no point in getting my hopes up for nothing."

"Baby, it was love at first sight."

"Second," Todd corrected him. "Second sight."

"Speak for yourself," Jacob said.

"So, how long did it take, before you were going out?" Sara asked. She had pulled her legs up under her on the couch. It felt like story time at camp.

They smiled.

"You're blushing," Sara said to Todd, delighted.

"Well. Um. We were going out, I guess, you know, that night," Todd said. Sara raised her eyebrows, teasing him, and Todd darkened a hue. "But we didn't, you know, do anything that first night, we—"

"Waited until the second night," Jacob broke in. "We decided to take it slow."

We laughed. It may have seemed rushed, but they'd never spent a night apart since that first, not even when Todd was in the hospital.

I wanted Nicholas here beside me, legs entwined on the couch. Someday, I vowed, we could sit here and tell our story like this. I'd tell how the first thing I noticed about Nicholas was his feet. I was enthralled by them the first time I saw them in Birkenstock sandals, at a rehearsal he was stage-managing at college. I'd been asked to help choreograph the show, so we were on staff together. His feet reminded me of the white marble feet of statues, long and unmarred, not one of the toenails scuffed or bruised or missing. I was used to dancer feet. I'd never held it against any of my dancer lovers for having ugly feet. Our feet were the tools of our trade. The women's feet were worse, but the men's feet were overmuscled, knotted with raised blue veins, skin so rough that it snagged on my sheets like sandpaper. Nicholas's feet, just one week after I'd noticed them, felt smooth and soft as a caress against my legs. When we awoke the next morning, I pulled back the sheets to gaze again at those feet. He laughed when I told him they were beautiful. A laugh of surprise and curiosity.

"No one's ever told me that," he said. "I've heard they're big, that's all."

"And you know what they say about men with big feet," I said, reaching for him again under the covers.

"Yeah, yeah, I know. Big shoes," he said, blushing.

He was so unlike a dancer in every way. His body fascinated me. I couldn't keep my hands off the texture of his skin, and his muscles, which gave slightly to my touch. He was toned, but he never worked out. So pleasing to touch, unlike a dancer in bed with a dancer, hard, unyielding, all bones and sharp angles, like "taking a bicycle to bed," one of my on- and offstage partners had commented.

We wore each other out, finding every opportunity to make love again, once even at the theater, standing between the crowded racks in the costume stockroom.

But what amazed me most was that when we weren't in bed, or on the floor, or in the shower, or over the kitchen table, we were fine. I liked him as much out of bed as in it.

I'd never had that happen before.

That first day I stayed, we made breakfast together and I'd seen the garden he kept on his fire escape. He crouched out there barefoot, wearing only soft, faded jeans. I sat in the windowsill in one of his shirts and reached out to run my fingers down the beads of his vertebrae, his spine curled like a C over his tomatoes, his basil, and his chives. He clipped some chives and we put them in our omelets.

Nicholas understood dance, without being a part of it himself. He'd stage-managed some dance and had seen firsthand the reality of it, the cruel work, the starvation, the handprint bruises left by partnering, the way we shaved dead skin off our bunions to fit into our shoes, like Cinderella's evil stepsisters trying to fit the glass slipper. He understood what I'd accomplished, and what I'd sacrificed to accomplish it. He also understood, then, what I'd lost. It was an important thing, that bit of knowledge, between us.

A log in the fireplace popped like a gunshot and snapped me back to the present. Dr. Sara was still quizzing Todd and Jacob about their early days.

"Todd, did you know at that point you were positive?" Sara asked.

"Positive about Jake? Or positively carrying the virus?"

She smiled. "Both."

"Absolutely about Jacob. Not a clue about the virus. It'd be another year."

"And even that was a formality," Jacob said. "We didn't really expect a positive result. Or, if we did, we thought it would be mine."

"We only went because we'd decided, when we were going to get married and have the ceremony and everything, that it would be awfully nice to be done with safe sex," Todd said. "Broaden our horizons a bit."

"But, alas," Jacob said, caressing the stubble on Todd's head, " 'twas not to be."

Everyone stared at the fire.

"So, where'd you guys go?" I asked, turning to Sara.

"We went shopping," she said with a bemused smile.

"Oh, yeah." Todd crossed behind the couch to several paper bags, moving quickly, confidently. I watched in awe. I'd never grow used to the pendulum of this disease.

Todd sorted through the bags and said, "I have gifts." He stood, hands behind his back, and said, "I wish to apologize in advance for the whining, annoying pain in the butt I will be by tomorrow afternoon." I saw Dr. Sara and Jacob exchange a glance.

"Tomorrow afternoon?" I said. "Try every day."

He threw my gift at me, and, laughing, we began to open our boxes. Toys. Silly, fun stuff, like crayons and superhero coloring books, bottles of soap bubbles and bubble wands, Silly Putty and green slime, wind-up frogs that hopped, pigs that oinked, and a parrot that repeated whatever we said.

Arnicia came in the back door from her training shift at the hospital. "What is going on here? It's way past all your bedtimes." Todd appeased her with the bright flower and star stickers she could apply to her long nails. She waggled them about and pointed to the still unopened boxes. "Whose are those?"

"Oh. Those are for Nicholas," Todd said. Jacob had rolled up one leg of Todd's jeans and was creating a giant special effects wound on Todd's shin with Silly Putty and red finger paint.

Dr. Sara stopped her creation of Play-Doh space aliens and asked, "Hey, how is old St. Nick, anyway?"

"He's great," I said, in midbite on my candy necklace. "He'll be back Saturday."

"Hey, Summer." Todd leaned over, contorting himself to watch Jacob's gruesome handiwork with his good eye. "Mom called while you guys were out and wants to know if Nicholas will be at Thanksgiving."

"Yep. He will." This would be his third with our family.

"I like Nicholas," Todd said.

"You like Nicholas too much," Jacob said. He grinned at me. "It's a good thing for us, Summer, that Nicholas is very strictly heterosexual." Todd rolled his eyes.

"If you don't mind my saying so," Arnicia said, looking straight at me, "I think it's a good thing that Jacob is very strictly homosexual." She slid a candy ring onto a finger and held out her hand to admire it. My face flushed hot.

Jacob laughed, then asked, "Why is your mom inviting everybody for Thanksgiving? It'll ruin it." Thanksgiving in the past had always been immediate family only. Mom had announced that, this year, all the relatives were coming. I didn't welcome the intrusion.

Todd shrugged. "I think, you know, for my grandma. I want to go."

"Okay. We'll go. I wonder if Her Royal Highness will be there? Will she deign to grace us with her presence?"

Todd looked up at Jacob and said, "Don't."

I, too, wondered if Abby would be there.

Todd stood and took one step, which melted into a lurch and left him clutching the mantel with both hands. We were all on our feet and at his side. A sheen of sweat had sprung from him— his face and neck, even his hands, and his one exposed calf shining in the firelight. The Silly Putty began to slide.

"Whew," he said. "I stood up too fast."

We let him have that. No one said a word.

He saw the finger paint trickling down his shin, between his toes. "Oh, no." He sounded so defeated, so surprised. "I'm bleeding again. . . ."

"No, no, no, don't worry," Jacob said. "It's just the paint, remember? It's okay."

Todd didn't remember, but he trusted Jacob. "I'm tired," he said.

Jacob knelt and wadded up the Silly Putty. He took several tissues and wiped the skinny shin and calf clean, then unrolled the jeans back down to Todd's ankle. "There, babe."

"Good night, everybody," Todd said, and, leaning on Jacob, left the room.

We three women stood at the fireplace. I shivered in spite of the heat.

"You should all go to sleep," Dr. Sara said. "Tomorrow's a big one." She put her Play-Doh in her bag, hugged us both, and left.

"You okay?" Arnicia asked me as we watched Dr. Sara's tail-lights disappear.

I shook my head, and she put a perfumed arm around my shoulder. Jacob came into the kitchen, opened the fridge, and began preparing the evening doses of medicine, the "cocktail hour," as they still jokingly called it . . . although Todd wasn't taking an actual protease inhibitor cocktail anymore. When those barely tested drugs had rushed onto the market three years ago,

Todd and Jacob had scrambled to get in on the promised Lazarus effect. The staggering expense and the inconvenience of the forty pills a day were at first well worth the steady dropping of his viral load. But Todd, like an unlucky many, couldn't tolerate the side effects of the potently toxic drugs. After four months of violent nausea, hives, and feet so numb that he could barely walk, Todd called it quits and our last line of defense crumbled. Since then, nothing new had loomed on the horizon.

I said good night and left the room. Before going upstairs, I stopped at Todd and Jake's bedroom and listened at the door. I heard nothing. I pushed open the door and saw Todd, asleep, on the bed. He wasn't tucked in yet and looked like a kitten in a ball on top of the quilt, curled up in the fetal position with his arms clutched to his chest. I remembered how he'd curl up like this anywhere, anytime, during hockey season and grab sleep wherever he could. His ride to the rink picked him up at the end of our long driveway at 4:30 every morning, while I was still buried under quilts in bed. Todd picked me up four nights a week during that same season from a ballet class that ended at 10:00 P.M. So many nights I'd step out of the dressing room to find him curled up just like this on the lobby floor, using his varsity jacket as a pillow, surrounded by all the adoring ballet moms, who shushed the people coming off the elevator lest they disturb him. We'd walk to the car hand in hand and sing to the oldies station on the hour-long drive home to keep him awake.

I wanted to keep him awake now. The illness seemed more in possession of him sleeping than waking. So thin, so frail, his slumbering breaths so labored. It seemed an impossibility that he would rise again and walk and talk.

I sat on the bed next to him and touched his shoulder. He didn't stir. I scooted closer and stroked his forehead, smoothing back the baby-fine hairs that were beginning to grow in, more red than blond. I bent and kissed the top of his sleeping head. He murmured something but didn't fully wake. "I love you," I whispered, and went upstairs to my room.

I wanted to say it to Nicholas, too, and I called him, ignoring the stack of poems and tests. What difference would one more day make? Hearing his voice was a massage on my soul. I burrowed under the covers, and we stayed on the phone, talking in whispers, long into the night. I didn't say good-bye to him until the pipes began to hiss and sigh, gearing up for their moaning lament that sang me to sleep.

Chapter Four

$\mathcal{I}$ spent most of the night fighting the urge to call Nicholas back or creep down the stairs to listen to my brother breathe. No urge to grade stirred within me during my hours of insomnia. Around three-thirty I slept, but not well, and when I woke, with a margarita headache, long before my alarm, I dressed and went downstairs. Everyone else was up, too.

"How ya feeling?" I asked Todd. He was working the cross-word puzzle at the kitchen table with Arnicia.

"So far so good."

"You're lookin' a little green, hon," Arnicia said to him.

"Oh, it's on the way," Todd agreed. "It's on the way. Give it a couple more hours." We might as well have been talking about an approaching hurricane.

"Do you want me to stay home?" I asked him. "I can call in sick."

"No, Jake's staying home. Save your sick days for when we can have fun."

"I'll be home no later than four," Arnicia said to Jacob, not Todd. "You page me if you need me before then." Jacob nodded, squeezing fresh orange juice with the intensity of a person performing CPR.

What an odd family we'd become. At first, Todd and Jacob had lived here alone and done fine. Todd had held his own for so long, but then began the endless barrage of infections and side effects. Every day some new crisis arose—he'd get a fever under control only to discover a purple lesion on the bottom of his foot. He'd get the lesion treated and reduced only to have a new medication scatter a rash across his torso. The medication that relieved the rash nauseated him. The nausea caused him to lose weight. The weight loss left him tired and weak. The fever came back.

And the T-cells kept dropping.

Overnight, last spring, he developed a flu so severe that he had to be hospitalized. He developed the tumor in his throat and started local radiation therapy. In May he got herpes sores in his mouth, some of them over an inch long.

The T-cells kept dropping.

He went through oral thrush, which, thank God, was easy enough to treat. Disgusting white fluff in his mouth and throat. It drove him crazy. The tumor grew so big, it hurt to swallow, and sometimes he couldn't speak. He changed to chemotherapy.

The clock kept ticking. The T-cells kept dropping.

And then he had the stroke.

We all believed he'd die. The day before was a good day. According to Jacob, Todd felt good enough to go across the street to the park by himself. He was cheerful and talkative, but after dinner, bending down to load the dishwasher, he had collapsed into a seizure.

He kept us in suspense for twenty-seven hours, loitering in a coma, then pulled through relatively unscathed. The key word is "relatively." It's amazing, when dealing with AIDS, the horrors you accept as fortunate.

The stroke blinded his right eye and subjected the left to weird, dizzying floaters. It stole his short-term memory—but only on some days, as though toying with him, refusing to let him get too confident. It impaired his movement enough to piss him off, but no more. His right hand sometimes failed to grasp on his brain's command. Until he recovered a little finesse, he'd dropped every one of his and Jake's crystal champagne glasses, smashing them on the floor. Visiting one day, I'd found two crystal flutes swept up and discarded in the trash. Abby had come by for a rare appearance and had gasped, "Your crystal!"

Jacob had looked at her, eyes narrowed, and said, "It's only money."

Jacob feared leaving Todd alone after the stroke, but they were both intelligent enough to know that Jacob couldn't keep watch around the clock.

"It would drive me crazy," Todd said. "What would we have to talk about? Don't think I'm being noble. I have very selfish motives—I need for him to be working."

"We can't be together twenty-four hours," Jacob agreed. "We'd kill each other."

They interviewed several people but weren't satisfied with any of them.

"Too geeky," Todd said of one.

"Too Christian," Jacob said of another.

"Too bossy."

"I think she was stoned."

And then, by accident, they'd met Arnicia at a theater party. She'd walked out of the host's bathroom just in time to see Todd do his melting act as he waited in the narrow hallway. Jacob eventually came to check on what was taking Todd so long and found them sitting on the floor, Arnicia's skirt hiked up—Jacob loved to tell how he'd seen her leopardskin panties—holding Todd's hand and chatting away, acting as though this were the most common occurrence in the world. Jacob most loved the way she'd looked up at him and asked, "Do you belong to this man?" and when he'd nodded, sighed and said, "Well, isn't that just my luck." During their conversation, they'd discovered she was a nursing student, dating an actor who'd stood her up that evening. She had classes and hospital work from one in the afternoon to around midnight. She could be home in the morning while Jacob was teaching acting students to use rapiers and daggers and to punch, kick, and choke each other. They'd left the party and discussed the arrangement over drinks at a nearby bar. Within two days she had moved in.

But Todd and Jacob wanted Jake to be acting again. They needed someone there in the evenings while Jacob had rehearsal. Jacob carried out another exhaustive search, but Todd found something wrong with every candidate. That's when I'd been called, late in July, living with Nicholas in Cincinnati, supporting myself teaching a college dance class of nonmajors while I finished the last class of my English degree. Two and a half years of taking nearly thirty-five credit hours every quarter had paid off. I'd been offered a job at the School of the Arts, where I'd student taught that spring. Nicholas and I were sitting on our balcony, toasting with beers, when Todd's call came. I knew my answer was yes, although Todd wouldn't let me tell him until I'd thought about it at least twenty-four hours. There was nothing to think about, and Nicholas agreed. I had to do this.

In two weeks I moved into the upstairs bedroom of their rented house, right across from Arnicia's room. We shared a bathroom and within a month were sharing perfume, lipstick, and nail polish. I liked her, and many nights found us sitting on our bathroom floor sharing secrets like sisters.

And here we all were, waiting for Todd's chemo sickness to strike, for the fourth time.

"I still can't believe you're in a play where you don't beat any-

one up," I said to Jacob, taking the glass of orange juice he offered. Bob Cratchit in *A Christmas Carol* marked his first role
since college, including the soap opera, that did not revolve
around stunt work or stage combat. The play opened the week
after Thanksgiving. "I thought you had rehearsal tonight," I said,
glancing at the schedule taped to the fridge.

"Nope." He pulled down the schedule. "This has all changed.
I have the night off."

Todd shook his head. "For such a good actor, you're the worst
liar I've ever seen," he said. Jacob shrugged, Todd reached for
him, and I slipped out of the room.

In my classroom, I wrote the quote of the day on the chalkboard. *"Do not fear death so much but rather the inadequate life."*—
Bertolt Brecht. Todd had sent me that on a card from Hungary.

Zackery never showed up. I'd hoped he wouldn't, since I still
hadn't read the poem, but I was annoyed all the same, on princi-
ple. He didn't know I hadn't read it, and I would've stayed with
Todd longer if I hadn't promised Zack this early meeting.

I wondered which was worse—watching Todd's condition de-
teriorate at home on these days or imagining it deteriorating, as
I did at school. Most days I guiltily lost myself in the little dra-
mas, the curriculum, the ridiculous rules and regulations, but images of Todd haunted me at school on the days after chemo. An
image of him sweating as homeroom started. Hyperventilating
and sweating that cold, sticky sweat.

I knew that Jake was changing sheets as second period started.
Peeling off the damp sheets thick with the syrupy odor of un-
healthy sweat. But I managed to sit through my class stumbling
their way aloud through *Hamlet* all the same. I bit my tongue and
breathed deeply to remain patient, trying not to compare these
kids with the students at the School of the Arts, who had cared

about *Hamlet* and had paid passionate attention to class, in case someday they were to act the melancholy prince, or dance Ophelia in the ballet, or sing Claudius in the opera, or design their own castle Elsinore.

I sat through the slow, halting soliloquies and told myself that at least this filled time and no more grading accumulated before I had the last batch returned. Another bonus presented itself as well. The reading was so excruciating that stopping for discussion was a welcome diversion to the class.

"Why's this guy so freaked out?" a student asked of Hamlet. Her clothes were way too tight; she couldn't be comfortable.

"How would you feel if someone you loved returned from the dead and told you something so awful?"

She shrugged and cracked her gum. She had no frame of reference. A few of them did, though; I could see it in their eyes.

I tried to imagine Todd coming back from the dead. I pictured him looking the way he used to, with a full head of hair and all the lost pounds. I wondered what he'd say to me.

Just before lunch I knew he was shivering. Convulsive shivers. Teeth clattering. Breath in ragged, panting gasps. But I made it through the review of the sophomores' grammar tests. The cocky one, who'd skipped on test day, slouched, sullen, during the review.

Now he's swallowing, I thought while the afternoon class continued with their poems. He can't stop swallowing, feeling as though he'll choke, fighting the nausea. His throat's feeling as if it'll close on him.

Zackery didn't show up for class, but he was on the official absence sheet.

Simon Schiffler came up to my desk during the last minutes of class. A nice kid, one I couldn't help but love, a hockey player, with blond hair always in his eyes. We'd already covered the answer to his question in class today. I'd pretended not to see him dozing off, remembering the cruel schedule the hockey team kept. I glanced around the room while Simon wrote down the notes I gave him.

Denny whispered to the kid across from him, and they both wheezed with laughter like hyenas. He was telling a joke, I could tell, and the punch line involved the sight gag of the stereotypical limp-wrist gesture. I wanted to rush across the room and slam him into the wall. I stood up. "What are you doing?" Everyone stopped talking and stared at me, slightly alarmed, it seemed, at my tone and posture.

He turned to me with that blank face. "You said we could talk. Class is done."

"Keep it appropriate," I said, wishing there were something, anything, I could say to him that would give me the same satisfaction as slapping that doughy face.

"It's appropriate. Relax, Ms. Zwolenick."

"Excuse me?"

"You're too uptight. Lighten up."

He reveled in my hatred of him; I could feel it. He goaded me, and I fell for it every time. Since it was minutes before the bell, I let it go. He broke off eye contact first, and I tried to take that for the small victory it was.

"Hey, I was talking about you last night at the opera," Carissa said. She wore a burgundy silk pantsuit and dressed as though she were going straight to an opera date from school every day. "I met your sister when I was there with my parents. My parents know your sister and Dr. Montgomery. I never knew Mrs. Montgomery was your sister."

I nodded.

"*The* Montgomeries?" Simon asked. "Like Montgomery Boulevard and Montgomery Park? You're related to them?"

"Only because of my sister's marriage," I said, my stomach clenching in its customary reaction to personal questions.

"So, you're rich," Denny said.

I laughed. "No. I'm not the one married to a Montgomery."

"She lives with her brother," the opera girl announced, proud of her newfound knowledge of me. "He's rich, too. He used to work on movies. A camera guy or something—"

"Sound," I said, looking at the clock. Ring bell, ring.

"Whatever. He's sick. He has cancer."

Everyone looked sympathetic.

"Cancer?" My eyelid began to tic.

"Yeah, that's what your sister said."

The bell rang. I stood, gripping the back of a chair, stretching my knuckles white, then blue, until every kid was gone.

I drove home tailgating some poor, flustered old man, screaming obscenities at an imagined Abby, but forgot her when I hit the back door.

Jacob knelt in front of the closed bathroom door, his elbows on the floor, his head in his hands, sobbing. I heard Todd inside the bathroom, sobbing, too. From the acrid, suffocating smell, I knew it had begun.

Jacob begged, "Please, Todd. Let me in."

In response, the door rattled three times as Todd kicked it from inside. I pictured him on his back, kicking the door, like a child having a tantrum.

"I have to come in. I have to help you." Jacob started to open the door.

"Stay the fuck out!" Todd screamed. "I don't need your help! I can do it!"

And with that, another bout began. My whole body recoiled

at the sounds. I feared the strength and will with which his body wanted rid of this poison.

Jacob saw me, grabbed my hand, and pulled me toward the door. "Summer's home, Todd," he shouted. "She wants to help you."

I managed to get the door open a few inches. The mess was everywhere—all over him, the floor, even the walls. He saw me and screamed. "Shut the door! I didn't fucking say you could come in! Get out!" He drew his legs up to his chest and bucked at the door with both feet.

I jerked my hand back, but not fast enough, and felt skin and bone grate as I yanked fingers free of the slammed door. I gripped my smashed fingers with my other hand, hunched over, curling up around a pain so sharp that my eyes and nose burned. A ringing began at the top of my spine, like the high, hollow pitch of glassware.

"Shit. Are you okay?" Jacob asked, reaching for my hands.

I turned away from him, keeping my throbbing fingers tight against my chest. "We have to go in," I said. "You can't just let him lie in that mess in there."

"He won't let me," Jacob said.

"Let you? For God's sake, Jacob. You have to do something. This is worse than last time."

Another bout began.

Jacob sank again to the floor, his back to the bathroom door. I slid down the wall beside him. "Jacob. Please. We could both go in. We could pick him up. He's not that strong—"

"No."

"How can you just sit here?"

He whipped around inches from my face. "I hate this," he said in a fierce whisper. "I can't even describe how much I hate this— sitting out here, listening to that, listening to him saying he can do it and knowing he fucking can't. Yeah, I could go in there, Summer. I could go in there and take over. I could stay in there and make him do what I want. But he doesn't want me to. So I won't. I've been sitting out here for twenty minutes, Summer. Twenty minutes listening to him wallow around in puke."

The ringing at the base of my skull grew in intensity. "Jacob," I begged, talking over the sound, shutting it out. "It's for his own good."

"How far do I go, for his own good?" Jacob asked me. "How far do I go in removing the last vestiges of dignity? You tell me that."

I buried my face in my knees, still gripping my hands in my lap. Jacob put an arm around me, and we huddled together outside that horrible room, which, for the moment, had fallen quiet.

After a while, we heard sounds. The sounds of Todd trying to clean up.

"No one in the world should have to do this," Jacob whispered. "No one. I can't think of a single goddamn person in the world, ever, that I would wish this on."

I paid attention to the ringing; heard it for what it truly was. With the clarity of a crack in the shin, I realized and whispered, "I can't do this." Once acknowledged, the ringing stopped.

"We're doing it."

"No. I can't do what you're doing. I can't love someone like you do. I couldn't do this."

"You are doing it. For Todd."

"But he's—he's not my lover."

"So?" His expression was that of a person who'd discovered green mold on a piece of bread he'd been enjoying.

The phone rang. And only because I couldn't stand Jacob's disapproval did I pick it up.

"Summer? Hey, it's me," Nicholas said. His voice, usually such a balm, tightened my throat. I felt caught; that surely he'd sense what I'd just revealed. Prickling heat crawled up my neck. I avoided eye contact with Jacob.

"Hey, love," I said in an artificial, sugared voice.

"Is it bad?" he asked, his own voice dropping serious.

"Yeah."

"How're you holding up?"

"I'm not."

He made the smallest sound, an "oh" of pain on my behalf. I imagined how, if he were here, he'd reach out and press me against him, his chin on top of my head.

"I can come tonight after rehearsal." It wasn't a question, it was a declaration. I knew rehearsal was scheduled until 11:00 and that he had to be the last out and lock up the theater. He wouldn't arrive here until 1:30 at the earliest. I also knew he was putting in hours on the set in the mornings.

"When's your call tomorrow?" I asked him.

He paused, and I knew he was trying to think of a lie, but he admitted, "Eight o'clock. But I can be late."

"You'd only be here five or six hours."

"I'd do anything for you," he said. I knew he meant it. "If you want me there, I'm there."

Todd coughed inside the bathroom. An obscene, strangling cough that made Jacob stand again and call through the door, "Are you okay?"

"Jesus," Nicholas said. "I could hear that. Is he all right?"

No answer from within the bathroom. Jacob slapped his palm against the door. "Answer me!"

"Don't come," I said. "I want you here, but I'd only worry. And I don't need anything else to worry about. I don't want you driving in the middle of the night."

"Are you sure? Is Todd okay?"

"Goddamn it, answer me, you little shit!" Jacob yelled. The doorknob wriggled in his hands. Todd had locked the door.

"Yeah. But get here this weekend. I'm living for that."

"I love you, Summer."

"Todd! You motherfucker! Say something!"

"I . . . I have to go." I hung up. My hands shook.

Arnicia came in the back door, dumping her armload of textbooks on the kitchen table. "How we doing?" she asked.

Before we could answer, Todd's weary voice came from inside the bathroom. "Nish? Could you help me a minute, please?"

"Of course, puddin'." We watched Arnicia gain access to the forbidden room. After a few minutes of murmured voices, she came out and headed for the kitchen. We followed her.

"What is up with that?" Jacob asked her. She looked at us and shook her head.

"I thought you all were some smart people. Don't you go and disappoint me."

"I tried for twenty minutes to get in there," Jacob said.

"And, of course, he wouldn't let you in. This is the worst one yet. He's embarrassed."

"He let you in," I said. It was an accusation.

"I'm an outsider," she said with exaggerated patience, as though talking to retarded children. "I was hired for this. I've only ever known him sick." She looked at Jacob while she rolled latex gloves onto her hands with a solid snap. "I've never made love to him." She took a jug of bleach from under the sink and an orange Gatorade from the fridge but stopped, frowning at me. "What's wrong with you?" she asked.

I opened my right hand, revealing a deep, blood-filled groove cut into the cuticles of my middle fingers. Released from my grip, the fingers began to swell, becoming purple. Although I hadn't asked her for help, Arnicia set down her bleach and

Gatorade, yanked open the freezer, filled a dish towel with ice, and handed it to me. Her movements were all too precise and forceful; I felt scolded in some way.

"You all get out of here and be patient," she said.

We did, sitting in the living room in silence, and soon we heard her soothing voice and the shower running. Before long, she had Todd tucked into bed smelling like baby powder and the bathroom so clean that my eyes watered.

"Jacob?" Arnicia called. "Your Todd will see you now."

Your Todd.

I thought of Nicholas as my Nicholas, but wasn't sure I was capable of being his Summer. I tried to picture Nicholas screaming at me with vomit in his hair. It just wasn't there.

I sat in the living room for a long time, ice wrapped on one hand, blowing the soap bubbles Todd had bought me with the other.

And after two nights of twenty-minute naps broken by the sounds of gagging and retching echoing through the house, it was over. That round, anyway. Todd weighed nine pounds less, I'd called in sick for two days, and we all looked like the walking dead, but it was over.

Dr. Sara came to visit to make sure we did the necessary work to get the nine precious pounds back on.

"I'm not going to do that anymore," Todd whispered. He'd trashed his throat from all the vomiting, bleeding large volumes from ripping up the tumor in the process. "I'm not going to do any more chemo."

Dr. Sara nodded and smiled. "Good," she said, looking at Jacob.

Jacob, behind Todd, stood up and turned away.

"You and Grandma Anna," I said, teasing him, hoping to distract him from their friction.

"Hey, I tried. How is she, anyway?"

"Hanging in there." They seemed to take turns, she and Todd, with their worst episodes.

"I want to go see her. Maybe tomorrow."

"We'll see," Jacob said.

"I'll go if I want." He was testy, rude.

"Sure, we'll go," Jacob said, unruffled. "I just meant we'll see how you feel."

Todd dropped off to sleep in midsentence, Dr. Sara went to visit other patients, and Jacob went to rehearsal.

I enjoyed the silence of the old house. I had so much grading to do, planning to do, but instead I sat in a chair opposite Todd's bed and watched him sleep. I flexed my hand, finally able to bend the damaged fingers. The groove from the door had sliced into the bottoms of both blackening fingernails, leaving them unattached at the cuticle beds. I expected they'd both fall off. I stared at them until my vision blurred. I yawned but put off going upstairs to my own bed. I missed Nicholas the most at night; it was our favorite time together back in our old apartment. No matter how late it was, or how early we had to get up the next day, we'd have the best conversations when we went to bed. Jacob had laughed when I said that, teasing, "Oh, sure you talk," but we did. Sex, for us, was rarely at night, and even more rarely in our bed. We favored the more spontaneous afternoon romps in less obvious rooms of the apartment.

Of course, privacy required that we stay in my bedroom since I'd moved here. But beyond that, there'd been a change, a gentling of sorts. Nicholas rarely initiated sex anymore, as if unsure how much he could ask of me. When we did make love, it felt careful, forgiving, more of a mutual comforting. I might miss the wildness at times, but I missed our conversations even more. We'd lie facing one another and talk in hushed voices, as though a child slept in the next room. It had never changed from the way we talked on our first date, when we'd hung on every word as a clue to each other's mystery.

When I caught myself nodding, unable to stave off sleep any longer, I crawled into the bed beside my big brother and wriggled under the double wedding ring quilt my mother's mother, my grandma Cailee, had made them. I snuggled up to him. "Hey," he murmured, surfacing for a fleeting moment and taking my hand. I wanted to talk to Todd, for him to talk to me. I missed his old voice so much—that fatherly lullaby, soothing and warm, his ability to make anything sound like a seduction. He could calm the wildest of dogs or horses and could talk Mom into agreements Abby and I wouldn't dare attempt. It pained me now that his voice was lost to me. Besides, he'd fallen back to sleep. So I slept, too, and we were still holding hands when Jacob came home and touched my cheek.

"Sorry, Summer," he whispered when I opened my eyes. "But the three of us in bed is just a little too weird."

He walked me upstairs to my own bed, my ankle already stiffening, causing me to limp. He kept his hand in the small of my back, guiding me, as if he didn't really believe I was awake. He tucked me in and kissed my forehead, leaving behind a comforting whiff of Ivory soap. "Thanks for staying with him like that," he said.

I smiled, feeling safe and cared for. We stared at each other, and just as the pause had grown the slightest awkward, there was a tap on the door and Arnicia came in. "You will never guess who just called." I hadn't even heard the phone. The ringers were off all over the house, except the kitchen. We were as paranoid about waking Todd as if he were a newborn infant. "Little Miss Abby."

And the peaceful mood yanked away from me like a curtain.

Chapter Five

I still seethed the next morning over breakfast. "Did she want to talk to any of us? Did she ask for me or Todd?" I asked Arnicia.

"Girlfriend, you are on my last nerve. I'm not gonna tell you again: She didn't ask for anybody. I said, 'Hello?' and she said, 'Arnicia?' and I said, 'Yes.' Or I might have said, 'Uh-huh,' or, 'Yeah,' or something—are you getting this? And she said, 'This is Abby. I'm just calling to see how Todd is doing.' And I told her and she said to give him her best and she told me she was leaving on a vacation to Costa Rica tomorrow and we both said, 'Good-bye.' I can't remember who said good-bye first—do you want me to call her back and see if she remembers?"

"Give him her best? What the hell does that mean?"

Arnicia rolled her eyes and poured cream into her coffee.

"Calling like that—like everything is normal. All casual. 'How is Todd doing?' Why doesn't she get her butt over here and see for herself?"

Arnicia sighed. She made a great show of opening the paper and getting out a pen. She settled into her crossword puzzle.

Todd made his zombielike way into the kitchen. He hung on to the wall as he walked but grinned and asked, "Hey, did you hear that Abby called?"

Arnicia chuckled.

"Yeah, I heard," I said.

"I knew she would," he said. I clenched my jaw and breathed deeply.

Todd took a few tenuous steps away from the wall and sank into a chair at the table. From his smile, you'd think he'd just slid into home base.

"Want some breakfast?" Arnicia asked.

"I'll get it in a minute. I need to rest." He panted and laughed at himself.

"I'll get it," Arnicia said. "What do you want?"

"You've done enough, Nish. I'll get it, really."

She put aside the paper and crossed her arms. "Mr. Zwolenick," she said, "I am getting paid an obscene amount of money to sit here and work the crossword puzzle."

"You earn every penny," he said. They studied each other a moment, both smiling.

"How about some Cream of Wheat?" she asked, getting up.

He gave in and made a face. "Mmm. Yummy," he lied.

She laughed. "Would you prefer a nice fluffy omelet with cheese and peppers and saus—"

His face went chalky. "Oh, no, no, no. Don't even joke like that." He shifted in his seat.

"Sorry," she said. "Not funny. Get me started on that"—she gestured to the puzzle—"and I'll serve you up the safest, blandest, kindest bowl of Cream of Wheat you ever had."

Returning to school for just a Friday didn't feel so bad. Just one day. Anybody can get through one day, right?

A knot thickened in my belly when I saw Zackery waiting outside my room. I'd never read his poem. I hadn't read anybody's. I'd entertained the thought of burning them all in our fireplace and claiming someone had stolen them but had settled, instead, on the plan to grade all night tonight so that there'd be nothing to distract me when Nicholas arrived on Saturday, so I could simply revel in his presence.

Zack coughed, his eyes met mine. "Sorry," he said, lowering them again, the miserable red splotches blooming on his neck. "I shouldn't have dropped such a bomb and then disappeared. I know that wasn't fair of me, after telling you, you know, but I was . . . embarrassed." We both took a deep breath, but before I could speak, Zack searched my face and said, "You didn't read it."

"No, Zack, I'm sorry. My brother's very ill. I'm helping take care of him, and the last few days have been bad ones, that's why I wasn't here. I wasn't reading or grading at home—"

"You've been gone, too?"

"Yes." Wait a minute. "You've been absent? All week? Since Monday?" He nodded. "That's not like you, Zack. Is anything wrong?"

He laughed, and it rang harshly in the empty hall. "Well. That's why—I—" His mouth formed half a dozen other words but discarded each before uttering a sound. He shook his head. He opened his arms in a helpless gesture, speechless.

"You know what?" I said. "I'll read it right now." I couldn't bear the look in those saucerlike eyes. Better to see them disappointed than in such suspense. I unzipped my briefcase and crouched down to go through it.

"No. No, b-because, actually, I think—I changed my mind—you shouldn't read it. I think maybe, I was, I don't know, out of line. If, if you could give it back to me, I—I'll just, you know, take a zero for it. I didn't—I wasn't—it wasn't for a grade—I just wanted you to know . . ."

I looked up at him, trying not to show how relieved I was. "I won't read it if you don't want me to," I said. He nodded. "And you can turn in something else, later. I won't give you a zero." He shrugged. I continued searching in my bag, to give it back to him and be done with it, when two other students entered the hallway, calling out a greeting to him.

"Give it to me later?" he whispered, almost begging. His tone made my scalp shrink, but I nodded. He walked away.

Of course, then, curiosity overcame me. I had to read it. At my desk, I opened the envelope, but a blank cover page was stapled in an elaborate pattern to the poem. I held it to the light, but his paper was a heavy, expensive brand, impossible to read through. I drummed my fingers on the desk. Part of me wanted to tear it open and read it anyway. Another part of me knew I could never replace this cover sheet and make it look untouched. I thought of Russ, the boy who'd had a crush on me when I student taught in Cincinnati. Russ had written poems describing my breasts as "sweetly swelling muffins"—just the tops, he'd pointed out, not the stems—and how they still held the "undeveloped promise of a freshman girl," his poetic way to suggest that I wasn't well endowed. Facing him, grading his work in class after my gentle reminder of appropriate boundaries, was so excruciating as to warrant its own level of hell, descending even deeper when his crush died away and I saw his own mortification set in. I liked Zackery enough that I didn't want him to go through that. He'd know for sure it hadn't been read, and we could put this entire idiotic episode behind us.

I had the manila envelope ready to hand over, but he didn't attend my class after lunch. This time he hadn't signed out. I knew he must be embarrassed, but after school I filled out a discipline notice. The kids always talked about fair. Well, I'd be fair—I wouldn't allow myself to make an exception for him.

I was glad I hadn't when I saw him outside. As I backed out of my parking space, checking behind me, there he was, lurking in the bushes by the bicycle racks. I stopped the car, but he slipped away around the corner of the building.

I leaned my head against the steering wheel. Now he knew which car was mine. I imagined him stalking me, spying, sighing in the bushes as he watched me unload groceries. Russ, in Cincinnati, had sat on a bench by the river, across from our apartment, every evening for weeks on end. Nicholas had wanted to call the police, but I'd convinced him the boy was harmless. Nicholas then took to waving and calling Russ's name from our tiny balcony, which was what eventually shamed him away. Don't do this to me, Zack, I thought. I can't worry about anything else right now.

When I got home, Jacob met me at the door with an air of patient long-suffering. "We're going to the farm," he said. "He's pretty damn tired, but determined. It took him most of the day to dress and shave and wash his hair—what little there is of it. He had to take naps between each activity."

"He's so stubborn."

Jacob laughed. "Look who's talking."

At the farm, Mom came out the back door, alerted by the pack of barking dogs, and waved for us to pull the car all the way to the back door. Todd wouldn't let us and instead walked up the path with me and Jacob on either arm. Once we were in the kitchen and Todd began the slow process of unwrapping the layers we had piled upon him, Mom kissed me and hugged Jacob.

"Hey, Jean," Jacob said. They held each other a tad longer than a typical hug. Mom appeared younger today, youthful almost, in her flannel shirt and work khakis, her hair in a single braid down her back, wild strands escaping all over her head.

Todd opened his arms and Mom embraced him, then held his face in her hands. He rolled his eyes and grinned, submitting with pleasure. "Let me look at you. You look good, sweetie."

"Don't exaggerate, Mom."

She laughed. "You look better than I expected."

"That's more realistic."

He did look good, though, all things considered. If you saw him today, and didn't know him, you'd see a man whose thinness and air of exhaustion suggested the completion of some highly physical feat. Like a man just come down from Everest.

Todd went to Grandma Anna's room. Mom, Jake, and I drank coffee at the kitchen table. We agreed to stay for supper, although Jacob would have to leave for rehearsal and couldn't stay long. Mom set us to work peeling potatoes. She decided to make a pot of stew for everyone but Todd—he would get his own plain potato soup. Jacob fussed over the potato soup, making sure Mom scrubbed the potatoes well, and that the pot was very clean, and that there wasn't too much heavy cream in it. Mom wiped her hand on her khakis, touched his cheek, and said, "I'm looking after him, too, Jake." He kissed her hand. She giggled. The two of them had been fast friends from the first Thanksgiving Todd had brought him home.

The back door opened and Dad came in from evening feed. "Hey there!" he said. He reached out and shook Jacob's hand—a hearty, manly handshake, with no eye contact whatsoever. I saw Jacob's amused grin and had to grin, too. Dad grabbed me in a big bear hug, ruffling my hair, snagging it with his callused hand. "Thanks for feeding the other day. Where's Todd? He did come, didn't he?"

"He's with Anna. Leave them be," Mom said without turning around from her pot.

"I can say hello, I think," he said almost to himself. He strode through the kitchen into the hall and went to greet his only son.

Jacob asked Mom if she'd "let him" set the table. He folded the cloth napkins and refilled the sugar bowl and salt shaker. He kept asking "What else can I do?"

Dad helped bring Grandma Anna to the head of the table in her wheelchair. She hadn't dressed today and wore a blue flannel nightgown with pink embroidered flowers, far too festive to suit her, with a brown afghan draped across her narrow shoulders like a shawl. She and Jacob eyed each other from opposite ends of the table.

"How are you, Mrs. Zwolenick?" he asked.

"I'm dying," she said.

He raised his eyebrows. "Yes, I know. I'm sorry." He sounded sincere, I'll give him that.

"There are things I would like to see happen before I die."

"Oh? So would I." They glared at each other.

"Fresh, homemade stew," Mom said with forced cheer, serving everyone.

"So, did Nicholas get that job in D.C.?" Dad asked me. It was always this way. We talked of the Arena, school, and Jacob's play.

"You're Bob Cratchit, right?" Mom asked.

"Bob Cratchit is a married man," Grandma said. That was a challenge. I saw Todd give Jacob a pleading look.

Jacob ignored Todd and said, "So am I."

She smiled. "Not in the eyes of God."

"All right, everybody," Todd said. "Let's not go there again."

"Yes, please," Mom agreed.

Outside, the dogs exploded in a flurry of barking and howling. Dad stood up and peered through the gathering darkness. "It's Abby."

The cancer comment from school replayed itself in my head. My fingers tightened on my silverware.

"Oh, no," Mom said. "What's happened now?"

"Aren't they supposed to be in Costa Rica?" I asked.

"They're supposed to be," Mom said. We watched through the window as Abby stepped out of her red Lexus, ignoring the dogs clamoring for attention, and picked her way up the stone path in high heels.

"How've they been doing?" Todd asked, his question burdened with the answer he already knew.

"Not good," Mom said.

"Is Brad still screwing all his nurses?" I asked.

"Summer," Dad warned.

Mom opened the door for her and gave her a hug. "Hi, honey. You're just in time for supper."

Abby wore a black cashmere suit with pearl buttons. She had no coat. Her red hair was down. I hadn't seen her hair down for years. "Hi, everybody," she said, sounding less than pleased at finding all of us here. She pulled her hair back with her hands, a nervous habit, then let it go. We had just a glimpse of the bluish, purple shadow outside her left eye and cheekbone. The stew went to sawdust in my mouth.

She hugged Dad, then Todd. "Hey, you. You look wonderful," she said to him.

"Yeah, right, but thanks. So do you. For real."

"Hi, Grandma." A kiss on the cheek. "Hey, Summer." A warm, forgive-me smile. "Hello, Jacob." No expression whatsoever.

They'd never been friends. I remembered the first time they'd met, in this kitchen. Abby had been sporting a split lip on that occasion. She'd stammered, "Y-you're Big Ed Baker."

"No, I'm Jacob Kenwood. I only play Big Ed Baker."

"Who's Big Ed Baker?" Dad had asked.

"A mean, stupid shit of a guy who beats women up," Jacob said. He looked at Abby. "Looks like you know one in real life." She'd hated him ever since.

Mom handed Abby a bowl, and Dad brought another chair from the living room.

We ate our stew in silence.

I'd never dreamed, when I first met Brad Montgomery, that he'd one day harm my sister. I'd liked him. I'd gone down to visit Abby for Little Sibs Weekend at her college, and Brad had taken us out to a hip restaurant and bought me a $60 university sweatshirt without batting an eye when he heard me say I needed a souvenir. He was tall, broad, and blond, his hair clipped short, the sort of cut Todd jokingly referred to as "young Republican."

Brad was dutifully impressed with my being a company member with the Dayton Ballet. "My parents have had season tickets forever. I'll have to tell them to look for you." And he did. At the next performance they delivered a box of two dozen roses backstage. That sold me.

Todd, however, had been skeptical from the start. He'd visited Abby on other occasions and come home saying Brad was "smarmy"—which I'd had to look up—and controlling. He teased Abby about wanting to be a doctor's wife. "See, this is the same reason why I hated that you were a cheerleader. Why not play the game yourself? Why be a doctor's wife if you could be a doctor?" But that year for Christmas, Brad gave Abby an engagement ring.

"You could buy our farm, all our property, with this," Abby had whispered to me as I'd admired her magnificent ring.

Eight years they'd been together. And here she was with no coat and a black eye.

Todd cleared his throat. "How many people are coming for Thanksgiving, Mom?"

"So far, everybody. It'll be a packed house." Mom had five brothers and sisters, and all of them had children. "Can you make it, Abby?"

"I'm not sure. I'll see." It was her standard answer.

"Will you be here, Mr. Kenwood?" Grandma asked.

"Of course he will," Todd said. "He's family."

"What about your real family?" Grandma asked. "Don't they want you?"

Jacob put down his silverware and folded his arms in front of his bowl. He leaned toward Grandma. "I think, Mrs. Zwolenick, that we've had this conversation before. I haven't been home for years, remember?"

"Why not?"

"Grandma, don't," Todd said.

"Is it because you're a homosexual?" Grandma asked.

"Oh, for God's sake," Mom said.

"Why is that all you ever want to talk about?" Abby asked. "Every conversation in this house revolves around homosexuality."

"I agree," Todd said.

"Can we please change the subject?" Abby asked.

"I'd like to hear about this trip to Costa Rica," Jacob said.

Abby turned on him. "Who do you think you are, anyway? What makes you think my personal life is any of your goddamn business?"

"Whoa. Sorry. Arnicia told me you were going, that's all."

"Abby, chill," Todd said. "Jesus."

Grandma hit the side of her bowl with her spoon. "Do not use the Lord's name in vain!"

We ate again. Our family dinners had been this way for years now. Abby helped herself to some wine in the fridge. She didn't offer any to anyone else.

"You didn't answer my question," Grandma said to Jacob.

"I thought we were changing the subject," Mom said, looking

at Dad. He simply opened his hands in a helpless gesture, and she glared.

Jacob didn't seem upset. His eyes twinkled as he said, "Yes, you're absolutely right. They don't let me come home because I'm homosexual. That's very perceptive of you."

"How long have they not let you come home?" she asked.

"Let's see . . . since I was a sophomore in college. That's what? Seven, eight years?"

"And in case you're getting any ideas, Grandma," Todd said, not looking up, "he's still homosexual. Abandoning him, banishing him, not speaking to him, didn't change that fact."

"Nothing will change that fact. Sorry if you don't like it," Jacob said, resuming eating.

"Do you?"

"Do I what?"

"Like it?"

"I like it fine," Jacob said. "Thanks for asking."

"I have a friend who went to Costa Rica last year," I said. "Remember Darci, from the company? She said it was unbelievable. A beautiful country."

"I have a husband who went to Costa Rica last night," Abby said.

"He went alone?" Todd asked.

"Oh, no, just without me."

No one knew what to say. I wondered what Brad looked like right now. To Abby's credit, she always gave as good as she got. Once, she'd broken his nose, although he claimed it was from playing racquetball.

"I'm sorry," Jacob said.

"Shut up."

Jacob laughed and held up his hands as if in surrender.

"You think you could be civil, Abby?" Todd asked. His voice

thinned, and his face shone with sweat. "Is that too much to ask?"

"Oh, like how civil you are to Brad?" she asked.

"Look," Todd said, "I never even see Brad. He wants nothing to do with me and doesn't work very hard to hide that fact. And it's hard to be civil to someone who bloodies my sister with regularity." There, someone had acknowledged it tonight. Normally, if Jacob didn't, no one would.

"It is not with regularity!"

"Abby, don't you understand that one time is too many?" Dad asked. He'd been waiting, too.

"What he does to you is inexcusable," Mom said. "You need help. So does Brad—"

"Would everyone just back off?"

"No. No, I won't," Mom said. "Because if I do, you'll end up dead someday—"

"Oh, for Christ's sake!" Abby stood, bumping the table. Grandma cringed at this blasphemy. Silverware clattered against china in rhythm with Abby's heels striking the floor. We heard her footsteps on the stairs and then over our heads. Then, silence.

Mom pushed her half-eaten bowl of stew away from her. Dad continued eating, and Mom looked at him with loathing.

Todd struggled to his feet. "I want to go talk to her." His voice cracked; he was tired. "Help me up the stairs?"

Jacob shook his head but said, "Sure, babe." He went to him, and they left the room.

"You are wrong to allow this." Grandma Anna pointed to Dad. "It is wrong, and because I love him, I will tell him so."

"Leave it alone, Ma," he said, using a dinner roll to mop up the remnants of his stew.

"You gonna tell Brad that what *he* does is wrong?" I asked

Grandma. "How can you tell us and teach us everything you have and not see how this makes every lesson of yours bullshit?"

"Summer," Dad said. "You leave it alone, too."

"Your language," was all Grandma said to me. A bitter laugh escaped from Mom.

Jacob came back into the kitchen. "Jean? Do you mind if I have some of that wine?" he asked.

"Help yourself," she said. "I'd like a glass, too."

He went to the refrigerator. Grandma Anna sucked in her breath as if in pain, and we looked at her in alarm. She pointed at Jacob. "What is that? What do you have on you?" she asked.

Jacob scanned himself, probably expecting to find a tarantula judging from her tone of voice. "What?" he asked with an edge of panic.

"That! That triangle! What is that?" She, too, had an edge of panic. There was a pink triangle pin, the point down, embedded in the knubbly folds of Jacob's thick black sweater. Grandma hadn't seen it until he'd stood. "I have seen them! I have seen them before!" she said. "What does it mean that you are wearing it?"

"Oh," Jacob said. He looked at the pin, then up at her. "I know where you've seen them." His voice was soft. Gentler than I'd ever heard it with anyone but Todd. "Didn't you know who they were?"

Grandma stared at him, nostrils flared as if she smelled rotting garbage.

"Gays had to wear them in the camps, just like the Jews had their yellow stars. Did you know they killed us, too? People like me? People like your grandson?"

"That's not true," she said without hesitation. I wondered what that felt like, to never doubt.

Jacob nodded. "Yes. It is true." He wasn't being disrespectful. His tone was neutral, cautious, even. "I've always wanted to ask you—but Todd will never let me. Would you have considered hiding any gay people in your hayloft if you could have, or . . . is that a different story altogether?"

"You mock me," she said, her eyes threatening to ignite. "You mock the sacrifice I made. You, who were never there, dare to wear that. These ridiculous lies. Why they allow you inside my home I will never understand!"

"Anna!" Mom said. "That's enough. Jacob is welcome here as my son-in-law."

"Jean," Dad said, frowning at her, begging her with his eyes to stop. They locked eyes while Jacob poured two glasses of wine. Dad dropped his eyes first and returned to scouring his bowl with the dinner roll.

Jacob handed a glass to my mother and sat back down at the table. "Okay, then, tell me," he asked Grandma. "Who did you think they were?"

Grandma didn't answer. She stared, but not at Jacob. She stared at the pink triangle and blinked. She'd gone a million miles and almost sixty years away from us, seeing horrors we could never comprehend.

"You know, Mrs. Zwolenick . . ." Jacob paused, took a sip of wine, and waited for her to return to us. "Your grandson showed me a quote the other day—you know how he is with quotes—because it made him think of you and me. It's funny because it made *me* think of you and Todd, and I just can't get it out of my head. It's from a heroine of yours: 'If you judge people, you have no time to love them.' Do you know who said that? Mother Teresa. 'No time to love them.' Time: I think that's the key word here. For you and Todd. Time."

Grandma trembled. Her eyes bulged.

But Jacob drank more wine. "Jean, this stew was fabulous." Mom smiled. There were tears on her cheeks. Dad studied a blister on his hand. Jacob looked at his watch. "I've gotta go. I need to get to rehearsal. To play Bob Cratchit." He looked at Grandma again and added, "The family man."

She wheeled away from the table, making a spitting sound between her teeth. "Lies," she muttered. "Lies. Lies." Dad scooted his chair back and rose to help her. They left the kitchen.

We went upstairs to get Todd. He sat on Abby's old bed, leaning against the wall. She lay with her head in his lap, and he stroked her thick, copper-colored hair. She sat up and wiped her eyes when we came in, and Todd prodded her and nodded.

"I'm sorry, Jacob," she said. It pained her, I could tell. "I've been under a lot of stress lately. I apologize . . . for how rude I was."

Todd looked at Jacob. "Thanks," Jacob said. Todd continued staring at him. "That's okay," Jacob added. "We're cool." He gave Todd a look that said, *Don't push it; that's all you're getting.* All he said out loud was, "I need to go, babe."

"I want to stay a little longer. Maybe Dad could drive me home. Or you could drive Summer home and she could come back to get me."

"I'll drive you home," Abby said.

I felt the vibes coming off of Jacob. "You're pretty tired. . . ." He faltered.

I expected Todd to get defensive, but he smiled. "I know. But we're in the middle of something important. Don't worry."

But Jacob would. He stood there. He didn't know what to say.

"I can drive, you know," Abby said.

Jacob didn't even take the bait. He just nodded.

"I'll stay, too," I said to him. "It's okay."

He nodded again, troubled. He kissed Todd, who wished him a good rehearsal. "I love you," Todd said.

"I love you, too. Please be home asleep when I get back."

"He babies you," Abby said when Jacob had left the room.
Todd beamed. "I know."

I sat on my old bed, but Todd said, "Summer, I need to talk
to Abby alone."

I sulked down the stairs, where Grandma Anna had disappeared to her room and Dad read the paper in the living room.
I helped Mom with the dishes, trying not to feel like the baby
shut out of the game.

"Well done," Mom said of Jacob. After a moment or two she
said, "I worry about him. How's he holding up?"

"All right, I think." I didn't tell her that last week I'd found him
in tears, lifting weights in the basement after midnight when neither of us could sleep. I sat on the wooden steps and watched him
working out. He wept the entire time. It was as if he had to
maintain his own healthy body in secret.

"They're so good together," Mom said. "And you? How are
you holding up?"

"This is . . . hard," I said.

"It's important, what you're doing."

I nodded. There was nothing but the soft slop slop sounds of
her hands in the dishwater.

"Mom? When did you know you were ready to get married?"

She snorted and looked out the window over the sink. It was
dark outside. All she saw was her own reflection. "I was pregnant."

"Oh." I stacked the silverware in their tidy drawer. I'd never
known that. I felt oddly unattached for a moment, as though
floating in space, looking down at the earth of my life.

"Are you in love, Summer?" she asked me. Her voice connected me again.

"Yes." There was no doubt in my mind that I loved Nicholas.
"But . . . I'm afraid."

She just kept washing, not looking at me, not asking me for more information.

"When you're ready, you'll know," she said. "There's no hurry. There are plenty of things to do for yourself first."

But I don't know what those things are, I thought. "You didn't," was all I said.

"Did it ever cross your mind that I wish I had?" She pulled the plug in the sink.

I floated through space again. And I saw from a great distance that my parents weren't bad parents. But their lives weren't what they wanted. I'd learned, these past three years, how preoccupying that could be. It makes it hard to see anything else. It overshadows. Buries. And I saw, for the first time, how well they'd done, all things considered.

"Hey, Summer," my father called from the living room. "You ever gonna ride? Or should I talk to someone else?" A woman who boarded her horse here was pregnant, in her last trimester. She'd asked him if he knew any competent riders who might like to work a horse. No strings attached—she just wanted him ridden while she was unable. He was nice, a big, gray Thoroughbred named Glacier. I went to the doorway, dish towel in hand.

"Yeah, I wanna come ride him. The weather's just been too bad. And then Todd, you know, after chemo—"

He nodded. "He's nice, but he's been off a couple weeks now. I don't want him getting too sharp or uppity for you."

I hadn't ridden since the accident. Not out of any fear, really, but from the logistical difficulty with a cast and then a series of braces that first year and a half. By the time I was free of braces, I lived in Cincinnati, where the only horses I saw pulled carriages around Fountain Square. But lately, visiting the farm so often, I'd been craving a ride. I woke from dreams about riding, every muscle alive with the long stored memory of the movement of a horse.

"You're free tomorrow, right?" Dad asked.

I nodded. "Yeah. Nicholas won't get in until late afternoon. But Jacob has rehearsal all day. I said I'd stay with Todd."

"Bring Todd."

"Bring me where?" Todd said from the top of the stairs. Abby had her arm around his waist, and he descended the stairs, one arm over Abby's shoulders and one clutching the banister. The picture they made together tightened my chest.

"Dad wants me to ride that horse," I said.

"No, I asked if you wanted to ride that horse. I don't care one way or the other. I thought you might like it."

"Do you want to?" Todd asked. I nodded. "Cool. We can come. No problem." His voice was barely a whisper. It was time to go home.

Abby brought the car to the back door, and we bundled Todd up and headed home. Twenty minutes later, at our house, she waited in the kitchen while I helped get Todd undressed and into bed. He fell asleep before I left the room.

I looked at him for a moment and wished he'd be sick. I wanted Abby to witness how ugly, how obscene, this could be. She only ever seemed to be here when all was quiet and tidy.

She stood in the kitchen, looking at a photograph strip taped to the refrigerator. It was one of those four-photo strips from a machine. Todd and Jacob had gone into one of those booths early last summer at an amusement park. It was before the weight loss started. They'd just moved back to Dayton. Todd had all his hair and a tan. Two of the photos were silly. In the third, they simply leaned their faces together, grinning smugly. Adorable, so in love. In the last, they were kissing. Abby stared. I couldn't read her expression. When she noticed me, she started, as if guilty.

We stared at each other. "You're telling people he has cancer?" Contempt made the words roll in my mouth, hard and crisp.

She exhaled and twisted the pearls at her neck. "He does."

"Oh, but that's not nearly the whole story, now, is it?"

"Summer." She always sounded so patronizing. So impatient with my childishness. "It's nobody's business. There is no need to explain the whole sordid story—"

"Sordid?" I wanted to rip out her hair. "You, of all people, have some fucking nerve, calling it sordid."

She paled. "Summer, don't—" Her eyeliner didn't run, but widened with her tears, making her eyes appear to sink deep into her skull. "Please. I have to say that. I have to."

"I can't even feel sorry for you anymore," I said.

She opened her mouth to speak, then closed it. She turned and left the kitchen. I heard her car start and drive away.

Chapter Six

⌒ discovered on Saturday morning that sleeping in had been destroyed for me. Sleeping at all was a struggle, but lingering was impossible. Tonight I'd sleep snuggled up to Nicholas, his arms and legs enfolding me. A safe, sweet place that inspired deep sleep and calm dreams. My body ached for it.

At eight, Jacob came upstairs to remind me that Arnicia had the day off, so I was in charge. "Here," he said, handing me a white plastic baby monitor. "Todd's up. You don't have to go down there—just keep your ears open."

"How long have you had this? I should have one all the time."

"I don't think so." He grinned. "I don't want you hearing everything that goes on in that bedroom." I made a face. "Hey, we still manage, babe, we still manage. And that is not for your listening pleasure." He left, laughing.

When the back door shut, the monitor crackled and Todd's voice, hollow and tinny, said, "It's true, you know. We still eke out a few romantic nights every now and then."

"More information than I wanted," I said.

He laughed. "Wouldn't these have been cool when we were kids?"

"Oh, my God, the things we could've done."

We talked that way, through the monitors, sprawled in our beds, a floor apart, for an hour, before Todd returned to his cross-word puzzle and I started in on the stack of unpromising poems. Zack's sat on the top of the pile. I held it in my hands for some time, remembering his disturbing behavior. What if it wasn't a crush? What if his girlfriend was pregnant? What if his parents abused him? What if he was suicidal? I removed three staples holding on the blank cover sheet, then chickened out. He'd told me not to read it. Let it go. I put it back in the pile.

After an hour of silence Todd crackled back on, asking, "So, are you gonna go ride that horse?"

"I don't know."

"You scared?" It wasn't a challenge; it was genuine.

"Yes."

"Then you have to do it."

I studied the scars on my ankle. "I know." I couldn't concentrate enough to grade well, anyway. The ride would occupy me in a real way while I waited for Nicholas. "Okay," I said. "Let's get this over with."

We didn't get to the farm for three more hours, since the simplest daily tasks took Todd forever these days. I tried not to fidget or pace, but at one point he looked up from the edge of the bed, where he perched, tying his hiking boots with absurd concentration, that birdlike tilt to his head to accommodate his one seeing eye. He saw my expression and said, "Sorry." I hated myself.

The day offered a swimming-pool blue sky and unseasonal warmth. Todd, bundled like an arctic explorer, was boyishly excited about being outside. He made his shuffling way up and down the barn aisles, peering in and talking to the horses, while I gathered all my tack. I was slow, with my still sore fingers and my choreography of the routine unpracticed and stilted.

"Do you remember hide-and-scare?" he called to me.

I laughed. We used to play our own strange version of hide-and-seek here all the time. We'd hide ourselves, with the object being to scare the finder when we were discovered. It was an ongoing game that could be picked up at any moment and lasted for nine or ten years of our lives. I learned to be wary in the barn and fields when I didn't know where my brother was.

"Oh, my God, do you remember when you hid in the grain bin?" I asked him. He'd gotten me so good one night, I'd peed my pants. It had been my turn to do evening feed, and when I'd opened the grain bin, there he was, curled up on his back with his knees under his chin. He'd sat up and screamed, *"Waaa!"* at me. I'd thought, for one horrifying second, that he was some mutant giant rat. That was how you "won" the game.

"That was my best one," he said. "What do you think was yours?"

It was years ago, and my face still grew hot. "Well . . ." I cleared my throat. "I think the hayloft after Abby's rehearsal dinner was a pretty big surprise."

Todd stood at the bottom of the ladder to the hayloft. He looked up. "Yes, well, that was a good one, wasn't it?"

"But I didn't win. I didn't scare you."

"Oh, yes, you did," he said. "As a matter of fact, I was terrified."

"I was, too, though, and that's not how the game works."

He laughed. "Jesus . . . what a night . . . I still can't believe you just sat there and watched."

"Todd! What was I supposed to do? It's not like, at that point, I could jump out and say, 'Boo,' and you two would have laughed. It was a point of no return, you know? There was no way to turn it into a joke. I was trapped."

We laughed, as we always did remembering that night. Todd groaned and hid his face in his hands.

I led Glacier out of his stall and into the aisle. Standing in cross ties, this generous gelding became a giant. It was a reach to brush his back, and I would've had to stand on a box to bridle him if he hadn't lowered his huge, elegant head.

"He's beautiful," Todd said. He came close, and Glacier stretched his neck toward him, flaring his nostrils to take in this new person. "Hey, handsome," Todd said, letting Glacier nuzzle his heavily padded arms and torso. Glacier let out a series of *whoosh-whoosh* snorts, and Todd said, "I know . . . not quite human, is it? Too much medicine."

I smiled, tightening the girth and double-checking every buckle. I loved this habit of his. He conversed with animals as if he knew their thoughts and had the uncanny ability to make you believe it. I was nervous with him so close to those soup bowl–size hooves and unable to move quickly, but Glacier stood, still and contained, in his presence.

Dad came down from the house when I led Glacier to the fenced-in arena. Todd walked along behind us, talking to Mario, the border collie, who followed his boy, this hero from his puppy years, with fervent devotion. Mario LeMutt, named the year Mario Lemieux won National Hockey League Rookie of the Year. Mario was old now, and the two of them moved stiffly together, on legs they no longer completely trusted.

"Your mom says you should go in," Dad said to Todd.

"Not yet," Todd said, and Dad nodded. He'd done what she asked, and his obligation was complete. He never fussed over Todd.

Todd settled on a bench, with Mario on his lap, the big dog's head on his shoulder, and Dad stood in the middle of the ring. I stood, too, my head just reaching the gelding's withers. I swallowed, and it stuck in my throat, as dry as the cinders we stood on. That sealed it: I had to ride. Up to that moment, I could have said never mind and wouldn't have felt embarrassed. Maybe it was just stubbornness, but fear affected me like a dare. That was the only way I'd survived New York. That was why I'd said yes when Todd asked me to move in with them. And that was why I'd ride. I'd lost, or was on the verge of losing, so much that I cared about. This part of my life, I could find again.

The stirrup seemed impossibly high, but Dad came to us and gave me a leg up. I scrambled onto Glacier's back, impatient with my inefficient, graceless movements. I sat for a moment, feeling the saddle, feeling the grand presence beneath me.

"You okay?" Dad asked.

I smiled and reached down for the other stirrup. I gathered the braided, leather reins. My sore fingers felt numb, almost tingly, but even those damaged nerve endings recognized the reins and knew where they fit in the curl of my fingers. I pressed my calves against the gelding's massive rib cage and he moved forward. So forward, so free. The familiar sensations returned to me in a rush—the soft pressure on the balls of my feet, his mouth in my hands—so trusting—the softening of my back and hips to move with him.

Dad was right: Glacier was a good one to start back on. His trot was floating and forward, perhaps a little too strong, but easily cajoled down. Dad gave me instructions, and we completed a series of schooling movements—circles, serpentines, changing directions frequently. We cantered, too, which was heaven.

After forty-five minutes we quit. I couldn't stop smiling as I dropped the reins and patted his woolly, winter neck. He wasn't even sweating, although I was. I could feel it trickling down my belly under my fleece jacket, even though my face felt nipped by the November air. I slid my feet free of the stirrups and stretched my legs long down Glacier's side, rotating my bad ankle, which had begun to ache as soon as I'd stopped.

Both Todd and Dad walked over to us, patting Glacier and looking up at me. Glacier, once again, posed near Todd, barely moving his head, as though not just colored like marble, but carved from it.

"Nothing so beautiful as a long-legged woman on a long-legged horse," Dad said.

Todd smirked and said, "Oh, yeah? I can think of one or two."

Dad coughed, his face instantly red. Todd laughed, then Dad did, too, giving Todd a push on the shoulder. From above, I watched this uneasy exchange. Dad always looked at Todd with an expression of utter puzzlement. Amazement and confusion combined. He sometimes shook his head, but in an admiring sort of way.

"You looked great, Summer," Dad said. "You're a natural."

Todd nodded.

"You should take some lessons with Kelly Canter. She's here on Sundays."

"Ha! Is that really her name?" Todd asked. Dad nodded. "That's hysterical."

"You let someone else teach here?" I asked.

"Sure. The boarders still take lessons from me, too, but this woman specializes more. The more advanced riders work with her."

A blush warmed my cold cheeks. I looked at Todd, who grinned and nodded, acknowledging that I had indeed just received a compliment from my father. "You ought to consider it, Summer," Dad went on. "You haven't lost a thing. If you're going to ride, you may as well ride as best as you can."

I led Glacier back to the barn. Todd and Dad stood talking at the end of the aisle. I wondered what topic they found, these two

men with so little in common. I put my tack away, brushed out
Glacier's saddle marks, and fed him an apple, which he ate in
three bites. I savored the muskiness of the barn: the rich sting of
manure, the damp, dirt floors, the soap-softened leather, and the
dusty sweetness of Glacier's coat that clung to my clothing. I savored, too, the oddly reassuring throb in my ankle, the bruised
feeling on my seat bones, the exhilaration of still feeling in motion—rising from the saddle with his outside foreleg.

Dad began turning out the horses, and without thinking or
discussing it, Todd and I fell into our old pattern of opening stalls
and shooing horses toward the open gates. "Been a long time
since I've had this team working for me," Dad said of us. Todd
and I smiled at each other across the barn lot, and he held out a
hand, inviting me to join him leaning against the mares' gate. He
pulled me into the crook of his arm. Beauty, a gnarled old mare
who'd taught us both to ride, lingered at the gate and pulled
Todd's sleeve with her sagging, lower lip. Her registered name
was Almost Beautiful, although neither of us had the heart to tell
her she wasn't even close. She butted him with her bony face, and
when he failed to produce a treat, she shied at an invisible phan-
tom and wheeled away, showering us with clips of earth.

When we made our way to the house, Mom banged around
the kitchen, slamming cupboards and chopping potatoes in a
dangerous fury. "Don't you ever think?" she asked Dad. "Do you
have any idea how long you kept that boy out there sitting in the
cold? I told you to send him inside."

Dad shrugged and said, "He didn't want to."

And in truth, Todd seemed fine. "It's such a beautiful day," he
said. He stood at the kitchen window, looking out. "God, this
place is gorgeous." He said it as if he'd never seen it before; he

sounded surprised. Turning away from the window, he said, "I'm not going to see fall again. I wished we'd gone camping."

No one knew what to say. The phone rang, and Mom turned to it as if a long-lost friend had entered the room. "Hello? . . . Oh, hello Jacob, how was— Yes, yes, they're here . . . everything's fine. . . . Of course, just a minute—" She handed the phone to Todd.

"Hey, love," he said to Jacob, "you know what I was just thinking? We need to go camping. . . . No, I'm serious; did you get outside at all today? . . . It's beautiful. . . ." I left the kitchen. I didn't want Todd to see me cry.

When I came back downstairs, after blowing my nose and patting water on my face in the upstairs bathroom, Todd reported that Jacob was coming over for dinner. "He says he has a surprise."

"So, you're gonna ride back with Jacob?" I asked.

"You may as well stay, too, Summer—"

"No, I want to be there when Nicholas gets in."

He took a breath and said, "He's gonna be late." His expression was gentle, as if he knew the disappointment I would feel. "Jacob says he left a message. He might not get in until ten or so."

"But—" The muscles of my face quivered. I couldn't control them, as though I'd been taken over by an alien. "They only had rehearsal until two."

"He'll get here," Todd said, coming to me, hugging me. "The schedule must've changed, that's all. He'll get here. So stay and have dinner with me, little sis?"

I wanted to be alone, to go home and pine in privacy, but how could I say no to Todd? I stayed.

"I wonder what my surprise is?" he said.

When Jacob arrived, though, he said the surprise had to wait until Todd returned to the house.

Another surprise came first. While Dad wheeled Grandma in, Todd, Jake, and I helped Mom put supper on the table—pork chops, green beans, mashed potatoes, homemade apple sauce, and cornbread.

I watched Todd devour two servings of mashed potatoes and some applesauce and cornbread. He'd been outside for hours and had been up with no nap almost all day, but the activity had charged rather than drained him. Grandma, on the other hand, like a dry, brittle corn husk, seemed fragile enough tonight to flit away to shreds.

She didn't say much, and the conversation at the table divided itself into Mom and Dad bickering about raising the board bill and Todd and Jacob talking about rehearsal for *A Christmas Carol.* I stayed on the periphery of both discussions, rather than trying to engage Grandma. I was buttering a piece of cornbread when she coughed and said, "You didn't lie."

We all fell silent. She stared at Jacob. "I beg your pardon?" he said.

"I read a book," she said. "I called last night. They brought it this morning. You didn't lie to me."

Jacob blinked, baffled. Todd touched Jake's arm and asked, "What is she talking about?" Jacob shook his head.

Grandma scowled. "It's on my bed." She pointed at me. "Bring it to him."

Rebellion flared in my chest, a familiar feeling from my childhood, but curiosity was stronger. In her room, on her bed was a book entitled *More Than Six Million.* Nothing clicked in my mind until I saw the subtitle, *Other Ethnic and Political Victims of the Nazi Holocaust.* One of Todd's postcards from Poland marked a chapter called "The Gay Experience." I took it to the kitchen, where everyone awaited my return in silence. I handed it to Jacob, who said, "Oh," as if recognizing someone.

"You told the truth," Grandma repeated. "It's as you said."

He still appeared somewhat baffled. He held the book in front of him with exaggerated care, as if it were alive. "Um. Good. I'm glad you read about it. I. Um. I thought you would like to know that."

"Know what?" Todd asked. Mom leaned in and whispered to him.

Jacob handed the book back to Grandma.

"I don't want it," she said. "I have no wish to think on such things. You take it."

He was stuck there, arm out, with the book. "But. It's a library book," he said.

"You take it back for me."

I'd never seen Jacob speechless in all the years I'd known him. He just stared at her. After a moment she waved her hands at him, as though brushing away flies. He put the book beside him. She coughed and asked us if we'd heard from Abby. That was that. She didn't mention it again. No apology, no "I was wrong," no explanation. I couldn't finish my dinner.

My agitation grew, as I drove home, alone, Todd in Jacob's car, to find Nicholas at our house. He'd never left a message about being late; he'd been there all along, helping Jacob set up a surprise for Todd.

I felt cheated of time with him, angry I'd been lied to. So angry that I didn't even hug him in greeting. "Why didn't you tell me?" I asked. "I could've helped you."

"Shh, you'll see," he said as Todd and Jacob came in the back door. He got hugged by both of them, and when Jacob asked, "Mission accomplished?" Nicholas nodded, legs jittering like a little boy.

Jacob turned to Todd and said, "Your wish is my command—with a little help from Nicholas here. Are you ready?"

"For what?" Todd was grinning, expectant.

"To go camping, babe," Jacob said. Nicholas led the way to the living room. Every window was open, and a fire blazed in the fireplace. Their tent stood in the middle of the room, flaps open to reveal the sleeping bags rolled out inside. Leaves, thousands of autumn leaves of every color, covered the floor. Their sweet, spicy smell embraced us.

Todd's mouth dropped open. "Oh . . ." He turned to Jacob. "You're wonderful." Jacob wiped Todd's tears away with his thumbs and kissed him on each eyelid.

"Forgive me?" Nicholas whispered. In answer I gave him the greeting I should have earlier.

We turned out the lights, so that only the fire lit the room. We kept our coats on, and Jacob insisted that Todd wear a hat. We gathered around the fire, and I snuggled close to Nicholas. I gained strength just being near him. I leaned my head on his shoulder and took in the deep musk of him; he smelled like earth and physical energy. I traced the calluses on his hands with my fingertips and pictured him raking the leaves in our yard and the park, hurrying, checking his watch, devoted to his mission.

Nicholas had bought marshmallows and graham crackers and chocolate bars.

"Oh, yes!" Todd said. "How can we camp without s'mores?"

Todd roasted marshmallows to perfection for everyone and even ate one himself. Nicholas suggested ghost stories. Jacob told the best ones, and we were still sitting in the dark, in tight knots of suspense, when Arnicia came home, well after midnight, and scared us all to death.

We scared her, too, and she screamed, for real at first, then in mock anger. "What are you all doing? You all are crazy. Crazy." But she joined us and told an even scarier story than Jacob's last one and finished off the s'mores.

Finally, that wrapping-up silence fell. The fire snapped less and less frequently, and we yawned more and more.

"You have a good day, sweetie?" Arnicia asked Todd.

He sat cuddled in front of Jacob, leaning back against his torso, his head just below Jacob's own. Jacob's arms wrapped around him. Todd smiled and said, "Every day's a good day."

"Amen to that," she said. "I don't know about you all, but I am tired."

"Let's get in the tent," Jacob said.

They crawled into their sleeping bags and zipped themselves into the tent, leaving their shoes outside.

Arnicia shook her head. "You all are loonier than goddamn toons."

"We're camping," Todd said.

They giggled inside the tent.

"You all better not do it in there," Arnicia warned. "It attracts bears."

They giggled some more. There was the crinkling sound of foil being torn open, and Todd said, "Oooh, you thought of everything."

"Man, I'm outta here," Arnicia said, and went upstairs to her room.

Nicholas and I stood in the dying light of the fire, smiling at one another. I opened my mouth to speak, but Nicholas put his finger to his lips and nodded his head toward the tent. A conspicuous silence hung in the air. We crept away up the stairs to my room. We closed the door, leaned against it, and kissed.

"That was wonderful," I said to him.

"I love you," he whispered, holding my face in both of his hands.

"I love you." I placed my hands on his, intertwining our fingers.

"Let's spend the rest of our lives together."

"Let's."

"For real," Nicholas said. "No more talking about 'someday.'" He produced a burgundy velvet ring box from the pocket of his coat.

My heart stopped, and for a panicked moment I wasn't sure it was going to resume. I closed my eyes and saw my mother stooped over the sink, saying, "I was pregnant." I saw Abby with her bruised eye. I blinked rapidly to shove the images away. I opened my mouth, but coherent thoughts did not materialize. "Nicholas, I—" was all I managed.

"You what?" he teased.

I felt trapped here, against the door, and I ducked under his arm and moved away from him. I stopped, standing in an uncertain balance. The floor slanted. "I can't get married now," I said, hardly able to believe my own ears. "You know I can't." But he didn't know. His face looked as though someone had just told him he was adopted.

We stared at one another a moment. He finally laughed and said, "Stop it. You're freaking me out."

He came toward me, but I halted him with, "I'm not kidding. I can't. I'm sorry."

He gave a little shake of his head. "You're saying no?" Incredulous anger rose at the end of the question. "Why? I—I mean, I never would've asked if I didn't think—I mean, we'd been talking about it for so long, and I . . . I thought I knew us."

He sat on the bed, near the stack of poems I'd left there, the ring box in one hand, and ran his other through the front of his thick black curls. I sat beside him, and without warning, I was in tears.

"Summer, what? Why are you crying?" He turned to me, the ring box tumbling into the folds of the unmade bedclothes and piles of papers, and brushed away a tear on my face with his finger.

"I have to figure out my life first. I have to figure out—" I faltered.

"You don't think I could help you figure it out? We can figure it out together."

I shook my head and said, "I have to do it myself," wiping tears with the back of my hand. "I can't think about this now."

He took my hand and looked down at it, not speaking. He touched my blackened fingernails, which moved like loose teeth, ready to fall off. "Is this from where Todd shut the door on you?" I nodded. He looked up as though he'd grasped some valuable point. "It's wrong to put it off, Summer. Don't you see—the focus would be on something new beginning, not . . . the end. Todd would get to be there. I want him to be there, don't you?" He took my hand in both of his, his face animated, as if he'd solved the problem.

I pulled my hand away. "I'm not ready."

He looked at me a long time. When I dropped my eyes from his gaze, he said, "I don't understand. I thought you wanted this, wanted us."

"I do. Please, believe me. But I have to find my own way for once. What if I can't make it as a teacher? I'm terrible at it so far. I mean, what if I end up a receptionist at some dance school?"

Nicholas stood and began pacing the room, and I went on, "I'd be an anchor on you. Like my parents are to each other. Think about it—your parents are divorced, and look at my sister's marriage, for God's sake."

He stopped pacing and turned to me. "Look at your brother's."

"That's . . . different. Todd's is different—the situation is, I don't know, exceptional, it's—"

"Because they're gay?"

"No!"

"Why, then? Because Todd is dying?"

I inhaled sharply as if he'd slapped me.

"You think that's why, don't you?" Nicholas came back to the bed but stood, facing me. "I watch you romanticize the illness. They would've lasted even without the drama and high stakes; they'd still be together in fifty years if they could. That's what makes them exceptional. I want what they have. Don't you? Don't you think we could do that?" He sat and tried to take my hand again, but this time I stood up and walked to the window. "Summer. I swear, all of a sudden I feel like I don't know who you are."

I turned to him. "Neither do I. That's why I can't do this right now."

He buried his face in his hands, elbows on his knees. Without lifting his head, he said, "Help me. Help me understand this." He raised his face, and his expression broke my heart.

I looked out the window, touching my fingertips to the cold glass. "I'm afraid of getting lost in this," I said, my voice barely above a whisper. I took a deep breath and struggled to speak without crying. "I can't be half a partnership until I'm a whole person, or I'm nothing but the partnership. I've done this before; I've already been married once—to the ballet. When I lost that, I was nothing. I don't want that again; I have to be something outside it. I want to come to our marriage without all this crap. I want to be like Todd and Jacob. I want to be as sure as they are . . . only I'm not yet."

He didn't answer me. I couldn't bring myself to tell him that I feared I'd never be that sure. That when it came to love like theirs I felt somehow lacking. I wasn't capable of dancing anymore because of a physical weakness. What if my heart, as well, was handicapped?

Nicholas stared at the floor, then stood and picked up his duffel bag on my chair. He hoisted it to his shoulder and zipped up the coat he was still wearing.

"Don't go. Nicholas, please."

"I can't do this anymore," he said, his voice changing, growing high-pitched with the effort to stave off tears. "I *am* sure. I want something more. You said this arrangement would be a test for us. Well, I finished the test. I'm sick of this weekend shit." He left the bedroom.

I followed him, not knowing what to say, what to do to make him stay, as he strode down the stairs and through the living room. I had to run, to catch him at the back door. I grabbed his coat sleeve. "Don't just leave," I begged. "Please don't walk away. I need to know you understand."

He paused. "I—I just wasn't prepared for this, okay?"

"I wasn't, either. Or I would've told you before. Please stay."

"No," he said. "I need to go. I need to . . . think. I can't be with you here right now."

"Will you come back, next weekend?" I asked.

He slowly shook his head at me, eyes glistening in the porch light streaming through the back door. "Jesus, you have some nerve," he whispered. He jerked open the door and stepped onto the porch, then paused and said, "Of course I'll be back. I want to see Todd." He stood on the top step and looked at me a moment. "Say good-bye to the happy campers for me." He went down the stairs and to his car.

But the happy campers were otherwise occupied. I walked through the living room, past the whispering and the unmistakable rhythm of the slow creaking in the old wooden floor.

Sleep wouldn't come, I could tell. I didn't even undress. I sat on the edge of my bed, phone in my lap, until dawn. When the pipes began to clang and moan, I pulled up my legs to lie down. Straightening my legs, I kicked the scattered poems. I sat again, to gather them and dump them on the floor. Zack's ended up back on top. I stared at it. What the hell. Why not see just how much misery could be produced in one day?

I opened the manila envelope and tore off the cover page:

12:01 A.M.

We finished tearing the set down at 12:01 A.M.

The play was already slipping behind us,

a spent breath,

less than real.

I had watched you all night. Thin T-shirt.

You swung a hammer and tore the fake walls down.

You'd destroyed a pretend world.

I watched the shifting muscles of your arms, beaded with glistening drops.

Your chest heaved gracefully.

I sat with my hands in my lap,

my body tensing and struggling against you.

In my mind, I fought images of my hands slipping over you,

touching a body full of gratitude,

and male,

like mine.

I saw the set crumble under these thoughts.

You'd destroyed a pretend world.

Chapter Seven

*M*y mouth turned to sand.

My head reeled.

I had not been prepared for this.

I took the poem in shaking hands and went downstairs. It was six A.M.

The tent stood empty. I found Jacob in the kitchen, sifting flour into a giant orange bowl. A bottle of Scotch sat on the counter.

He turned, startled, when I came in. He glanced at the clock. "I couldn't sleep, either," he said.

"Where's Todd?"

"I put him in bed last night, after . . ." He grinned. "Well, later. He's too thin to be lying on the floor." The baby monitor lay next to the liquor bottle. Jacob appeared to be making bread. Without looking at me, he said, "I think the question of the morning is: Where's Nicholas? What the hell was going on last night?"

I didn't answer. Jacob stopped sifting and looked at me, frowning. "Are you okay?"

"No. Um . . . could you read something?"

"Sure." He took the poem in his flour-coated hands and read

it. "Whoa. Is this a high school kid?" I nodded. He read it again, and I saw a light, penciled note on the back of the page.

"What's that say—on the back?"

Jacob turned it over. His eyes scanned the words. "Christ," he whispered, handing it to me.

It read, "Things are bad. I bought a gun. I got rid of it because of that quote you put up. Thanks."

A gun? Oh, my God.

"What do I do? Jake, help me—I can't screw this up."

"You won't screw it up." He smiled at me. "What's this quote he talks about? You're doing something right or he wouldn't have given this to you."

"But he gave it to me a week ago. I ignored him. I was—I was actually mad at him. Oh, Jesus, I shouldn't be allowed anywhere near these kids. I'm a horrible teacher, I'm—"

"Settle down," Jacob said. "He wouldn't have given this poem to a horrible teacher."

"Do you think he means . . . was he going to kill himself?"

Jacob nodded.

"Did you—did you ever think about that?"

"Oh, yeah," he said with no hesitation, making my breath stop as if I'd plunged into icy water. "Lotsa times. I don't know the specifics of what this kid is going through, but I can imagine. Living like that makes it tough to think that living at all is such a great thing."

"Living like what?"

"Thinking you're an alien, babe. A threat to society. To believe that you're responsible for 'the breakdown of family values,' like you hear everyone saying."

"Hey—" Todd stood in the doorway, in Jacob's robe, rubbing his eyes. "What's going on? Why'd Nicholas leave?"

"What are you doing up?" Jacob asked.

Todd looked at us, hands on hips, as if scolding us. "You know, those monitors don't have to be two-way. There's this little switch. Amazing technology."

"Oh, shit, I'm sorry, babe." We'd woken him up with our conversation. Jacob messed with the monitor. "There. Sorry."

"What's this thing you're reading? What's wrong?"

I handed it to him. He read it. "Wow. How old is he?"

I shook my head. "Seventeen, eighteen, maybe. He's a senior."

Todd sat at the kitchen table. "Damn. I envy him. I can't imagine being so brave at that age."

"What do I say to him?" I sat across from Todd, my knees up to my chin. "I want to tell him the right thing."

"What do you think is the right thing?" Todd asked me.

"I don't know. That—that life will get better. And that he's a beautiful person, not a freak, and he'll be all right."

We were all silent a moment. Jacob and Todd looked at each other.

"Well," Jacob said, going back to the counter. "That sounds like the right thing to me. You've got it down, babe." He began to knead the bread dough.

Todd studied the note again. "What's this quote he talks about?"

"I don't know. I put up a quote every day." I tried to think of one that would have changed his mind. "Oh. Maybe it was the Rita Mae Brown quote you gave me."

"'The only queer people are those who don't love anybody'?" Todd asked. I nodded.

Jacob hooted. "You put that on your chalkboard? No wonder you're always in trouble with that greasy little principal. Why'd you put that up?"

"Denny, this asshole kid in my class, said that we ought to deport all the queers to an island to stop the spread of AIDS."

"Charming," Todd said, a red flush spreading across his cheeks. "Was Denny in this kid's class? What's his name, anyway?" He turned the poem over. The name was nowhere on it.

"Zackery," I said. "And, yeah, he heard this little exchange. The whole class did. I was pretty pissed off. The quote went up the next day."

"Well, see, that meant something to him. It would have meant a lot to me at his age, too."

"I wish you'd talk to him," I said.

"I will if he wants me to, but you have to talk to him first. And he has to choose to talk to me; don't push it on him. He knows about me, right?"

I shook my head.

"You're kidding," Jacob said.

"I don't know. I think some kids know, because their parents know Mom and Dad, but I don't think Zack does. I've never talked about you to anybody at school."

I wasn't sure how they felt about that. I wasn't sure how I did, either. After an uncomfortable silence, Jacob asked, "Does he know anyone else who's gay?"

"I don't know. The poem talks about this other person, but it doesn't sound reciprocal. The way he's acted about this poem, I doubt if the other person is even aware."

Jacob covered the dough with a dish towel, then washed his hands in the sink. "Well, it could be good for him to talk to one of us," he said. "To meet a gay person who's alive and well and functioning in the world. To see someone who 'survived—'"

"Then he'd better talk to you, not me," Todd said.

"No," Jacob said, turning sharply from the sink, spattering us with water. "No. Think about it, babe. You could be the greatest lesson he'll ever learn in following his heart. And being true to himself. And the fucking awful things that could happen if he's not."

I arrived at school an hour and a half early the next day.

While I waited for Zackery, I put a quote on the board: *"And the day came when the risk to remain tight in a bud was more painful than the risk it took to blossom."—Anaïs Nin.* That was on a postcard Todd had sent me from Cairo.

Zackery never showed up.

I was a wreck all morning. It was one of those rare days when no one seemed to have questions or demands, so that the five minutes between classes tortured me. Five minutes was a long time, time when thoughts of Nicholas flooded my brain. Todd and Jake had not let the Zackery situation keep them from returning to their question yesterday: Where was Nicholas? They'd heard our angry voices, they'd heard us running past the tent, they'd heard his car start and drive away. And they knew what had happened. Nicholas had already shown Jacob the ring, while they'd set up the tent.

I told them the truth. Far from giving me the third degree, as I expected, they exchanged a glance and were then oddly silent on the subject, although Jacob did ask me while we bagged the leaves in the living room, "Are you out of your mind?"

I pushed away the thoughts of Nicholas. No good. They were simply replaced by images of Zack with the back of his head blown out. Oh, God. I put myself in that image instead. A crush? I could hardly stand myself. I thought he'd had a crush on me.

At lunch I was walking a different hall in search of a bathroom that didn't have maintenance men working in it, when I saw him.

He was kneeling at his locker, digging around for something

at the back of it. His soft brown hair fell into his eyes. I watched him for a moment before I approached. "Zack?"

He looked up at me with his dark, serious eyes and blanched so completely, I feared he would faint.

"I read it."

He nodded but didn't speak.

"You wanna talk?"

He nodded.

"Is now a good time?"

He nodded again.

"Let's go someplace more private." He closed his locker and followed me mutely. We headed to the library and found a study cubicle with a door we could close. The cubicle had huge glass windows that made me feel like an exhibit at the zoo. I put his poem on the table in front of us, so that even a quick glance would reveal a reason for us to be here. We looked at each other, neither of us knowing what to say.

"I feel really stupid," Zack said.

I laughed. To my immense relief, he laughed, too. "I do, too. I don't know how to start. I guess, first of all, I should apologize. I read it when you asked me not to."

Zack shook his head and said, "I—I'm glad."

"I thought you might be. I'm glad I read it, too. I want you to know how together and brave I think you are for this. This took a lot of courage. And it has to feel good to have told somebody."

"Well, someone who understands, anyway. I've told someone before . . . and, um, that's what led to the gun. I, um, told my mom."

"I take it not a very good reaction?"

"That's the understatement of the year—" He stopped.

"What'd she say?"

"She didn't say anything. She hit me."

My pulse quickened. My face burned. I sat up straighter. "How did she hit you? Did she—"

"Hey, calm down." He relaxed and seemed amused by my reaction. "She just slapped me, then told my father." Zack sighed and rubbed the back of his neck. He recited in a bored monotone how they'd told him he was evil, blamed it on him hanging out with the drama crowd, accused him of doing this as an act of rebellion, to humiliate them. He'd tried to explain to his mother that maybe he wasn't gay; maybe he was just confused. He'd practically begged for counseling, but they'd forbade him to tell anyone else, fearing it would "shame" the entire family.

Some students looked in the window. I picked up Zack's poem and pointed to a word with my pencil. Zack leaned forward to study the word. The students walked away.

"So," I said. "You bought a gun." I swallowed. I wiped my hands on my skirt. I was walking a tightrope, only I was walking it for someone else. One wrong step and he fell, not me.

"Yeah." He made a face. "But I'm not a psycho, I promise. I felt so bad. I wrote that note on the back of the poem really fast. I almost called you at home. I kept thinking about what I wrote and what you must think."

"I'm sorry you had to wait so long. Truly I am," I said. "Did you really throw the gun away?"

"Oh, yeah. It's long gone."

He told me how he'd actually prepared a letter to his family. He'd gone so far as to choose a Friday when his younger siblings would be visiting their grandparents so that none of them would see him dead. But on that Friday I'd risked the principal's disapproval and had put up my Rita Mae Brown quote.

He took a deep breath. "You're right. It does feel good to just tell somebody."

"I'm flattered that you trusted me. Really."

"Well, I figured, you know, you could relate."

"Because of my brother?"

He frowned, and his eyes didn't register recognition of any sort. "No," he said, "I just thought, because, you know, you're . . . you know . . ."

I shook my head, confused.

"You are . . . too. Right?"

The carpet whipped out from under me. "Gay?"

Zack turned so red, it looked painful. "Oh, God," he said, "now I feel really stupid. I'm sorry. God, you must think I'm some freak."

"No, Zack, no. I don't at all. But . . . why? Why did you think I was?"

"You always . . . the things you say to Denny . . . I just . . . Oh, God, I'm sorry."

"Don't, Zack; it's all right. I'm . . . glad you thought so, if that's what made you tell me. If that's what made you feel you could talk to me."

"I really . . . I really thought you were. I'm sorry. I hope . . . God, I'm sorry if I . . ."

"Don't be sorry, Zack. Honestly. My brother's gay."

"Your brother who's sick?"

I nodded. "I live with him and his lover now. I'm around gay people all the time. I don't think you're a freak."

"I never knew. About your brother." He looked somewhat stunned.

I shrugged. "I never told you. It never came up. I hope you don't care, but I showed him your poem. He thinks you're very brave."

"Yeah?"

I gave him an index card with my home number on it. I told him to call anytime, that Todd and Jacob would talk to him, too, and showed him a brochure they'd given me for a local support group for "sexual minority youth." Jacob had been a guest speaker for the group once. Zack frowned, a rigid stubbornness setting in his jaw, but he took the brochure.

The bell rang. "I guess I can't be tardy if I'm with the teacher, can I?" Zack asked. "I can't afford another one, not with the Saturday school I already have thanks to you."

"Hey, you skipped my class, buddy."

And we headed for class like that, bantering and laughing. At my door I stopped. "We can talk some more," I said. "You know where to find me. Here or at home. I mean that, okay?" He nodded, and we went inside. The rest of the students sat, chatting, waiting for us.

"Hey, I saw your sister again last night," Carissa said. "We were at the ballet."

"Well, you certainly make the social and cultural rounds, don't you?" I asked. I tried to make it a joke, but it sounded hard and bitter. Carissa didn't seem to notice.

"Did you know there are pictures of you in the lobby at the ballet?"

My heart sank. "Yes, I know."

"What for?" Simon asked.

"She was a dancer. My parents say you were famous!"

"Well, *here,* I was," I said, aware that the entire class was listening. "You know, in Dayton. I was a big fish in a small pond."

"So what happened to you?" Denny asked me. "You're not famous now."

"Nope. I got injured."

"So you're just a has-been?" he sneered.

"Not even that," I said with a smile, but hating him. "More like an almost-was. I wasn't so famous in New York. The pond got lots bigger."

There was silence. Fearing other questions, I asked Carissa, "So, how's my sister? I think you talk to her more than I do."

Bad move. "She says your brother is lots better. Maybe out of danger altogether."

"Cool," another student said. "Like in remission? What kind of cancer does he have?"

"He doesn't have cancer!" I hadn't meant to yell. The class was a frozen tableau, staring back at me.

"He doesn't have cancer," I repeated in as calm and rational a voice as I could muster.

"But . . . but your sister said—"

"My sister wasn't telling the whole truth."

"He doesn't have a throat tumor?"

"Well, yes, he does, but it's more complicated than that. . . ." Why didn't I just say it? I was as bad as Abby. "He has AIDS."

Their faces registered new levels of shock and amazement.

I braced myself for the inevitable question to follow.

"Is he gay?"

I opened my mouth. This was harrowing territory with judgmental high school seniors. I felt fiercely protective; they would think only in stereotypes, caricatures, and not see the incredible person I saw every day. I took a breath, and my eyes fell on Zackery Hauser.

Those big dark eyes were watching me. He knew the truth and watched me hesitate. I was still on that tightrope.

"Yes," I said, lifting my chin without meaning to. "Yes, he is, but that—"

"Told ya so!" Denny said to Karl beside him. Karl shrank in his chair, looking up at me, pale and apologetic.

The class and I stared at each other, except for Zackery, who seemed suddenly fascinated by his own shoes. No one breathed.

"Well," I said. "Ask. I know you want to."

They all stared at their hands or at the floor. I sat on the edge of my desk and waited. Finally a hand raised.

"Do your parents know?" Carissa asked.

Zackery lifted his head, but his eyes flashed panic when I glanced in his direction.

"Yes," I said. "And they still speak to him. They see him almost every day."

"How'd you find out he was . . . you know?"

My cheeks flushed pink. I couldn't help it. "Um . . . he told me," I lied.

They went on and on. A few kids, Denny included, sat quietly with ill-concealed contempt on their faces. Someone asked if he "had someone."

"Do you remember the guy who came and did swordwork with us when we started reading *Cyrano?*" I struggled not to look at Zackery.

Several girls' eyes lit up. "Oooh, yeah, that guy from the soap opera?"

I nodded. "Well, that's him."

Silence.

The girls looked crestfallen. "He's your brother's—?"

"Yep. He's my brother's."

"That's sick," Denny said. "He shouldn't have been allowed to come in here and teach us."

"Why?" I'd made it across the tightrope and felt cocky, reckless. I risked a glance at Zack, but he'd shut his eyes. I imagined that I could hear his heartbeat from across the room.

"He could have . . . you know," Denny said. "What if he was scoping out guys while he was here or something—"

"Oh, for God's sake," I said. "That's ridiculous. Don't flatter yourself, Denny. Just because I'm heterosexual doesn't mean I'm trying to seduce every boy in class, luring them into the book-room with me."

"I wish," Zack said. The class erupted in laughter, a release for them from the nervous tension. Stunned, I stared at Zack, who grinned back at the class, basking in their admiration for a good joke. I bit my lip at his defensive charade.

"Keep it appropriate, please," I said, rolling my eyes, but my voice caught in my constricting throat.

"Sorry, Ms. Zwolenick." His eyes lit on mine for just a fraction of a second.

"It's repulsive," Denny said. "It's just wrong."

"And it's in the Bible," Chen said. She was a pretty Korean girl.

I smiled. Years of listening to Jacob battle it out with Grandma Anna had me fully armed to take on the Bible. Grandma Anna had read books on "homosexual behavior" to "arm herself against the enemy," and Jacob had done the same with the Bible. He'd trained me well.

"Ah, you must be referring to good ol' Leviticus."

Chen nodded. "That and some others."

"A cheery little book." I quoted: "'Do not lie with a man as one lies with a woman; that is detestable. If a man lies with a man as one lies with a woman, both of them have done what is detestable. They must be put to death; their blood will be on their own heads.'"

Denny, Chen, and a few others looked smug and righteous.

"Denny, I saw you eat a hotdog the other day at lunch, right?" I asked him.

He shrugged. "So?"

"Well, did you know that a pig is an unclean animal and you're not supposed to have anything to do with it? Leviticus 11:8."

He blinked. "I'm not Jewish," he said.

"Oh, so *all* the rules in the Old Testament apply only to Jews?" He snorted.

I took stock of my classroom of sinners and pointed out that Chen's rayon shirt broke a law in Leviticus 19:19 that forbade wearing clothes of more than one fabric, and that according to Deuteronomy 22:5, every girl wearing pants was sinning, since "a woman must not wear men's clothing." I informed them that I Timothy 2:9 declared that "women are to dress modestly with decency and propriety, not with braided hair or gold or pearls," and watched Carissa finger her braid thoughtfully and several other girls touch their earrings. "As a matter of fact," I went on, "remember this next time we have group presentations or discussions: 'A woman should learn in quietness and full submission. I do not permit a woman to teach or to have authority over a man; she must be silent.' "

"Right on," Denny said, but even Chen looked disgusted with him.

"But, I mean, times have changed," Simon said.

"Oh, so we're allowed to say some rules don't apply anymore, but some others are set in stone?" I asked. He blushed.

"It's still repulsive," Denny repeated.

"Denny, shut up," Carissa said. Several others murmured agreement.

"Two guys just can't love each other," he insisted. "It's not how things work, you know? Sure, they can get off on each other, like guys do in prison and stuff. Personally, it makes me wanna puke, but they can't be in love."

"Oh, and you know all about love, right, Denny?" Carissa asked.

"I know what's fucking right and wrong."

"Hey!" I said, feeling for all the world like my grandmother. "Watch your language."

The bell rang. Denny gave me a deliciously evil grin and ducked out the door as fast as he could. I turned back to the class, but everyone was gathering books, hefting backpacks, filing out the door. Only Carissa stood by her desk. "I'm sorry," she said. "About your brother. It must be hard, taking care of him."

I nodded.

"Thanks for telling us." She smiled sweetly and left the room. Zackery was the last out, and we faced one another, unsure what to say or do. I opened my arms in the hug I'd been afraid to give him for so long, and he accepted it. We both had to wipe our eyes.

"Sorry about the bookroom thing," he said. "I was just . . . you know . . ."

I nodded. "Come see me. Tomorrow morning?"

"I'd like that," he said. "I'll be here."

Only after he left did I feel light-headed at having revealed so much.

I wanted to call Nicholas and tell him, hear the stage manager in him give me calm advice. Everything had a solution; nothing was a crisis. But I couldn't just call Nicholas. Not now. Not when I had nothing to offer him in return.

I'd told Todd and Jacob I'd go to the barn after school. Todd had felt so well, he and Jacob had talked of going out. Jacob had instructed me to relax and treat myself; I didn't need to hurry home.

A long trail ride on Glacier sounded therapeutic, soothing. I tried to muster my enthusiasm, but when I got to my car, I realized the riding clothes I'd packed that morning were still in my room at home.

Something crumbled in my bones. I drove home, planning to steal from Todd's stash of appetite-inducing marijuana, get good and stoned, and bury myself in quilts in bed. I drove slowly, feel-

ing already drugged. Adding to my heaviness were Denny's
words, which wouldn't leave me. I wanted to make Denny see, I
wanted to make Zackery see, I wanted them all to see that yes,
indeed, two men could love each other.

I remembered realizing it myself for the first time when I'd
gone to visit them in L.A. during the dance off-season. They
were different there, different from how they were at the farm,
home for the holidays, but only different in the sense that I was
seeing them together on their own ground, in their own home.

They were any couple, madly in love, without Grandma Anna
or anyone else around to stop them from reveling in it. They'd
settled easily into a comfortable series of "always." They always
made waffles on Saturday mornings. They always spent Sundays
in bed, working the crossword and watching the week's worth of
Jacob's soap opera on videotape, occasionally shutting their door
and turning up the stereo a tad too loud. They always ran together on weekday mornings, leaving in the dark, returning
sweaty and panting, as the hazy Los Angeles sun rose. Then they
always stripped down inside the privacy fence of their backyard
and swam. The splashing and their quiet laughter would wake
me, and I'd watch them from the guest bedroom window.

All that was before I knew. Before I knew how it all would
change. They'd known, of course, but Todd wasn't ready to tell us
yet. I just thought he overreacted to my using his toothbrush and
thought he must be joking when he flipped over my borrowing
his razor to shave my legs. I'd teased him about Jacob babying
him, how Jake asked him, "Are you tired?" all the time, as we'd
gone to Disneyland, movie studios, and Lion Country Safari.

I was so stupid. One day, the morning I left, actually, I asked
Todd for some lotion. My skin flaked from the afternoons spent
poolside. He directed me to the top drawer of their bedstand

table. I found it, a weird brand called Corn Huskers, right next to a huge box of condoms. A box of 150, about half gone.

"Jesus, Todd! What do you have all these for?"

"What do you think?" he said, flustered.

"What kind of weird lotion is this?" I asked, pouring the clear, silky fluid into my palm.

"Water based." He closed the drawer. "Any more questions?"

"Not until you answer my first one."

"Read a newspaper lately?" Jacob asked from the doorway.

"What's that supposed to mean?" I asked. Todd's shoulders sagged. He'd shot Jacob a look, full of meaning, but that I didn't understand. And even though in my dance world the plague had already begun to take its toll, I was too self-absorbed to put two and two together.

"Forget it. It's no big deal," Todd said. "You need some?"

"I told you: I'm on the pill!" I said for the hundredth time.

Jacob snorted and left the room.

And I knew something had happened there. Some hint of something lurking under the surface. But it had gone somewhere over my head, and try as I might, I couldn't reach it. Later, of course, it got pulled down and handed to me. Now it was always around, in the way, and I could never stop bumping into it.

Didn't the sickness alone prove Denny wrong? That they stayed together in spite of it? I pulled into our driveway. Jacob's car was here. They were home after all.

I let myself in the back door with customary quietness and tiptoed through the kitchen, in case Todd was asleep.

He wasn't.

He and Jacob were making love on the living room floor.

I froze in the doorway, and in the few seconds before they became aware of me, it was as if I took a mental Polaroid.

"Uh," Jacob said.

"Oops," Todd said, and they started to scramble, both of them reaching for the point of connection.

"Sorry, sorry, sorry," I said, fleeing the room. "God, I'm so sorry, you guys," I said from the kitchen, where I couldn't see them. "I'm going to the barn—I didn't mean—I just came home because—please—go ahead—I—I'm sorry." I stood by the oven, hands over my face, shaking my head.

In a few minutes they peeked into the kitchen, fully dressed, red faced, and grinning.

"I'm sorry!" I said, wincing.

"Hey, we're sorry. Um, look, we thought you were going to the barn. We wouldn't have been out here, you know, otherwise," Jacob said. He couldn't look me in the eye without laughing. Todd kept clearing his throat. And he wouldn't look at me at all.

I explained why I was home, changed my clothes, and left, promising to be gone "at least two hours, maybe more. I'll wait in the driveway if I'm back early." We joked about it, but we all still blushed.

As I drove to the barn, the image seeped into my view, becoming clearer and clearer as I recalled every detail.

It surprised me because it wasn't what I had pictured. It wasn't what I'd pictured them having sex to be like. Or any gay men, for that matter. After all these years, I had that stupid notion in my head of how gay guys "do it." And this wasn't it.

They were face-to-face.

I felt stupid admitting this, but it had never occurred to me that they could do it face-to-face.

The image developed in my mind. *Todd, lying on his back, on the carpet, Jacob's back moving so slowly, so gently, over him that it hardly seemed like sex.*

At the farm, Dad's truck was gone, and I went straight to the barn without going inside the house. A few boarders were there, and after some obligatory small talk, I brought Glacier in from his field, groomed him, and tacked him up.

In the arena, a fine, misty rain began to fall. The other riders went inside, but I kept working. Glacier pinned back his ears in the drizzle but otherwise did not protest.

Todd's arms reaching up to Jacob's face, his thumbs following the outline of Jacob's lips.

My fingers stiffened in the cold. Glacier turned dark, gunmetal gray in the rain. The rain grew heavier, and he lifted his head and wrung his tail. Still I worked on. My clothes soaked through. Steam rose off Glacier's neck and shoulders, until I led him into his stall and covered him with a blanket, the wet wool filling my nose with deep musk.

I put the tack away with fingers that could barely function to unbuckle and snap. One of my damaged fingernails caught in Glacier's leather halter and tore off, the raw, exposed skin stinging in the sharp chill of the evening.

Before leaving, I said hello to Mom and Grandma in the house, turning down an offer of dinner and dry clothes. I drove home with the heat turned high in my car, the windows steaming, my ankle throbbing.

It was so tender and so . . . beautiful. Their deep, searching kiss, savoring each other. It was when their lips parted from the kiss, Jacob tugging on Todd's lower lip with his teeth, that they saw me.

"Look what the cat dragged in," Jacob greeted me at the back door, still blushing—(I had honked in the driveway, knocked, and shouted, "I'm home!"). "You're a mess. Good way to catch pneumonia, babe."

"Have you forgiven me?"

"Of course. Have you forgiven us?"

He left for rehearsal. Todd was "watching a movie," asleep on the couch wrapped in a blanket. I took the baby monitor and went upstairs to take a bath.

The hot water embraced me, soothing and shocking at once. I sank in up to my chin, with only my bent knees not submerged. I leaned my head back against the white tile and closed my eyes.

Oh, Denny, I thought, you are so, so wrong.

And I'd been wrong, too.

I hadn't realized it until now. It wasn't until today that I saw them and knew what I should have known outside the bathroom door that awful chemo day. I'd seen their love in the moment it was most intimate, most private, in the moment we all feel most in love.

They had something better than I had ever known.

And I wanted it, more than anything.

Tears, hotter than the bathwater, stung my cheeks.

Chapter Eight

Tuesday morning, Arnicia met me in the kitchen with, "I understand you got quite a show yesterday."

"Todd! You don't have to tell everyone," I said.

He sputtered, crimson. "I didn't."

"Where's Jacob?" I asked, hands on hips.

"Gone already," Arnicia said, smiling. "But he gave me the scoop. Said the look on your face was priceless." She set Todd's breakfast in front of him. This morning it was pancakes, with butter and syrup. A good sign.

Arnicia looked around the kitchen, then sat and took Todd's crossword from him while he ate. "I like it when you feel good," she said to him. "I get the cushiest job in the world."

"Anything to please," he said. "I'll have to feel good more often for your sake."

"You do that." She watched me toast a bagel and said, "And you. I don't even know what to say to you. What are you thinking, saying no to a man like Nicholas?"

Todd froze, fork midway to his mouth, and waited for my answer.

"So," I said. "Jacob gave you the scoop on that, too?"

She nodded. I wrapped the bagel in a napkin and shoved it

into my briefcase. I picked up my coat. "Oh, now, don't be mad at me," she said.

"I'm not mad; it's just everyone has an opinion about it. This is between me and Nicholas. Nobody else."

She gestured to the clock with her long, sculpted nails. "Where you headed in a huff so early?"

"I have a meeting with a student. Zackery. A gay boy. Get Jacob to fill you in. He knows all about him." I went out the back door and shut it just a tad too hard. I wasn't even sure it was intentional.

Of course, I regretted it a few miles later when I realized I hadn't said good-bye to Todd.

I called Todd from the empty office when I arrived at Old Mill High School, deadening any dramatic effect of my exit. He laughed at me and said not only did he plan to live through the day, he and Jacob were heading to a hockey game that night. It was with a much lighter heart that I waved to the custodian and headed to my room down the quiet hallways.

Zackery was already there, with a box of doughnuts. I poured coffee for us in the teachers' lounge, where two teachers were frantically preparing and photocopying for the day. The sight of them sent flutters through my belly, the way finding someone practicing in an empty studio between rehearsals used to do.

"Well, no messages in my mailbox this morning," I said, sitting down with Zack in my room. "No angry parents complaining about our little Bible lesson."

"It's still early," Zack said. "Give it time."

I laughed. "Thanks for your reassurance." We ate in silence for a few minutes. "So, how's it going at home?"

He lifted his shoulders. "It sucks. But, hey, what can you do?"

"That's what I want to know. *Is* there anything I can do?"

He smiled. "This." He nodded to the doughnuts, the coffee, the two of us. "And really, it sucks, but it's not that bad. We just don't talk to each other. I've got a debate tournament this weekend, though, which helps. The weekends are the worst. It'll be good to be out of the house."

"Who's the poem about?"

He started, hints of pink splotches whispering upon his neck. He lifted his shoulders again. "A guy. . . ."

"What guy?"

"None of your business." He smiled but wouldn't meet my eyes.

"Does he know?"

Zack burst out laughing. "No. No way. And he never will. He does not feel the same. Of that I have no doubt."

"Tell me. Come on."

"No." One of my homeroom students came in and plopped her pile of books onto her desk. Zack stood up, grinning at me, and said, "Thanks, Ms. Zwolenick. See you sixth period."

I looked forward to sixth period but found it just my luck that every poem we worked on that day shared the subject of love. Love lost. Love unrequited. Love thrown away. Regrets. Anguish. Lots of teenage angst. By the time the bell rang, I was wrung out and exhausted. Today I had packed my riding clothes—no way was I making that mistake again—and found a trail ride on Glacier to be more therapeutic, and lots colder, than I had expected.

I met Kelly Canter as I was walking down the driveway. She was thin, with a boyish figure and a square, determined jaw. Her voice, though, was soft and lyrically feminine, soothing to both man and beast. "Your father told me you might be interested. I'm sure we could set up a time," she said. Her hands and face were the only clues to her age, but if Dad hadn't told me she was in her sixties, I'd simply have attributed the worn, leathery skin to a livelihood earned outside. It was hard not to be inspired in the presence of her elfish energy. "You seem hungry," she said, peering at me, and I knew she didn't mean food. She opened the trunk of her car and loaned me some videotapes of top Olympic riders and a classic text on riding.

I drove home knowing I'd get the house to myself that evening to watch the tapes, but Todd stood, frowning, panting slightly in the kitchen. "You wouldn't want to go to this hockey game with me tonight, would you?" he asked me.

"Jacob's not going?"

"I guess not."

"Excuse me?" Jacob's voice hit flat and hard as a slap. He blocked the kitchen doorway, body stiff and coiled in some dangerous way, like a horse tensed and ready to kick. With a jolt of adrenaline, I was reminded why he got cast so often as terrorists, rapists, and wife beaters. "When did I say I wasn't going?"

Todd rolled his eyes. "Well, since you've been such a dick all afternoon, I just assumed—"

"Hey, now," I interrupted him. "You say that like it's a bad thing." I was repeating a joke they'd made countless times, but neither of them laughed. I couldn't tell yet if it was a fight brewing or the wake of one already past. "What's going on?" I asked.

Jacob slouched in the doorway. "Your brother thinks he's always right about everything."

"And Jacob's an asshole," Todd said.

"Fuck you."

"Fuck you right back, you stupid shit."

"Okay," I said, startling myself, sounding like a teacher, "I don't think I want to go anywhere with you guys right now." I held up the videotapes. "I have my own plans for the evening. See ya."

Upstairs, I showered off the horse smell and changed clothes.

When I came out of the bathroom, I interrupted what looked to be a violent, almost predatory kiss taking place on my bed.

"For Christ's sake," I said. "Is this your new kink or something? Wanting to get caught?"

They laughed and sat up. "Please come with us," Todd said.

"We'll be good," Jacob promised. "We want to cheer you up."

Of course, I agreed.

We called a cab so that we could get out at the front door of the Nutter Center and spare Todd the walk through the inefficient maze of the parking lot.

"Stop it," Jacob said to me as we rode along, me in between them.

"Stop what?" I asked.

"You're thinking about it again." He gestured to himself and Todd and nodded. "You can't do that, you know. You can't have erotic thoughts about your own brother."

"Jake!" Todd and I protested in unison.

"Was it erotic?" Jacob asked, teasing me.

"Why are you asking me this?"

"Yes, why *are* you asking her this? Are you going to ask her to videotape us or something?"

"Hell, she doesn't need to videotape. She was there."

"Stop it! I said I was sorry!" The cabdriver looked in his mirror at us, feigning boredom but intrigued.

"I'm just curious," Jacob said. "I find it odd that most straight men have this thing about lesbians. You know, there's a token lesbian shower scene in almost every straight porn movie ever made—"

"How would you know?" I asked, catching the cabdriver again.

"Don't try to change the subject: Because it's the safest way for a high school faggot to look at naked men—"

"Naked men with huge dicks," Todd added.

"Would you quit interrupting me? Now, as I was saying: Straight guys—even straight guys who are completely homophobic—get off on lesbians. But the same is not true for straight women and gay sex scenes. Why is that?" He looked at me and waited, as if he truly expected me to have a thesis on this subject.

"I think it's because women's bodies are considered works of art," the cabbie said.

Todd and Jacob leaned forward and looked at each other over me.

"Works of art?" Jacob repeated.

"Yeah, and everyone likes to look at naked women. Naked men—they're not so beautiful, y'know? Not so sensuous."

"Speak for yourself," Jacob said. Todd hid his face in his hands, shaking his head.

The cabbie went on, "And—there's just something, I dunno, inherently violent about men fucking each other. Pardon my French. With women, it's soft and sweet—even more than when a woman and a man are fucking. But two men—that's always violent, y'know?"

"No," I said. "That's not true. I've seen two guys having sex that was very 'soft and sweet' like you said. Very sensual."

Now the cabbie raised his eyebrows.

Jacob leaned forward, past me, and asked Todd, "Soft and sweet?"

Todd held up his hands. "I am *not* participating in this discussion."

Jacob leaned back and said, "Summer, just so you know, never use the adjective *soft* to describe a man having sex with *anyone*."

I laughed but argued, "It was a compliment."

The cabbie shook his head, coming to a stop in front of the Nutter Center. "You said you were going to the Bombers game, right?"

"Yep," Jacob said, paying him. "It's my first one."

"No kidding."

When the cab pulled away, I asked Jacob, "Have you really never been to a hockey game?"

"Nope. Never. I'm a hockey virgin."

"Well, I'll be gentle," Todd said. "I'll go nice and slow."

"You mean 'soft and sweet'?" Jacob asked.

"Shut up!" I punched him in the arm, relieved that all seemed friendly again.

Inside, we stood in line for beer, and when our turn came, Todd ordered three.

"What the hell are you doing?" Jacob asked.

"What's it look like?"

"It'll fuck up your meds! Are you fucking crazy?" People in line pretended not to look at us.

"You seem to think everything I say today is," Todd said, plunking down his money, picking up his plastic cup, and walking away from Jacob without his change. Jacob followed. The woman behind the counter waved the dollar bills and feebly called, "Sir?" after them.

"I'll give it to him," I said. She handed it to me along with the carrier containing the other two beers. "Thanks."

I caught up to them where they had stopped outside a men's rest room.

"You're only doing this because you're pissed at me," Jacob said.

"Now who thinks they're always right?"

"Give me the fucking beer."

Todd began to chug it instead. I closed my eyes, and when I opened them, he'd drained the cup. He tossed it toward a trash can, where it almost went in but bounced back onto the floor with a hollow plop.

They stood, facing off. Jacob picked another cup out of the

carrier I held, upsetting the balance, almost making me drop them. "Fine," he said. "Why not have another?"

Todd took it and raised it to his mouth, but I knocked it away, splashing beer all over the wall. He reached for the third, but I simply let go of the carrier. Beer spattered all over our shoes and pant legs. They kept their eyes locked on each other.

"Who's got the goddamn tickets?" I asked.

Jacob pulled them out of his pocket without looking at me. I snatched one, let the other two drop into the beer and left them. I passed our section twice before I calmed down enough to really read the ticket, then made my way down the steep concrete stairs to our seats inside the stark whiteness of the rink. The crowd was thin compared to weekend games, and I sat conspicuously alone, watching my breath slow in the frosty air. The game was already under way, and I followed the zipping puck without really seeing it.

Almost ten minutes passed before Jacob took a seat beside me. "Where's Todd?"

He shrugged.

I turned in my seat and looked up at the entranceways. "You just left him?"

"He's a big boy, Summer."

"What the hell is going on?"

He sighed and slouched down, leaning his head on the back of the seat, not even pretending to watch the game. "He's mad because I won't go to Thanksgiving at my parents' house."

"What?" I wanted to slap him. "You were gonna let Todd swill three beers for *that?*"

He closed his eyes.

"I thought your parents didn't speak to you."

"Today was the first time in three years." He opened his eyes, his look venomous. "Todd acts like I should be jumping up and down for joy."

"What did they say?"

"Nothing important." He sat up straight and looked down at the ice. So did I.

I envied the players their strength. The sure way they moved. The cavalier abuse they heaped upon their muscled, athletic bodies. They knew they were invincible. Immortal, even. One player stopped short, shaving ice into a powdery spray. He raised his arms in triumph at the announcer's words. So cocky, moving with the irresistible arrogance of a Thoroughbred yearling.

Jacob tilted his head at the penalty that was announced. "Icing? What the hell is icing?"

"He shot from too far behind that line." Todd's voice made us jump. He stood in the empty row behind us and pointed over our heads. "And there was nobody in this half of the rink, so it's considered an act of desperation." He climbed over the row and sat on the other side of me from Jacob.

"There are guys blatantly fouling each other all over the place, and they think icing is a bad thing?" Jacob asked.

"They are not 'blatantly fouling,'" Todd said.

"Hello? Babe, look at that! Is he allowed to hang on him like that? Look—he pushed that guy on purpose."

"This is hockey," Todd said. "Don't complain about people pushing each other, okay?"

"I just think in light of the flagrant disregard for sportsmanship, icing seems a pretty wussy thing to be worried about."

A silence fell. "Well," I said. "I'm sure having a great time. Thanks for inviting me."

They both mumbled, "Sorry."

The Bombers scored. I dragged both Todd and Jacob up by the elbows and taught Jacob how to "count 'em down" with the crowd. "Look, we may as well go home if you're just going to sit here and sulk," I said when we sat back down. They both shook their heads and leaned forward, as if determined to get involved in the game.

Play resumed, and two players bashed into the glass near our seats. Jacob winced and exhaled through his teeth. "Damn! I can't believe you used to do this!"

"Why can't you believe it?" Todd asked. His tone held a challenge, and I sighed loudly and deliberately. Jacob didn't answer, and Todd let it drop.

We focused on the game for several minutes, the silence growing more natural, less strained. A drunk man in our section shouted that the goalie "sucked dick." Jacob leaned across me and whispered to Todd, "So, is that like a regular thing with you goalies?"

Todd cracked his first smile of the night.

In between periods I left them alone and went to buy us hot pretzels. When I returned, they were sitting side by side.

Shortly into the second period, a fight broke out on the ice, and players whipped off gloves, threw down sticks, and laid into each other. The crowd went wild.

"This is sick," Jacob said as people farther down front stood on their seats for a better view. Todd stood, too, although we could see just fine from our higher seats. "Not this many people stood up when they scored a goal."

The refs separated the players. One of the Bombers took off his helmet, and the coach peered at a cut above the player's eye. The coach touched the cut, assessing the need for stitches, perhaps. I winced, but the player didn't even blink. Blood trickled down his face and dripped onto the snow white ice. Todd's lips parted slightly, and he went still and silent. He stared, enthralled.

"Babe?" Jacob asked him, tugging on his shirtsleeve. Everyone else had sat down. Todd gave himself a little shake and took his seat.

"What?" Jacob asked.

Todd shook his head. "It's just—" He stopped and shook his head again, watching the bleeding player, who stood talking to his coach and the refs while other players milled around on their skates, picking up their discarded equipment. The player's curly brown hair was wet with sweat and matted down from his helmet. His face was sharp and angular.

Jacob and I looked at each other and shrugged.

"I was still playing in college," Todd said.

Jacob and I looked at each other again. "I know," I said. "So?"

"So, I was positive then." His eyes never left the injured player. All three of us watched him wipe some blood and flick his fingers casually, spattering the ice and the coach's pant leg with crimson.

"Oh, please," Jacob said. "No one's gonna get it playing hockey."

"They *could*," Todd said. "What if you bashed heads together? What if you both break skin at the same time?"

"Pretty unlikely."

"What's fucking unlikely about it?" Todd's face reddened.

"It just is. It'd have to be a lot of blood and—"

"You don't know—"

"What do you mean I don't know? I know a fuck of a lot about—"

"For Christ's sake!" I stood up. "I'm going home. You all have done a great job cheering me up. I had about as much fun as I would've going out with Mom and Dad." I climbed the stairs as quickly as my ankle allowed me. At the top I looked down. They were still arguing. Jacob was standing up.

I called a cab and waited for it outside in the cold. The cabbie was a young woman, thankfully quiet, almost sullen. I looked out the window at the pale, swollen sky, about to split with snow. By the time she delivered me back at the house, steady flurries were falling, darting in the sharp gusts of wind.

I stood in the bay window of the living room, watching, not wanting to go to my cold, empty bed alone. It seemed unreal to me that I had left, had fled in my panic. Just like a little girl, how I'd climbed to the hayloft when the shouting in the house grew too loud. Only then, I could count on Todd coming after me. It had never been Todd doing the shouting.

I wrapped an afghan around me and sat on the couch in the dark. I pulled the phone into my lap. Twice I dialed all but the last number, then replaced the receiver in its cradle. What would I say to him, after all? But finally I completed the number and listened to his phone ring three times before a sleepy, gravelly, "Hello?"

"Hey . . . it's me."

The voice became sharper. "What's wrong? Is Todd okay?"

A warmth spread through me. "Yes, he's fine. I just . . . I wanted to hear your voice. Were you sleeping already?"

"Yeah."

"I'm sorry."

Silence.

"I miss you," I said.

"I miss you, too."

"I wanted you to know that. And I wanted you to please believe me, that it's not you; there's nothing wrong with you; it's me. This is my problem I'm sorting out."

He exhaled a short laugh. "That's only the most classic breakup line there is," he said.

More silence.

"Are you doing all right?" he asked me.

"No. Are you?"

"Not exactly the best time of my life, no," he said.

"Are you coming for Thanksgiving?"

After a long pause: "I don't know. I don't think so, Summer. I think it would be really hard for me, okay?"

"Please come."

"Maybe. I don't know. I'd like to see you. I'm sorry I just left like that. It's good to hear your voice."

"It's good to hear yours. I'm sorry I woke you. Good night."

"Good night, love." We both breathed on the line before the click and the tone. I'm not sure who hung up first. I continued to sit there, staring out the bay window, until a car pulled into the driveway. I stood to look. It was a cab. I dropped the afghan and slipped upstairs to my room.

I undressed and climbed into the tall antique bed, pulling the covers up to my chin. I stared at the high ceiling and listened to the angry symphony of slamming doors and heavy footfalls from downstairs. About the time I was ready to yell at them, they quieted down.

I lay there for about an hour, then admitted to myself that I wasn't going to sleep. I turned on my lamp and tried to grade. I heard Arnicia come in and go to her room. The noises of her moving about in her nighttime routine comforted me for a while, then her room fell silent along with the rest of the house.

After another hour I pulled on Todd's giant sweatshirt and tiptoed back down to the kitchen. I opened the fridge and stared for a moment at the door shelves stocked with medicine bottles. The shelves inside didn't offer much in the way of comfort food. I settled for a strawberry yogurt, but even after I closed the refrigerator door, a cold draft blew across my bare calves. I looked around, confused as to its source, and saw, with a start, that the back door was open a crack. It pulsed open and closed with the wind. I went to latch it and saw a small orange light flare briefly on the porch. I caught my breath—it was just Jacob smoking.

I stepped onto the porch, my skin prickling and shrinking in the cold. "Hey."

"Holy shit! You scared me," Jacob said. He was sitting on the top step, wrapped in a thick wool blanket, only his head and hands visible.

"Aren't you freezing?" I asked.

He shook his head. He handed me a cigarette and the lighter. I took it without a word and stood beside him, shivering, arms crossed tightly in front of my chest, looking out at the snow falling.

"So pretty," I said.

He nodded. "But none of it's sticking. In the morning, it'll all be gone."

We smoked.

"Sit down," he said. "Want under the blanket?"

I nodded, grateful. He opened it up, and I slid in next to him, surprised by the amazing amount of warmth held inside the blanket. I snuggled in and said, "Oh, my God. You're naked."

"Yeah, so? Do you want under the blanket or not?"

I pulled it up around the back of my neck, tucking myself into this toasty cocoon. His hard, ropy thighs touched mine, and I was thankful for the dark as the blood rushed to my face. My gaze had lingered on his bare legs before, whenever he wore shorts or slipped out of their bedroom in his underwear to grab the morning paper. But I'd never had myself pressed up against him, bare skin to bare skin. He shifted his weight slightly to flick his cigarette ash into the wind, and his muscles rippled along mine. This was what Todd felt, every night, lying beside him in bed. Or lying under him, like yesterday, on the living room floor.

I thought of how different Nicholas's thighs felt. Not as long and lean as Jacob's, but more sensuous and compact. The difference between a Thoroughbred and a quarter horse. And that difference went for their temperament as well as their conformation, Nicholas as bombproof in a crisis as the red quarter pony I'd had as a child.

Jacob felt me shiver and scooted closer, thinking I was cold. We each used one hand to keep the blanket closed tight in front of us and the other to handle our cigarettes.

"I hate that I can't just enjoy the good times," he said out of the blue. "So many great days in a row and I get terrified."

"You call this a great day? That was horrible."

He looked at me, surprise in his eyes, and asked, "You aren't going to give us any credit for that?"

"For what?"

"For going at it. Unlike you; first sign of trouble and you're hightailing it out of there."

I tensed, and he smiled. Side by side, he felt the change in my body and knew he'd gotten to me.

"So, did you make up? Is it over?" I asked, ignoring his comment.

"Hell, no."

"You allowed to sleep in there?"

"Don't know that I want to." He looked out across the yard, at the lacy designs being etched in the sky. "But I will."

"Could you please not slam any more doors?"

He looked at me. "This really has you freaked, doesn't it?" He laughed. "This is nothing. This is tame. We've broken furniture before. Your damn brother once got out of the fucking car on the Los Angeles Freeway and started walking. Hell, once, re-member the apartment before the big house? I came home and the motherfucker was throwing all my shit off the balcony like some crazy woman in a movie. He'd changed the locks on me. I had to go up the fire escape and break in."

My breath snagged in my chest. I couldn't see my brother doing any of these things. "Why?" I whispered.

"That first time? After we found out, you know, about the virus. He thought it was my fault. You know, from fucking around." He shrugged. "And you know, to be honest, I thought it was, too."

I twisted my torso to face him. "Did you? Fuck around?"

He opened his mouth. He shut it, pursing his lips. He looked up at the sky. "Never after we were married." He looked me in the eyes and said, "Not once after we were married. When I said the vows, I meant them."

He lit another cigarette and offered me one, but I shook my head. I watched him smoke and felt crushed, deflated. "When else?" I asked.

He looked at me, confused.

"You said 'that first time.'"

"Oh. Two other times he tried to throw me out when he thought I couldn't handle it, the whole sickness thing. He wanted to get rid of me before it got ugly and he was depen-dent on me. He was convinced I would bail when he needed me most." He took a deep drag on the cigarette. "He was really just scared, though. You know? Still is. And so am I."

I said nothing. He'd finished that cigarette and stubbed it out on the porch before he spoke again. "God, I hope I can do this."

"Do what?" I asked.

"What it takes to get him through it. To the end."

I closed my eyes. I didn't want to know Jacob felt this way, too. My poor brother. What a crew of chickenshits he had on his side. "You have to," I whispered.

"I don't know, baby. I don't know. What if he's right?"

"He calls you the love of his life," I said.

Jacob smiled. His cheeks glittered in the blue light of the snow.

"So, go eat some turkey with your parents," I said. "What's the big deal?"

"That's not the point."

"Well, isn't this what you wanted? I mean, it's like you won."

He laughed. "No. It's not what I wanted. And it's really none of your business."

"Okay," I said. "Fair enough. Then how is it any of your business to blab about me to Arnicia?"

"Please. Arnicia's family." He lit another cigarette, shaking his head. "Besides, that's different. We all were involved in that—Todd and I helped shop for the goddamn ring. None of us know what the hell you're thinking." I said nothing, and he went on. "Don't get me wrong. You don't need to be married, and you sure as shit don't need all these people telling you what to do. You're the only straight woman I've ever known who's smart enough to believe she can find herself with*out* a man. Most of you think a man is required to even be happy. So . . . if you don't want to marry Nicholas, that's fine. Problem is, I don't believe that. I think you've got something else going on that I can't figure out. I don't think *you've* figured it out yet. I think you do love Nicholas and you do want to marry him and you're on the verge of really fucking it up."

I pulled away from him, permitting a huge gust of wind into our blanket. We both gasped. I huddled back in close to him.

"Sorry," I said. "It's just—look, I don't want to talk about it. There's just so much . . . going on right now."

Jacob nodded. "But life goes on, babe. Don't be afraid to plan a future without Todd. It won't hurt his feelings. It doesn't mean you're wishing him dead. I've been through all that mind shit. Life goes on. He wants it to." He tossed his cigarette into the yard and wrapped his arm around me.

"It's scary," I whispered.

"That's okay," he said. "It's always gonna be."

Again I shut my eyes. I didn't like his answer. I slipped a hand under the blanket, too, to pat his leg, but he yelped and said, "Your hands are *really* cold, baby!"

I giggled and tucked it under my sweatshirt to warm it up.

After a moment he yawned and said with surprise, "Hey, maybe I *will* sleep."

"I'm jealous," I said.

"You got school tomorrow?"

"Yeah. Last day before Thanksgiving."

"You coming with us tomorrow night to help your mom get ready?"

"I thought I had to," I teased. "Didn't you volunteer us all?"

"Hey, I think it will be fun." We sat there, neither one of us wanting to break out of the warmth yet, even though the door was only a yard away.

The kitchen light snapped on, and as we turned to it, we were blinded when the porch light came on as well. We squinted at Todd silhouetted in the doorway. "Just leave the fucking door open," he said. "It's freezing in here." He swung it shut so hard, it didn't catch and bounced back open, but he was already fuming his way back to the bedroom.

I abandoned the safe, soothing warmth of the blanket and felt flayed by the cold as we went inside. Jacob closed the door quietly, locked it, and took a deep breath. "For better or worse, baby," he said to me. "For better or worse." He went into their bedroom, and I went up to mine, but even the moaning pipes didn't drown out the angry voices.

Chapter Nine

$\backsim\!\!\!\sim$

$\mathcal{W}$hen I got home from school the next day, I walked into cold silence and stiff body language; the fight was far from over but had moved into a quieter phase.

Jacob drove to the farm, and Todd stared out the window. I sat in the backseat and said, "Well, this should be fun." Neither said a word the entire trip. I counted every minute of the drive and wondered why I hadn't driven myself separately.

Mom put Todd and Jacob to work peeling apples. I could tell she sensed the tension, too. She sent me upstairs to get the silverware box from under her bed, and as I came down the stairs and back into the kitchen, the problem was finally being aired. I'm not sure who asked or broached the subject.

I sat down as Todd was saying, ". . . and some man says, 'Jacob?' No one mistakes us for each other. No one. I would have thought it was a salesperson, except they used his first name. So, I was like, 'No . . . but I can get him for you . . . can I tell him who's calling?' There's this really long pause, and I finally say, 'Hello?' again. And a woman's voice says, 'We're Jacob's parents.' So I try to be warm and gracious, and I assure them that I'll get Jacob right away and he'll be so glad they called, but he's rude to them right off the bat."

Jacob flung his peel into the white basin between their chairs the way a mean-spirited child would hurl a rock at a stray cat.

Todd went on, "I try to leave him alone; I go stroll around the yard. I figure I'll give him plenty of time, but I look in the window and he's already done! He only talked about five minutes! And he admits he hung up on them. You've waited for this conversation for what? Three years? And you hang up on them?"

Grandma Anna wheeled herself into the kitchen doorway behind me. I was surprised to see her up and dressed in decent clothes—a tan skirt and a rich chocolate sweater; she'd been having terrible headaches lately that left her largely bedridden. "What did they want?" she asked Jacob.

"To fucking invite me to Thanksgiving dinner," Jacob said as if the very thought were outrageously inappropriate.

"Jacob! Your language!" Grandma said.

"Sorry." I'm not sure he noticed she called him Jacob. It was the first time I'd ever heard her do so. Mom handed me the silver polish.

"Wouldn't you expect him to say yes?" Todd asked, peeling his apple in a slow, meticulous manner. "I don't get it. I told him I'd go. I've been feeling great. I mean, the timing's perfect. There's no reason not to go."

"You should go," Mom said. "You must go."

"No. We're going to be here like we have been the last four years."

"You're such an asshole," Todd said, shaking his head.

"No, I'm not. They are."

"They're trying not to be. What do they have to do? Send an engraved invitation? Give them a break."

"Why? Why should I give them a break? Did they ever give me one? I don't owe them a goddamn thing. I don't want to eat their goddamn Thanksgiving dinner."

"That is such bullshit," Todd said. His peeling grew slower and more deliberate as Jacob's grew more reckless.

"Look, babe, you can think that all you want, but I already have plans. This family has made me welcome for years, and I'm spending Thanksgiving here. You do what you want."

"You said you didn't want to do Thanksgiving here if all the relatives were invited. You hate them, so don't even pretend you'd rather hang out with Marnee."

"Jacob, it would be great for you two to be with your parents," Mom said. "Please. We understand."

"No," he said. Todd exhaled in frustration.

I watched Grandma, head tilted, brow furrowed, listening to their conversation. She seemed troubled by Jacob. As Jacob went on, she looked concerned for him, which confused me. "Why?" she asked.

We all looked at her. "Why?" she repeated. "Why did they call you after so many years?"

Now we all looked at Jacob. I hadn't even thought of that. Jacob glared at Grandma as though he might slug her, but then he sort of slumped as if defeated and said, "Because I wrote to them."

"What?" Todd said. "You didn't tell me that."

Jacob picked up another apple and peeled, not looking at us. "I thought . . . I wanted to give them the chance. I wanted them to meet you. I wanted them to see. I needed them to know that . . . they were . . . running out of time."

Todd put down his apple and knife and touched Jake's arm. Jacob kept peeling, taking big thick chunks with the red peel, whittling the apple almost to the core. "Jake. Then, that's beautiful. I don't understand . . . why don't we go?"

Jacob bit his lip. He set the apple core carefully on the table and wiped his hands on his jeans. He looked Todd square in the eye. "Because they didn't invite you. They didn't even ask about you."

Todd blinked.

Jacob's mouth twitched as he went on, his anger hiking his voice higher and higher. "I kept bringing you up. I kept talking on and on. They'd just change the subject like I hadn't said a word."

"Why didn't you tell me this?" Todd whispered.

"Why would I fucking want to tell you this?" Jacob yelled, the tears finally breaking and rolling down his cheeks. "You think I wanted you to know my parents don't give a shit about the most important thing in my life?" He brushed an arm roughly across his face and breathed deeply with his eyes closed. After a pause, he opened his eyes and said in an almost inaudible voice, "I wanted you to like them someday."

Todd pulled his chair closer and leaned his head on Jacob's shoulder, one arm across the back of Jacob's chair, the other reaching for one of Jacob's hands. Jacob stared at the table of apples, allowing his hand to be taken but otherwise not responding. Todd kissed his shoulder, and, finally, Jacob brought his other hand to Todd's arm.

I stood, caught Mom's eye, and nodded toward the living room. Grandma Anna turned her wheelchair around and followed us.

"It's a step, isn't it?" Mom asked.

Grandma surprised me by saying, "No. He took a step, but they did not." She nodded, as if to herself, and went into her room.

Mom and I sat on the couch, watching about twenty minutes of Jacob's old soap opera until he came to the door and said, "Turn that awful shit off. Are we going to make a pie, or what?"

While I turned off the TV, Mom hugged him and gave him a kiss.

We sliced and diced vegetables, cleaned the house, and made three pumpkin pies, two apple pies, and one pecan pie. We went back home at ten o'clock.

Nicholas had left a message on the machine. He wished us all a happy Thanksgiving, but he wouldn't be joining us. "I got a second interview at the Arena," he said. "Since we're dark for the holiday weekend, and so are they, I thought I'd drive over there tomorrow. The artistic director will meet with me on Friday. Wish me luck."

"Go on, Nicholas!" Jacob shouted.

"I knew they'd want him," Todd said, beaming as if Nicholas were his son. "He's as good as a stage manager gets."

I smiled and tried to quell the skittering of my heart. This was fabulous news for Nicholas. I didn't want it tinged with what I was feeling. Of all my blood being pulled down through my feet, running out, escaping down a drain. The realization that I would not have the luxury of muddling my way through this with him nearby.

I went to my room to call him, to congratulate him, but heard voices on the line. Todd or Jacob was already on the phone. I tried once more half an hour later but gave up and fell asleep around eleven.

In the morning there was a note from Arnicia under my door, reminding me that she was visiting her family this weekend and wouldn't be back until Saturday. *"Try to get Todd to eat as much pumpkin pie as possible. It's actually very nutritious,"* she wrote in a P.S. With Todd doing as well as he was this week, her absence meant no extra chores for me at all.

Jacob and I puttered around, waiting for Todd to wake up of his own accord. We watched cartoons in our robes while he painted my toenails. He opted not to paint my fingernails, since one was missing and there was no way to disguise the red twist of angry skin left behind. The other damaged nail had shifted from black to purple and looked as though it might stay connected. When my toes were dry, he helped me pick out clothes. After several outfits we settled on a long red wool sweater, a short red-and-black kilt-style skirt, black tights, and black clogs. "You've got the best legs," he said, appraising me. This outfit flaunted them. I left my hair down long.

Todd emerged around ten-fifteen. Somewhere in the night he'd acquired a new cough—a single, dry cough like a faraway gunshot. Although Jacob said it was no big deal, the worry in his eyes matched the worry churning in my stomach.

"You stayed up too late last night," Jacob said while we watched Todd eat his breakfast of canned pears and Rice Krispies. "How long did you talk to Nicholas, anyway?"

"You were talking to Nicholas? I was trying to call him "

"Sorry." He glanced at the clock. "He's probably on the road already."

I thought of him making the eleven-hour drive alone. We'd traded back and forth every three hours when we went together last summer. We'd read to each other and eaten cashews and M&Ms. I'd liked D.C.; it was a cleaner, easier city than New York. We'd stayed three days, our last vacation before I moved in with Todd and Jacob. We'd wandered through the zoo, the National Gallery, and all the major monuments. We'd found a giant bronze statue of Albert Einstein, and Nicholas had kissed me as we'd sat on Einstein's knee.

It was hard to believe that was only five months ago. I wondered if Nicholas would think of that when he was there. I wondered what he was thinking of right now.

We made it to the farm around noon. Several cars already

lined the driveway. Over the years, the family gatherings had strengthened again after the shaky period following Todd's rather forced coming out the night before Abby's wedding. There'd been two or three years where there'd been no reunions here at the farm; then slowly, they'd reappeared. And many old wounds were scabbing over. They still itched a little and were red around the edges, but healing was visible.

My mother's mother, our grandma Cailee, came out in the yard to greet us. Ceidlih is the true Welsh spelling, but she'd abandoned that shortly after coming to this country. Her brogue and raucous laughter seemed to warm the snow flurries falling through the gray air. She kissed us all and giggled with delight when Jacob picked her up and spun her. "Thank goodness you've arrived!" Grandma Cailee made me laugh at the way she made fun of and imitated her own children. She'd whisper to me that they were "a moaning lot of dullards." In fact, she seemed younger than any of them, with her bawdy songs and her practical jokes. She'd barely blinked an eye at Todd's disclosure and now claimed that he seemed to be the only one of her children, or grandchildren, for that matter, who'd chosen well when it came to spouses.

"Where's Nicholas?" she asked me. I was grateful for the easy answer I'd been given and for the fact that Todd and Jacob didn't elaborate in any way. "Well," Grandma Cailee said. "I wish him well, but I'll miss his handsome face. Come and liven them up inside!"

Inside was chaos, but warm, cheerful chaos. My dad and several of my uncles and cousins were watching football in the living room. Most of the women were in the kitchen, but there were a few overlaps, and already there was enough bustle to make it a party.

My mother's oldest sister, my aunt Marnee, hugged me primly in the kitchen. "Where's Nicholas?" she asked.

"He can't come. He's going to Washing—"

She interrupted me, saying, "Let me see your hands! Let me see your hands! No ring yet? Better get a move on, young lady!"

She turned to Todd and Jacob. "Well, hello there, Jacob! I'm never sure if I'll see you or not!"

"What's that supposed to mean?" he asked, bristling.

"Ignore her," Todd said.

"Todd! Shouldn't you be lying down?"

"No, Aunt Marnee. I can still walk and talk."

"Hi, Todd." Her son, Bobby, now in college, shook Todd's hand. There'd been a time Bobby wouldn't even stand in the same room with him.

"Hi, Bobby."

"Bobby, wash your hands," Aunt Marnee said.

"Ignore her," Bobby said, smiling, mimicking Todd's own tone. He didn't wash his hands.

"You just can't be too careful," Aunt Marnee said to my aunt Emma, her sister-in-law. She'd meant to whisper it, but it was a skill she didn't quite possess. Aunt Emma nodded, wobbling her double chins. Jacob narrowed his eyes at them. Todd put a hand on Jake's arm.

"How are you feeling, Todd?" Aunt Emma asked.

"I'm doing good. It's been a good week. I've started this funny cough this morning, though—"

Mom turned around from the turkey, her eyes full of question, her face pale.

Aunt Marnee and Aunt Emma nodded to one another and clucked their tongues.

"May I escort you, ma'am?" Todd asked Grandma Cailee, offering his arm. She took it, and they headed for the living room.

As they passed, Aunt Marnee said to Aunt Emma, "I'm just amazed that Jacob will stay with him."

Jacob froze in that coiled, threatening posture that earned him his living. Only he wasn't acting. "Excuse me?" he said.

"I wasn't speaking to you," Aunt Marnee said.

"Then you better not speak *about* me in front of my face."

Marnee had the good sense, at least, to blanch a little.

I saw Mom's face. All she ever wanted was a nice holiday. Just some peace and togetherness. Every attack on Todd and Jacob was an attack on her as well, and she was weary of defending herself.

"Come on, Jake," I said, looking at Mom. "I want to show you Glacier, the horse I've been riding." I all but pulled him out of the kitchen.

"Fuck them!" he exploded in the yard. "It makes me fucking furious! Those simple bitches are allowed to take marriage vows, and they have no concept of what those vows mean. And us, we can't even call it a marriage legally—and Jesus—it offends me that those cunts would even consider that I'd leave him!"

He hurled obscenities at the sky. The horses lifted their heads and stopped their chewing, shocked by such behavior. They snorted to show their disapproval. We both smoked three cigarettes in a row, leaning on the mares' gate. Jacob calmed down, and we hiked through the fields in silence. It was an effort to keep my clogs on, so our progress was slow and solemn. I reached out and held his hand.

"I'm having déjà vu," he said.

I nodded. I'd been thinking that this reminded me of another Thanksgiving. The Thanksgiving I'd met them at the airport and had felt such foreboding. I'd gone to meet them, happy and inspired, wanting to show off my walking without an ankle brace. I'd even worn low heels, and I'd been taking college classes. I was so excited to show Todd, but they'd both seemed preoccupied and edgy. At the house, Todd had napped and Jacob and I had walked in this very field. I'd taken him to the pond and shown him the treehouse and the rocks that Todd had told him about, and he'd started to cry. I'd taken his hand then and had said, not asked, "Something's wrong."

"Yes," he'd said. "Todd's going to tell you."

"Is it something awful?"

He'd nodded. It was snowing that day, too. Lightly, like this. It had gathered on our hair, our lashes, and our shoulders.

I hadn't asked any more questions. For once in my life, I wasn't nosy. In spite of the urgency, I somehow knew I didn't want this information.

That Thanksgiving I was so aware of savoring every ritual, every aroma, every crescendo of laughter in that crowded kitchen. I watched everyone, drinking in every detail. I didn't know yet how, but I knew that all this was about to be threatened. This was the part in the horror movie where the camera would look in on us from outside, through a window—an outside force, the evil creature—watching and awaiting its chance to destroy us all, its hideous, raspy breath audible over our voices and laughter.

Abby had been there. It was the first time she'd left Brad, and she and I had stayed up late in our old bedroom, a sacred slumber party of whispered secrets. Secrets she resented sharing once she went back to him.

Nicholas was there. I'd met him at the college, both of us standing out as older than our classmates—he, like most theater tech majors, had taken forever to graduate because he kept getting work in "the real world" that took him away from school for quarters at a time. We'd been going out for three months. Jacob had cornered me against the refrigerator and had asked if I wanted Nicholas there for the news. Was he "a keeper," he'd asked me. I'd said yes.

We'd eaten, but I could hardly swallow. My imagination hurtled over all the possible crises and scenarios I considered, refusing to settle on the one I'd thought of first. The one I couldn't allow it to be. I tried not to think about Robby, my former ballet partner, and how he'd come to my apartment one night—after missing a rehearsal here or there, giving up one role, then another, finally missing class for two entire weeks—to tell me he wouldn't be back next season and why. I tried not to think about his funeral I attended just four months later. Or the three other funerals by the time that season ended. That was a different world, a past life, and had nothing to do with my brother. My big brother, whose hands shook as he tried to eat that night. I remember he put down his fork and Jacob held his hand. No one else seemed to notice.

Over dessert Todd cleared his throat. And he told us. "Um. I tested positive for HIV." And then he frowned, as if the words, said out loud, had not quite sounded right. He looked at Mom and whispered, "I'm sorry."

My heart was absent in my chest. A low keening filled my ears, my head, blocking out all other sound. Nicholas wrapped his hand around mine and prompted me to breathe again. He put an arm across my shoulders and pulled me to him. He put his lips to my ear and said, "Shh." I realized the keening sound came from me. I put hands across my mouth to stop it.

Mom blinked. Dad shut his eyes. Grandma Anna prayed to herself, moving her lips and touching a bony hand to her forehead, and her chest, and shoulders. Abby appeared stunned, almost exasperated, as if Todd had just told her they were planning to move to Tibet.

Todd and Jacob watched us and waited. The silence lengthened until I thought we would never speak again. Each minute made me fear we'd lost the skill entirely and would become deaf and mute to one another. Finally Mom shook her head. "It's a mistake."

Todd got up and knelt beside her chair. He took both her hands in his and kissed them. "No. It's not a mistake. It's for real. We've been through all kinds of testing and screening. It's for real."

"Jacob?" Mom asked. To this day I wonder if she was asking not just did he have it, but if he were responsible for Todd's. I wonder if she'd have forgiven him if he had been. I wonder if I could have. But Jacob shook his head.

"No, Mom. Jacob is okay."

"Alejandro?" Mom asked, of Todd's college boyfriend.

Todd sighed and smiled, looking at Jacob. They had thought of every conceivable question we would ask.

"No. Alejandro is okay. He's married, too . . . to a woman. Quite a lovely woman, I might add. And he has two gorgeous children. Both sons. He tested negative four different times last year."

It took a moment for us to realize the implication of what he had just said.

"Wait—" Nicholas said, looking up.

"How long have you known this?" Mom asked.

"Since January two years ago," Todd said.

I squeezed Nicholas's hand. I could hardly bear to look at Jacob. They had gotten married, here on the farm, in July. I watched my mother, who turned to Jacob with a look of such gratitude, such love, something so akin to awe, it almost pained me to see it. With Todd still kneeling at her lap, she reached for Jacob, too, and he'd folded his long frame down beside her and she'd pressed his head into her bosom as if he were a little child. She pressed her cheek against his shining black hair and kissed his hair over and over again. We sat watching, crying, for what seemed like hours.

Of course, we eventually came round, that Thanksgiving, to the question of how, then, had Todd contracted the virus. There'd only been two lovers. He wasn't nearly the slut his two sisters had been. He'd never had a transfusion. He'd never had surgery. He'd never used drugs.

"Some doctors are curious about his time spent in Africa," Jacob said.

"I did get my ear pierced there," Todd said, but he didn't sound convinced. "And I had to have stitches there when I dropped that glass lantern on my foot."

"Or that tattoo you got in Ireland," Jacob said halfheartedly.

Although he considered it a long shot, Todd was planning to look up a friend from fifth and sixth grade—Timmy Tatalovitch. Apparently they'd "messed around" rather extensively up in the treehouse during some of their summer sleepovers.

"Todd," I said, "if you're going back as far as sixth grade, what about your senior year?"

Abby gasped as if stung by a hornet.

Todd looked at her and said, "Oh, yeah . . . there is someone else. . . ."

"What's his name?" Jacob asked.

"It's a she," Todd said slowly. "I hadn't even thought of her, Summer."

"A she?" Jacob raised his eyebrows.

"Who?" Mom asked, looking at Abby. Abby had turned pale green.

"Becka. Becka Maynard," Todd said. "Yeah. If I'm gonna panic poor Timmy, I guess Becka is a more likely candidate. I'll have to call her, too."

"Oh, sweetie," Mom said, her face changing.

"You can't," Abby whispered.

"Why?" Todd asked.

"Sweetie, she died last summer," Mom said. "I didn't know you knew her."

"Becka Maynard," Grandma said sharply to Mom. "He took her to the prom." Mom looked ashamed somehow, almost heartbroken, as if not remembering this or even knowing it in the first place made her responsible.

Todd looked at Grandma and nodded. In a delayed, almost stunned manner, he turned back to Mom. "She's dead?"

Mom nodded.

Abby's lips trembled and she looked down at her plate. "She had cancer."

"No," Mom said, "it was pneumonia."

A heavy silence descended. Todd and Jacob looked at each other.

"I'm . . . what sort of cancer?" Jacob asked carefully.

"Skin cancer." Abby's voice was barely audible. She looked up at Todd, and their eyes met and held for several minutes.

"Oh, shit," Todd said at last. I thought he was going to cry, and I couldn't tell if it was for Becka or for himself. Maybe both. "Why didn't anyone tell me?"

Through her tears, Abby said, "For God's sake, Todd. You don't talk to anyone from here. You don't even go to your class reunions."

Todd just stared. "Oh, shit," he said again.

"Becka Maynard came to the farm one day," Grandma said.

"She was here lots of times," Todd said. Mom blushed again.

"No," Grandma insisted. "After that. I was working on the flowers. She asked for you. She wanted your address, your phone number, but you didn't have one. I told her you were traveling the world and may never come back. She laughed. She said she might do the same."

"I remember that," Dad said, his first words since Todd's announcement. "I remember you telling me a friend of Todd's from high school had visited."

"But . . ." Grandma's voice grew hoarse. "I never told you. I didn't mean to forget to tell you. I didn't do it on purpose."

"I didn't call sometimes for weeks," Todd said gently. "It would be easy to forget."

"Tell me," Grandma Anna said. "What does the death of this girl have to do with you? She died of pneumonia. Or cancer." She waved her hands impatiently at Abby and Mom. "You, you have something else."

"She had AIDS, Grandma," Todd said. "And no one here either knew or would admit it."

"You don't know that," Mom insisted.

"I can find out," Abby said. "I know her doctor." We all looked at her. "It's not Brad; it's someone else. I can find out for you."

"Oh, God. She's already dead." Todd looked so lost. Jacob put his arms around him. "If that's it, that's . . . ten years. That was ten years ago. Christ."

"I can find out now," Abby said, standing, her cloth napkin falling to the floor. She left the room.

Abby was on the phone a long time. This doctor, who Abby'd been having an affair with for over a year, had indeed been Becka's doctor, and she had, indeed, had AIDS. Her skin cancer was basal cell carcinoma, usually seen only in the elderly, or in people with AIDS, and had eventually ravaged her former beauty. Her pneumonia was none other than pneumocystis carinii pneumonia—PCP. The family had kept her secret quite well. She'd apparently contracted the virus from her high school boyfriend, Chet Cotter, who had contracted it by sharing needles taking steroids during a football camp one summer. His secret had never been known in Old Mill because shortly after graduation, his family—a military one—had moved out of state and lost contact with their friends and neighbors.

"Well, well, well," Todd said. "Interesting bit of irony isn't it?"

Today, Jacob and I stood, dusted with snow, holding hands, looking down at the pond.

"I fell in love with you that day," I said. "Because you married him knowing he was sick."

"I can't comprehend my life without him," he said, not meeting my eyes. "I'm not prepared at all."

We stood there a moment longer, until he laughed. "I can't get too sentimental. I'm freezing my ass off."

"Me too," I admitted. My feet were numb and my hair wet and stringy from the snow.

Laughing, still holding hands, we took off back to the house.

In the yard, I saw a tall, thin woman I didn't recognize going in the kitchen door. "Who's that?" I asked.

"Oh, my God," Jacob said, stopping, staring after her. I had to pull him to the house.

I opened the door, and there stood a woman I'd never seen before in my life. But there was no question at all who she was— the resemblance was so startling.

"What the hell are you doing here?" Jacob asked.

"Happy Thanksgiving," his mother said, smiling weakly.

"Hello, hello!" Grandma Anna said. She wheeled into the wide breach between Jacob and his mother. "I'm Anna Zwolenick. We spoke on the phone. I'm so glad you could accept my invitation."

"Your invitation?" Jacob asked, staring down at her. "You . . . I . . . who the hell asked you to invite my mother?"

His mother cleared her throat and looked as though she might be sick.

Grandma Anna only laughed and slapped his hand, scolding, "Jacob, your language!" I almost choked. No one else was in the kitchen at the moment to witness this, and I knew that no one would believe me later if I recounted this exchange. "And I invited your mother and your father." She turned to Mrs. Kenwood. "Couldn't Mr. Kenwood make it?"

"Um, no," she said. "He—he wasn't feeling well."

Jacob laughed. "How clever. That's not even a lie. The thought of me always makes him a little sick, doesn't it?"

His mother flared her nostrils and narrowed her eyes. Hell, she should've gone to Hollywood, too; Jacob's talent for terrorism was clearly inherited. "If you'd rather I left . . . ," she began.

"No, no," Grandma Anna said. "Jacob, where are your manners? Aren't you going to introduce us?"

He stared at Grandma a moment before saying, "This is Anna Zwolenick, Todd's grandmother. This is my mother, Patricia Kenwood. And this is my sister-in-law, Summer. She lives with us."

"I am so pleased to meet you," Grandma said. "Summer, take her coat."

But Mrs. Kenwood folded her arms, as if I might try to take it from her by force when she said, "I—I don't know how long I'll stay, actually."

There was an awkward silence. "You drove three hours," Jacob said softly. "You can take off your coat."

She looked at him and nodded. She turned to me, handed over her coat, and said, "Thank you."

"Want me to get Todd?" I asked.

Jacob hesitated.

"Yes, please," Mrs. Kenwood said. She looked Jacob in the eye when she said, "I want to meet him."

I dumped her coat on Grandma Anna's bed and found Todd, with our cousin Sheila, tending the fire in the living room. "You're not going to believe this, but Jacob's mother is here."

"No way!"

"You better get in there."

"Oh, man. I'm scared," Todd said. "Do I look okay?" He messed with his stubbly hair in the mirror above the mantel.

I laughed and pushed him ahead of me into the kitchen. We arrived just as Aunt Shannon, my mother's youngest sister, and her daughters, Samantha, twelve, and Daniela, nine, burst into the kitchen.

"Jake!" Daniela screamed, and ran to him, jumping into his arms. He gave her a big kiss and hug.

Mrs. Kenwood's eyes widened. I looked at the scene through her eyes and decided I was a vengeful person. It made me glad to think how sad it might make her to hear this beautiful young girl greet with such love the son she'd ignored for years.

Samantha, too, hugged him and said, "Hey, they mentioned Big Ed Baker on the soap yesterday!"

"Did they?"

"Yeah . . . they're trying to find you and get you out of the cult. You've changed your name to Sparrow!"

"Sparrow?" Samantha watched Jacob's former program religiously. She programmed her VCR to tape it while she was in school and had saved every episode that Jacob appeared in or was mentioned in.

"Yeah. Will they find you? Are you going to be on it again?" she asked.

"Now, Samantha," Aunt Shannon said.

Jacob knelt, so that he was looking up at Samantha, holding both of her hands. "Remember what we talked about? Someday I might be on it again . . . but I hope it's not for a long, long time."

She nodded. "Me too."

Todd made a small sound—a laugh and a sigh combined. I squeezed his hand.

Daniela spied Todd. "Todd!" She ran to him.

"Easy, easy, easy!" Aunt Shannon cried, but Todd knelt so she would not be tempted to jump into his arms.

Jacob tried to introduce Todd to his mother in a meaningful way, but people kept arriving or coming into the kitchen. Todd and Mrs. Kenwood made their own introductions, and we all had snippets of conversation in between the interruptions.

At two o'clock the line for food started, and we heaped our plates from the many steaming platters lining the kitchen counters. Todd still tried to converse with Jacob's mom and was talking to her a great deal more than Jacob was himself, when Aunt Marnee butted in, saying, "Todd, I brought your favorite cranberry Jell-O salad. Can you eat that?"

"Sure, I can have some."

"I just wondered if you were still having all that diarrhea—"

"Mom!" her son, Bobby, said. Mrs. Kenwood coughed and looked pained.

"Well," Todd said. "Remind me to thank my mother for sharing that little bit of information. Aunt Marnee, I'd like you to meet Jake's mother—" But Marnee had flown off to boss someone else around.

We did manage, eventually, to get Mrs. Kenwood out of the kitchen and into the living room like a real guest. We sat in crowded rooms, eating too much good food. The fire crackled. The windows steamed. I thought of Nicholas and wondered if he was weary of driving yet. I thought of Zackery and wondered what his Thanksgiving was like. I wish I'd thought to invite him here. Mom wouldn't have minded.

I glanced over to check on Mrs. Kenwood. She'd relaxed somewhat but had set down her plate with only a few bites taken. It bothered me to see Todd's plate looking much the same. "Want a piece of pumpkin pie?" I asked him, remembering Arnicia's advice.

He wrinkled his nose and shook his head.

"You okay?" I asked.

"I think I just ate too much." He pressed a hand to his belly.

I frowned. But he turned his attention back to Mrs. Kenwood, so I let it go.

She retained her stunned expression until she left late in the evening. I thought her eyes looked just a little watery when she said good-bye to Grandma Anna, but Jacob claimed they didn't.

"I wasted too much time," Grandma Anna said to her. "And, as you can see, now I have not much time left. Enjoy your son . . . and my grandson, too. Do it now. Or you will regret much."

Mrs. Kenwood nodded, pursing her lips into a grimace of a smile. She seemed somewhat irritated by Grandma. "Jacob," she said. "It—it was good to see you. And Todd, I'm glad I met you."

Todd shook her hand, but Jacob and Mrs. Kenwood never once touched.

Jacob thanked her, rather formally, for coming. She nodded and left.

Jacob pointed at Grandma. "You," was all he said. He shook his head but didn't seem all that angry.

"That was my Christmas gift this year to you both," she said.

"It's a little early for Christmas gifts," Jacob said.

"I don't think I'll be here this Christmas," Grandma said,

pressing a hand against her temple. I'd seen her do it many times today.

Todd nodded. "I don't know if I'll be, either."

"Stop it," Jacob said. "I hate it when you get like this."

"I have something else, as well," Grandma said. She reached for Todd, who gave her his hand. She held out her other hand for Jacob, who offered it, not reluctantly, but with just the slightest hesitance. She put their hands together on her lap, forcing them to kneel beside her chair, and pushed up the sleeve of her blouse, exposing her tattoo. My scalp shrank. Shivers whispered across my shoulder blades. Even with her living in our house my whole life, I had seen that tattoo, her number from the camps, on only two occasions. She tapped the tattoo with a finger and nodded. She pulled her sleeve back down, put her gnarled hands on top of their two, and whispered, "I would do it again. All of it. I would do it all again to protect you."

That was enough.

That was plenty.

But then she added the topper: She looked at Todd and then Jacob and said, "Any of you."

Todd smiled. First he laughed, almost nervously, then he kissed her on the cheek. She grabbed his face and kissed him, and they held each other. This had been a long time in coming. Todd had believed that one day she would see that she was wrong and ask his forgiveness.

Now here they were, laughing and crying. I watched in wonder. Then, after a few minutes, she sort of pushed him away, cleared her throat, and asked, "And do you know what I want from you?" That was that. As far as she was concerned, the last ten years were over and behind them. Just that simply. And I found that I wanted to grab her dried-twig arms and shake her and tell her it wasn't that easy.

But it was. For her, it was. One look at Todd's face made that clear.

"What I want from you is to go to church, the way we used to."

"Not me," Jacob said. "No way."

"Oh, come on," Todd said, and coughed his gunshot cough.

"Let's go right now," Grandma said.

"It's too cold. It's too late. You're both too sick."

"All the more reason we need you to drive us," Todd said.

"I will not go in a Catholic church!"

"Then wait in the parking lot," Todd said, grinning.

"And freeze my butt off?"

"Suit yourself. I'll get your coat, Grandma, and a blanket for the car."

Jacob threw up his hands and went into the living room, following Todd.

"There she is! Stop, Summer!" Aunt Emma cried, unaware of their argument. "We're playing a relationship game."

Uncle Orin was videotaping us.

"No, Summer can't play," Aunt Marnee said. "Nicholas isn't here."

"Todd and Jake can play," Aunt Shannon said.

Aunt Marnee made a face but caught herself. "Oh. Okay. We'll let you boys do it. You have to tell us the worst part about being together and the best part."

"Jacob's driving me and Grandma to church," Todd said, going up the stairs. "We need to hurry."

"Jacob, you do it! It only takes a second!" Aunt Emma said.

"I don't know. . . ." He was still preoccupied with the church situation.

"What's the worst part about being with Todd?" Aunt Marnee asked, like a pushy news reporter. The camcorder just kept going.

Jacob looked at Grandma and cocked his head to Todd's foot-steps above us. "Living with him," he said with feeling.

"I knew this would happen," Aunt Marnee declared.

"And the best part?" Aunt Emma asked.

Jacob considered this. Todd came down the stairs, hat, coat, and scarf on. He was holding Jacob's coat. He paused at the bottom of the steps and looked at the expectant crowd. He didn't know what they were waiting for. Jacob looked at him for a long time, and something shifted in his face.

"What's the best part?" Aunt Marnee repeated.

Jacob smiled and shrugged and said, "Living with him." He reached out his hand and said, "Come on, let's go."

Chapter Ten

The Saturday after Thanksgiving the world fell to pieces.

Friday I saw hints, but nothing prepared me for all of it at once.

By the time Jacob and Todd came home from church Thursday night, Todd's cough had changed. Distant thunder rumbled deep in his chest. He'd close his eyes and exhale slowly, trying to suppress it. Staccato coughs jerked his shoulders and back as they came erupting forth out of control.

Added to this was an abdominal pain that made Todd sweat and grind his teeth. He said he'd grown used to general discomfort, but this pain was new, and there was no telling what it might portend. They scheduled a doctor's appointment; but the earliest they could get was Saturday morning.

On Friday Grandma Anna's vision blurred to the point of blindness, and she suffered terrible spasms of pain in her temple. It grew worse throughout the day, until my father and his brother, Dan, would not leave her side.

Saturday began at three A.M. as I came scrambling up out of sleep to Jacob shaking me awake. I'd spent a year expecting every morning to bring my brother's death, but here it was and I felt completely unprepared.

"No, no, it's not Todd," Jacob said. But he was pulling me upright. "It's that kid. The gay kid. I don't know his name. Hurry!"

"Zack?" I asked.

Jacob picked up my phone. "Are you still there?" he asked someone. "Good. Stay on. Here she is." He stretched the phone toward me. "He's a mess. I think he's drunk."

I took the phone. Jacob turned on my lamp, then went downstairs to hang up the other extension.

"Zack? What's going on? Are you all right? Where are you?"

"I'm at Denny's." He did sound drunk.

"Denny Robillard's?" In my murky-mind, heart-racing state, I envisioned Denny holding Zack hostage.

"No . . . Denny's the restaurant."

"Why are you at Denny's?"

"Denny's the restaurant, not Denny Robillard's," he said, offended. "Why would I go to Denny Robillard's? Do you think I like Denny Robillard?" He was definitely drunk.

"No, no, of course not—"

"Denny Robillard is an asshole."

"Yes, yes, he is," I said. "You wouldn't go there. I was just sleepy. I wasn't thinking right—"

"Oh, God. I'm sorry. You're sleepy. I'm sorry." Then he whispered, "Go back to sleep. I'm sorry." He was hanging up the phone.

"Zack!" I screamed. "Zack! Wait! Don't hang up!"

"Ms. Zwolenick?" He sounded surprised, as if I were the one who'd called him in the middle of the night.

"Yeah, it's me. Listen: Why are you at Denny's?"

"Denny's *the restaurant.* By the fairgrounds. Downtown."

"Okay. Good. Now, how come you're there? Why aren't you at home?"

"People like me don't deserve a home."

"Did someone tell you that? Did you get thrown out?"

"I should have done it." He was crying.

"Done what? Zack, sweetie, talk to me." Jacob came back upstairs and stood in the doorway.

"That's what he said—"

"We're coming to get you. You just sit down and order something."

"—when they read the note on the back of the poem—he said I should have done it." And he hung up.

"Oh, shit. He hung up. We have to go get him."

Jacob handed me clothes. "I can't go, babe. Arnicia's not here. Todd's stomach hurts too much to leave him alone."

"Shit. Shit. I don't know what to do!"

"Just get there. Denny's at the fairgrounds, right? I heard that much. I'll call the manager there." He called information while I pulled on jeans and a sweatshirt and fumbled for some shoes under my bed.

Jake convinced the manager to call the police if Zack left, telling him he was a runaway for simplicity's sake.

I sped through the empty streets, running red lights, expecting to see red and blue ones in my mirror, but managing to make it to Denny's ticket free. I could see Zack through the window as I parked. He was sitting in a booth, eating onion rings and apple pie à la mode.

"Hey," I said, sliding in across from him. "Whew, you're drunk, Zack." He reeked.

He waved his hand cavalierly and shook his head, but then had to steady himself by gripping the edge of the table.

I managed to get from him that his parents had taken to going through his room. They'd discovered the poem. And the note on the back.

And that man had told his son, "You should have done it." He'd said that to this bright, beautiful young man.

What did it do to a person to be told that? Grandma Anna had once told Todd he was not her grandson, that he was a disgrace, that only Satan made people like him. But his own father had never said, "You should have killed yourself." I shivered.

"Come home with me. You can stay with us."

His drunk was wearing off, leaving his face gray and haggard. "You can't do that. I'm not eighteen yet."

"We can get you removed. Do you want me to talk to some-one—?"

"No!" No amount of coaxing persuaded him. I quizzed and quizzed him, but his parents had not done anything beyond screaming at him. Twisted as it was, I wanted them to hit him, harm him in some visible way, so that I'd be required by law to report it and have him removed from that awful home.

I paid for his meal and waited for him while he threw up a few times in the bathroom, then walked with him around the snow-encrusted racetrack at the empty fairgrounds while he mustered the strength to go back home.

"Remember," I said, taking him by the shoulders, "that you deserve a good, loving home because you're a good, loving person. Do you hear me? You are a good, smart, brave person, and there is nothing wrong with you. Nothing."

He burst into tears and hugged me, crumpling until he embraced my knees, sobbing into my legs as I stroked his hair and the sun rose over the bleak, deserted racetrack.

I dropped him off at his house and then sobbed myself. I parked a block away and cried for a long time before I drove home.

Jacob's car still sat in the drive, and Arnicia's car was in my spot out front, but inside, the house was eerily silent. I called, then

ran through the rooms, stopping in Todd and Jacob's bedroom. I
froze, panting, and took in the dark stains on the rumpled bedclothes, the pools of water leading from the bathroom to the pile
of bloody towels on the floor, my box of Kotex from upstairs,
covered now in red smears and handprints. I backed out of the
room slowly and tried to catch my breath.

In the kitchen, I pressed the blinking light on the answering
machine. Jacob's voice on the machine sounded distant and de-
tached, like an android version of himself. "Summer, I'm at the
hospital. Um . . . your grandmother died this morning. I'm here
with Todd. I mean, we brought Todd—we're not here for your
grandmother. Todd's . . . Nish found him . . . I mean . . . oh,
shit." There was a moment with only the muffled beeping of
hospital paging codes in the background. "Um . . . you should
get here . . . as soon as you can."

I looked at the clock. It was only nine A.M. Could so much
have happened? I hadn't even taken off my coat. I got back in the
car and headed for the hospital.

I found Arnicia first, and she filled me in. She'd come home
earlier than expected, thank God, and had, simply on a whim,
gone to check on Todd while Jacob showered. She'd wanted only
to say hi, she hadn't suspected anything wrong, and felt guilty
about possibly waking him, when she'd discovered him, unconscious, head and upper back still in bed, the rest of him sprawled
over the edge, a pool of blood gathering at his feet. She'd
screamed for Jacob. He'd called 911 while she'd stopped Todd up
with Kotex from our upstairs bathroom and started mouth-to-
mouth when he'd stopped breathing. The paramedics said she'd
saved his life.

He was conscious, but barely. He couldn't speak. And he
couldn't write—he would only scribble if we gave him paper and
pen. The bleeding this time was not from low platelets, as before,

when he'd still been doing chemo, but from Kaposi's sarcoma lesions that had developed in his intestinal tract. He'd had respiratory failure and consequent heart failure due to the anemia—his poor heart having to work so hard because of the KS. A sadistic domino effect. His chest bubbled when he breathed, from the KS that had crept into both lungs as well.

"Oh, God," Jake whispered when a coughing fit started. He sat on the edge of the bed and took one of Todd's hands. Todd's other hand, looking fragile and sore, rudely poked full of IV tubes, clutched a handful of bedsheet, stretching the bruised skin tight. He braced himself, holding his breath. He turned to Jacob, his eyes open wide in supplication. His face turned red.

"Baby, you have to breathe," Jacob said sadly. Todd nodded, just as sadly, and finally did. The breath he sucked in sounded like someone gargling and spawned an interminable series of rattling, agonizing coughs. The coughs seized him for long two- and three-minute stretches at a time, holding new breath hostage until he opened his mouth wide and gasped for air like a man drowning. Each gasp for new air set off a new series of coughing, some so long that I feared he would drown in the thick mucus that came in a rolling boil up out of his throat, spattering droplets of blood on his sheets and on his shirt and on his lover, who didn't flinch a bit but held his hand in his own.

When it ended, Todd was drenched in sweat and exhausted. Before he could rest, though, his other bleeding began again, which seemed to pain him mentally as much as physically. His expression of humiliation and disgust tore at my heart when we saw the sheets staining burgundy between his legs. He made an angry growl and tried to lift himself to sitting. The nurse herded us all out; only Jacob was allowed to stay. My mother, father, and I followed Arnicia out of the room like dumb sheep. Arnicia sat in the hallway in one of those huge, square orange chairs, and I started to as well, but my father kept right on walking. We got up and followed him at first, until we realized he was just walking blindly.

"Joe?" my mother kept asking. "Joe?" But he just kept walking, walking, walking. We stopped him in the parking lot, none of us with coats on, standing in the gray wind and the snow flurries it whipped off the hospital roof. He burst out sobbing. Really sobbing, bawling like a baby.

"I've seen animals suffer less than this that I put down to end their misery," he said. My mother walked away from him.

Arnicia followed my mom, and I led my dad inside.

We met again outside Todd's room. The room with the biohazard warning on the door. We sat and waited. My mother sat, staring, hands clutched over her heart as if she could physically stop it from breaking.

My father wouldn't stop crying. He'd lost his mother already this morning, and for all we knew he was about to lose his son.

He didn't, though. Not yet, anyway. Todd lived through that day and the next.

Jacob wouldn't leave his side. For two days Jacob didn't sleep or shower or shave but stayed there, holding Todd's hand and talking to him nonstop. Talking of nothing. Talking of everything. And trying to breathe for him.

It was obvious Todd wouldn't be able to go to Grandma's funeral. We didn't even know if he knew she was dead.

He knew. And on the evening of his second day there, when he was finally able to write, he scrawled, *"I'm happy for her."*

It was Arnicia who made us eat. It was Arnicia who reminded us to sleep and change our clothes. It was Arnicia who stayed with Todd in the hospital—his third day there—while the rest of us attended the funeral. Jacob didn't want to go, but Todd insisted. It was windy and sleeting, and we huddled shoulder to shoulder under the swaying tent at the cemetery. Mom stared at a space in front of her. Dad and Uncle Dan wept. Abby, who hadn't been to the hospital yet, cried, too, but silently, the tears dripping untouched off her chin. Brad held her close and looked appropriately subdued. This, apparently, was a proper family function for him to attend. I searched both their faces and noted two small scabs near Brad's left ear. They could be cuts from shaving, but I eyed Abby's nails as she squeezed Brad's arm. Seeing them together, touching in this loving way, struck me as comedic. I looked around. Why was no one else noticing this absurdity? When I looked back at Brad, our eyes met and held. I couldn't read his expression. I was holding Jacob's hand but let it go and put my arm around his waist. Jacob lifted his arm to my shoulders and pulled me against him. I never took my eyes from Brad's. My own heart felt hard and indifferent. I hated that. I hated him. Soon my brother would be in this same ground, and I knew he wouldn't come to Todd's funeral.

When the service ended, Jacob and I left the tent and walked to his car. We drove back to the hospital without saying a word.

Nicholas was with Arnicia in Todd's room. Todd's eyes were open, and the good one lit up in recognition as Jake and I walked in.

"Hey," I said to Nicholas as Jake embraced Todd.

"Hey," he answered. "I'm sorry about your grandmother."

I nodded and swallowed. We stood there.

"Oh, for Christ's sake," Todd rasped in a voice that hurt to hear. "Hug each other."

We did, and to touch him felt like coming home; a surprising feeling, from far away.

Todd was back. Or, at least, part of him was. His voice remained a shredded, raw whisper painful to emit. He couldn't walk at all on his own. Reaching for the TV remote seemed enough physical exertion to set off a coughing fit. And eating had become a continual battle with his rotting, cancer-riddled intestines. His body had fallen into shambles around him, but Todd, our Todd, the spirit of Todd, remained. That's what was back that day. That was why we celebrated.

Nicholas and I didn't talk much, with the commotion of relatives coming and going after the funeral, but he was there. I didn't get to thank him until late that evening.

"Of course I'd be here," he said in one of the hospital lobbies. "I came as soon as Jacob called."

"Jacob called you?" It hadn't crossed my mind to wonder how Nicholas even knew about Todd's hospital stay.

"Yeah." He crossed his arms. "And it's a good thing, since you didn't."

I flooded with shame. I'd never even thought to call him. I didn't think I could. "Nicholas. I'm sorry. I'm so sorry. I—I—you were gone, in D.C., and I didn't think I could just . . ." I stood there, mouth open. I looked around the lobby. The other people weren't part of Todd's entourage. "You were gone," I repeated. "You felt so far away."

"Tell me about it," he whispered. We stood in the lobby, yards apart, but those miles separating D.C. from Ohio seemed to stretch between us even still.

"Will you come with me to get a coffee?" he asked. He turned and started walking before I answered.

I followed him through the hospital halls in silence. We got coffee and sat at a table in the abandoned cafeteria, both of us burning our lips, trying to drink too soon.

"When were you going to call me?" he asked. "What if Todd had died?"

"I—I'm sorry," I said. "I felt selfish, calling you to comfort me when I—"

"Summer." He leaned across the table close to me. I'd never noticed how cold, how blank, his blue eyes could get—like a wolf's. "I'm not talking about comforting you. I didn't come here today to impress you or try to endear myself to you. I'm here because I care about Todd. This was serious. He almost died. You should've called me."

I nodded.

He stirred his coffee even though he hadn't put cream or sugar into it. He sighed. "We're worried about you." He looked down at his cup. "Todd was really disappointed about us, did you know that? He . . . he cried. He thinks it's because of him."

The room began to spin. I'd never had anyone tell me something about Todd that I didn't already know. I'd never entertained the idea that someone could be closer to him than I was, except, of course, for Jacob.

"He's worried about you. He says you're a wreck. And I agree—and not just because you said no to me. You're overworked and overwhelmed. He knows you're not sleeping. You've lost weight—"

"Look, I know. I admit I'm a wreck. That's what I tried to tell you, the night you . . . you gave me the ring."

"Hey." He lifted his head. "Where is the ring? Do you still have it?"

"Yes. Do you want it back?"

He paused. "Do I? You tell me."

"I don't know." The words just floated out before I could think about them or grant them permission. My eyes welled. I searched for the bottom of my Styrofoam coffee cup through my blurring vision.

After a pause Nicholas asked, "Have you, you know, done any thinking?"

I nodded. Then I shook my head. I could hardly meet his eyes.

"I just can't—I'm not ready. I have so many things I should do for myself first. I just—I don't know."

He dropped his head in a barely discernible nod. "Are you . . . do you want to try?"

"Yes," I whispered.

"That's all I needed to know." He looked at his watch and stood. "I need to get going to make rehearsal on time." He kissed my cheek. That warm peach scent of him, his skin, his hair, filled my head. I sat there after he walked away and tried to imagine never breathing that scent again.

I stayed and finished the bitter coffee by myself.

For two days in a row, the principal had left messages on our machine at home, expressing sympathy for Grandma, then saying that we needed "to discuss some issues of utmost importance." I obsessed over these calls, trying to imagine what we had to discuss. I didn't return the calls but went back to school Thursday and made an appointment to see him during my lunch hour. I made sure I wore panty hose.

I'd called Zack's house, desperate to know he was all right in my absence, but his mother said, "He doesn't live here," and hung up before I could ask where I might reach him.

Zack waited in my classroom Thursday morning. "You okay?" he asked, standing as I came in.

"Yeah, are you?" I wanted to hug him, but another student was in the room. As it was, she gave us a quizzical look before returning to her homework. She was in my homeroom and here early, apparently cramming for a test of some sort.

Zack wasn't okay; I could tell. Dark circles ringed his already serious eyes. "You want some coffee, hon?" I asked. He nodded.

The girl looked up again. "You want some coffee, Leslie?" I

asked quickly. "Don't spread the word around, but since you both are here so early . . . ?"

"No, but thanks. I've got my caffeine fix, already," she said, gesturing to the Mountain Dew can half-hidden under her desk.

When I returned from the teachers' lounge, Leslie had taken her books and her Mountain Dew can somewhere else, and Zack fell on the coffee and doughnut I brought back for him like a scavenging stray cat. "So, don't they feed you where you live now?"

He glanced up, startled.

"I tried calling you. Did they throw you out?"

He shook his head. "No, I left."

"Don't lie to me. They can't legally throw you out if you're under eighteen."

"I'm not lying. I left. I couldn't stand it there. They don't care that I left, but they didn't make me."

"So, where are you staying?"

"At a friend's. It's cool."

I exhaled. "What friend? Are you safe?"

He paused. He saw my face and laughed. "You think I'm somebody's sex slave or something, don't you? Relax. I'm staying at Simon Schiffler's. His mom's really cool. They don't know about the gay thing. They just think I don't get along with my parents. Which is true." He scribbled down the phone number for me.

I told him about my upcoming meeting with the principal. "I should never have told that stuff, I guess, to the class," I said. "I think I'm in big trouble."

"It needed saying. A lot of us, we're glad you said it."

"Tell that to Mr. Vortee?" I asked. He laughed.

He reminded me to put up a quote of the day when the bell rang and he left for his own homeroom. I shuffled through my book of memories and found a quote that gave me chills. *"What are you waiting for? What are you saving for? Now is all there is."—George Balanchine.* It was on a postcard of the U.S. Show Jumping Team at the Olympic Games in L.A. I wrote it on the chalkboard. I put the postcard in my blazer pocket, though, instead of back in the book.

The morning dragged since the classes themselves were doing nothing. I gave them permission to "use" the day to catch up on whatever they needed because I'd been too exhausted to plan anything. Several students slept, some did other homework. A few listened to Walkmans, and one or two had hushed, whispered conversations. I let them talk, but every whisper stabbed my heart, and all were accompanied by quick glances in my direction. I'd told only one class about Todd, but I could tell they all knew now. There was a difference, however subtle, in how they looked at me. In some eyes it was sympathy, in others curiosity, and in a few it was disdain.

At lunch I steeled myself for my meeting with the principal. He shook my hand, the top of his head level with my breasts. The students called him Shorty Vortee. I sat down as quickly as possible, and we looked at each other eye to eye across a desk of sports trophies.

"Ms. Zwolenick, first let me say that I am very, very sorry about your grandmother."

I nodded. "Thank you."

"I know this is a difficult, delicate time for you, which makes it all the more difficult for me to bring this up"—my stomach wrapped itself into a fist—"but I think we need to address it and soon. There are a number of ugly rumors surfacing, which are quite damaging, not only to you, but to the school itself, and our reputation as an institution of the highest quality."

"What rumors would those be?" I asked.

"Well, I . . . hardly know where to begin. I'll simply be blunt, Ms. Zwolenick, and you'll have to forgive me: I have had students and parents alike tell me that you are promoting the homosexual lifestyle in your classes—"

"I would hardly call it promoting—"

"—which would make you an inappropriate role model for impressionable young people."

"Why?"

"Oh, Ms. Zwolenick, really. Is your brother, in fact, a homosexual?"

"Yes." We stared at each other. He broke away first.

He coughed. "I'm sorry. I'm very sorry to hear that. I always thought he was a fine, upstanding young man when he attended school here."

"He still is a fine, upstanding young man. He was gay while he attended school here, you know. He was gay when he took the hockey team to the state playoffs. He was gay when he was the prom king. He was gay when he—"

"Ms. Zwolenick, please! This is all beside the point. It is not appropriate for you to tell a literature class that your brother is a homosexual, that he has AIDS. It is not appropriate for you to invite a known homosexual in as a guest speaker. It is certainly not your place to use class time to try to refute the Bible's stance on homosexuality!"

"I did not, in any way, *refute* the Bible's stance on homosexuality, nor was I the one who brought it up." I took a deep breath. "Mr. Vortee—if students ask me these questions, don't you think it's appropriate to address them? I won't lie or make up answers. Isn't it always appropriate to turn a student's curiosity into an educational experience?"

"Educational! Is this the sort of casual morality you espouse in your classes? You are troubling me a great, great deal, Summer."

Summer. Now I was a student again, not a colleague. Before I could answer, he went on. "So, it is true that you live with your brother and his . . . lovers?"

"He doesn't have 'lovers.' He has a spouse. They've been together five years."

"Yes, well. You know this is a small town. The students see the teachers outside of school—there's no avoiding it. You have an obligation, therefore, to be a positive role model—"

"Which is exactly what I am doing! I'm helping to care for a member of my family who is now terminally ill—"

"But under the circumstances, given the illness in question, surely you—"

"What exactly are you saying, Mr. Vortee? I'm not sure I understand you. Aren't I being a positive role model by speaking up against discrimination?" I squeezed the arms of the chair until I felt my nails embed in the wood.

"It is troubling, Ms. Zwolenick. Very troubling. Students make assumptions. It changes how they view you, and if they cannot view you with absolute respect, well then—"

"Well then, what?" I asked. I stood up. I pressed my hands to my thighs, fighting the urge to pick up a trophy and bring it down on his head. "Please be clear, Mr. Vortee—what is it, exactly, that you wish me to do?"

He cleared his throat. "I'm simply asking you to consider, since we have the levy up for vote again this spring—" His phone buzzed. He smiled an oily smile. "Please excuse me." As he picked up the phone, the bell rang. "Have a good class," he said.

For a moment I thought I might vomit, but then anger fueled me. I walked into the afternoon class with as poised and oily a smile as Mr. Vortee's himself.

"Ha. Look who it is," Denny said. "I didn't think you'd be back."

"Here I am." I said. I looked right at him. "You're stuck with me, buddy. You couldn't get rid of me if you tried."

"Oh, yeah?" he asked, curling his lips into a sneer.

"Yeah," I said. "I just came from a meeting with the principal." I repeated: "You couldn't get rid of me if you tried."

He looked a tad uncertain, which was all I really wanted. I turned away from him and began class. This class would be working, damn it. No day off for them. Even if Denny was the only one to blame, I couldn't sit and listen to the whispers of this class. No way.

We worked until the bell rang, no quitting early. And as the students filed out, Zack turned to me and asked, "Did it . . . go okay?"

I shook my head. I felt the tics begin in the corners of my mouth. Goddamn it, I was going to cry. I tried to set my lips, to stop the tremors.

"Hey, hey," Zack said. "It's okay." I sat at a desk, and he sat in a chair beside me, patting my shoulder. I saw two girls look at us, then one another, before leaving the room. Simon stood in the doorway.

"I'll catch you later," Zack said to him. "I'll get another ride home." Simon nodded and seemed relieved to walk away.

I rubbed my eyes. I took deep, hiccuping breaths to quell the sobs trying to leap out of my chest. "It's just like my mother said," I told Zack. "I asked her once—a long time ago, the night of my sister's wedding. I asked my mom if she was upset that Todd was gay." Zack raised his eyebrows. "She said yes. She was upset, but not at Todd. She was upset because she knew his life would be harder. This is what she meant. Stupid Vortee. People like Denny." I sniffed and shook my head, willing anger to replace this ridiculous crying.

"Your mom said that? That she wasn't upset?" His eyes were wide with awe and longing.

I nodded.

"How did your brother tell you? Did he tell you first and then your parents? Did he sit everyone down and, like, announce it?"

I laughed. "No, he didn't tell us. I found out quite by accident. It was—"

"But you told the class he told you."

I blushed. "I know. But he didn't."

"What happened? What was the accident?"

"It's a long story."

"Tell it," he said. He slid into a student's desk across from me. "Tell me. Please?"

The thought made my head spin. "I wouldn't even know where to start."

"You said it was your sister's wedding," he prompted me.

Chapter Eleven

It was the eve of my sister's wedding, actually. The rehearsal dinner. More of a rehearsal bash. The Montgomeries had rented the entire country club. Everyone invited to the wedding was invited to this bash. Our family was no more singled out than any other.

Todd arrived home that evening from his summer hockey camp in Canada, with a friend from the college hockey team, a Venezuelan who'd learned to play hockey at the American military institute he'd attended for his high school years. His name was Alejandro Hidalgo. Todd hadn't asked Mom if he could bring a guest—the house was already overflowing—but she was too overwhelmed to argue and was as charmed by Alejandro as the rest of us.

Alejandro's skin was the color of coffee with lots of cream, especially in contrast with his ivory linen suit. He had dark, jewel-like eyes and shining black hair that curled just down to his collar. A rather hawkish nose kept him from being conventionally beautiful but rendered him all the more striking. I loved to listen to him talk. He hummed while he searched for a specific English word, eyes flashing impatience, then he'd snap his fingers, curl his lush lips into a smile, and say the word with relish. Each time made me giddy.

I watched him dance with my cousin Sheila, who pressed her torso against his, both arms around his neck. Todd stood beside me, sipping champagne and watching, too. After Sheila monopolized Alejandro for three dances, Todd said, "I need you to save him, Summer." He led me toward them as Sheila caressed Alejandro's curls with her fingers. "What a slut," Todd said. "Good thing I warned him about her."

"And did you warn him about me?" I teased.

Todd started, but Alejandro turned to us gratefully, saying, "I hear you are a dancer, yes? Your brother tells me you are an artist. I would be honored."

I danced with him and saw him exchange a knowing smile with Todd. I thought maybe Todd had planned this; maybe he'd brought Alejandro home on purpose. To set us up together.

He hadn't, though, as I soon found out. But, still believing this, back at the farm, I snuck out of our house full of relatives and climbed to the hayloft, where Alejandro and Todd, who had graciously given up his room to Aunt Marnee and Uncle Orin, had agreed to sleep. Too old for hide-and-scare, but doing it anyway, I crept out there and chose my spot, twelve bales above their sleeping bags.

When the barn door swung open and I heard their voices, warm and unsuspecting, I wanted to leave, to greet them at the top of the ladder and say, "Hi, I was just leaving." But I didn't. I suddenly felt ridiculous; it wouldn't be funny, but I pressed myself down flat and waited.

Alejandro sat on a sleeping bag, setting the electric lantern beside him. Illuminated by that golden light, he transformed into an angel with a halo of curls. "Do they know?" he asked.

Todd sat near him. "I'm not sure," he answered after a pause. "I think my mom might. Maybe."

"Will you ever tell them?"

Todd pushed his hair out of his eyes with his hand. "Oh, yeah, sure. And I think they'll be completely cool about it. It's just . . . when exactly is the best time to bring that up? You know? Make some official announcement?" They laughed. "You ever gonna tell your folks?"

"No way. They would not be 'completely cool' about it."

"God, that would suck."

The silence swelled. Alejandro picked up a piece of hay and pulled it between his teeth, then twirled it about his lips. Todd exhaled.

"You know," Alejandro drawled, "I have never understood that expression."

"What? 'Sucks'?"

"Yes. Used to describe something horrible. Dreadful. I have never found it to be so bad. Have you?"

"No." Todd's voice was no more than a breath. "Can't say that I have."

Alejandro licked the length of the straw. "I have always found it to be quite . . . satisfying."

It grew difficult to breathe in the close, humid air of the hayloft. I didn't know yet what was going to happen, but I knew the tension and the electricity in the air were somehow dangerous. Something I should not see. I could sense it.

And I couldn't wait.

When Alejandro reached for Todd and their lips met, that kiss stole my breath as quickly as if I'd been punched. I watched in a dumbfounded stupor my brother's hands—those hands that had picked me up and brushed me off countless times—as they grasped and kneaded and caressed. Those hands unbuttoned and unzipped with a choreographed familiarity, and Alejandro's did the same. I watched in amazement Alejandro's mouth and what it did to my brother's earlobes and throat and chest and nipples.

My ears burned.

I was sweating.

There was no way to turn this into a game of hide-and-scare now.

I watched, but I didn't see. I saw other moments in my mind. I saw the clues I'd missed. I saw puzzle pieces fitting neatly into place. I never realized I held my breath until Todd gasped, once, as though he'd been held underwater and finally released. The sound reminded me to breathe again, and the thick perfume of hay warmed my nose, my throat, my head.

And then my mother called from the back door of the house, scaring all three of us to death. I drew myself back from the ledge of the bales and pressed myself flat, willing myself to disappear. When she called a second time and the back door slammed, I heard zippers, suitcase snaps, and hushed laughter. They were clothed and respectable by the time she opened the barn door and turned on the lights to tell them I was missing and would they mind walking down to the pond to see if I was there. Everyone went searching for me. I couldn't just walk out the front barn door in full view of the house, so I opened the loading window, in back of the barn, to jump out and sneak back as though I'd been out walking.

That moment changed everything. I've often wondered what would've happened had I simply gone to the house with my discovery, carried it with me at the wedding with my bouquet, and waited to confront Todd on my own. How long would I have waited for him to tell me the secret of his heart? But as I dropped to the ground, falling hard on my hands and knees, it was decided for me. I stood, tried to brush myself off, and ran around the corner, bumping smack into my brother. In my peripheral vision, I saw Alejandro peeing against the barn wall.

"Whoa! What are you doing?" Todd said, grabbing me around the waist and picking me up. Pressed close to his bare chest, I felt the blood rush to my face. I could smell his sweet sweat and another smell—like fresh mushrooms with a hint of chlorine. "Thought you could sneak by me, huh?"

"I wasn't doing anything!" I said.

Todd's tone changed and he set me down, holding my shoulders. "Mom was worried—where were you?"

"Nowhere. I was just walking."

He pushed me around the corner into the light from the loading window to look at me, then noticed the window itself—open and blazing light. He looked at it and looked down at me. He didn't look angry, he didn't look scared, he didn't look upset. He looked lost. Alejandro came around the corner and looked up at the window. Todd asked quietly, "Where were you?"

My heart sank and melted for him. "I was walking."

He brushed the hay chaff from my hair and turned me to the light. My front was covered in straws and seeds. Alejandro disappeared back around the corner.

"Summer?" It was a question and a plea all at once.

"I'm sorry," I whispered.

And I took off running toward the house.

Once I was "found" and scolded for disappearing, everyone in the house had gone to sleep, except for me—sitting panic-stricken in the living room amid my slumbering cousins—and Todd and Mom, who talked in the kitchen a long, long time. Eventually they slipped out into the side yard and sat on the swing between our two oaks. I stood in the dark, in my nightgown, and watched them from the kitchen window. I couldn't hear what they said, or if they were speaking at all, only crickets whirring in the yard, the house whirring with its pulsing electricity I never noticed in the daytime. The crickets stopped and I turned to see Alejandro open the kitchen door and whisper into the darkness, "Todd?"

"No, it's Summer."

He paused, took a step back, then said, "You must tell me, where is the airport? I must go. You must tell me which direction to walk."

His bag was packed. He said we could blame it on him, to "save Todd's honor." He kept saying that. I tried to convince him to stay, that it was my fault, not his, when I saw Mom pass the kitchen window on her way to the back door.

I grabbed Alejandro's hand and bolted for the living room, then remembered all the cousins sleeping on the floor. I stopped and Alejandro crashed into me from behind, his chin bashing into the top of my head like a hammer. Small purple sparks burst in front of my eyes, but I pushed him into the narrow pantry just as Mom opened the kitchen door. I pulled down on his shoulders and he sank to the floor with me, our legs entwined, arms in an odd embrace. I ducked my head so we wouldn't be staring face-to-face, and with my nose rubbing his chest, I smelled chlorine again.

I waited for lights to come on, but they didn't. Mom was dialing the phone from the green, glowing numbers in the dark. "Abby?" she asked. Abby? Why was she calling Abby? Abby was staying the night, in spite of all of Mom's pleadings, at the apartment she already shared with Brad. She'd refused to stay at the farm if relatives would be there. "I know, I know, honey, this isn't about the wedding . . . I really need you right now, and you know I would never ask on this night unless it was important." She sighed and said with such significance that I couldn't mistake it, "Todd told me . . . Yes . . . he said you knew already, and it would— Are you sure? . . . Oh, Abby, thank you . . . I love you, too, sweetie." Click. And the back screen door yelped, and she was gone.

I reached up to rub the back of my throbbing head, and my hand came away sticky. I lifted my face, and something dripped onto my eyelid. I wiped it; it was dark. "Alejandro! You're bleeding!"

He kept saying, "I must go," but not moving. He took off his T-shirt and pressed it to his chin to stop the bleeding. I tried to get him to stand, but our legs were entangled, and I lost my balance and bumped into a cupboard. The canning jars began a chorus of high-pitched clinking, followed by the crash of a mason jar of peaches hitting the floor—the immediate, sickly-sweet smell giving them away.

I snatched my hand back to avoid the broken glass, lost my balance, and fell onto Alejandro, shoving him down onto his back.

Then the lights came on. And there stood my aunt Marnee.

"Summer Marie! What on earth is going on?" Her scowl of disapproval turned to outright horror as she had a moment to register the scene before her: Alejandro, bare-chested, sprawled on his back, with me, in an almost see-through summer nightie, straddling his pelvis in a lewd squat, my hands on the shelf above as if for leverage. Adding the final, bizarre twist was the blood streaming down his chin and spattered on my still hay-covered hair, my face, and chest.

"Oh, my God!" Aunt Marnee started screaming. The cousins woke up. Aunts and uncles swarmed from every room, and all tried to squeeze in the tiny pantry doorway. Alejandro's eyes flashed panic and he lunged forward, seized my face in his hands, and kissed me passionately with his bloody mouth.

I was so taken aback that I couldn't respond. Just a split second, but time enough to think that these were the very lips that less than an hour ago had been wrapped around my brother's . . . well . . . all sorts of my brother's anatomy. I also registered in that split second that this kiss was exceptional. I also registered that blood tasted like metal and made me think of rust.

I wrestled my head free, yelling, "Stop it!"

Amid all the noise and confusion, Alejandro whispered in my ear, "Please, Summer. Pretend. It is better this way, less of a disgrace."

Not understanding what he meant, I tried again to stand. Aunt Marnee pulled on my upper arm; Alejandro pulled down on my hips.

My father, hearing me plead, "Stop it," plowed through the crowd and slipped in the peach juice, knocking me into the corner shelves and down onto Alejandro for a third time, this time with force. Dad scrambled for balance, grasping for a shelf as I had earlier. His flailing arms caused a dozen more mason jars and miscellaneous pots and pans to rain down upon us. Three jars thudded into my back and shoulders before breaking on the floor, bathing us in soft, mushy cherries, tomato sauce, and green beans. Alejandro and I huddled, clinging to one another for protection as kitchenware crashed around us.

A cast-iron skillet hit Alejandro on the bridge of his nose. His eyes rolled back into his head.

The kitchen door slammed. "What in the world is going on?" It was my mother's voice, although I couldn't see her through the crowd.

"Todd's friend was trying to rape Summer," my cousin Bobby said, looking almost gleeful at the prospect.

"He was not," I said. I slapped Alejandro's cheeks, to no effect.

"Summer looked more than willing to me, Jean, I'm sorry to say," Aunt Marnee said to my mother. "I hate to think what would've happened if I hadn't found them."

"What was all that crashing?" Todd asked, trying to push through the relatives.

"Back up, everybody!" Dad shouted. "Back up! We need to get him out of here." Dad tried to lift Alejandro, but he kept slipping in the wet muck on the floor.

"Oh, my God! Alejo?" Todd rushed forward to help Dad. The two of them managed to drag him out of the treacherous footing. They put him on the kitchen table, where Mom pressed a dish towel to his chin.

"What did you do to him?" Todd turned to me, his eyes bright and hard.

"Really, Todd," Marnee scolded. "I think it should be the other way around. We all know how Latino men can be."

"Shut up, Marnee," Todd said.

Marnee turned to Mom, but Mom only sighed and said, "Perhaps it's better if you did . . . be quiet."

Marnee huffed out of the kitchen.

"What did you do to him?" Todd repeated.

"I didn't do anything, honest. The cans just fell—"

"Why were you in there?" Mom asked. She propped up Alejandro's head on a pile of dish towels and pot holders.

"We were . . . hiding."

"From?" Mom asked.

"You."

Mom and Todd exchanged a glance. Dad looked baffled. Bobby gawked at the body on the table. Uncle Orin shuffled in the doorway to the living room, looking after his offended wife, then turning back to the scene in the kitchen. Grandma stood silently, clutching her walking stick, staring intently at whoever spoke.

"Summer, are you hurt?" Dad asked. "Did he make you go in the pantry?"

"No. He came up here looking for Todd and—"

"Where was Todd?" Dad asked.

"With me," Mom said. "Is your mouth bleeding, Summer?"

I wiped the blood from my lips. "No. That's Alejandro's."

Now Mom and Todd looked baffled. "He kissed her," Bobby reported. "We saw him."

"I saw him, too," Dad said. "Summer, you need to explain."

"They were gonna do it," Bobby sang.

"No, they weren't," Mom said to Dad.

"Jean, I saw what I saw."

"Joe, Alejandro is not interested in *Summer*." She said it that way mothers have, of making a statement significant.

It took a moment to register. Dad blushed and raised his eyebrows. He looked at Todd, who swallowed and nodded. Dad didn't seem upset, only more confused. "But . . . he did kiss her."

"What do you mean, Alejandro isn't interested in Summer?" Bobby asked. "You mean he's a faggot?"

Mom bristled. Todd's face flooded red.

Uncle Orin fluttered in the doorway, gesturing for Marnee to come back.

Grandma scowled. She stared at Todd now. He met her gaze and held it.

"He told me to pretend," I tried to explain. "He said it would be less of a disgrace."

I thought my mother might cry. She kept swabbing the blood from Alejandro's nose and chin. "Less of a disgrace," she whispered.

"Than what?" Grandma Anna demanded of Todd.

He dropped his eyes.

"He meant that being kicked out for sleeping with the girl would be less of a disgrace than being kicked out for sleeping with the boy," Grandma spat out, enunciating every syllable. Her eyes never left Todd. "Is that right, boy?" She slammed her walking stick on the floor. Todd met her gaze again. "Is that right?"

"Yes," Todd said.

"He wants to sleep with you?"

Todd nodded.

"And you? You want to sleep with him?"

"Yes."

Grandma pointed her walking stick at Todd and said, "Then you are the disgrace here! A disgrace to this family! You! You are not my grandson!" She hobbled out of the room, muttering Polish. I never forgave her for the look on Todd's face. I think that hurt pierced him deeper than even testing positive for HIV.

It was a wound he was unprepared for, from a source he didn't expect. From a source, in fact, that all his life had prepared him for tolerance, at least, if not support and understanding.

I remember Todd staring at the spot where Grandma had stood. He kept staring but raised his voice. "I suppose it doesn't matter to you that I love him, Grandma."

Aunt Marnee gasped and looked at Mom with condescending pity. Mom cried, cradling the still unconscious Alejandro's head, as if to shield him from the physical blows of the words in the room.

"Love!" Grandma repeated, coming back into the doorway. "You cannot know what love is! This is not love!"

"This is love, Grandma. This is as real as what Abby and Brad have—"

"No! No! This is not! This is not natural! It is a sin! Abby and Brad are blessed by God! You! You are damned!"

"That's enough, Anna!" Mom yelled at her, shocking us all.

The kitchen door creaked and we turned to Abby, her face red, her eyes swollen. "What's going on?" she asked.

"Abby?" Dad asked. "What are you doing here? Is anything wrong?"

Abby nodded, grimacing to fight back tears. "I'm not—I'm

not going to marry Brad." She sat on the kitchen floor with her head in her hands, crying.

"You see," Grandma Anna said, pointing at Todd, "you are a curse! You curse your sister's happiness!"

"Shut up!" I screamed at her. Dad stopped me. I have no idea what I was going to do, but I wanted to hurt her. What a strange trio of couples we were—Todd had gone to Abby. He knelt on the floor and took her in his arms, where she sobbed into his chest. Mom was holding Alejandro's head, where he was stretched out on the kitchen table. Dad had his arms crossed over my chest, hugging me to him from behind. And Grandma, alone in the doorway.

We held those poses so long, I'll never forget them. Grandma moved first, leaving the doorway and slamming her bedroom door shut. When the echo of it silenced, Mom said, "We need to go to the emergency room."

It gave us something to do, something to focus on, and an excuse to escape the other relatives. Alejandro didn't come to until we were at the hospital. He'd collected a severe concussion, a broken nose, a broken rib, and many cuts to be stitched. Like most hockey players, the next day he acted as if nothing had ever happened, but that night he was hurting. I was examined, too, but had only bruises. A nurse gave me a blue icepack to put on my shoulder.

Dad and Todd went with Alejandro to X-ray, and Mom stopped me from joining them, suggesting that it might be good to let them be alone together. So we three women sat in chairs around the empty bed, and Abby told us that Brad had been a little too bothered that Todd was a "faggot." When Abby had told him where she was going, he hadn't taken it well and had gotten so ugly that she'd been scared. I remember she'd said she always thought he wouldn't find out.

"Always thought?" I asked, confused.

"I knew he was that way," she said, not looking at us. "They're all racist. Last night, the things they said about Alejandro . . . before the added bonus of him being queer."

"You knew he was like that?" I asked. "How could you even consider marrying him?"

She looked at me, then looked at Mom for a moment before turning back to me and whispering, "There's no ballet career waiting for me."

I wanted to ask her more, but she and Mom both started to cry.

We returned to the house full of relatives. All the relatives, even the ones who'd been staying in hotels, summoned by Aunt Marnee. Cars lined the driveway. Cousins sat waiting on the front porch. Every light in the house was on. Once we were inside, Uncle Orin said, "I think we deserve an explanation," when Marnee punched his arm.

"An explanation?" Mom asked.

"Absolutely right," Sheila said. "This is some pretty serious stuff that affects the whole family."

"Look," Abby said. "I'm sorry I changed my mind about getting married, but it's—"

"Not you," Uncle Orin said, rubbing his arm after another punch. "Todd."

Then things got really nasty. Questions became accusations. Poor, concussed Alejandro was left on his feet too long and turned and retched into the kitchen sink. Sheila called Todd a "repulsive little faggot," and Todd answered, "You're just jealous because you wanted to fuck him yourself." She slapped him. Hard. I could tell it surprised Todd, but not half as much as his backhand surprised her, knocking the gloat right off her face. Mom started crying again, begging them to stop it. When Aunt Marnee asked Todd, "How could you do this to your mother?"

Mom had thrown everyone out, screaming, "He didn't do this to me! You did!"

It was quite a day.

Uncle Dan called the church, the pastor, and the caterers. We discovered that if we canceled without twenty-four hours' notice, we didn't get our money back. So we didn't cancel. It was decided that at three o'clock that afternoon, there would be no wedding on the lawn, but a party.

Everyone slept, except me and Todd. We met, without planning to, out in the hayloft. We stared at the sleeping bags, and both of us colored red. "Where were you?" he asked. I pointed. His eyes narrowed as he replayed the movie in his mind. He winced in recognition of my view. "Some show, huh?"

I grinned. We were silent for a long time, standing there. Finally he sat on a sleeping bag. I lowered myself stiffly beside him, the soreness settling into my back and shoulder blades. I kissed his shoulder and whispered, "How come you never told me?"

He sighed. "I always meant to, Summer, but . . . it took a lot of time to sort it all out. I told Abby, but she was older. That's the only reason. She'd been through the dating . . . and the sex and everything."

"What makes you this way?"

"I wish I knew. Not a clue. But I am. I've known as long as I can remember."

"But you had sex with Becka! Or did you make that up?"

He closed his eyes and rubbed his temples. "No, I really had sex with her. I shouldn't have. Abby talked me into it. It was stupid. We thought maybe it would 'cure' me." He laughed.

"Did you like it?"

"Well . . . yeah, I liked it. Of course I liked it. It felt great, but . . . Look, the vagina is quite nice, thank you, but it's no cure. There's a hell of a lot more to loving somebody."

"You didn't love Becka?"

"No, and she didn't love me. We both needed something else and settled for each other."

I snorted. "What could Becka need?"

He looked at me and frowned. "Somebody to be nice to her, for starters." He ran his hands through the hay, twisting an alfalfa stalk in his fingers before he said quietly, "She didn't even know women could have orgasms."

"Did she? Have any?"

Todd nodded, blushing but smiling slightly. "So we both knew we were being needy as hell, and that was—"

"You told her?! Weren't you scared she'd tell all those snooty friends of hers? When she got back together with Chet, weren't you—"

"Hey, she kept my secret. I trusted her. I still do. I think she's pathetic for settling for Chet, but she was a good friend."

"God, still . . . if Chet knew you'd slept with her—"

"Summer, that was the point. That's why Abby wanted me to do it. That's why it was stupid. Stupid and tacky. I wanted Chet to know I'd slept with her. I wanted Becka's cheerleader friends to know I'd slept with her. I wanted the whole school to know I'd screwed Becka Maynard. Don't you get it?"

I did get it. And it made me unbelievably sorrowful.

Not as sorrowful, though, as my observation that the first emotion to cross Abby's face when Brad showed up at the party was fear.

Not as sorrowful as watching them drive away after they had talked for less than an hour.

Not as sorrowful as seeing my mother's face when Mrs. Montgomery had called to tell her that Abby and Brad had eloped and were officially married.

The sorrow changed, though, later that evening, when Todd

said that in spite of Grandma's reaction, he was relieved the truth was known. We sat on the front porch for hours, talking. Alejandro's stitches, in the eerie light of the citronella candles, made him look like Frankenstein. We'd stared out at the true darkness of a country night, watching the fireflies, low to the ground, evenly dispersed as if a person had strung yellow Christmas lights through the neighbor's soybeans across the road, content to absorb all that had happened.

I was drunk with sleepiness. I fell into a limbo-land stupor, sleeping and waking, unable to hold my head up in that wicker chair on the porch. Somebody scooped me up and carried me up the stairs. Even if I didn't recognize the comforting smell of my brother, there was only one person capable of lifting me with such ease. I couldn't even open my eyes.

He drew the cover under my chin, and I turned and curled up on my side. He sat on the edge of the bed and unplaited my hair, running his fingers through it instead of brushing it.

He sniffed, a sniff that spoke of welled-up tears. I forced my eyes open and rolled over to face him. He grinned and sniffed again, wiping his eyes with the back of his hand.

"Thank you, Summer," he whispered. "You saved my life, you nosy little hussy."

Zackery shook his head. He'd sat enthralled for the entire story, hanging on every word. The distant sound of the choir practicing for the holiday concert carried to us through the deserted hallways, offering an eerie score to my tale.

"What happened to Alejandro?" he asked. "You said Todd's with someone named Jacob now?"

"They eventually broke up."

He looked so disappointed. "Oh, no . . . they can't."

I laughed. "This isn't a movie, Zack. But you know, I thought the same thing. I adored Alejandro. Whenever I had a weekend without a performance or rehearsal, I'd go stay with them at their apartment at school. I spent weeks with them in the summers. Alejo would make sangria and cook—damn, he was a great cook—and teach us Latin dances on their hardwood floors. They'd take turns dancing with me, and sometimes they'd dance with each other."

"So what went wrong?" Zackery asked. He looked so sweetly concerned.

"Alejandro wouldn't come out. He wouldn't tell his family. When they'd come to town, Todd had to move all his stuff out of their apartment. Alejandro would take some girl he barely knew out to dinner with them, and Todd wouldn't even get introduced. And it wasn't just when his folks were in town, either, which was just once or twice a year. Alejandro would go jogging with Todd, or go grocery shopping, but he'd never go out, to movies or restaurants, unless it was more than the two of them."

"Still, though," Zack said. "Just to have somebody, even if it's secret."

"No," I said. "Don't kid yourself. It was awful. It becomes something shameful, dirty. Todd loved Alejandro; he really, truly did. But he made himself leave it because he saw there was no future there, at least not a future he could accept as his own."

Those words. Oh, my God.

Would Nicholas one day say of me, as Todd had told me of Alejandro, "I'll never regret our time together. I'll never say it was wasted. It was a stepping-stone. A preparation. It's helped get me ready for when I meet the one, you know? The one that's for life."

Chapter Twelve

◇'d managed to save Todd once, but I hadn't known he needed saving; it was an accident. This time I knew, and it tortured me to stand by and watch.

The drive to the hospital after school was like a nightmare—when you run and run down the ever-lengthening hallway, getting nowhere. Time and traffic crawled. A whole school day now felt like decades, and I fought to quell my mounting hysteria until I got to Todd's room and saw him. There he lay, sucking in breaths, the dark smudges of his eye sockets in sharp contrast with the unearthly pallor of his face. He smiled at me, and the skin of his lips cracked. But it was a smile all the same.

Dr. Sara stood at the foot of the bed, looking at his newest bloodwork. She turned a page and shook her head. "Six T-cells. Six. And you're still here. It's that goalie mentality, I guess."

"Okay, okay," I said, sitting on the edge of the bed, facing him, "you win. I was a big, fat whiner when I was injured. You made your point. Isn't this a little drastic just to prove me wrong?" He grinned and rolled his eyes.

After Dr. Sara left, Todd wrote on his ever-present notepad (talking was too excruciating and was saved for special occasions), *"Tonight's Jake's opening night."*

"Oh, my God," I said. "I forgot all about it. He hasn't—he hasn't been to rehearsal all week."

"Buy some flowers. Big. Huge. Not roses. Something fun—tiger lilies, sunflowers. Get those flowers that look like dicks. He'll laugh. He needs to laugh."

I read the note. "Dicks?"

"You know what I'm talking about. You said yourself they look like dicks."

"But what are they called?" He shrugged; he didn't know. "Look, I'm not calling a florist and asking for flowers that look like dicks! You have to at least give me a name!"

"Starts with an a."

I glared at him, shaking my head. "I can think of an appropriate name for *you* that starts with an a right now."

"Please?" he wrote, and I knew I would do it. I reached for the phonebook, but Todd waved me away from it and wrote, *"Jacob will be here any minute."* As I left the room he held up the notepad again, with *"Fill the dressing room"* written there. I nodded.

I found a phone tucked into a back hallway, by the stairs no one used. I called the first florist whose ad caught my eye in the Yellow Pages. Thank God I got a witty man who understood when I tactfully described them as "you know, they have this long, pointy sort of thing coming out of them, like, you know, a finger. . . ." He laughed and said, "Oh, you mean antherium. Honey, I've always thought they looked more like penises than fingers!" It was expensive, this request made so late, but possible. The dressing room would, indeed, be filled. And the funny man had asked, "Do you *want* them to look like penises? Because I could send you all pink ones." I agreed.

When I returned, Jacob sat in a chair pulled close to Todd's bed, facing him, holding his hand. He stood up when he saw me.

"Hey," I said, hugging him, feeling that exchange of strength we managed to muster for each other. "Break a leg tonight."

"I shouldn't be going, but this butthead is making me."

"Well, for once, I agree with the butthead," I said. Todd wadded up a piece of paper and attempted to throw it at us. His feeble effort fell far short, and we laughed. He flipped us off. Jacob kissed him.

Todd wrote, *"Has Abby come by?"* Jacob and I stared at the note.

"No, babe, not that I know of," Jacob said. Todd nodded. He folded the paper and dropped it into the wastebasket.

"She sent a bouquet, though—" I started to say, but Jacob stopped me with a ferocious glance. Too late. Todd's face was animated, questioning.

"They wouldn't let us put it in here," Jacob said. "You know, the room's already so crowded. It was huge. Gorgeous."

It was huge, but I wouldn't say gorgeous. To me, it had seemed only expensive and prepared in a way to make that fact obvious. There really had been no room to put it, the diameter of its girth being almost three feet. It had taken another person to help me haul it to the car; I'd lugged it home but had found its remains protruding from the garbage disposal the next day after school. The disposal hadn't worked quite right since, but I'd never mentioned it.

Todd mimed a card with his hands and raised his eyebrows. "Um, yeah," Jacob said. "There was a card. I think it's at home. I'll look for it later. I've gotta go, babe. I'll be back as soon as I can." I stepped out of the room while they said their good-byes.

"Have a good show," I said to Jacob as he came out into the hallway.

He sighed and slumped against the wall. "I don't want to go. I don't want to be anywhere without him right now."

"Me neither," I said.

He took a breath. His face changed. His energy changed. "But we have to. You know that, don't you? Todd wants us to."

Back in the room, Todd had written, *"Nicholas opens tonight, too."* He was stage managing *A Christmas Carol* in Cincinnati. *"Would it be too weird for you to send flowers for me there, too?"*

"No, sure." A nurse came in and asked me to excuse them, so I returned to my hallway phone. This call took a while, and I had to settle for the flowers arriving for tomorrow's show, not tonight's. I almost added my name to the order but let it remain Todd's gift, since he'd thought of it. When I returned, the nurse was leaving.

"He wanted me to wait for you," she said, indicating the needle in her gloved hands. "But I couldn't, sorry. He's on so many medications that timing is everything. He'll be out for at least an hour, maybe two. He left you a note, though. I promised that you'd get it, but I don't think you can miss it."

His yellow notepad was on his chest, under his chin. The note read, *"You look awful. Promise me that you'll do something for yourself tonight. I'll ask about it, later, and you've never been able to lie to me. I'll know. Have fun. I love you, Todd."*

I took the notepad and tore off this page. I folded it and put it in my pocket, with my postcard of the U.S. Show Jumping Team. I thought about the quote and asked myself and Todd, in a whisper, "What am I waiting for? What am I saving for?" He'd ask about it later, and by God, I was going to have something to tell him. I kissed his peaceful face and drove to the farm.

Maybe things are meant to be, I thought as I stopped Kelly Canter walking up the driveway to her car.

"Sure," she said, looking at her watch, "I've got time for another lesson. Go saddle up. I'm going to warm up a little in my car."

It was the coldest day I'd ridden, but I didn't care. I told Kelly to be ruthless with me and told her that I wanted to do this "for real." She smiled and nodded and said that there was a lot wrong with me, but nothing that couldn't be fixed. For the entire lesson she worked me on a longe line with no reins, to improve my seat and balance. Glacier was accommodating to a point, then got bored and silly, putting in a halfhearted buck or two in the wind to liven things up. We laughed at him. It was a good lesson, and when I wrote my check with stiff, frozen fingers, Kelly said, "You know, Glacier's owner isn't going to ride again until June. I'll ask her if she'd mind if you showed him. There's an easy event in April that'd be just right for you."

I wanted to do a jig.

Dad came down to do evening feed and told me that Mom had gone to stay at the hospital until Jacob got back from his show. An idea flashed into my mind. I couldn't think about it too much or it would be too easy to convince myself that I was too tired, it was too far, I had schoolwork I should be doing, all of which were true. I got in my car and drove for Cincinnati.

I listened to NPR, and when that was over I flipped through the stations, singing out loud to songs I knew, filling the silence so that I couldn't hear myself thinking all the reasons to chicken out. A flock of pigeons lifted off in my chest as I took the last exit before the bridge over the Ohio River. I had done it. I was here.

On our street, the pigeons beat their wings against my ribs with a new frenzy. I parked on the river side of the street. The apartment was dark; Nicholas was at the theater. I looked at my watch. The curtain had gone up half an hour ago.

I opened the street door and noticed my name still on the mailbox alongside Nicholas's. I climbed the narrow stairs to our door, unlocked the apartment, and almost cried when the smell hit me. The smell of home. I'd never noticed it when I lived here, but I recognized it instantly.

I moved through each small room as though I were in a museum. There was the couch we'd bought at the Salvation Army when we'd first moved in together. The curtains I'd made with the neighbor's sewing machine. The table Nicholas's mother bought for us. The framed print of Gustav Klimt's *The Kiss* Todd and Jacob had shipped to us for Valentine's Day last year. The stained glass we'd bought at a flea market that played with the morning light. At night, the street lamps caught it, and when we made love on the living room floor, we'd move our bodies so that we were covered in color. A red stripe across my belly. Green diamonds on Nicholas's back.

A photo of us sat on top of the TV. A commercial photo we'd bought after Nicholas took me white-water rafting in West Virginia. In the photo, our blue-and-yellow raft stood almost vertical against a wall of raging water. Although the river guide looked worried, Nicholas and I were laughing.

That trip was a birthday present from Nicholas. I found riding a raft through white water similar to staying on an ill-behaved horse, and I was intensely aware of my body the entire day. I smashed my knuckles passing too close to a rock, got *thwack*ed in the shoulder with a paddle, and rubbed my shins raw as I braced for dear life. "Damn," I said as the guide stopped us on a sandy island for the provided lunch of pasta and salad, "people could get hurt doing this."

Nicholas laughed. "But isn't it fun?"

"I could never have done this for fun when I danced. My limbs were a little too expensively invested in."

"Yeah, right, how about being on top of a huge, unpredictable animal?" he asked, tracing a finger across the scars on my ankle.

It had never occurred to me to avoid horses or to think of

them as dangerous. They were too much a part of the background of my childhood, like Grandma's Bible lessons or Mom and Dad being gone in the evenings.

Later that day the guide told us we could swim through the last rapids if we wished.

Nicholas grinned and said, "Come on!" He slipped off the raft before I could blink. I slipped off, too, and laughed so hard that I sucked in great lungfuls of the New River as I tumbled through the rapids. I saw Nicholas in flashes, like a jumbled music video, the water roaring in my ears, and at one point I felt his hand touch mine. We tried to grip fingers, to hold hands, but we were jerked apart and met again, coughing and sputtering, a hundred yards apart, on the bank. My knees were bleeding, and by evening I had a huge green purple bruise blooming on one hip, but the wounds felt like badges of honor.

I picked up the photo. It needed to be dusted. The phone rang and I jumped, almost dropping the picture. I fought the urge to hide. I didn't live here anymore; I was an intruder. But when the machine clicked on, it was still my voice saying that "we" were not at home, please leave "us" a message.

"Hey, Nick, it's Cindy." The voice of our friend, a lighting designer, made me smile. "If you need to drown your sorrows some more, come on over after the show. See ya."

My smile soured. Drown his sorrows? It was like overhearing someone gossip about you. I was the cause of any sorrows Nicholas had. And come on over? Cindy lived alone. I turned in a circle, looking at the room. What the hell was I doing here?

I walked through the living room into our tiny bedroom. Our box spring and mattress welcomed me from the floor. Neatly made, with a few *American Theatre* magazines by the lamp. I knelt and crawled onto the bed, closing my eyes and breathing deeply when I laid my head on his pillow. The gentle scent of his skin, his hair, soothed me, lulled me into a deep sleep.

The threatening growl of an animal woke me with a start, and I didn't know where I was. The red eyes glaring at me from the void of blackness focused into the red numbers of a digital clock, and I remembered. But the clock read 11:17. Shit. Nicholas should've been home from the show by now. What had I expected? It was opening night, after all. He'd go out, meet up with Cindy, drown his sorrows.

I sat up and noticed the blanket covering me. The room was darker because the curtains were pulled shut against the streetlights and the door was closed; only a line across the bottom let in light. A faint, rhythmic cadence confused me for a moment, until my stomach began to gnaw on the aromas of garlic, onion, and beef. That was the animal that had frightened me. Nicholas was home, and he was chopping something. I sniffed, and the animal roared again. Nicholas was making chili.

"Hey," I said, rubbing my eyes in the steamy kitchen. "Why didn't you wake me?"

He turned from chopping an onion, his eyes pink. He looked at me a moment, smiling, before returning his attention to the cutting board. "You need to sleep. And you were out. Really out. Plus, I called the hospital to get the daily scoop. At first, I thought maybe you were here because Todd . . . you know . . ."

"Todd's fine," I said. He nodded and chopped.

"So, aren't you going to Cindy's?" I hated the venom in my voice.

Nicholas kept chopping, but his body stiffened. "Nope," he said with no emotion. "Not tonight."

I swallowed, and something in me softened. "I—I was afraid you might not come home."

"I wasn't planning to. I had to change clothes. Fog machine started leaking. I had to crawl under some platforms with duct tape to wrap up a tube. Got that slimy fog juice all over me." He scraped the onion off the cutting board into the pot and stirred.

"Happy opening night," I said. "Did it go well, other than that?"

He smiled. "Yeah. Even considering that Tiny Tim was exposed as a fraud in front of the entire audience."

"Oh, my God. What happened?"

"Charlie, the kid playing him, dropped his orange—he gets this orange in the first Christmas morning scene, you know, when Scrooge looks at the Christmas present. And he dropped his orange and it started rolling downstage toward the orchestra pit. And the kid jumps off his stool, runs after the orange, catches it, then freezes, caught. He slowly looks back at his stool and his little crutch. The audience laughed; they loved it. The kid was mortified. Backstage, we were all saying, 'That damn Cratchit! His kid's not crippled. He's been faking it all this time!'"

I laughed. I missed his stories from the theater. He held the wooden spoon up to my mouth to test the chili. I "mmmmed" my approval. Then he kissed me—a hot, garlicky kiss. I "mmmmed" my approval of that, too. He stirred the pot and said, "It feels really good. Having you here. Even just knowing you were back there, asleep."

I didn't know what to say.

"So, why'd you come?" he asked.

"I wanted to see you. Todd told me to treat myself, and I thought it would be a treat. To be with you."

He turned from the pot, his eyes still pink and watery. "So, be with me, Summer."

I knew he didn't just mean tonight. I blinked, my own eyes burning from the onion.

He stirred some more, and with his back to me he said, "So, are you just here because Todd told you to come?"

"No." I touched his back, then wrapped my arms around his waist, hugging him from behind as he worked at the stove. I pressed my cheek against his shoulder blade. "I wanted to come. I miss you."

He turned around, and we embraced face-to-face. I stood on tiptoe to kiss him again—the crook of his neck, his earlobes, his lips. Under his sweater his skin was warm, and my hands went there. He dropped the wooden spoon to the floor and seemed to be searching for where my skin was warm as well.

On the floor, amid dropped pieces of chopped onion and peppers and spatters from the spoon, we began with a hint of desperation. The bubbling pot soon lulled us into a more luxurious mode, however, and we savored and explored. Time seemed to slow as tongues lapped and the stove flames licked, and my eyes streamed with tears.

"What's wrong?" Nicholas whispered. I shook my head, unable to speak. He lowered his face to mine and kissed away the tears. He found tears where I knew there weren't any. I wanted to melt and float away on the waves rippling through me.

When we finished we stayed on the floor, catching our breath, basking in our smugness. I wished I could purr. Eventually we filled bowls of chili, careful to avoid the bottom of the pot we'd allowed to scorch, and carried the bowls to bed, where we ate cross-legged, wrapped in blankets. My lips tingled, full and swollen, from the needles of the hot spices.

"I missed a sound cue yesterday, for the first time in my life, thinking about making love to you," he said.

I grinned. "Sorry. I'll try not to be so inspiring."

"Don't you dare."

For some glorious moments it felt like the old, safe days when

I'd believed I had all the time in the world to figure it out, this mess of my life. But something shifted in the room; I felt it even before Nicholas spoke.

"I need to know—did you mean 'no' or 'not yet,' Summer? Are you working on this or not? I need to make a decision."

My stomach bottomed out, as though I'd hit a dip in country road.

"I got the official call from the Arena. They offered me the job."

I nodded, tried to smile, but my face was frozen, numb, and all I mustered was a twitch.

"I've thought a lot about what you said that night, Summer. I know what you're going through. I understand. But I need you to understand me, too, okay? The more I think about it, the more miserable staying here alone becomes."

I frowned. "But you won't be here. You'll be in D.C."

"Maybe not."

I stared at him.

"That's why I need to know," he went on. "I've got some time before I have to tell them. If we're really going to try to make this—"

"You can't give that up because of me."

"It's not giving up. It's choosing."

"And you'll hate me for it later. I didn't ask you to do this. Don't push this on me."

He narrowed his eyes. "This is my move. I know what's important to me."

"But this job is important to you. This is big time."

"I thought we were, too."

I scraped the bottom of my bowl with my spoon. "Don't do this for me," I whispered. "I don't deserve it."

Nicholas slumped. He opened his hands. "What the hell does that mean?"

I stared at the bottom of my bowl and whispered, "I'm screwing things up left and right. I'm about to fail at caring for Todd just like I'm failing at being a teacher. Why should I risk failing at this, too?"

He ran his hands through his curls. "What do you mean, you're failing to care for Todd?"

"I'm terrified. I hate it. I didn't think about any of this. I thought it would be noble to be his caregiver, more noble than being a teacher, and—"

"Of course you're terrified," Nicholas interrupted. "What do you think *he's* feeling?"

I closed my eyes.

"And, as for failing at teaching, we all told you it was crazy to go through your first year of teaching while you were taking care of Todd. You look horrible. Jacob says you never sleep. It's too much. It's making you not do either one very well."

"But I had to," I insisted. "I was running out of time to show Todd I could be something . . . be the best at something again."

Nicholas shook his head. "You are so desperate to please him, Summer. He already loves you. Why are you so obsessed?"

So I told him. I told him about the promise I'd made to Todd years ago. How he'd snapped me out of my self-pity. About my terror that I wouldn't fulfill the promise in time. I'd never told Nicholas before. He lay on his back on the bed, one arm thrown over his face.

When I finished he rubbed his face, like a weary, old man. He stared up at the ceiling. I put my hand on one of his, but he took my hand and put it down. I drew it back as if he'd slapped it away. He ran his hands through the front of his hair, still staring at the ceiling. "Oh, so now I get it: marrying me is a big fat compromise, right? The giant anchor on your plans of fame and fortune. How exactly is that supposed to make me feel?"

"Nicholas . . . I—that's not what I meant."

He rolled off the bed and walked through the living room into the kitchen, where he retrieved his jeans and pulled them on. I followed slowly, relieved that he stood with his back to me, hands on the counter, while I sorted out my own clothes and dressed.

I pulled on my sweater, and when my head popped through the neck, he was facing me. "I need a reason to stay here," he said. "You need to know that."

Those pigeons in my chest tried to fly again. I nodded. "I should go back."

"Yes," he said. "You should."

He stood in the kitchen window and watched me cross the street to my car. I flicked my lights and held a hand to the window, but he didn't respond. I looked back, at the end of the street, and the apartment was already dark.

Chapter Thirteen

⁙

I unlocked our back door, bone weary, cursing myself for abusing my body this way. It was a quarter to three. Arnicia blazed through the kitchen in her red kimono, her hair wild, like some crazed Medusa. "Where the hell have you been?" she demanded. She hugged me savagely, as if welcoming and punishing me at the same time. "I called the hospital, thinking maybe you were staying." She shook my shoulders. "You think your brother needs to be worrying about you disappearing in the night? What are you thinking, girl?" Before I could speak, her eyes filled with tears and she asked, "Are you all right? Nothing happened to you, did it?"

I pulled away and held her at arm's length. "Nish, what's happened? Why are you acting like this?"

The tears stopped, and she narrowed her eyes into a hateful squint. She took my hand. "Come listen to this," she said, jerking me to the phone, where she stabbed the flashing message light with a long red nail.

An unfamiliar voice, breathy with dangerous intimacy, said, "Where's the faggot? Is he dead yet?" A beep, and then the next message, the same voice half an hour later: "So, who all goes with who here? You all mix and match? Trade around? Or is it always a group thing? Ever invite an audience?" A beep and then something about Sodom and Gomorrah. A beep and then something about a "den of iniquity." A beep and then something about "AIDS-infected motherfuckers." On and on. I couldn't catch my breath.

Arnicia pressed the delete button. The light stopped flashing. "That fucking piece of shit has called all goddamn night. Every time I think I'm going to get to sleep, he calls back. I tried the star-69 button, but it keeps telling me that number is 'not known.'"

"Unplug the phone," I said, my mouth not wanting to work properly.

"I would have loved to unplug the goddamn phone! But what if you were trying to call? I had no idea where the hell you were."

"I'm sorry, Nish. I'm so sorry." I hugged her, and she calmed down.

"Girl, you have onion in your hair," she said. "Where the hell have you been?"

"I went to see Nicholas."

She twirled around, her kimono flapping. "Oh, I knew you'd come to your senses. Good for you, sweetie. Good for you."

"Um, no. I think it ended rather badly," I said.

She stopped dancing and shook her head. "Come on. Tell me."

We sat on the couch. I told her all about the promise and my visit to Nicholas. When I finished she rolled her eyes. "All this worry about defining yourself. I listen to you yammering on and on to Jacob, saying how much you've learned from your brother, but I don't think you've learned anything from him at all." She paused for a second, giving me a chance to rebut, but when I wasn't quick enough, she shrugged and pointed one of her magnificent nails at me. "See, your real problem is that you've always defined yourself as Todd's little sister and you have no idea who you'll be when he's gone."

I stared at her with an open mouth.

She stood up, yawned, and padded upstairs to her room.

I followed and never felt so glad to climb into that giant bed. Of course, the one night all week I was able to sleep well, I only had two hours left to do it.

In the morning, my eyes stung as if they'd been pickled, and my mouth was thick with the taste of garlic. I stared into my haggard reflection with disgust.

I packed a weekend care package for Zack while Arnicia read the glowing review of last night's opening of *A Christmas Carol*. Jacob had been singled out for much praise and, according to this reviewer, had been responsible for conveying more of this "classic story's warm message than Ebenezer Scrooge himself." We toasted him with our coffee cups and avoided the topic of our anonymous caller.

At school, I met Zack in my room. I gave him my gift, and he blinked hard when he saw the granola bars, apples, jar of peanut butter, and loaf of bread. He didn't speak, but the look he gave me was enough. I hugged him. Leslie entered and put down her books. "Zack, man, you are always in here!" she said before leaving to roam the halls with her friends.

I forced myself, later in the day, to make eye contact with Denny. I smiled at him. I made small talk. I was sickeningly cheerful in his presence. I was not going to give him the slightest hint of my exhaustion or my suspicion that he was making the calls.

I didn't want Todd to get the slightest hint, either, so at the hospital after school I told him of the lesson with Kelly and the possibility that I'd ride in competition this spring. He smiled as he listened and nodded. Jacob laughed and said, "The girl has got a mission. Oh, and I understand I have you to thank for my dressing room full of little pink penises?"

I laughed. "It was Todd's idea."

Todd requested everyone's Christmas wishes. Jacob and I looked at each other, and I skirted the issue by asking Todd what he wanted.

He wrote on his notepad and held up, for both of us to see, *"You mean, besides a cure?"*

My throat closed. Jacob's mouth crumpled up. Todd's eyes widened, and he shook his head. "No, no, no," he whispered, his face contorting. "Kidding." He reached for Jacob's hand and pulled him in to sit beside him. He patted the other side of the bed and gestured for me to sit. "I'm sorry."

"I'd just—" Jacob wiped his eyes. "I'd do anything for you, babe. You know that." Todd nodded and kissed Jake's hand. "Anything in my power." Jacob stroked the down on top of Todd's head. It was an inch long now but had grown in delicately fine, like an infant's wispy hair. Todd raised his eyebrows and cocked his head. "Yes, anything," Jacob said. Todd repeated the gesture, teasing, flirtatious. "Really," Jacob said, laughing a little.

Todd picked up his notepad and wrote: *"I want to go home."*

Jacob read it and closed his eyes. "Todd, that's not fair," I said. He gestured for me to shut up.

"Babe," Jacob said. "It's so dangerous, with . . ." He stopped. He looked around at the paraphernalia in the room. The oxygen tank. The million different monitors chirping out their cryptic messages from Todd's heart and liver and lungs. He didn't need to tell Todd. Todd knew. "What about the IVs?" he asked. There was a tube in Todd's arm, dripping in antibiotics, and a tube in his stomach for food.

"*Nish knows how*," he wrote. "*You can learn.*" I wasn't sure I wanted to.

Jacob read it. He chose his words carefully. "I think you need to be here, babe."

Todd snatched the notepad back and wrote quickly, "*I can leave here whenever I want. No one can stop me. Don't you want me back?*"

Jacob read it and didn't look up.

"Todd, stop it," I said. "You know that's not what he means."

He ignored me and scribbled, "*Sick of it? Easier to keep me here and come for visiting hours? I told you that you wouldn't——*"

Jacob yanked the notepad from his hands and hurled it across the room. "Fuck you," he said in a cold whisper. "That's pretty fucking ungrateful of you, you little shit."

Todd opened his mouth, red faced, but of course couldn't speak. He wheezed, gesturing to me for another notepad, but before I could hand it to him, Jacob left the room, kicking a chair into the wall with a splintering crash.

Todd froze, staring after him, until a nurse opened the door gingerly and asked, "Everything all right in here?"

Todd smiled at her and nodded, and I said, "Yeah. Sorry."

When she went away, he picked up the new notepad I'd given him and began to write, slowly, deliberately, in big block letters. He finished and looked at it, frowning. I had just opened my mouth to ask what he'd written when Jacob came storming back.

"You know what?" he asked Todd, and I could see he had gathered steam on what must have been an angry walk down the hall and back. "What I'm fucking 'sick' of is——"

Todd held up the notepad. It read, "*THERE IS NO POINT IN MY STAYING HERE.*"

Jacob stopped. I had to catch my breath—as though my heart had stopped its rhythm. Jacob sat on the bed. After a moment he stroked Todd's face. "If you go home . . . it . . . it means . . ." He couldn't finish. He kept tracing that thin, gaunt face. "And I—I can't. I'm not ready. I'm not ready to . . . admit that, babe, I'm not."

Todd sighed. The sigh rattled in his chest. He pressed Jacob's hand to his cheek. "I am," he mouthed. Not a sound came out, but we understood. Jacob nodded and bowed his head. Tears dripped onto Todd's face from his. Todd touched one with the tip of his tongue and closed his eyes.

Finally Jacob lifted his head. Todd opened his eyes. They looked at one another for a long time. I ceased to exist. Time ceased to exist. Jacob inhaled and sat up straight. He nodded. Although his mouth trembled, his voice was sure and strong when he said, "Okay."

Todd kissed his hand. He put Jacob's hand on his own heart, pressed it with both of his own, and raised his eyebrows. "Yes," Jacob said. "I promise."

The doctors at the hospital balked, but Dr. Sara supported Todd's decision. "He needs to be where he wants to be. He'll be happier. And the happier he is, the better chance those six lonely T-cells have of getting anything done."

They settled on a compromise. They convinced him to stay until his fever went down, figuring that would give them three or four more days to treat his lungs. Todd agreed. He just wanted to be home for Christmas, and this would get him there with two weeks to spare. Two weeks, though, now seemed as distant and unplannable as two years had before his illness.

Word traveled fast among the family members that weekend. Jacob suggested that Christmas Eve dinner be at our house, not the farm. That way Todd could stay in bed but still see everyone. The relatives agreed, and knowing this seemed to buoy him.

Everyone wanted us to have more help at home, and Dr. Sara

did all in her power to sell Todd on a good home health care agency. He had the money. But he remained insistent that he didn't want strangers around him or our comfortable routine broken. Maybe it was denial on our parts, but we foolishly agreed we could do it all.

There was much work to do, and I lost myself in it. Nicholas came to help. It was Nicholas's idea to turn the living room into Todd and Jacob's bedroom.

"Think about it," he said to Jacob, getting excited in that boyish way of his, "having your bed in that bay window alcove. Todd can look across at the park, have the morning sun hitting him. We could put bird feeders outside, in those trees. He's right next to the fireplace." Jacob liked the idea, so we hefted furniture and rolled up carpets. It was as though they were just moving in.

Mom and Dad came to help, and Uncle Dan brought Grandma Cailee. We made paths for the wheelchair, built a bench in the shower, and decorated the house. We wrapped garland around the stair banister and draped it across every door frame and the mantel, with burgundy velvet ribbon wound through it. Wreaths adorned every door. We put a Christmas tree in the living room, their new bedroom, and covered it with the ornaments from our childhood.

As I unpacked the boxes, I recognized many of Grandma Anna's handmade creations among the ornaments. I held a crocheted snowflake in my hands and realized this was the first time I'd thought of her since the funeral. I hooked the snowflake to a prominent front branch of the tree.

Abby stopped by, for exactly two hours, and kept checking her watch the entire time.

"Where are you supposed to be?" Jacob finally asked her.

"None of your damn business," she said. "Do you want my help or not?"

"Look," Jacob said, "we don't need your help. Your brother, however, needs your company every now and then. Think you could manage that?"

"You are such an asshole," she said, picking up her purse to leave.

He grabbed her wrist and whispered, so that the others, in the living room, wouldn't hear, "You think I'm an asshole? Fine: I admit, I'm an asshole. But what about Todd? I don't care if you hate me, but please, Abby, don't take it out on him. He needs you. Do you know what it's done to him that you've never come to the hospital? He asks about you every fucking day!"

"I . . . I . . . sent flowers," she said.

"Abby. He never got to see your flowers. They took up more room than his goddamn bed! He's got money, too, Abby. He can buy all the fucking flowers he wants himself. And I kept hoping he'd forget, but I finally had to bring him that goddamn little white card with the typed message: 'Get well soon. From, Abby.' 'From, Abby?' Couldn't even muster up 'Love, Abby,' could you? 'From, Abby,' for God's sake!"

She stared at him, her lips trembling. She pulled her wrist from his grasp.

"Abby." He said it so gently, so kindly, that she stopped and looked up at him. "He's not . . . getting well. You do know that, don't you?"

She nodded.

"I just wanted to make sure," he said.

She took her purse and left.

The ugly, harassing phone calls continued. In someone's ordinary life I would have just turned off the ringers and ignored the phone. But I was afraid of missing important news from the hospital.

I sometimes went to the hospital in the morning as well as after school. Knowing that we were bringing Todd home carried me through the next days. It was a relief to be so busy.

Zack worried about me. He didn't want me to spend so much time fretting over him, with all that was going on at home. But he needed someone to fret, and I was good at it. He worried about being a burden on the Schifflers, who were housing him. I took great pleasure in shopping for him, selecting items he needed with care.

The three or four days turned into five or six, as Todd's fever hung on. Just as tenaciously, however, Todd clung to his determination to go home for Christmas. The nurses half loved, half hated him. He could be charming and inspirational one moment, a petulant child the next. He threw tantrums and sometimes his hospital tray or his water pitcher, and there were times I wanted to slap him upside his little chick-fluff head. One day Arnicia actually did. In response, Todd grabbed hold of her hair and pulled with all his might. His might wasn't much, but it was enough. They cussed at each other a long time at the tops of their lungs—of course, the top of Todd's lungs was barely an audible voice, and he paid for it by not being able to utter a squeak for the next twenty-four hours—and then burst out laughing. I stood there, eyes wide, while Arnicia laughed and laughed. She put her hands on her hips and said, "Well, do you feel better?"

And he rasped, "Fuck you. Yes. Yes, I do feel better. So fuck you." And they laughed.

Jacob and I arrived at the hospital one afternoon to find Nicholas there. He'd set up a small artificial tree in the room and had brought a VCR and a boxful of taped Christmas specials.

They were watching some black-and-white classic I knew I should recognize but didn't. I couldn't remember watching any Christmas specials as a child. The season, for me, had long been about rehearsing a world full of toy soldiers and rats and Sugarplum Fairies.

Jacob hugged Nicholas, then sat on the bed and kissed Todd. There was only one chair—the nurses had taken away the broken one and had never replaced it—and Nicholas stood, offering it to me, but I shook my head. He shrugged and sat back down. I shifted my weight from one foot to the other. We were saved by a knock on the door.

Jacob looked at Todd, who nodded, and Jacob called, "Come in."

The door opened, and it took me a dreamlike moment to recognize who it was. In his unforgettable voice, sultry and Spanish, he said, "Hello, Todd." He nodded to us. "Jacob. Summer." Turning back to Todd, he asked gently, "Are you well enough for a visit?"

Todd's mouth dropped open, and he whispered voicelessly, "Oh, my God."

"I do not believe we've met," the man said to Nicholas. He reached out to shake hands. "I am Alejandro Hidalgo." Always suave, always the gentleman. He looked great, though just the slightest bit thicker. Not fat, but more stiff, less supple. What struck me was the dead look in his black eyes. Eyes of defeat.

Todd smiled and made a questioning gesture with his hands. Alejandro bent and kissed him on his cracked and blistered lips. For the first time in weeks, color appeared in Todd's cheeks. Jacob looked on, nostrils flaring. It was unlike him to be so gracious in this respect, but he showed great restraint.

"Why are you here?" Todd wrote.

"Because you are sick."

"How did you know I was in the hospital?"

"Your sister called me."

"No, I didn't." Then it hit me. "Oh." My face tingled with heat.

Alejandro showed us pictures of his gorgeous wife, Mariana, and their two sons, Andres and Philipo. Todd scribbled as fast as he could, and soon there were pages of yellow paper all over the bed and floor. They reminisced and talked of all they'd learned from each other. Alejandro revealed his unhappiness, how he lived a lie. How he envied Todd's and Jacob's courage. When Todd gave up writing and forced out his horrible, grating voice, both of them growing teary, the other three of us left the room.

We stood disoriented in the bustling hospital hallway. Jacob said, in a voice full of wonder, "If ever there were two people who were meant to be together . . ."

"Jacob!" I protested. "If ever there were two people who were meant to be together, it's you and Todd."

He shook his head. "No. I got lucky. Alejandro had a good thing. A damn good thing. And he blew it." He looked at me and then Nicholas. "He blew it," he repeated. "I cannot imagine what he must feel like living with that every day." He walked down the hall toward the cafeteria, leaving me and Nicholas to stare at one another.

Later that evening, when Jacob had left to play Bob Cratchit in Dayton's *A Christmas Carol,* and Nicholas had driven back to stage-manage Cincinnati's *A Christmas Carol,* and Alejandro had left to take his wife and children to see *A Christmas Carol* in his wife's hometown of Indianapolis, I sat with Todd in his darkened room. A hockey game was on, with the sound down low. The Vancouver Canucks vs. the Los Angeles Kings. Todd watched and was unusually silent, the pad and paper lying on his lap unused for almost half an hour. "You okay?" I asked.

He snapped on his lamp and wrote, *"I feel like I swallowed ground glass."*

"Nice," I answered.

Then he wrote *"Waa-waa-waa,"* and pointed to himself.

"I think you're allowed to every now and then."

He made a face and shook his head. He pointed to the clock. It was a waste of time, he was saying. We were all getting good at interpreting his sign language.

"Do you worry about time?" I asked. We'd never had a conversation close to this subject.

He nodded yes.

"Are you afraid . . . to die?" I asked.

He paused. He shook his head. He thought a minute, then picked up the notepad. *"I just don't want to yet. I like life an awfully lot."*

I looked at that note a long time before I could meet his eyes again. "I like life, too . . . with you in it."

He smiled. He reached for me. We hugged as best we could with him in a hospital bed.

Then he took the notepad and wrote, *"Want to talk about Nicholas?"*

"Yeah." But I had no idea where to start. I asked Todd, "You really like him, don't you?"

"I think he's the nicest straight man in the world."

I laughed.

"Do you like him?" he wrote.

"I love him," I admitted. "I adore him."

In big block letters: *"THEN WHAT'S THE PROBLEM?"*

I shook my head. "I don't know . . . I'm afraid, I guess. . . ."

"What?" His voice pinched something in my spine, like teeth scraping on a fork.

"I'm afraid. . . ."

He stared at me. I felt as stupid and lowly as I had when I'd stood in the kitchen dragging my cast, telling him my life was over.

"Of what?!" he screeched.

"Todd, don't talk—" I said.

"Of happiness? Of love?"

"Stop it! Please! You're hurting yourself!"

He coughed, then wiped blood from his lips on the back of his hand. He wrote on the notepad, the words barely legible: *"Do you know how ANGRY you make me? If you just didn't love him, that's one thing, but to make a lame excuse like that!"* He made a growling sound and ripped off the page, handing it to me. While I read, he scribbled off another. *"Do you know how insulting that is? Haven't you learned anything from this?"* He shoved that page at me, too, and sat, jaw clenched, breathing hard, shaking his head while I read it.

"I'm sorry," I whispered.

"You will be," he said aloud, with much struggle. "I warn you, Summer, you will be." He shut his eyes and rubbed his neck.

"But Todd, I just—"

He shook his head. His eyes were glued to the TV and the hockey game. Players bashed into the glass near the camera, the bone-crunching crash audible even with the low volume. Todd smiled.

"I'm afraid that I have nothing to bring to a marriage," I said. He looked at me. He frowned. "What can I offer Nicholas?" I asked.

Todd wrote, *"HELLO?"* in big block letters, then added more calmly, *"What did I have to offer Jacob? This?"* He gestured to himself and all the bags and tubes attached to him.

He frowned at me again, tears forming in his eyes. I opened my mouth to speak, but he held up a hand to stop me. He stared at the notepad, pen poised, and I knew he was thinking, composing. He wrote, *"What I have to offer Jacob comes FROM Jacob, if that makes sense. And what he offers me is because of me."* He bit his lip and crossed that out, but not before I'd read it. He tried again: *"We bring out the best in each other. I have an attentive, adoring audience I can count on. I can dare and take risks and walk on the edge. I can't fail, as long as I'm with him."*

He handed it to me and then wouldn't speak or write again the rest of the evening.

All he would do is point to the clock.

I read his note over and over again and realized that if I was set on burying Nicholas with Todd, I might as well throw myself in there, too.

I went home and called Nicholas.

Chapter Fourteen

*H*e answered on the first ring and seemed spooked that it was me.

I'd taken his ring out of its box and put it on, a delicate Celtic weave of gold, with a tiny chip of diamond. Although I didn't wear much jewelry beyond earrings, it suited me; it looked at home on my hand.

"I—I was just going to call you," he said. "I've made a decision."

"Oh?" I said, smiling at the ring, feeling buoyant and bold. "So have I."

"I just told the Arena I'd take the job."

The words made me flinch like the crack of a whip. I said nothing.

"I was sitting here thinking of how to tell you. How to explain how much it hurt me to hear the truth last week when you came over, but how much I appreciate that you told me."

"The truth?" I whispered. It hurt to push sound out.

"I just—I really thought we were something that we're not," he said in a rush that spoke of rehearsal. I pictured him sitting on our bed, selecting his phrasing, practicing. "And I'm sorry that I pushed you. I understand, what you said about marriage. And . . .

I was wrong to pressure you, with Todd, and all you're going through. Telling you that you had to be the reason that I stayed. God, I'm sorry, Summer."

I closed my eyes and tried to breathe. My entire body had stopped, including my brain. The only thing functioning was my heart, but haphazardly, and my pulse pounded out the passage of seconds, minutes, before he spoke again.

"I hope . . ." He paused. "I hope we can stay friends. I can't stand to think of losing you."

I made some strangled sound.

"I mean, you're the one who made me realize how important this job was to me. You're right: it's the chance of a lifetime. I'd always regret it if I didn't jump at this chance. I . . . I just—I need to go and find out if I'm up to this. It reminds me of how you said you were almost too terrified to say 'yes' to the role of Myrta. How you said it would be almost easier to pass and not make a fool of yourself, but then you always would've wondered."

But I never danced the role, I wanted to remind him. I'd said yes, but I'd broken my ankle and my life had turned upside down and led me to him.

"Are you there?" he asked.

"Yes."

"This is . . . so hard."

He had no idea. No idea how close I'd come to making a muck of his life. I'd almost grabbed hold and pulled him under. "You'll be brilliant," I said. Todd had said that to me before every performance.

"What was your decision? You said you'd made a decision, too."

I laughed, a little too maniacally. "Oh, nothing like that. I just . . . um, I think I'm going to enter that gelding, Glacier, in an event in April. Get back in competition."

"Good for you, Summer."

And we talked on like that, Nicholas sounding almost giddy. Like all stage managers, he thrived on a sense of closure, on one more item marked off a list, a decision made so action could follow.

When I hung up, I put the ring back in its box. My hand looked pale and naked without it.

I spent the night baking, full of relentless energy, like the days I'd expertly inhaled thin lines of cocaine to dance through injuries and a body spent with starvation. I didn't even make a pretense of going to bed. Arnicia studied in the kitchen while I baked and iced sugar cookies and made caramels, but eventually she went upstairs to her room. Not even the anonymous caller bothered with me the rest of the night.

In the morning I prepared another care package for Zackery. It was the last day of school before winter break, so I filled a big box, even including Kleenex and soap and toothpaste.

The day was a silly day at school, a waste. Half of the students were gone already—left town with their parents for ski trips or warmer climates. The other half couldn't be convinced to do anything productive and were manic with the sugar from candy canes and chocolate Santas. I added to it with my homemade treats. The students seemed surprised when I passed them out, as if some alien being had borrowed the body of their teacher.

All day, I simply tried to keep order. The students milled about and chatted. A few asked how my brother was doing, and each time the room fell silent. Did they want the polite, brief answer or the real one? I settled for something in between. "He gets to come home soon," I said. "I can't wait. I miss him."

"I'll miss you," Zackery said, lingering after his class. "God, two weeks seems like a long time. I'd wish for it to go fast . . . but I won't. Not for you."

I smiled at his sweetness, his generosity. "You take care of yourself. Call if you need anything. Even just to talk."

He nodded, walking backward, hands stuffed in his pockets. "Bye," he said. "I guess I'll see you . . . next year." He smiled at the corniness of the old joke. My chest ached as he walked away.

I called the nurses' station for an update after school. They reported that Todd's fever was down.

"That's great!" I said, but the nurse seemed hesitant. I knew it was what we'd been waiting for, and I drove to the barn glad for one small, hopeful thing to latch on to and for an activity that would fill my time, my brain. I feared what would become of me if I stopped moving and succumbed to the emptiness howling inside.

Kelly was walking from the back door of my parents' house and greeted me with, "You sure you want to do this today? We could reschedule, no problem." The weather was fine. I had no idea what she meant. When I wanted to go ahead, she shrugged and said, "Sure. Your call."

She followed me on foot in the arena, calling, "Relax your wrists! Lower your hands! Get out of his mouth like that!" I tried to relax and open to it, but her impatience made me tense, mechanical. I could do this, I knew I could do this. I focused, bit my lip in concentration, tried to visualize myself doing the moves correctly as I used to in ballet. "You're jabbing him in the mouth! Lower your hands!" She lacked her usual soothing tone and repeated the same direction over and over. Glacier pinned his ears back and lifted his nose ever higher. Kelly finally stepped into our path and stopped us. "You're in no condition to be on a horse today. I'm not going to subject him to this any longer."

Her words slapped me across the face and left my cheeks burning. I dismounted, sure my misery branded me as red as Glacier's quilted saddle pad. "I just want to work," I said. "I need to work. You mentioned the event in April, and we have so much to do—"

"Summer, you're dealing with a live animal here. A living, feeling creature. You can't just set deadlines and make decisions without considering him. You either ride the horse to ride the horse and learn from him, or I won't work with you. Maybe you'll be ready for an event in April, maybe you won't. That can't matter. There are no shortcuts in this."

I nodded dumbly and led Glacier away. I gave him two apples, as a way to apologize.

Both my parents were gone, so I drove to the hospital. As I walked down the hallway toward Todd's room, a nurse recognized me and stopped in her tracks. "Summer, what are you doing here?" she asked.

"I'm here to see Todd," I said. They knew that.

"But—but . . . didn't you know? Didn't anyone tell you?"

The worry on her face froze me. She started to say something else, but the gentle smile on her face was too much to bear. I didn't want to hear her. I didn't want to know why she was mustering up her kindness. I turned and walked down the hall toward the room.

"Summer?" she called.

I broke into a run.

I hit the door—the last door in the hallway—with both hands. The slap of my hands echoed as I stared.

I stared at the empty room. The bed stripped bare. The monitors silent. The Christmas tree gone. No sign, no trace.

The room went green and wavy before my eyes. The floor hurtled up toward me, compacting my legs, and it grew closer and closer, the room drawing shorter and shorter. I tottered.

Strong hands grabbed my arms. "It's okay, Summer," the nurse said. "It's okay. Sit down, hon."

She drew me toward a chair, but I crumpled on the floor, my head in my hands. "That's right," she said. "Put your head between your knees. Breathe, hon." I heard running footsteps in the hall. I looked up at two other nurses.

"Is she all right?" one asked.

"Where is everyone?" I whispered.

"They're at home, hon," the first nurse said, squeezing my hand, smiling. "It's all right."

"Already? But, where's Todd? I want to see him."

They were silent a moment, frowning. Then one nurse said "Oh. . . ."

My nurse took both my hands and said, "Oh, Summer, no. No. Todd's at home. They took him home. Everything is fine. His fever went down. Not as much as we liked, but enough that he was driving us crazy."

"You mean—?" I breathed again, but too much. My relief came as hyperventilation.

"And he cheated," the third nurse in the doorway said. "We found this in his trash can, hidden under a bunch of paper towels." She held up a box of Popsicles, flattened and empty. "He was bound and determined."

"Oh, my God," I said, hysterical laughter bubbling up through me.

"You okay?" the first nurse asked, releasing my hands.

I nodded. I tried to catch my breath. "Yes. Yes. Yes. Oh, my God. I've got to get home. Thank you. Oh, my God, thank you." I took off running again.

"Be careful!" they shouted after me.

*   *   *

I passed my parents, leaving, on our street, but they didn't see me. I burst in the back door and flew to Todd, in his bed in the bay window. "Oh, my God, Todd! I thought you were dead!"

He looked at me, amazed, laughing at my manic energy.

"Where have you been?" Jacob asked. It was *A Christmas Carol's* first dark night since opening.

"Long story. Oh, my God. You're home."

Todd opened his arms as if to say, "Here I am." I kissed him.

"Oh, my God," I repeated. "I really thought you were dead. I saw that empty room. Oh, God."

They laughed. "Jesus, Summer, I'm sorry," Jacob said. "We kept trying to reach you."

"And you've been discovered," I scolded Todd. "They found your evidence. What did you do, eat a whole box of Popsicles to get your temp down?"

They all burst out laughing. "Oh, honey," Arnicia said. "Boyfriend didn't just eat them!"

"What?"

Todd shook his head. *"Enough! Stop!"* he wrote, giggling.

"I don't get it," I said.

Jacob laughed so hard, he could barely speak. "Oh, God," he gasped. "I'd have given anything to see that!"

"What did you do?" I asked Todd. He rolled his eyes and shook his head.

"He—he," Arnicia tried to say through her laughter, "he—did something obscene!"

Todd put the notepad over his face.

"He really wanted to come home," Jacob said with admiration. Then, teasing, "Tell me, did it feel good?"

Todd removed the notepad and shook his head, eyes wide. They convulsed with laughter again.

This time I laughed, too. "Okay," I said. "I get it, but I still don't get it. Why? Why didn't you just eat them, you freak?"

"They'd already caught him doing that, days ago, with ice," Arnicia said.

"They wouldn't even bring him ice anymore," Jacob said. "And . . ." He started giggling again.

Todd sighed and picked up the notepad and wrote, *"They started getting mean and nasty about WHERE they'd take my temperature. They didn't think I could cheat there."*

"Didn't think you *would* cheat there," Arnicia corrected him.

"Who brought you the Popsicles?" I asked.

They fell silent and lowered their eyes. Todd wrote, *"Nicholas."*

Having Todd home was work. An exhausting, intricate regime of medicines. Tubes and needles to grow familiar with. Rules and regulations to follow. Red plastic biohazard boxes in the kitchen and bathrooms. I had to get used to using latex gloves at times, something I'd avoided to this point. I felt awkward and ridiculous whenever Todd saw me put them on. He couldn't do anything for himself—it was a major accomplishment for him to sit up and put his feet on the floor and never repeated in the same day—and although Dr. Sara and Arnicia had warned us, and told us nothing but the ugly truths, I found myself quite unprepared.

"This is terrifying," I whispered to Jacob one day as Todd slept and I finally got a sluggish IV bag to drip.

He nodded but said, "I'm glad he's here. Home where it's just us. I hated sharing him with all those people who came by the hospital for obligatory visits, sucking up all his energy." I knew what he meant. Our time was running out, and we were selfish with it.

Jacob monitored the visits to the house and sometimes sent people away without seeing Todd. I'm sure our relatives didn't understand him. I think a lot of them thought he was cold and aloof. I heard Aunt Marnee say Jacob was tired of all this. Well, yes, of course, he was tired of it, but it didn't mean he was complaining.

Arnicia had warned Jacob about our caller, and he'd taken to answering the phone with a cheerful, "The Wholesome House, how can we help you?"

The first time Todd heard the caller, though—when we didn't make it in time and the machine picked up and conveyed the hateful obscenities—and we saw his eyes, that was it. That day we took the necessary steps to get an unlisted number.

I tried and tried calling Simon's house, to give Zackery the new number, but there was never an answer. He hadn't said anything about his plans for the holidays, so this troubled me. There was plenty at home, however, to keep me busy. I lost myself in tending to Todd, and when Todd napped, I graded and planned and read, in the endless preparations for school, so grateful for this respite, a chance to catch up.

His third day home, Todd announced that he wanted to see *A Christmas Carol.* He wanted to see Jacob act, he said, one last time.

"Oh, babe," Jacob said. "That's too far. It's too long. All those people. All those germs. You don't want to do that."

Todd bristled. *"Don't tell me what I want."*

"Well, I'm not taking you. It's a stupid idea."

"I can always call a cab," he wrote.

"You can't talk," Jacob reminded him, laughing. Todd flipped him off. Jacob tried to kiss him, but Todd turned his head away. "Fine," Jacob said, leaving the room. "You go right ahead and call a cab, babe."

Nicholas saved the day when he visited that afternoon. He knew the artistic director of the Dayton company; they'd worked on a show in Chicago together four years ago. Nicholas made some calls and arranged for Todd to watch the performance from the sound booth. We bought a little portable hospital cot that folded up like a chair. If Todd fell asleep, no big deal. No one would stare at him, and even better, he would not be exposed to an entire audience's germs. Nicholas agreed to sit with him, ready to wheel him out if . . . anything should happen.

"*Nicholas is brilliant,*" Todd wrote.

"To Nicholas!" Jacob said. He opened the bottle of champagne Dr. Sara had sent him for opening night. We toasted, with the fancy champagne glasses they'd bought to replace the ones Todd dropped after the stroke. Todd, of course, just had water. I toasted, too, but I could hardly swallow the champagne. It was hard to look at Nicholas, who seemed to feel the same and avoided being alone with me. We hardly made eye contact all day, and when he hurried off the back porch to his car instead of lingering to talk with me, I had the sensation of sand running through my fingers.

It was my mother's idea that, just like the old days when I'd danced Her Royal Highness Herself, the Sugarplum Fairy, here in the local *Nutcracker,* all of the relatives get tickets and plan to go to the closing matinee performance before dinner here on Christmas Eve. Jacob, at Todd's request, bought the tickets for everyone, as gifts. It was a good thing, too, since the next day that performance sold out.

Aunt Marnee protested, "It's morbid! Todd shouldn't see it, and neither should the rest of us. All those ghosts and tombstones. All that death being foretold! What kind of Christmas spirit will that put us in? I won't go!"

So it was with two tickets to spare and my new unlisted number that I looked up Simon Schiffler's address and drove by his house on Christmas Eve morning on my way back from the grocery store. For two days now no one had answered the phone.

I knocked on the door and waited. There were no signs of life. Just as I was walking back to the car, the side garage door opened.

"Ms. Zwolenick? What are you doing here?" It was Zackery, safe and all right. He stepped into the yard and hugged me. He was wearing his coat and hat and gloves.

"You going somewhere?" I asked.

"No, I was just—" But he stopped himself and stammered as if I'd just caught him rifling through my purse. "Yeah, I—I thought I might, you know—"

A bell went off in my brain. "Are you living in their garage?" I asked.

He put his hands in his coat pockets and looked at the ground. "Just these past couple of days."

"Oh, Zack." I didn't know what to say to him. "Zack." I shook my head.

"It's not that bad." He looked up, but past me, at the street beyond. "They're gone for Christmas. Grandparents in Florida. Simon's mom didn't want me alone in their house, you know. I can still live here when they get back; she's really cool. I told her I was spending Christmas with my parents. But—" His eyes met mine for a second before he returned his gaze to the ground and whispered, "I called them and they said they didn't think that was a good idea."

I reached out and touched his cheek with my fingertips. "You're not spending Christmas alone," I said.

"I don't want to."

"Do you want to come home with me? Until the Schifflers get back?"

He looked up at me and said too readily, "Yeah. That'd be great." The corners of his mouth twitched.

"Go pack," I said. "You need something nice. We're seeing *A Christmas Carol* tonight."

He nodded, and I followed him into the garage. As he sorted through his belongings in black garbage bags, I took in the electric space heater, the cot with a sleeping bag, the cooler, the water jugs. A stack of books was piled near the cot. The garage smelled of oil, and I could see my breath.

"Where do you go to the bathroom?" I asked.

He looked up from shoving clothes into a backpack. Red mottles blossomed on his neck. "Oh . . . you know. It's like camping," he said. "And there's a McDonald's right down the street." He saw my expression and added, "It's not that bad, really. Look at all the stuff Simon gave me. It's only for four days."

I nodded and walked back into the yard, desperate for clean, cold air to quell my nausea.

We got in the car after he'd locked the garage. We drove for a mile or two in silence. "I was really . . . scared," he said, looking out the window. I thought about the gun he'd bought. Those fears had power when you were all alone in a dank dungeon of a garage.

"You are going to be bombarded by my crazy relatives," I joked. "You don't know what fear is yet." He laughed, grateful. He knew I understood him and was not making light.

At the house he was welcomed warmly by Arnicia and Jacob, who acted as though I always returned from the grocery store with young homeless men in tow. Arnicia did say, "You didn't tell me he was so cute," and set Zack to blushing, though.

"You need anything?" Jacob asked him as we all unloaded groceries. "Soft drink? Juice? Tea? A beer?"

"Jacob!" I said. "He's not even eighteen. Besides, it's only ten in the morning!"

"Oh, honey, that has never stopped boyfriend from having a beer for breakfast," Arnicia said.

"Hey, hey, now," Jacob said. "Only in extenuating circumstances!"

"Such as?" Zackery asked, grinning.

"Well . . . you know . . . if I'm out of coffee."

We laughed, and Zackery took a Coke. I took him in to meet Todd. Todd shook his hand and smiled. He gestured for Zack to sit and wrote to us, *"I want to talk to Zack a while. There's some things I want to tell him."* We left them alone, and they talked for over an hour. Several times we heard Zack's laughter from that room. And several times it was silent.

Jacob left for the show, and I took special care preparing for the play, knowing I'd see Nicholas. I even curled my hair and pulled up the sides, fastening them with a pearl clip Grandma Anna had given me years ago. I hadn't even taken that clip with me to New York but had recently rediscovered it. I held up a hand mirror to see the fall of strawberry blond curls shimmer against the navy blue velvet dress I'd selected.

Nicholas arrived, freshly shaven and stunning in a suit and tie. He hardly looked twice at me before helping wheel Todd to the limo Jake had arranged.

"I've never been in a limo before!" Zack said.

"Me neither," Arnicia said. "I like living with these rich boys. They treat me like a . . . like royalty." She laughed. "You all take note: I did not say they treat me like a queen. Get it?" We groaned.

We got Todd situated at the theater. "Thank you," I said to Nicholas. He nodded at me, saying nothing. I wanted to grab him around the knees and tell him I was sorry, I was stupid, I took it all back and would marry him and follow him anywhere, but in the time it took me to think that, he turned away from me to talk to the sound board operator. I kissed Todd good-bye and took Zack to meet all my relatives in the lobby. His presence confused a few. "His folks had to leave town," was all I said, "and he'll be with us for Christmas."

My mother knew the story of Zack. She hugged him and adopted him for the evening. When the lights flickered to warn us to get to our seats, she led him, arm in arm, to the one beside her own.

I settled into my seat and looked around the grand old theater and the sellout crowd. My chest tightened. I should be on that stage. This many people had stood and applauded me under this very same gold-and-green marble ceiling. Not a one of them knew me now.

The houselights fell, and I discovered that my aunt Marnee was wrong. It wasn't the ghosts or tombstones that haunted those of us who had come.

It was Bob Cratchit.

I expected brilliance from Jacob but had not given much thought to the role he was playing. He wrung our hearts as he looked with such love and adoration upon his poor, ailing Tiny Tim. He looked with the eyes of a man who was prepared for inevitable loss. Who knew the loss would come, but who did all in his power to stave it off just a month longer . . . just a day. . . .

And when that terrible, hooded Ghost we'd grown familiar with showed us the poor Cratchits of the future, without their beloved Tim, all three rows of us were quaking and sniffling. Grandma Cailee held my hand. Arnicia, on the other side of me, blew her nose. I stole a glance up at the dark booth but saw only the lights reflected on its glass windows. My father, on the aisle, got up and left. He didn't return until the curtain closed, and his swollen red eyes gave him away.

Jacob looked up at the booth for the entire curtain call. His face shone, with sweat or tears, I couldn't tell. When I made it to the booth to take Todd home, Jacob was already up there, and Todd had a swath of greasepaint on his cheek and the collar of his white shirt.

Back at the house, Todd's pride for his Jacob transformed him like a blood transfusion. We propped him up, in full view of the party, a fresh stack of his yellow legal pads beside him. There were always two or three people around him and two or three people waiting, like a receiving line.

We'd been back only thirty minutes, and already Todd had asked me almost twenty times if Jacob was home yet. "Why are you asking me what you already know?" I teased him. "You know darn good and well that the very first second he gets here, he is coming straight to your side. He adores you."

I did go peek out the kitchen window, though, just to appease him. The driveway and narrow brick street were lined with cars. Jacob might have to park a block away.

A cab slowed, then stopped. It sat there a full minute before anyone stepped out. I couldn't believe my eyes. The cab drove away, and she stood there. I watched, unmoving, ignoring some cousin who called, through all the voices and music, "Whatcha lookin' at, Summer?"

Just standing there for what seemed an eternity.

And then turning and walking away, up the street. I bolted out the back door. The cold air seared my lungs, burned the inside of my nose.

"Abby?" I called.

She stopped. I wove my way between all the cars to reach her. "Abby, where are you going?"

She wore an open black cape over a gown of green satin and spangles, obviously coming from or going to some formal event.

"What was I thinking?" she asked. She didn't ask me, as much as she seemed to ask herself.

"What, Abby? What do you mean? Please come inside. Todd will be so happy."

She held a wrapped and ribboned box in front of her as if it contained a severed finger. "I wanted to find him the perfect present. I spent lots of money—lots. What was I thinking?"

I pulled on her arm. She took some steps, allowing herself to be led. "Come, give it to him. He'll love it."

She stopped. "No."

"Abby, it's freezing. You're here. Come inside and give him his present."

She shook her head and wouldn't meet my eyes. "He's not ever going to win his Academy Award," she said, looking at the box in her hands. "He's not ever going to be attending the premiere of Jacob's first feature film. He's not ever going to leave that house again, is he?" She stared at the house, streaming light and cheerful noise.

"No," I said. "He's not."

She looked me in the eye. "So what the fuck is he going to do with solid gold cuff links?" She dropped the box on the frozen dirty ground and began walking up the street. Her heels sang with a clear ringing on the sidewalk.

"Abby!" I called. "Come back! Please? What am I supposed to tell him?"

But she rounded the corner and was gone.

I wanted to run after her. Everything in me wanted to run and find her and hug her. But I made myself turn and go back in the house.

I left the box on the ground.

Chapter Fifteen

I opened the back door, and although the heat enveloped me, it could not warm the cold pit in my stomach. I made my way to Todd, who gestured me over from across the room.

"Is he here yet?"

"Would you chill?" I laughed at him. "No, not yet!"

"What were you doing outside?"

"Oh, there was a parking problem." I surprised myself with how easy and ready the lie was. "One of our neighbors. I schmoozed a little; everything's okay."

He frowned, but just then the door opened again. Jacob stepped in, and everyone applauded. Todd's pride shone from him, his face aglow. I'm sure the raging fever helped, too.

And, as I'd predicted, Jacob did come straight to Todd with an unabashed kiss that made Aunt Marnee cluck her tongue and Aunt Emma flutter her double chins. He took Todd's hands, and Todd whispered to him, close to his ear. They stayed like that, with Jacob "monopolizing" Todd's company (according to Aunt Marnee) for ten or fifteen minutes.

I found Zackery, to make sure he was surviving. Now Grandma Cailee had adopted him. They sat on a couch, deep in conversation about Dylan Thomas poetry. He looked up at me and smiled.

"You doing all right?" I asked him.

"This is great. Thanks. Really."

"He knows his Thomas!" Grandma said as though that were the highest compliment imaginable.

"Hey, he has a good English teacher," I joked.

"I do. I really do," Zack said, those eyes of his suddenly serious and deep as the dark wells on Grandma Cailee's farm.

The chant of "Presents! Presents!" drew us to the bedroom. Everyone had gifts for Todd. Aunt Marnee gathered everyone around to watch the opening of the gifts, probably so she could keep track of whose was most expensive. She started off with her own, of course. Little Daniela sat on the edge of Todd's bed and opened the packages for him. Aunt Marnee had bought Todd pink silk pajamas, a bold, if tactless, gift for her. Everyone oohed and ahhed, and Todd nodded and smiled. He didn't wear pajamas, even now, and was fanatical about getting dressed in real clothes every day, even when it took him close to an hour to do so.

He received a lot of clothes, which was all well and good, I guess, but I could feel Todd's growing exasperation as he opened items like wool socks and expensive sweaters and even new track shoes. He smiled politely, but the bemused furrow in his brow deepened.

Aunt Emma gave him a magazine subscription. A year's subscription. He laughed out loud.

He opened the gift from Nicholas. Two handmade birdhouses to hang in the bay window, just as he'd promised, with seed to go with them. Todd smiled, and the furrows disappeared. He clapped his hands together like a little kid and looked around for Nicholas.

"He had to leave after the play," Arnicia said. "He's driving tonight to spend Christmas with his dad in Indiana." My face burned. I hadn't even gotten the chance to wish him a Merry Christmas.

Young Daniela and Samantha gave Todd a photo album scrapbook. "This is all the stuff we know you would've come to, if you could have," Samantha announced, and everyone said, "Ahh . . ." in unison. Inside were photos and captions from Samantha's school play and choir concert, and Daniela in her gymnastics class, and progress of their new puppy. The captions were written by the girls themselves, and it was obvious Aunt Shannon hadn't interfered. Things like "The girl behind me in this one picks her nose—I've seen her!" and "We think the boy on the right is cute—do you?" Todd pored over the pictures, tilting his head to take it all in with his good eye.

Aunt Marnee grew bored with the photo album when Todd spent too much time on it for her liking. She turned and looked across the bed at Jacob. "And what did you get for Todd, Jacob?"

He appeared taken off guard. "Um . . . well, I didn't get him . . . you know, a traditional present, like—"

"You didn't get him a present?" Aunt Marnee asked, her words a condemnation.

A silence fell. "No," Jacob said. He opened his mouth, but no further words materialized.

I saw Todd prod Daniela and point to another package at the foot of the bed. "Oh! Here's another one," she said, getting the hint. "There's lots more. Open this one—it's from Sheila." Todd diverted attention back to the bed, away from Jacob. After a moment Todd caught my eye and tipped his head toward the kitchen. I looked. Jacob was gone. I nodded at Todd and slipped away myself.

Jacob had poured himself a drink and stood staring out a window. "Hey," I said. "Don't let her get to you."

"It's just, it had never crossed my mind, you know? And I know she doesn't get it. She thinks I think it's a waste of money, or worse, that I didn't think he'd live this long."

I put an arm around his waist. "You don't care what she thinks."

"No . . . but . . . shit. I just wish that for once, she'd get it. She'd get us. We don't need presents. All those people giving stupid, obligatory gifts because tradition requires it. I wasn't going to fucking buy him some material object that would be worthless to him. Some ridiculous thing to add to the inevitable haul to Goodwill when this is over. That man in there knows the secret to life. He's traveling lighter than any of us. What could I buy him that he could use or need?" He downed his drink and reached for the Scotch bottle. I took it from him.

"Jacob. You did give him a present. Something he could use and need. You didn't have to buy it, and it's by far his favorite one." I stood on tiptoe and kissed him on the cheek. "You brought him home."

He took the bottle from me and replaced it in the cupboard, then turned and hugged me. "Thank you," he whispered. "You just gave me a present."

The back door opened and Abby stepped in, still in her gown and cape. She held a basket in front of her and seemed strangely protective of it. She didn't look at me; she and Jacob stood face-to-face, expressionless, the usual hint of challenge between them. "Todd will be glad you're here," Jacob said.

"I have a present for him. I—I want to know if it's okay to give it to him."

Jacob shrugged. "Sure. You don't need permission to give your brother a present—"

She turned to me and said, "This gift didn't cost me anything. I found it, as a matter of fact. But I love it. It's been one of the few things in my life that I do love lately, and because of that, I want to give it to him." She opened the basket and took out a sleeping yellow kitten, its eyes shut tight.

Jacob's expression melted, and he reached for the kitten. Abby handed it to him. "Is—is that okay?" she asked.

"Abby, this is great," he said. He held it up and looked between its legs. "What's his name?"

Abby blushed, and I was struck by how beautiful she was. Exquisite, with her red hair swept up in a regal French twist, emeralds at her ears and throat. That throat, that long white neck, the envy of any ballerina. "I found him on Cooper Street behind the hospital one night. I just call him Cooper."

Before I could ask her what she was doing behind the hospital at night, the back door opened again and Brad came in. He was still deep tan from his trip to Costa Rica, the lines around his eyes and mouth white in contrast. His hands looked brown at the end of his tux sleeves, the tux I knew he owned instead of rented. He wore too much cologne.

"Forget something?" he asked Abby, holding the box of cuff links. A dark smudge from the driveway soiled one corner of the box, and the ribbons were flattened now. "Jesus, have you been drinking? These cost a fortune. We're not made of money, you know."

"Oh, thank you, hon," Abby said. "I didn't realize I dropped them." She took the box from him and kissed him on the cheek.

"Hey, Summer," Brad said to me. He nodded at Jacob, then noticed what Jacob was holding. "Jesus Christ, what's that cat doing here?"

Abby blushed again, but this time darker. "Well, I thought since I—since we can't keep him, Todd might like him."

Brad shook his head at her. "You're passing this stray off as a gift?"

"I think Todd will love him," I said.

Brad smirked. "The last thing a man with AIDS needs is a cat to give him toxoplasmosis."

Abby's blush faded. She looked at Brad, her eyes frightened. Brad cleared his throat, as if gearing up for a medical lecture, and said, "You see, cats can transmit—"

"We know what toxo is," Jacob interrupted him.

"Well, then, you realize that it would be unwise to—"

"We're keeping the cat," Jacob said.

"You seem rather cavalier about the danger."

"Todd can't stand up," Jacob said. "Don't worry about him cleaning out a litter box."

"That'll be my job, I'm sure," I said.

Abby looked uncertain. She twisted the emeralds at her neck. "I didn't know there was any danger. I—I didn't mean—"

"I think he'll love it," Jacob said. He said it in a soothing tone meant for Abby, but he looked straight at Brad.

"What's his viral load?" Brad asked Jacob. It was somehow a challenge.

"Three hundred thousand," Jacob said. No emotion.

Brad whistled a low note. "T-cell count?"

"Six."

Brad shook his head. "Forget it. He doesn't have time to get toxo."

I looked at Jacob's face and feared for Brad's life.

Abby's expression might have looked the same if Brad had sliced a knife across her throat.

Jacob turned to Abby, handing over the kitten. "Why don't you give Todd the kitten? I think he's going to love it. He'll be really glad you're here."

Abby nodded and left the kitchen. Brad called after her, "Hurry up, Ab. We're late to the party."

Brad turned to the platter of Christmas cookies beside him. He selected one and bit into it without asking.

My gaze traveled back and forth between Jacob and Brad as if I were watching a tennis match. Jacob watched Brad and appeared relaxed, leaning against the kitchen counter, but his hands gripping it behind him were white across the knuckles. He was still, too still. I looked at his abdomen and was relieved to see him breathing slowly, evenly.

Brad ate the cookie, checking his Rolex every so often, none of us saying a word.

When he finished he wiped the crumbs from his tux, very busily, very involved, giving us this little show of flit-flit-flit swipes. He held out his arms and examined himself, then washed his hands at the sink, whistling softly. Holding up his forearms, as though about to walk into surgery, he eyed the dish towel looped through the refrigerator handle and asked me, "Got a clean dish towel?"

"Top drawer, right beside you," I said. He frowned, then opened the drawer and lifted out a dish towel, unfolding it from one corner and studying the whole towel before drying his hands with it. He dried very mechanically, very thoroughly, then tossed the towel onto the counter. Rubbing his hands together, he moved toward the doorway, looking over my shoulder into the room. He opened his mouth to call to Abby, but Jacob interrupted him.

"Give her a minute."

Brad turned. "Excuse me?"

Too loud, too clearly, as if Brad had honestly not heard him, Jacob repeated, "I said: Give. Her. A. Minute."

My heart began to pound.

Brad raised one eyebrow. "I'll speak to my wife any damn time I—"

"Get the fuck out of my house." Jacob pushed himself off the counter and stood, weight distributed evenly on both feet.

Oh, God, I thought. "Guys, come on, it's Christmas."

They faced off.

Abby swept back into the room, her green skirt brushing past me. Although she wiped tears from her cheeks, she looked radiant. "Sorry I took so long, hon," she said. Brad finally took his gaze from Jacob's. His eyes took her in and softened. "Thanks," she said. "We can get going now." She wrapped both her arms around one of his and kissed his shoulder as they walked to the door. "Oh! My purse!" she said. "You go ahead, I'll be right out."

"I'll bring the car around front," he said to her. "Just wait. Don't stand out in the cold." She closed the door, and instead of going to get her purse, she turned to us.

"Abby, I just want to say . . . ," Jacob floundered. "Look, I'm really glad you came, too. Your gift was the best one."

She nodded, avoiding his eyes. "Um . . . I have something for you, Jacob." She fumbled in the pocket of her cape and pulled out the box of cuff links. "I was going to give it to Todd . . . but he won't be able to use them. Um, maybe you could." She held out the box to Jacob. He took it from her warily. "Open it," she urged. He did. "His name is on them," she said. "I thought you might like them . . . because of that."

Jake's breathing changed. He nodded. "Thank you."

They looked at one another for a moment. "I'm sorry," Abby whispered. Jacob shook his head at her. "I just wish . . . ," she said, and her words encompassed more than the illness, more than this animosity. They encompassed all the history of their lives.

"Me too," Jacob said.

They took a hesitant step toward each other, but a car horn tooted outside. Abby put a hand on the doorknob.

"Don't forget your purse," I said.

Abby smiled at Jacob. "It's in the car." She slipped out the door.

They would have liked to comfort each other, I thought, but they didn't know how.

The party went late. Late enough that it officially became Christmas Day. Todd held up for some time but finally fell asleep, little Daniela curled up by his side. Cooper crawled into Todd's sweater and curled up on Todd's chest—it was probably warm as a radiator—with just his golden ears peeking out. Jacob herded everyone out of that room and closed the door.

Samantha and Jacob bundled up and went outside to hang the bird feeders. I watched them through the window. I thought how wonderful it would have been for Nicholas and me to have our announcement to make, here at the party. To have that ring, perhaps, to show people, but more important, to have each other. I put my forehead against the frosty glass.

"You okay, Ms. Zwolenick?" Zack asked.

"Yeah." I turned around. "Just a little sad."

A few hours later everyone went home. Mom and Dad were last to leave. They stood together at the foot of Todd's bed, looking down at him. Jake, Arnicia, and I watched them. Zack had fallen asleep in the living room.

"Remember when we used to do this?" I heard my dad ask my mom. As an answer, she put an arm around his waist.

They turned and saw us. "We used to wake up in the night, and go watch you sleep," my mom said. "When you were babies." My dad put an arm across her shoulders. They looked at each other, surprise in their eyes. After long embraces and Christmas wishes, they drove away.

We went to the living room. Zack sat on the couch, rubbing his eyes. "C'mon," I said. "Let me show you where you'll be sleeping." He followed me groggily up the stairs. He protested a bit but was too tired to put up much of a fight about taking my room.

He went to change in the bathroom. "Oh, Ms. Zwolenick," he said from inside. "What half the guys in your classes wouldn't do to trade places with me right now." I'd forgotten that hand-washed lingerie hung in the shower.

"Zack!"

"And it's all lost . . . completely lost . . . on me." He held up a red lacy bra. "Ah, the irony. . . ."

"Give me that!" I grabbed the bra from him and snatched down the others, laughing. I put them away and gathered myself a pillow and some blankets while he changed. He came out in a pair of sweats and no shirt. There was something so touching about that healthy young, unblemished body that I had to look away. I think he was embarrassed. He slid under the covers and pulled them up to his chin. "Thank you," he said. "I had the greatest time. I can't imagine . . . being at Simon's right now."

"Neither can I. Merry Christmas."

"Merry Christmas, Ms. Zwolenick."

"I think, under the circumstances, that you should call me Summer. After all, you are in my bed."

He laughed. "The rumors we could start, huh?" We both fell silent, thinking. He looked at me with those saucerlike eyes and said, "I wish—now don't take this the wrong way—but I almost wish that we were . . . you know . . ." He blushed. "Somehow that would seem a lot less complicated."

I nodded. He was right. A lot less complicated.

"Make a Christmas wish, Zack."

"I already did. It came true. Thanks."

I took my pillow and blanket and turned out the lights. I closed the door and began to make my way down the stairs.

Arnicia sat curled up at the bottom of the stairs, head leaning against the wall.

"Nish? What's wrong—?"

She turned with her finger on her lips. She motioned with her manicured hands for me to creep quietly down beside her. I had no idea what we were hiding from. I set the bedding down silently and sat on the stair beside her, and she brought her mouth to my ear. "I'm waiting to hear the toast," she whispered.

I shook my head and mouthed, "What?"

"You've never seen this?" she whispered. I shook my head again. "Oh, honey. It's wonderful."

Again I asked, "What?"

"You just wait," she whispered, and leaned back against the wall.

It was late, or early, however you wanted to look at it, and I was tired. I felt a little curious, but more irritated by this strange request to hide in the stairwell. Minutes crawled by. Arnicia appeared to fall asleep. Just as I was ready to gather my bedding and give up this odd vigil, the door to Todd and Jacob's bedroom opened. Arnicia sat up and patted my leg. Once again she put a finger to her lips.

We couldn't see anything, but we heard Jacob go to the kitchen. "The crystal glasses," Arnicia whispered. I heard a cupboard open and glasses tinkling. More footsteps, back toward the bedroom. "The request," she whispered.

We heard Jacob ask, "So . . . what'll it be?" It was a one-sided conversation, as Todd was obviously writing. "Uh-uh, no way." Pause. "I don't care. I want to get some sleep tonight." Pause. "Club soda it is." More footsteps, the fridge opening.

Nish leaned in again and said, "Sometimes it's only water.

Sometimes Alka-Seltzer or some medicine. Sometimes shots of tequila. It all depends. Now listen."

Jacob was back in the bedroom. In a somewhat formal, but loving, voice—a voice unveiled, unlike I'd ever heard him—he said, "To this day, another day lived together, the one thousand nine hundred and eleventh day we've been together." There was a clink of glasses. There followed a long, silent pause, then Jacob padded back to the kitchen, washed the glasses, put them away, and went into the bedroom and shut the door. I heard the slight creak of the bed shift as he must have climbed into it beside his Todd.

I turned to Nish. "How did you know they would do this?"

"They always do it. Every damn night, even when they've been pissy all day with each other. They did it in the hospital with paper cups. Those days that Todd wasn't . . . really here, Jacob still did it—whispered it in Todd's ear." I shook my head. I didn't know what to say to this. Nish knew and continued. "Some days, girl, when the world is spinning out of control and I'm out of money and behind in classes and everything seems just bleak and bad, I sneak down here and wait. I've waited hours before, until I'd hear one of them go to the cupboard and get the glasses. As long as there is this, I can go on. I'll be all right."

I nodded. She patted my leg again. "You'll be all right, too."

I hoped she was right. I fell asleep dreaming of toasting with Nicholas.

Chapter Sixteen

On Christmas morning I awoke to the sound of coughing. A rattling, bubbling cough that hurt to hear and must have hurt to endure. It lasted a long time. Peace on earth, I thought. Good will to men.

There were no gifts to exchange between us in the house. Somehow we were beyond that. It was a gift enough that the coughing fit ended and Todd could watch the fat red cardinal who came to Nicholas's feeder. It was a gift enough to watch the kitten, Cooper, twitch all over as he crouched and spied on the feeding bird.

I went upstairs to wake Zackery. He slept on his stomach like a baby, his face turned to the side, lips parted. I leaned in my door frame a moment and watched him before I touched his foot peeking out of the covers and shook it. He opened his eyes, and that angelic face drew itself in again, lined and watchful. "Merry Christmas . . . again. Want some breakfast?"

He joined us downstairs, and we sat in our sweats and pajamas around Todd's bed, eating coffee cake Grandma Cailee had left us, basking in the quiet and the calm of our little family, doing nothing more strenuous than playing with Cooper.

Cooper ventured off to explore this new house, but he never

strayed too far without coming back to Todd. He seemed to understand that Todd was his person. He would sit on no one else's lap, he would allow no one else to pick him up, and he answered to no one else's call. All Todd had to make was a kissing sound and Cooper would come loping in his awkward way like the most loyal trained dog. Any of the rest of us trying this were met only with golden eyes of scorn.

"Are you ready for your present?" Todd wrote to me when Arnicia left for her family's gathering.

"I thought we weren't doing presents," I said. Todd handed me an envelope that held instructions for me to buy a horse of my own. Any horse I wanted to pursue my new sport with. I could do the "shopping," and Todd would fund the vetting and the purchase and the board at Mom and Dad's for as long as the horse lived. "Todd . . . that's too much. You can't do that."

He wheezed. *"I CAN do it!"* he scribbled. *"You want this and I want you to go for it. Have no regrets, little sister."*

I read that and smiled. "Okay. It's a deal."

I began the next day. I took Zackery back to the Schifflers' once we knew they were home, then drove to the farm.

I expected Kelly Canter to be excited when I enlisted her help. To my surprise, she seemed skeptical. "What's our price range?"

"We have no range," I said.

"None at all? Hmm."

We visited the best breeding barns and an auction the following week, looking at warmbloods with the average price of $10,000. But although I could afford any horse my heart desired, I couldn't find one my heart did. Kelly, too, burst my bubble by pointing out that just because I bought a horse that could do advanced levels of dressage didn't mean that I could.

"You're in a hurry," she said to me one day in January, after school resumed. "I don't like that."

Well, of course I was in a hurry. I wanted Todd to see my purchase. I took Polaroids of each prospect to him. He would nod his approval and write, *"Is this the one?"*

I'd shrug and say "I don't know. . . ."

"Then it's not. Don't rush it."

Everyone telling me to slow down seemed ludicrous under the circumstances.

Todd got bad. He spent most hours of the day sleeping. His belly hurt so bad, he ground his teeth even in his sleep. His cough grew worse, and he coughed up so much blood—it looked like a cupful once—that we forced him to go to the doctor. Todd kicked and punched when Jacob tried to pick him up and carry him. Jacob finally set him down, both of them sobbing.

"I want to die at home," Todd wrote over and over again. We had to promise he would not be readmitted at the hospital before he'd settle down and ride willingly in the car. It's a good thing, because even Dr. Sara wanted him hospitalized. Although she couldn't get culture results for several weeks, she suspected he had *Mycobacterium avium* complex, or MAC. She did know already that his fever was too high, his liver and spleen too large, and his red blood cells too low. He was anemic again . . . or still; I couldn't keep track anymore. And, as had become expected, new KS lesions had crept in, including three that had snuck into his left lung.

"You promised," Todd forced out again and again, knowing it pained us to hear that trashed voice of his, until Jake agreed.

I knew what it meant when the doctors gave in so quickly. Dr. Sara was the one, though, who said it out loud. She pulled us into a waiting room. "We're at the point where we can't keep up with the opportunistic infections. He's being bombarded, and his body simply has nothing left to fight with. Rather than try to aggressively treat each ailment—and deal with the side effects and discomforts that come with each medicine and treatment—I think we should consider simply making him comfortable."

So we took Todd home, where he retched up blood, he coughed and hacked, he suffered terrible night sweats, and he had a fever that hovered between 103 and 104 for weeks. Cooper loved all that heat. He'd lie on Todd and purr, kneading Todd's skin with his snowy white paws.

But even so, there were days that stood out as relatively good. God, how AIDS could change one's standards.

There was the day we had a deep, diamond snowfall that canceled school. Jacob stamped out "I LOVE YOU TODD!" in the snow. We lifted Todd and held him up at the window, and he laughed.

There was the freak day, out of the blue, when Todd could speak in a normal voice. He babbled all day long. He made phone calls to everyone he could think of. He even ordered a pizza he couldn't eat, just because he could use the telephone. It lasted only a day, and he was rendered silent once again. For weeks we received gift packages in the mail from all the catalogs he'd called.

There was the day I brought Chaos over, the horse trailer blocking our narrow street, for Todd to view from the window. Kelly and I had changed tactics, searching cheap, hanging around the racetracks. We'd tried many lovely Thoroughbreds failing at racing careers and destined for dog food, but Chaos, whose name seemed to suit her, was the first I thought I might buy. And, of course, she was the only one Kelly wasn't crazy about. I fell in love with her scrappy sweetness, the crooked blaze between her long-lashed eyes, and her high-pitched whinny that made one turn, expecting to see a yearling. Even with her woolly winter coat, the color of chili powder, she shone with a careless sort of elegance. She wanted to please but was rough and reckless in her impulsive enthusiasm.

I unloaded her in the street and she barreled out backward, skidding on the bricks, wheeling, and whipping my arms at the end of her leather lead shank. She snorted, her red tail lifted high, and jumped the curb to the sidewalk as if it were a fence. She pranced about the yard, bumping me with her shoulders. I tried in vain to stand her still for Todd to look at.

Jacob came out on the porch and yelled, "You've got to be crazy! This horse is psycho!"

Chaos jerked me off my feet as she shied away from Jacob's voice. I almost tumbled into the snow but caught myself in a wild scramble. Kelly stood by the trailer, shaking her head.

I kept Chaos for a month's trial, at my parents' farm. During her weeks there she chased dogs, fought her way to the top of the pecking order in the mares' field, and kicked down boards in the pasture fence not once, but twice. Lessons with Kelly consisted of trying to get the mare to walk.

"SHE'S the one?" Todd wrote in disbelief.

I grinned.

"But you'll have to start from scratch."

I sighed. Kelly had complained of the exact same thing. "I don't care what people think," I told Todd. "I want to school her, I want to teach her, even if Kelly doesn't think I have enough patience. And I think Chaos can teach me as much as I teach her."

Todd looked at me a moment. *"How can you be so smart about some things?"* he wrote in his ever disintegrating scrawl. *"And so dumb about others?"*

"Nicholas doesn't want to marry me, Todd. It's not my fault."

He blinked, a startled look on his face, as if that was not what he meant at all. He shrugged and wrote the check for $1,500. Chaos was officially mine.

Chaos of another sort belonged to me at school. Denny continued his disparaging "fag" remarks, and I found no support from the principal when I wrote Denny up for disciplinary action. When I suggested that he might let it go, then, if Denny made "nigger" remarks, Mr. Vortee protested that this "was not the same thing at all!"

So I had to endure the presence of this boy five days a week. It was only for an hour at a time, but I wanted to shower before I returned home to Todd so as not to taint him with this hatred. One day I found a bingo game drawn up on scrap paper left behind on Denny's desk. Instead of letters, the blocks consisted of dates. Possible dates of when the "faggot" would die. I stood staring at that paper and thought for a panicked moment that I would never begin to breathe again.

I had no idea why, but I kept it. I smoothed it out and put it in my briefcase.

Every time I looked at Todd, I thought of that grid of dates.

At the beginning of February, Todd's weight seemed to halve itself overnight.

"He's wasting," Dr. Sara told us. "This is the end result of many contributing factors—malnutrition, prolonged bed rest, depression, cancer. It's called cachexia. His body can no longer be nourished. It's consuming its own muscles." She cleared her throat. "Including, eventually . . . his heart. His organs will begin to fail."

Food passed straight through him, if it got down at all, in a most unpleasant and painful manner. Most of it was full of blood, and, Todd reported, it burned like scalding water. Even IV supplements distressed his digestive system. Every time he ate, he was in agony. His few waking hours became nothing but convulsions of stomach cramps and an exhausting farce of sheet and clothing changes.

When Dr. Sara explained to Todd that his cancers monopolized any nutrients he did manage to keep in his body, he decided to stop eating.

It took us a minute to adjust to that, Todd waiting patiently while we convened yet again with Dr. Sara.

"He'll starve to death if you don't force the issue," she said, her voice void of judgment, her eyes avoiding Jacob's. "And it won't take long."

"It won't . . . take long . . . either way, will it?" Jacob asked her. She shook her head. Jacob nodded and said, "It's his call."

Todd studied our faces when we rejoined him. He weighed a few ounces over one hundred pounds as of that morning, and his face was stretched and cracked with the taut, tight skin of starvation.

The effect of his fast was immediate. When he was awake, he seemed sharper, more playful than he had in months. He wrote long conversations with us, he laughed out loud, and he wanted to leave his bed and go to other rooms. He was so light that it was easy, even for me or Nish, on our own, to get him into a wheelchair.

That first evening, Todd and I were home alone, and he wanted to take a bath. He ached much of the time, especially in his knees and elbows, which now seemed enormous compared with his spindly arm and leg bones. Nish had been trying out her massage techniques on him, from the class she was taking. Since she wasn't home, he thought a hot bath would be soothing. I ran the tub, wheeled him in, and began to help him undress when he stopped me and gestured for me to leave. I hesitated, and he sighed and reached for the notepad.

"I just want to be alone," he wrote. I looked at the light, wavy letters and knew that soon I'd be unable to read his writing. *"A little privacy seems like a luxury. Please?"*

He'd been poked and prodded, and bathed and dried, and handled and wiped, and generally subjected to a million indignities and invasions as of late. "Can you get in the tub without hurting yourself?" I asked. He nodded. "Okay. I'll just wait outside the door until I know you're in. There's the bell"—I pointed to the edge of the tub—"if you need me for anything." I looked at him, unbuttoning his shirt with feeble, unbending fingers, and thought there was no way he could manage this feat.

I closed the door, though, and stood waiting. I heard slight rustles of clothing. I heard the chair squeak as he shifted his weight. I heard the thump of his hand on the wall. Excruciating minutes passed, but I finally heard the plunk of one foot going in the water . . . followed by the other . . . then a squeak of skin sliding on the porcelain, a big splash and the breathiness of his laughter. I couldn't help myself, and I opened the door. He was in, and smiling, but there was water all over the floor. I mopped it up with a towel, "just so you won't slip later," and left him to his coveted privacy.

I parked myself outside the bathroom door with a stack of tests to grade. The end of the quarter loomed near, and I needed these tests finished. I read the same response to an essay question five times in a row, though, and gave up. Sitting there, back to the door, reminded me of Todd's last chemotherapy treatment, the day I'd believed I couldn't love Nicholas. Mere months ago. I examined the fingers Todd had smashed that day in this very bathroom door. The skin under the lost nail had toughened itself into a new one, surprising me. I'd expected it to grow from the cuticle out, but I realized a new nail had materialized without my even noticing it. The other damaged nail grew slowly, the purple stripe now midway across it, drifting day by day farther from the faint scar at my cuticle. Neither one hurt anymore.

Todd stayed in the tub over an hour, running more hot water twice. Finally I heard the water moving and the unmistakable sounds of him getting out. I put down the tests but bit my tongue and made myself wait to be summoned. There were more squeaks and thumps and splashes that sounded like unsuccessful attempts, but I was determined not to pester him. At last I heard two soft plops of feet on the floor and felt dizzy as I breathed normally again.

The relief was short-lived as Todd rasped out loud, "Oh, my God."

I whipped open the door.

He stood, naked, before the full-length mirror. It was steamed over, except for a clear swath he'd wiped with the towel now crumpled at his feet.

"How can someone look like this and still be alive?" he wheezed.

I'd wondered the same thing for days. Skeletal, sunken gaps between his ribs, his torso peppered with lesions, he looked alien, lizardlike. He turned away and leaned on the towel bar. "It's disgusting," he rasped.

I wrapped my arms around his still dripping body and pressed my face into the side of his leathery own. "You are not disgusting. Only the disease is."

He turned and looked at his image again, rapidly steaming over. "Hard to tell the difference anymore," he whispered.

And because I was there, he let me help him dress again. When Nish got home, complete with almond oil, Todd refused a massage. Even when she offered to pull his bed right next to the fire.

"Not in the mood," he wrote. *"Thanks, anyway."*

After two days of fasting, his body began its methodical shutting down. In the morning he got dizzy, or *"floaty,"* as he called it. By afternoon excruciating headaches seized him. *"Like ice cream too fast. Only won't stop."*

"There are painkillers, Todd," Dr. Sara told him. He'd avoided morphine, thinking it would send him into oblivion, but she convinced him to try a small amount to temper the pain.

I went to school for half a day, to tell Zackery and to leave sub plans. I told Mr. Vortee I didn't know when I'd be back. He looked a little too pleased, and I couldn't tell if it was because Todd was dying or he thought I was resigning. "You'll need to turn in grades for the quarter, of course."

Oh, God. "I'll do my best," I said.

He frowned. "I'll expect them by the end of the week."

I stared at him, then repeated, "I'll do my best." He began to stammer something, but I walked away. I knew it was rude and unprofessional, but I was too exhausted. Maybe he'd fire me, I thought with a certain amount of longing.

The next day was Todd's birthday, and he requested a celebration of sorts. Mom, Dad, and Abby came over, and we made all of Todd's favorite foods so that he could smell them and watch us eat them. We wrapped chicken enchiladas oozing cheese and sour cream and had chips and salsa and guacamole. Jacob stirred up a pitcher of margaritas and consumed most of it himself. Abby brought dark, juicy strawberries. Todd held one and breathed in its aroma. Cooper yowled to inspect it, and Todd held it out for him. The kitten bit it and hissed.

For dessert, Mom baked a pan of homemade brownies. Before

she cut them, still warm, and topped each one with a scoop of mint chocolate chip ice cream, she lit thirty birthday candles and told Todd to make a wish. He closed his eyes for a long time, finally opened them, and gestured for the rest of us to blow them out.

I'd have given anything to know what he wished.

Mom and Dad left first, but Abby lingered, cleaning up the kitchen with me as Jacob tucked Todd into bed. She picked at the last bit of brownie in the pan. "Remember what Todd did for my thirtieth birthday?"

I hoisted myself up to sit on the counter, near her. "Same as he did for my twenty-first."

He'd given me twenty-one gifts on my twenty-first birthday. A delivery service had knocked on my apartment door that June morning five years ago, with the first gifts from him, a card labeled #1, a box of Pop-Tarts labeled #2, gourmet coffee beans and a coffee bean grinder labeled 3 and 4. An index card, labeled 5, that read, "I'll pay your phone bill this month if you call me and let me listen to you eat Pop-Tarts." So I did, and he answered, groggy with the time change, but he sang "Happy Birthday" to me and made me describe how it tasted to consume more calories in one sitting than I normally did in a day. He'd contacted other company members so that everywhere I went that day, someone was handing me a gift wrapped and labeled #9, #12, and on and on, culminating with #21, a bottle of champagne to celebrate my legal age.

"I should've done that for him this time," Abby said. She stared down at the brownie pan.

It struck me that she might make a mental note to perform this ritual for my thirtieth birthday, when it came, and with that thought I felt suspended in air a sickening second, that feeling when a frightened horse shied from beneath you. I saw myself at six sitting in a blanket tent under the kitchen table with my brother and sister. Rain poured down the windows, and lightning and thunder ripped through the black sky. The air inside the tent was close and muggy. "Will you always be older than me?" I'd asked them.

"Always," Abby had promised.

"Always," Todd had promised.

But it wasn't true. On my thirty-first birthday, what they had promised me would always be, would be no more.

"Hey." Abby laid a hand on my knee as she stood beside my perch on the counter. "How's that kid who stayed here? Zackery? Was that his name?"

I tried to smile. "He's doing okay, I guess. I should call him tonight. I'm taking some time off school until . . ."

She squeezed my knee and looked at her watch. "I—I should get going. I've stayed too long."

"Too long?" I asked. "Don't you get it, Abby? That this is it? This is where you should be."

She blinked and swallowed. She shook her head.

"Todd won't be inconveniencing you—or Brad—much longer."

"That's not—I just—" she twisted the gold chain at her neck. "That's not what I meant."

"I'll tell him you'll be back tomorrow," I said.

She opened her mouth and paled stark white under her red hair. She nodded and left, closing the door as if it were an eggshell.

In their bedroom, Jake lay in the newly purchased hospital bed with his arms around Todd, Todd's head resting on Jake's chest. I heard the low murmur of Jacob's voice, talking close to Todd's ear. They both looked out the window at the milky sky.

I tiptoed to my room. I sat on the bed and dialed Simon's

house. A woman's voice, open and cheerful, answered and took my request to speak to Zack as the most natural thing in the world. She called his name, and he answered her, just a room away. He wasn't back in the garage, as I feared.

"Hey, it's me," I said when he answered. "Just checking in with you since I'm not at school." He seemed touched that I'd called. We chatted about this and that, and he inquired about Todd. I gave him the update, then asked about school.

"You didn't hear about it?" he asked. "God, there was an awful wreck in front of the school at lunch. Police and ambulances all over the place. The whole afternoon no one was having class; but we couldn't leave because the wreck was blocking the parking lot entrance. They finally let us drive across the lawn when school let out. Vortee was out there directing traffic."

"Was anyone hurt?"

"Yeah, a bunch of people. Nothing major, though. The only one seriously hurt was Lisa Robillard."

"Robillard? She related to Denny?"

"Yeah. His sister. She's a sophomore. She'd just started to drive, too. And it wasn't her fault. Some other kid was high. Last I heard today, she was in a coma. But I don't know if that's really true. The rumors kept getting more and more out of hand. Like people were saying someone had been decapitated. You know how people get."

I closed my eyes. "Oh, God. Do you know her?"

"No, not really. I mean, I know who she is."

"Oh, God. That poor family."

"Yeah, you missed a wild day. But we're holding down the fort." He went on blithely, and I knew he'd never had to hang around a hospital and wait for someone, anyone, to tell him the fate of someone he loved. "Carissa and I are going to make sure that we still get a quote of the day while you're gone. I hope you don't mind. We take them out of that book you have on top of your file cabinet. Today we put up *'Be kind, for everyone you meet is fighting a hard battle.'*"

A rush of goose bumps erupted across my body.

"Hey, listen," Zack said. "There's another call coming in. Do you want to hang on?"

"No, I should go. Keep me updated, okay?"

"Sure. Thanks for calling. Bye."

Todd had sent that Plato quote on a postcard from Nairobi after a long conversation we'd had about Grandma Anna. I'd tossed it aside flippantly, thinking Todd too idealistic for his own good. I touched my hot cheeks. I'd never appreciated, until this moment, how hard it had been for Grandma to release those prejudices, in spite of all she'd seen.

I'd never told her that I admired her for it. I'd never acknowledged that she'd even changed. I'd simply watched that night when she'd exposed her tattoo, and then they'd driven away to church. Two days later she was dead.

I thought about Todd's postcard. Even back then he'd understood her and waited. She was fighting a hard battle. Accepting Todd and Jacob together had forced her into a corner. She could reject the teachings of the faith that had enabled her to survive the camps, or she could reconcile herself with the image of her Angel burning in hell. What had she decided? What had gone through her mind? What event had turned the tide? I'd never asked her.

I wiped the tears from my cheeks. Grandma had loved Todd fiercely.

There was no love lost between me and Denny.

The battle would be all the harder.

I called the hospital and asked for a nurse I knew. She told me that yes, Lisa Robillard was there, in an intensive care unit, and yes, she was in a coma. I thanked her and hung up as Jacob appeared in my doorway.

"Hey, baby," he said. "Todd wants to talk to you."

I looked up into Jake's eyes and nodded. I stood, and he took my face in his hands and kissed my forehead, then led me downstairs to where Arnicia sat beside Todd, holding his hand, her fingertips pressed inside his wrist. Jacob kissed Todd awake and helped him get oriented. "Summer's here, babe. You wanted to talk to her." Over Todd's head he told me, "He wanted to talk to you alone." He and Arnicia went away.

I crawled into the hospital bed and held his cold, twiglike hands in mine, both of us lying on our sides, face-to-face.

"It's here . . . ," he whispered, not bothering with the notepad. He whispered without voice, so that I had to look intently at his mouth, getting the words from the shape of his lips and the percussive consonants he could spit out. I nodded and leaned my head into his. He patted my hands. "Don't be . . . so afraid. . . ."

"I'm just— Oh, God, Todd—there was so much I wanted to do, so much I wanted you to see—"

"Sum—" The last syllable of my name was only an exhalation. He poked me with his finger again, indicating "you." "Just don't . . . get it. . . ."

"Get what? Get what? Tell me."

He smiled and rested before speaking. He took in a deep breath and pushed out, "Nick."

"Nicholas? But Todd, he wants to go to D.C. He doesn't want to marry me. He thought all the things I told him—" Todd lifted a hand, tried to put it to my mouth, but he hadn't the energy. I stopped and waited for him.

He sucked in breaths between each word with effort. "You'll figure . . . out. But don't . . . be so . . . afraid. Risk."

"I don't understand, Todd."

"Help Jake. . . ."

"Don't," I said, fighting hard not to cry. "Please, Todd. What will I do without you?"

He managed a shrug. "You'll be . . . brilliant."

"Oh, God, I'll miss you," I said, sincerely believing I was dying, too, it hurt so unbearably to breathe.

"I'll . . . miss you . . . little sis . . ." Again the last syllable was a faint breath.

"I love you, Todd. I hope you know how very, very much I love you." It seemed utterly impossible to convey this.

He nodded. He knew. "I love . . . you." Sweat stood on his forehead. His breathing was labored. "Good-bye, Sum . . ."

I couldn't say it. I even shook my head. He smiled again, with a look of patience, like the dark, liquid eyes of an old horse. I think he understood. After a while he said, "I want . . . Jake now." I kissed him and left.

Arnicia sat on my bed, brushing my hair, as I called Nicholas. I got the machine. A new recording, one without my voice on it. No more "we" or "us." "Nicholas," I said, "are you there? Please pick up."

Silence.

"It's here," I said. "Can you come? Todd didn't ask for you, but . . . I am. I really need you here. I couldn't even say good-bye to him. Please come, if you can. I love you."

Arnicia hugged me when I hung up, and she held me while we slept in our clothes, on my bed.

I woke with a start at 3:11. Had I heard a noise? I listened. Arnicia breathed slowly and deeply beside me. I became convinced that this was a "sign." That Todd was gone, and Jacob would tell me he'd died right at 3:11. My heart pounded in my ears, and I slid carefully off the bed, remembering to keep weight off my bad ankle. I balanced there, rotating it, then folded the bedcover over Arnicia before creeping out of the room.

When I heard his ragged, labored breaths before I hit the bottom step, my own breath began again. I went to their doorway, and Jacob turned his head toward me. "Summer? What're you doing?"

I came close so I could speak to him. He held Todd against his torso. Sleep would be impossible for him with that noise. "Just . . . checking," I said.

He nodded.

I leaned over, kissed them both, then wandered the house. I couldn't sleep. I couldn't rest. I couldn't cry. I needed something, some task, some mindless chore, to hold me in place, keep me grounded. I imagined myself breaking into pieces I'd never be able to collect and repair. I had to do something.

I brought my briefcase downstairs and took out my gradebook and a calculator. I sat at the kitchen table and slowly, methodically, averaged grades. I didn't even look at names—I just added up the rows of numbers, double-checking each one. Recording the translation each time with a sense of completion: 75%=C, 89%=B+, 26%=F-, and on and on. I never looked up; I never checked the clock. I just listened to that grating breath and desperately added and divided. Added and divided.

When I came to the last class, I checked each student three times, not wanting to be done, not knowing what I'd do then.

Finally I closed the book. I lifted my head. Traffic moved on our street. Bleak sunlight struggled in the gray sky. Still, the breathing rasped from the bedroom.

I went to Jacob, who sat, just as I'd left him hours ago, holding Todd. Just sitting and listening to him breathe.

"Think I can make it to school and back?" He knew what I meant.

He nodded. "Going strong. But don't . . . linger, or anything."

"Just turning in grades."

I put on my coat and took the gradebook to the car. I guess I could've called someone to come get the grades, but I suddenly wanted to go. Was I running? I looked at the house as I scraped the heavy frost off my window. Would I come back? I got in and started the engine. Yes, I'd come back. But being outside, away from that unsettling gargle of his lungs, felt like getting extra oxygen.

I hated myself for even thinking that.

Half an hour still remained before homeroom when I arrived at school. I parked illegally by the back door and glimpsed my reflection in the window as I shut the door. I hoped I wouldn't see anyone—I wore no makeup, my hair was down and slept on, and I looked like a zombie from a horror film.

In and out, I told myself, and I did just that, handing the gradebook to the secretary, who said sweetly, "Hang in there, honey."

As I stepped out the back door, though, I bumped right into Denny Robillard.

He stared at me blankly a moment, as if he didn't recognize me. Then his bloodshot eyes went hard and glassy, his face setting in a mask of contempt.

"Denny, I heard about the accident. I'm so sorry about Lisa."

The mask slipped, but the eyes remained suspicious.

"Are you okay? You need anything?"

He shook his head.

"Is she—is she any better?"

He held my eyes a moment before he shook his head, ever so slightly.

"Why are you here?" I asked him, making my voice as gentle

as I could. "I mean, you should be with her, Denny. You should be with your family."

He shrugged. "Nothing I can do there." He moved sideways to step past me.

I put a hand on his arm. I didn't grab hold; I just touched him. He didn't have to stop, but he did. He kept his eyes on my hand on his arm. "I've been there, Denny," I said. "My brother had a stroke and was in a coma last spring. And it was horrible. God, Denny, it's awful, but he pulled through it. He told me when he came out of it, that when we sat with him and talked to him, he could hear us." Denny looked up, and from his expression I saw he did know a little something about love. "He could hear us," I repeated, taking my hand away. "He remembered things I read to him, stuff I said to him when he was under. It made me really glad I stayed with him as much as I did." Denny's mind was somewhere else. All kinds of thoughts were racing through his brain, behind his eyes, fixed on me, but not seeing me. "So, look, I need to go, but I want you to know that it can be really confusing at the hospital. The doctors will rush you, not explain things. If you or your parents have questions, call me at home, okay? I know a lot of the doctors and nurses. I'd be happy to help you."

He leaned in the frame of the door, holding it open, staring at me as if I'd just offered to give up my firstborn to him. "I mean it," I said. "I won't be at school for a while, but call me at home if you need to. Here." I fumbled in my coat pocket, found an old receipt and scribbled our new number on the back of it. "The number's unlisted." I shoved it into his hand.

The mask dropped completely for a split second, and he nodded. He slipped inside the door and was gone.

It had begun to snow hard, little pellets that stung my skin. I paused for a moment, at my car, and turned my face up to the sky. I allowed myself the luxury of remembering curtain calls for *The Nutcracker* at Lincoln Center, the fake snow falling down upon us, sticking to our sweating bodies. Never mind that, swept up and reused night after night, it contained gritty dirt, stray sequins, and the occasional bobby pin—it was glorious.

I opened my eyes to the quiet lot and the few sugar-dusted cars.

This felt pretty glorious, too.

Chapter Seventeen

⚮

$\mathcal{I}$ arrived back at the house as Nicholas was getting out of his car across the street. I began to cry at the sight of him. We met in the street; he hugged me, and I clung to him. He wore a black turtleneck, black cords, and black Reeboks—still in his backstage "uniform."

"I didn't check my messages until this morning," he said into my neck. "I'm sorry. I got here as soon as I could." I didn't even care where he'd been—I only cared that he was here now.

Inside, he hugged Arnicia, too. We peeked into the living room, and Jacob motioned us in. He sat beside Todd on the hospital bed, holding his hand.

I could tell Nicholas was shaken by Todd's appearance. Maybe by Jacob's, too; he had also lost weight and smiled at Nicholas with wild hair, unshaven face, and bloodshot eyes.

Todd grasped one of Nicholas's hands and smiled but said nothing. When Todd released his hand, Nicholas left the room.

I followed him and watched him step onto the back porch and take deep breaths of cold air. When he came back inside he blushed to see me. "Go be with him," he said. "I'll make break-fast."

So I went to be with Todd, who soon sniffed and nodded his

approval at the aromas of coffee and sausage filtering in from the kitchen. Arnicia sat at the foot of the bed, massaging Todd's feet. Jacob and I sat, each of us holding one of Todd's hands, saying nothing, until Nicholas served us fluffy omelets stuffed with cheese, green peppers, and sausage.

Around nine o'clock Dr. Sara came in. Todd agreed to a "full-strength" morphine drip. It was the last joke he ever made. He'd said his good-bye to Jacob last night. He was ready.

Mom and Dad came over, and Uncle Dan brought Grandma Cailee. Although everyone knew they were saying good-bye for the last time, it was serene. After an hour Todd dropped off to sleep.

"He'll come in and out," Dr. Sara informed us. "But he'll be largely incoherent."

We nodded, but she didn't rise from her seat by his side. She leaned in close to his head and brushed his cheek with the backs of her fingers. "Oh, God," she said to no one in particular. "This has to stop." She stood, businesslike again, but faltered and sat back down. Jacob, sitting on the bed, took her hand without meeting her eyes. Several minutes passed before she tried to stand again.

Abby arrived, and although Jacob offered her his seat nearest Todd, she shook her head. She looked into Todd's face, and tears fell down her own, but she never touched him like the rest of us.

Todd surfaced twice that day. He made eye contact, and I knew he was still in there. I put the pen and pad in his hands, but he didn't try to grip them or even seem to recognize them in any way.

"Leave him be," Jacob whispered. He sat next to my mother, and the two of them spooned Todd ice chips. I put balm on his chapped lips.

The first time Todd seemed present, Jacob encouraged him,

updating him. "Your skin is different now, babe," he said. "It's yellow, but not like hepatitis yellow. It's changing. You're getting closer."

Hours later he said, "Your fingernails are blue now. It won't be long. You're doing great, babe. We're all here with you."

Nicholas made everyone sandwiches for lunch, and in between his cooking and cleaning, he sat beside me and held my hand.

He had to leave around four o'clock. I walked him to his car. "We close tonight," he said. "I'll be back as soon as we strike the set."

"Hurry," I whispered.

He started to cry, and I hugged him. "I love you, Nicholas," I said.

"I love you, too." He sniffed and opened the car door. Once inside, he rolled down his window and nodded toward the house. "That's the most beautiful thing I've ever seen you do."

He rolled the window back up and drove away. I stood in the driveway long after his car left my view.

The next morning Todd smiled vaguely at the voices of Mom, Dad, and Grandma Cailee, but his one good eye strayed and rolled, not focusing, having gone blind. The skin on his face drew so tight, he couldn't close his eyes completely. Jacob put in drops when they got dry and red.

Toward noon Todd's breath grew shallow and choppy, and his pulse skittered in an erratic dance. His hands curled up. I unfurled his fingers and straightened his wrists, but every time I looked, they were clenched tight and bent inward again.

"Um . . ." Jacob cleared his throat. "I'd really like . . . um, Todd wanted . . . it to be private."

Mom started to cry but nodded. Mom and Dad both kissed

Todd again and whispered final messages to him. "We'll be at the farm," Dad said to Jacob, gently pulling Mom away.

"You don't have to leave," Jacob said. "Just—"

"Yes, we do," Mom said. "We should. Todd talked to me about it. Call us when . . ." She couldn't finish.

"I will," Jacob said, his own voice breaking, and they embraced. I wondered what strength either of them had left to offer to the other.

"Should I go?" I asked. Jacob shook his head.

It seemed later than it was, for the skies had been dark and threatening all day. Around 10 A.M. it had started to snow, and it had been snowing steadily ever since. We didn't turn on a television or radio, but if we had, we would've known that we were getting a blizzard.

Jacob and I passed the afternoon and evening side by side. We held each other's hands. We didn't say a word. Sometimes Todd moaned, and we whispered over him and stroked his wispy, featherlike hair.

The phone went dead. The lights flickered with growing frequency and finally went out.

Nish was trapped at the hospital.

Nicholas was forced off the road and into a hotel on his way to us.

We made a fire and lit candles all around the room. Cooper curled up on Todd's chest.

We continued our vigil.

Hours passed.

Todd's hands and feet curled up so tightly that I couldn't force them straight and so resigned them to their fetal state.

More snow fell.

More hours passed.

And Todd stopped breathing. No dramatic "death rattle" or convulsion. He just stopped breathing.

When he died, it was as if Todd had gotten up and left the room. Cooper jumped down from the bed, hair puffed out like a porcupine, and immediately left the room himself. Trying to follow his person, perhaps.

We watched as Todd's face released its tension-filled grimace and relaxed into as peaceful a look we had seen on his face in months.

Other parts of his body released as well, and without a word we gathered what was necessary and bathed him. Handling his battered body with care, we sponged away the mess and patted him dry. I changed the bedding while Jacob held Todd's body. We dressed him in clean dry clothes, even putting on his new Christmas shoes, and tucked him back under the down comforter.

I thought of Nicholas's words and knew that seeing my brother off on this journey was my greatest accomplishment. And there'd be no audience, no fanfare, no mention in the paper, except my name in a list of all who'd survived him.

Jacob leaned over and kissed Todd.

Then he stood and turned to me.

We went to each other and slowly rocked each other before the fire. I closed my eyes and breathed in the comforting, Ivory soap smell of my brother's lover. I rubbed my cheek against his soft sweater and the hard muscles beneath it. His own cheek rested on the top of my head, nuzzling my hair.

I have no idea how long we held each other in that dreamlike state, but we held each other desperately. I lifted my head and looked at his lined gray face. "We should sleep," I whispered.

He shook his head and said, his voice brimming with child-like fear, "I . . . I don't want to sleep by myself. . . . I c-can't . . . sleep in that bed by myself. . . ."

"Shh," I tried to comfort him. "I'll stay with you. If you want."

"You would . . . do that?"

"Come on," I said. We covered Todd's face with a sheet, blew out the candles, and closed the screen on the fire. "Do you want to sleep in my room?" I asked.

He shook his head, and I followed him to the double bed in the bay window, abandoned since the last hospital stay. "These pillows still smell like him," he said. He climbed into bed under the covers, fully clothed. He even had his shoes on.

I followed, leaving mine on as well.

We lay on our backs, side by side, staring at the snow drifting up in each windowpane.

"We never spent a night apart," Jacob whispered. "From the time we moved in together, we never spent a night apart, even when we were fighting. I haven't slept a single night without him by my side for five years."

I reached for his hand and held it.

"Do you . . . do you think we could . . . just hold each other?" he asked, more tears appearing, glistening in the snowfall's glow. "Is that too weird?"

"No, Jake, it's not too weird. I'll hold you." I turned on my side and reached out my arms. He turned, too, but his back to me, then scooted into me so that we were like spoons. We slept that way, me behind Jacob, his arm over mine across his chest, hands clasped, holding one another all night long.

We each were, for the other, as close as we could get to Todd that night. And we weren't equipped to do without him just yet.

I spent the night awake, exhausted as I was, holding Jacob, listening to him breathe, and watching the endless snow falling. Finally, as the pipes began to howl out their dirge and the sky turned gray with hints of dawn, I drifted off. Only an hour later I awoke when Jacob stirred beside me. He rolled over toward me, not quite awake, and fumbled through the folds of the quilt until his hand caressed my hip. He frowned. His eyes flew open, and I watched the realization and the memory flood into his face.

"God," he said. "Sorry."

"It's okay."

"Um . . . thanks. Thanks a lot, for last night."

"Why do I feel like it's the morning after a one-night stand?"

He didn't laugh. He pushed the tousled morning hair out of my eyes with his fingers. "I mean it, Summer. Thank you."

"I know. I didn't want to be alone, either."

And that was all we ever said about it.

The blizzard was a blessing, in that it allowed us our time to be in this emptiness without him, to test it, and find our way, without the intrusion of others. We couldn't begin to carry out the formalities, since the phones still held silence and the roads were impassable. We couldn't see the garage from the back door, the snow was so heavy.

The morning seemed so calm compared with the others of months past. Was it only months? Why did it seem as if my whole life had happened here and nothing had existed before this—this room and the routine of changing sheets and IV bags and bleaching down the bathroom and marking off pills taken and counting out pills to come and taking temperatures and drawing blood and hanging on to every word written on those yellow notepads or whispered from those yellow lips.

There was nothing to do this morning. Todd lay there and needed nothing from us any longer.

I sat beside his body and waited for myself to recognize the loss. To feel something, to do something. I breathed slowly, carefully, and listened to my own pulse.

Jacob smashed some things in the kitchen—plates and glasses and flower pots—then sat in a corner and wailed. I knew not to go to him. I sat beside Todd and waited. I didn't cry.

When Jake started cleaning up, I joined him, and we scrubbed and swept and filled garbage bag after garbage bag . . . not stopping with the broken pieces of china and the dirt and dead plants, but adding all the vestiges of the disease that had robbed us—a half-used box of latex gloves, all the medicines (a bag by themselves), disinfectants, lotions, plastic bedsheets, bedpans, piles of pamphlets, folders full of lab results, sheet after bloodstained sheet, IV bags, IV tubes, IV stands . . . the giant stack of yellow notepads.

"Stop," I said, out of breath. "I want these."

He sat down, panting, hugging his garbage bag to his chest. I thought of news footage of flood victims clutching sandbags, realizing the futility, stepping back to let the water flow.

We sat for hours, leafing through the notepads and the weeks' worth of one-sided conversations recorded there. Some pages contained doodles, some contained lists.

One list I found was headed "Things to Do Before I Die." This list began with some practical matters: 1) Funeral plans; 2) Talk to Sara re: checking out options; 3) Double-check with Kenny [his lawyer in L.A.]. Then the list became personal: 4) Sunrise w/Jake; 5) Talk: Dad; 6) Design quilt w/Mom and Grandma C.; 7) Talk: Abby; 8) Plan: Nish; 9) Package: Nicholas; 10) Morning feed w/Summer. All these things were crossed off except for number ten. We'd not done morning feed together since we were teenagers.

But the list went on, and the remaining items were what moved me most:

11) Be present

12) Risk

13) Love

14) Travel light

"The secret to life," Jacob said. He looked up at me. "What did we do?" he asked.

I shook my head, not understanding.

"What did we do to deserve him?"

By two o'clock that afternoon the snow stopped, the roads were slowly cleared, and we were converged upon. I was grateful for the time alone with Todd, before the coroner carted him off and relatives filled the house, all bearing food and talking far too much.

Nish took charge, when she finally got home, and was protective of Jake, who wandered from room to room, dazed and bewildered.

Grandma Cailee hugged and rocked Mom, who howled at the ceiling.

Dad sat next to Todd's now empty bed and put his hands on the slight indentation left there, hard, stony lines engraved upon his face. Abby sat next to him, rubbing his back as she stared at nothing, her face exhausted, her eyes dead.

Other relatives milled about, murmuring and whispering.

So many formalities, rituals, silliness. It grew difficult to breathe.

Nicholas burst through the back kitchen door and froze. He looked at Arnicia organizing food on the table and counters. He looked at all the people. He looked at me, and he knew. I went to him and hugged him. "Oh, Summer, I'm sorry. I'm so sorry. I tried to make it—"

"Shh," I said. "I was okay. I did all right."

He pulled back from my embrace and asked, "Can I—? Is he still—?" He looked toward the living room.

I shook my head. "They took him away."

Nicholas sank to the floor and wept. I crouched behind him and wrapped my arms around him.

Jacob came into the kitchen, looked down at us, and said, "I have to get out of here."

"Go," Arnicia said to us. "You need to get out. Go. I'll tell your folks."

So we did. Hideously underdressed, we trudged through the deep, drifted snow in the backyard to the driveway. Our cars were buried, so Nicholas led us to his own, parked on the street. The wheels spun on the bricks but finally rolled forward. We skidded and swerved away.

We didn't discuss it, but I wasn't surprised when Jacob drove us to the farm. I remember thinking how absurd it was—Mom and Dad had come to our house, and we had left to go to theirs.

We sat in the driveway. I thought of Todd's list and that unfulfilled number ten. Morning feed with Summer.

I got out of the car and waded through the knee-deep snow to the barn. The horses were all gathered at the gates. They whinnied and tossed their heads when they saw me coming. I went into the empty barn. The grain sat cold and hard in every feed box. I looked at the geldings rattling one gate. Ice encrusted their manes and tails, pearls of it strung in their whiskers. They'd been out all night. It was only snow; it hadn't been that cold. These horses were hardy and healthy and turned out all winter, anyway. It just surprised me; Dad was usually such a softie when we had bad storms.

And they hadn't been given breakfast.

There was not a one of them in danger of starving. But I felt the extent of Dad's distraction with the tenderness of a bruise.

I opened the geldings' gate, the aluminum sticking to my bare hands. They filed past me, and I followed them to their stalls, shutting and latching each door behind them as they began grinding their corn. "Like one giant machine," I said out loud, remembering.

The ponies, too, went dutifully to their stalls.

But not the mares.

Their feet crunched in the snow as they came in for breakfast, big clouds of their breath hovering in the air. I quaked from the cold—for I had no hat or gloves or coat—and from the sorrow bubbling in my chest. They stopped inside the gate and clustered around me, just like the mourners at a funeral. Their boxes of grain lay waiting in their freshly bedded stalls, yet they all stayed with me and gently lipped my sleeves and hair in sympathy, blowing hot breaths of comfort across my face. Chaos laid her velvety head into my chest, her long ears tickling my chin.

I sank to the snow, amid all those hooves, and sobbed until my throat ached and was raw. The mares lowered their heads to me, watching with kind, maternal eyes.

"Summer?" The heads lifted, ears pricked, and turned to this intruder. It was Nicholas. He held a blanket for me. "Come in from the cold, love," he pleaded.

I stood and let him enfold me in the blanket. He even covered my head and kissed my frozen cheeks and eyelids. The mares stayed in their huddle and watched us walk to the house.

"What package did Todd give you?" I asked him as he led me up the stairs to my old room. He patted my back as if he believed I were delirious. "His list mentions a package to give to you," I said, "and he marked it off."

"Oh . . . yeah, that was weird. He gave that to me a long time ago. Something he wanted me to mail for him."

"Oh." It seemed so anticlimactic. "Who was it for?"

"It was addressed to the postmaster."

Nicholas tried to tuck me into my old bed, but I held fast to him. "Nicholas, please," I said. "I was wrong. I want to marry you—"

"Shh," he said, prying himself free from my grasp. "You can't decide that today. Not today."

I wouldn't let him go. "I love you, Nicholas."

"I love you, too." There was a pause. "But . . . I don't believe you."

I blinked.

"I just think," Nicholas said, "with all that's happened, you can't trust your emotions right now."

"I'm not just doing it for Todd; this is what I want."

He slumped his shoulders. "Summer, I'm not going to listen to you today. You can't tell me this today."

I had to laugh. "You sound just like Todd when he asked me to move in."

He looked into my eyes. "I'm not Todd."

My laugh died. "I know."

"And I don't want to be his substitute," Nicholas said, his voice thick with emotion.

And he left me. I slept for fourteen hours straight, like a woman in a coma.

Nicholas told me later that he'd gone back to the barn, but the mares had wandered back to the field without eating their breakfast. Not knowing what else to do, he'd shut the gate behind them again.

Somehow that day ended, and the next began, and the next day ended, and another began.

There was a funeral. Jacob said some things. My father said some things. Both of them managed to finish, although they both wept their way through it.

Todd was cremated. It took five hours. Five hours, and all that remained of thirty years of life was a silty, splintery boxful of ashes, an amount smaller but surprisingly heavier than I expected.

A few days later Jacob took the ashes and scattered them around the pond and the big rocks where we used to sun dry. I stood on the hillside and watched him. The ashes lay gray and stark on the snow, reminding me of Todd's lesions. Then they sank through the snow and disappeared, leaving delicate, coral-like lace behind. Jacob sat on a rock, hugging the empty urn, and I walked away and left him there. He didn't come back in until dinner.

I took two weeks off from school. I couldn't get my mind to wrap around any clear thought or my body to perform any simple task. I walked a lot, in the snow, often wandering down to the pond, where I found myself regretting there was no marker, no stone, no way for Jacob to one day be buried alongside his Todd, their love memorialized in death like millions of married couples.

I didn't ride Chaos but spent many hours in her stall, standing beside her, my face against her long winter coat. She let me be there, sometimes releasing a sigh heavy with contentment.

Nish went to stay with her sister for a while. She called every day.

Neither Jacob nor I ever went back to spend a night in the house. We retrieved Cooper and returned every other day to carry out more belongings, but we never went alone, and we never stayed. Mom invited Jake to live at the farm until he made plans.

We were a muted, lost little group.

Once, at two in the morning, I met my mother in the hallway outside my old room. Hand in hand we went to the kitchen.

Jacob was already there, in the dark, on the floor, leaning against the refrigerator with a bottle of bourbon in his arms. He looked up at us, eyes raw and weepy, and said, "I can't sleep without him."

We'd meet there often, the three of us. We'd make cocoa we never drank. We'd look at childhood photos. We'd tell stories.

One night Jacob said, "I have to go." My mother nodded, but I resisted. Everyone was abandoning me.

"I can't just stay here, wallowing in this," he said to me. "I've got to work. I've got to do something. I think I need to go back to L.A. It's time."

It was time for me, too.

The next day I went back to school.

Chapter Eighteen

The first thing I found, opening my briefcase, was that bingo game.

It haunted me the entire day, through all the mumbled I'm sorrys and sympathetic glances. Through the stack of tasteful cards piled in my mailbox. Through all the eyes that wouldn't quite meet my own. Through all the bowed heads and hushed, polite voices.

Other than Zackery greeting me with a wordless hug in the morning, I didn't feel a real connection to another person all day long.

I saw the grid. I saw the dates. And I finally saw Denny Robillard.

He wouldn't look at me at all.

But when the bell rang and his class got up to leave, I heard myself saying, "Denny? Wait a second, okay?"

He turned warily, not sure what attitude to adopt. He opted to slump back down in his desk, casual, legs splayed. I sat opposite him and laid the bingo game on his desk.

"What's this?" he asked.

"You know what it is. Nobody won, I guess. The date's not on there. Although this one is close." I tapped the block marked March 2.

He looked at the game. He didn't know what to say. I didn't, either, but again I heard words coming out of me. "He died. My brother. The faggot, you know." The words weren't angry. I guess that's what scared him, because he nodded meekly.

"How's your sister?"

"The same," he whispered.

"Do you talk to her?"

He nodded.

I looked at him and remembered all the times I'd wanted to slug him. "It feels like she's gone, doesn't it?" He didn't respond. I pushed my luck. "Do you miss her?"

He pursed his lips, creating dimples where I'd never noticed them on him before. He nodded.

"Ah," I said. "Then you can probably relate. My brother's gone, Denny. My big brother, who taught me how to swim. And to ride a bike. Did you teach Lisa to ride a bike?" He stared at the desktop. I went on. "He was thirty for three days when he died, Denny. Barely thirty. Think about that. That's not very old. And think about this: From the time he was a high school senior, his days were numbered. He didn't know it, but already there was a limit to what he would accomplish and experience in the world. You just never know. And that's why maybe you shouldn't be wasting time, Denny." I handed him the bingo game. I made him take it. "On so much hate."

I got up and left the room on legs that felt as though I'd just finished a full-length ballet. I could barely feel my feet hit the floor. I went to the bathroom and washed my face. I stood in there a long time, but when I came back, Denny was just leaving my room. He didn't see me, down the hall. He walked slowly.

*   *   *

Jacob decided to take very little with him when he returned to L.A.

He gave me Cooper to keep. Cooper had really been Todd's cat, not their cat, and Jake found it hard to have him around. At the house, after Todd died, and then, at the farm, whenever anyone came to the door Cooper rushed into the room, full of expectation, and then shrank when he saw it wasn't his person. He looked from the visitor to the floor and blinked his golden eyes.

Jacob took clothes off hangers and tossed them into his suitcase. "Todd wanted you guys to have him."

"You guys?" I asked.

He shrugged. "He meant you and Nicholas. Cooper was supposed to be, you know, a housewarming . . . a wedding gift. . . ."

I bent to fold a shirt he'd wadded up.

"But, that's okay," Jake said. "He wanted you to have him anyway."

That "anyway" left a bitter taste in my mouth.

I took Jacob to the airport by myself. We left early and stopped on the way to say good-bye to Arnicia at her sister's.

"He paid off my student loans," she told us. "I'm gonna name my first son Todd."

Jacob teased her, "You're gonna name your son after some white guy?"

"Honey, and a faggot to boot."

We left her and drove to the airport. At his terminal we sat far from the rest of the travelers and held hands. "We made it through together, Summer," he said, looking straight ahead.

I nodded.

He turned and studied me, and I watched his gaze travel over my forehead, my nose, my jaw. "You are so like him," he said. "You even look like him. The way his face used to be. Before."

I brought a hand to my face, and my fingertips explored my lips and chin.

"Is it ruined with Nicholas?"

I nodded.

"No hope at all?" he asked.

"I was ready to marry him," I said. "I called him, but he told me he took that job in D.C. He thanked me . . . for setting him free."

Jacob chewed his lip and watched me a moment. "What did you say to him?"

I shrugged. "What could I say?"

He clapped a hand to his forehead. "Jesus, how this race perpetuates is beyond me, you all are so unimaginative."

I laughed. "What? What would you have done?"

He cradled my cheek just a moment with his palm, and I couldn't help but know he was thinking of Todd. He drew his hand away in the same second the thought occurred to me. "Get your shit together, Summer," he said, looking out the window at the planes taxiing in and out. "And dump half of it. Remember that list."

He got up and boarded his plane without further ado. I stood at the window long after the plane carried him away.

March turned into April.

I turned in my resignation letter for Old Mill High School. Vortee never commented.

I mailed a résumé to Cincinnati's High School for the Arts.

Nicholas didn't return several messages I left him on his machine.

I tried to train Chaos, who remained true to her name.

Zackery went on spring break with Simon and missed two weeks of school.

Mr. Vortee paid "casual" visits to observe my classroom twice a week.

Denny refused to look at or speak to me.

Living in my parents' home again felt oppressive. I longed to be alone and felt more lonely than I ever had in my life.

Lonely enough that I called my sister.

I went to Abby's house after school on a Thursday late in April. She assured me Brad would be working.

Her home was breathtaking, if formal, in its modern luxury. Outside, it looked like a designer greenhouse, appearing from a distance to be made solely of windows. Inside, it felt like a museum. I'd been in it on only two other occasions, and much of what I remembered was redecorated or remodeled. "My little projects," she said, blushing, when I mentioned them. "I need something to keep me busy. I just might go crazy, otherwise."

"It's gorgeous, Abby. It's a beautiful home."

"It's not a home at all," she said, walking away from me before I could answer.

I followed her through the marble-floored hallway to a small dining nook where chocolate brownies awaited us on antique china and coffee in a sterling silver service.

We sat across from each other, and neither one of us knew what to say. I began to regret that I'd arranged this visit. I took a sip of coffee.

"You hate me, don't you?" Abby asked.

I spat my coffee, spattering brown droplets on the ivory tablecloth.

"I don't hate you," I said, wiping my mouth with the cloth napkin.

"I can feel it, how much you hate me, how much you think it was all my—"

"Abby, I don't hate you. I only wish you weren't with Brad. I don't understand how—"

"No, Summer, you don't. And it's none of your business."

"Okay," I said, more than happy to let this subject go.

"Todd never let up about that, you know, about Brad. Every phone call. Every letter. Even when he was gone—you know, traveling. Those postcards he sent us? He was even doing it then! Here, look." She stood and pulled a tea tin off the shelf. Todd had brought it to her from India. "I've been looking at these every night for the last month and a half." She pulled out the stack of postcards and handed two to me. One was of a monument in Innsbruck:

"And remember, we all stumble, every one of us. That's why it's a comfort to go hand in hand."—Emily Kimbrough.

And the other featured sleeping lions in Kinshasa:

"The things which matter most must never be at the mercy of the things that matter least."—Goethe.

"See?" she said, leaning over my shoulder. "It was years before I understood about the postcards. I always thought they were about him. That's how I read them. But, see, he understood that I wouldn't listen to him. All those postcards from all over the world. They were about me. He was still trying to give me brotherly advice all the way from Zaire." She looked at the postcard and repeated "Zaire." She looked up at me. "He went to Zaire. When it still *was* Zaire. I wish I could do something like that."

"You could," I said.

She shot me a look. "Not brave enough. Besides, I'm stuck here, in my little prison. You know, Todd never saw this house? I've lived here, what? Seven, eight years? And he was never once invited inside."

This was not at all what I wanted this visit to be. "Um . . . he would have loved it," I said, looking around, knowing I lied but not having the courage to say anything else. "It's beautiful."

She laughed, a harsh, one-note exhalation. "Well, all this beauty comes at a price."

"Everything has a price, Abby. Everything."

"Some people have to pay more than others. Like Todd." She stared down at the postcards as her face quivered in her effort not to cry.

I stood up. I didn't know what to say or what to do. A minute stretched out into a decade as I stood there.

"So I can pay this," Abby said through her tears. "This one is easy."

"Oh, Abby, no," I said. I saw her with new clarity, as though a dirty window had been scrubbed clean. I crossed to her and took her in my arms. "No, no, no. Are you staying to punish yourself? You can't do that. You don't need to do that."

"It's all my fault," she said.

"No. No, it isn't. That's such bullshit! You're not responsible for Todd's death. You're not responsible for him getting sick." She buried her face in my neck. I stroked her hair. I rocked her. "And you know who would be the first to say that to you?" I took her by the shoulders and held her at arm's length. The years between us felt reversed. "Todd, that's who. He'd say this was utter bullshit, Abby, and you know it."

"But—but . . ." She sniffed. "But I told him—"

"You told him what? That if he told people he was gay, he might get beat up? He might be embarrassed? That we all might be embarrassed? You were probably right, Abby. What—because you were a few years older you were supposed to be an expert? You're not a psychiatrist. You didn't hold a gun to his head and say, 'You must fuck Becka Maynard'—did you? Did you?"

She laughed just a little and shook her head. She wiped her eyes with the back of her hand, smearing her eyeliner.

"Well, then," I said, "how can it be your fault?"

"I suggested it."

"But he actually did it. Not you."

"He regretted it."

"Abby, we all do things we regret. That's just life. We're human. We make mistakes."

"But it was a horrible mistake. I should have told him that it didn't mat—"

"Abby, listen to me: Maybe you wish you'd said things differently. But the bottom line is this: You are not responsible for Todd having AIDS."

She closed her eyes. She took a deep breath. She opened her eyes and blinked. "Say it again," she whispered. I did. A change went through her body, as if she'd just stepped into a warm bath. She opened her arms. We hugged each other. "Thank you," she whispered into my hair. "Thank you. I always thought you thought that."

There'd been some years I thought I thought that, too, but all I said was, "No."

And as we ate all the brownies, every last one, and drank wine instead of coffee, I felt so light, so buoyant. As though I'd float out of my chair if I didn't keep a hold on the table.

When Abby and I stood on the porch saying good-bye, her mailman walked, whistling, up the driveway.

"Oh, good," Abby said. "I like the chance to go through it all first."

"Do you have something to hide? Or does Brad?" I asked.

She laughed. "Both." I shook my head as she thanked the mailman and sorted through the mail. "Bill, bill, bill," she said, going through the hefty pile. "Radiology lab, my ass." She held an envelope up to the fading afternoon light. "Bastard." She tucked the offending letter into the pile and stopped cold. She blanched so rapidly, her childhood freckles stood out on her white skin.

"Abby?" I asked. "Abby? What is it?" I moved to her side and saw the unmistakable, beloved handwriting on the envelope she held.

"How?" she whispered. "H-how—"

"Open it!"

She dropped all the other letters. Some fell off the porch onto the soggy spring ground. She opened the letter with shaking fingers, reverent in her attempt to keep every word written by his hand intact. Inside was a piece of yellow notebook paper. I thought I might have to grab the porch rail to keep from lifting right off into the sky.

She read it. She smiled.

"He's still at it," she said. She handed it to me.

My dearest Abby,
"Life is too short to be the caretaker of the wrong details."
—Alexandra Stoddard.
Let it go. I love you.
Todd

I handed it back, and she pressed it to her heart, then looked at the envelope again. "This is postmarked yesterday. How did he manage it?"

I felt that sensation of bird wings fluttering against my ribs. "Nicholas!"

"What?" Abby asked.

Todd couldn't be sure of a date when he'd prepared these. Our brother had been playing a bingo game of his own.

"The package he— Nicholas took it to the post office— Oh, my God! I have to go! I have to check my mail!" I ran to the car. I glanced in the rearview mirror at the end of the long, winding drive. Abby stood on the porch, her hair and the discarded letters lifting gently on the wind.

Chapter Nineteen

I sprayed gravel pulling into the drive at the farm, one foot on the ground before the car was completely in park. I fumbled with the metal post box by the road. I yanked it open. Empty.

I roared up the driveway, slammed the car door shut, and ran, my heels sinking into the spring ground, to the back door.

My parents sat at the kitchen table. They each held a letter in their hand. Yellow notebook paper. "Did I get one?" I asked, panting.

My mother nodded and handed it to me.

I opened mine. I wanted to tear it open but, like Abby, wanted to keep even my own name and address written by my big brother's hand.

Inside was:

Dear Summer,

Don't hurry with Chaos. She's a lot like you. She's out to prove things that don't matter, and she misses the main point. It's gonna take some time.

"The pleasure of love is in loving. We are happier in the passion we feel than in that we arouse." —François La Rochefoucauld.

I love you,

Todd

I tried to call Nicholas. Again there was no answer. All I said, after the beep, was, "Call me, please? Or come over? I miss you."

Jacob answered at his new number, though. He was working again. By the end of next month he'd be back on his old "daytime drama." Big Ed Baker was leaving the cult in a Waco-like fiasco.

He had a letter from Todd, too. Todd had addressed it to their own old Dayton home, and Jacob regretted that a yellow forwarding sticker obscured Todd's handwriting. His read:

My dearest love,
I have nothing left to tell you. We have no unfinished business. All I
can do is thank you, and remind you:
"Wherever you are and in every circumstance, try always to be a lover
and a passionate lover. Once you have possessed love, you will remain
a lover in the tomb, on the day of resurrection, in paradise and for-
ever." —Rumi.
I'll be waiting, lover.

He stopped twice as he read it.

I read him mine, and he said, "I might just have to come take that cat away from you if you don't get a move on."

"I'm trying, Jacob. Really I am. And you couldn't take this cat from me if you wanted to."

As if in answer, Cooper chirped and leapt into my lap. He was growing up big, as yellow tomcats often seem to get, complete with boxing-glove paws with the spare toe—all four of them white to match his bib and belly. He sat upright, stiff and formal, facing me as I talked to Jacob, his eyes level with my own. He watched my lips move as if he were a deaf person, sometimes even reaching a paw to my lips as if mesmerized by their movement.

"I miss Todd," I said. I hated that I said it.

There was a long silence.

"Yeah, me too." I felt stupid, knowing what a gross understatement that was. After another pause Jacob said, "But we've got to move on, Summer. Let it go."

Move on. Let it go. Just phrases in a language I couldn't speak.

As the weather grew warmer, Chaos began to shed her winter, chili-powder coat for a slick, sassy one of red pepper.

Kelly worked with us, and I marveled at how she managed to conceal her boredom. Our lesson on this particular May evening was trying to cajole Chaos into a relaxed walk. She wanted to trot, and to trot fast. When she stopped trotting, she didn't really ever admit to walking. Instead she jigged—a nervous, staccato gait, like a marionette puppet of a horse. I exhaled. I tried to weigh more than I did. I envisioned myself a torso of butter melting down her sides. I kept my shoulders back. I left the reins long and low, my knuckles growing grimy with her sweat and shedding hair.

After an hour of jigging and prancing and fussing her way through serpentines and circles and diagonal lines, she snorted and walked. She seemed to gain two inches on each side of her ribs as she just relaxed.

"What a good girl," I said, leaning forward to rub her shoulder with one hand. "See? It didn't have to be so hard. That's all I wanted."

"That's all she wanted, too," Kelly said, smiling in the orange pink glow of the setting sun. "She just thought you expected something more."

The warm weather brought trouble at school. The students were restless, weary, and mentally already long gone from this building, especially the seniors. Every day became a struggle just to capture attention spans, much less maintain them. Classes wandered in insolently after the bell—and I just stood, biting my tongue, trying hard to pick my battles in these last weeks.

Even Zack was worthless as a student. Our morning meetings remained routine, however, and I looked forward to them.

As I was heading to the parking lot one day after school, Zackery fell into step beside me. He giggled, and I looked over at him. He was almost skipping. "What's up with you?" I asked.

"Look!" He handed me an envelope. "I just got it from the guidance counselor last period." Inside was an acceptance letter from an out-of-state university.

"Congratulations! This is great!" We hugged each other and spun around. He gave me a big kiss on the cheek. "We have to celebrate," I said. "What sounds good?"

He thought a moment. "Ice cream."

"Ice cream it is."

He went straight to my car and let himself in the passenger seat. It wasn't until I backed out of my parking space that I saw our small audience by the door.

We indulged ourselves at an old-fashioned ice-cream parlor on the outskirts of town, where our waitress was a student from school who raised her eyebrows when we came in. Zack ate some monstrous thing that came in what looked like a fish bowl, complete with bananas, a giant crown of whipped cream, and not one, but five cherries atop the several scoops of ice cream and flavors of topping. I ordered a restrained root beer float.

Zack had pictures from the spring break trip he and Simon had taken to Cancún. In one photo Zack stared morosely at Simon, who had his arm around a tan blond babe with oiled breasts spilling out of her white bikini.

"Yikes," I said. "Who's that?"

"Some slut Simon fell in love with," he said.

I looked up at his expression of desolation, every bit as raw as when the photo was taken. "It was Simon, wasn't it?" I asked. "In the poem?"

He bloomed in red mottles and lifted one shoulder.

"I remember," I said. "Simon worked set crew for extra credit for his theater class."

"No," Zack said with a bemused smile. "He worked set crew because Leslie Cambridge was in the play." He sighed. "I worked set crew because he did." He lifted his shoulder again. "I'm over it."

"Oh, Zack." I reached across to squeeze his hand just as our waitress brought the check. She could barely contain her curiosity.

"People ask me about us," Zack said when she wandered away, looking back at us over her shoulder. "They all think we're doing it in the bookroom every morning. I tell them you're not my type."

"Zack."

"They just think I mean older women."

"Oh, thank you very much."

He grinned.

"It's a good thing I resigned before I got fired for having an affair with a student."

"So, it's true? I heard you were leaving."

"Word travels fast."

"What are you going to do?" he asked.

"Honestly? I have no clue." I slurped my float. "I hope I'm back teaching at the School of the Arts in Cincy. I student-taught there and they wanted me to stay, but I needed to be closer to Dayton, for Todd."

He nodded. "I'm glad you'll still be teaching," he said. He took another bite of his obscene dessert and laughed. "Hey, I've been meaning to tell you, Denny Robillard defended you the other day."

"Defended me?"

"Yeah, you walked by at lunch, and some football players said, 'There's the fag hag,' or something equally charming, and Denny told them to shut up. I was behind them in line."

"You're kidding me."

"No, seriously. He said you were 'cool as shit.' I guess that's a compliment. He said, 'She's the best.'"

The best. Neither of them had any idea the impact those words had on me.

I pulled into the drive at home just as my dad was walking back to the house from evening feed. He waved and opened the back door. Cooper cantered out into the yard in his cougarlike way. I called to him, and he ran to my feet, hugging my leg with his forearms. I lifted him like a child, under his armpits, and hoisted him to my shoulder. He purred in my ear as I strolled behind the barn to study my red mare in the early evening light.

Chaos stopped chewing and froze, muscles tensed. She raised her head, ears pricked at me. My heart melted when she nickered softly. I called to her, "I'm just looking at you, you pretty girl."

I was discovering her bit by bit. I'd finally begun to understand her secrets. And my own.

Chaos nickered again and lowered her head to resume grazing.

Knowing her was the consolation prize of loss.

Cooper yowled, and a voice answered him, "Hey, Coop." It was Nicholas.

"Hey, you," I said, a thrill of adrenaline jumping through me. "What are you doing here?"

He shoved his hands into his pockets and grinned. "You said to come over. I'm a glutton for punishment, I guess."

"No, you're a sadist. You like to punish me. I thought you'd dropped off the face of the earth."

We laughed and let the unspoken remain so for a while longer. "So, how's Chaos?"

"She's good," I said. "We've made progress lately. She's really blossomed here. I hope once I move her, it's not like starting all over again."

Nicholas leaned on the fence. "Why would you move her?"

"I've been trying to talk to you about that. I left you a million messages. I—I'm moving back to Cincinnati."

Something shifted in his face. He opened his mouth and stammered, "But—but, what'll you do?"

"Well, I'm interviewing for a job at the School of the Arts."

"You're going to keep teaching?"

I shrugged. "I think for another year, at least. And somewhere besides Old Mill. To see how it is when I'm not dealing with . . . well, you know, without all that going on . . . you know what I mean."

He nodded. "Wow. This is a switch."

"Well, I think, maybe I'm good at it. Maybe not all the actual classwork stuff, but I could get better at that."

"What about making your mark?"

I sighed. "I was stupid, okay? Besides, this job is important."

"Hell, yes, it's important." Chaos began to amble away from us, toward the other mares. "Good for you, Summer."

Cooper squirmed out of my arms and onto Nicholas's shoulder. He began licking Nicholas's ear in earnest. I watched Nicholas tousle with Cooper, who would not be dissuaded from his vigorous cleaning of Nicholas's ear and neck, before I said, "I'd like to keep our apartment. Have you given them notice about the lease?"

"No. I was going to keep it, actually. You know, to have a home base between shows. See what happens after the Arena season. I was thinking I'd sublet it or something, while I was gone."

"Oh. Well, I'd . . . I'd love for you to use it as home base. If, you know, you wouldn't mind my living there, too."

He plucked Cooper from his shoulder and lowered his head, petting the cat in his arms. I couldn't see his face.

"I'd like it to be our home base," I said. "Our home again."

He looked up at me. He started to speak but stopped and nodded. He finally whispered, "We could give it a try."

I kissed him. Cooper mewed and muttered, getting squashed between us.

The kiss lasted, and Cooper jumped from Nicholas's arms to the fence and from there to the ground, stalking away in disgust. We sank to the ground as well and sat together, looking up at the emerging stars in the violet sky.

"What did Todd say to you? . . . You got a letter, right?"

Nicholas nodded. "Rainer Maria Rilke said it." He quoted, " *'For one human being to love another; that is perhaps the most difficult of all our tasks, the ultimate, the last test and proof, the work for which all other work is but a preparation.'*"

The next day, after school, I stepped into the hot parking lot. The weather had finally turned. The blacktop gave slightly under my feet, and the edges of the parking lot shimmered and danced in waves.

As I drove home, my blouse soaked through with sweat and the back of it stuck to the seat. I rolled down all the windows and let my hair fly in the wind. When I pulled off the interstate onto my parents' road, the air was sugary with honeysuckle and lilac, the dogwood trees lining the driveway in full, resplendent bloom.

I didn't stop at the house. I walked straight to the pond, carrying my heels in one hand. I shed my clothes on the bank and slipped into the cool dark water. I ducked under, like a porpoise, then climbed up to the big rock and lay on my back in the sun, looking up into the bright blue sky. I felt the water evaporate from my skin, the breeze drying my hair.

I lay there for over an hour, listening to a dog barking in the distance and the occasional whinny from the fields above. I lay there remembering. I lay there letting go.

When I sat up, my legs were bright pink. I pressed my fingers into them and watched the white fingerprints fill up with pink again, then noticed my fingers themselves. Only a thread of purple remained on the tip of my once bruised fingernail, so thin that a quick filing would erase the last trace. The scar on my fingers glowed white against my tanned skin. The scars on my ankle flamed red.

There was dirt on my toe. Light, flaky gray dirt. I dipped it in the water and watched the flakes drift away, bobbing and twirling. Doing a dance.

"Bye," I whispered. I'd never said it.

I drew my knees in to my chest and wrapped my arms around them. I threw my head back, closed my eyes, and breathed. The algae on the water's edge. The sunbaked horse manure. The fresh, new grass. The hot, cooking rock. The watercress. The mint. The air. The air, heavy with promise, of summer just beginning.

About the author

About the book

Insights,
Interviews
& More ...

Read on

Meet Katrina Kittle

I LOVE QUOTES. I've kept notebooks full of favorite lines from books and movies since I was a kid. My love of quotes is apparent in my first novel, *Traveling Light*. It's apparent to anyone who sees my writing office, too—Post-its and postcards with quotes cover every inch of bulletin board. Some quotes are painted directly on my multicolored walls. The newest one that inspires me is from Julia Cameron's *The Sound of Paper*. She writes, "In order to make art, we must first make an artful life, a life rich enough and diverse enough to give us fuel."

I feel my life is sometimes almost "too" artful! And it always has been, for as long as I can remember.

I grew up in Dayton, Ohio, in a home where books were prized possessions and reading was a treasured pastime. My dad encouraged me to read great books long before the same titles were required in school. A voracious "chain reader," my dad still greets me at the door whenever I visit with, "Did you bring me any books?" My sister Monica and I have a friendly rivalry, competing for Good Daughter points based on how many books we deliver. I feel the competition is slightly unfair for two reasons: her husband works in a bookstore and gets access to advance reading copies, and the books I actually write myself should count at least twice! When I read a good book, it's a habit to pass it on to my dad and discuss it with him, a tradition we've kept since my junior high days.

Left to right: Dad, big sister Monica, Mom, and Trina (doing the infamous "say cheese" face), Christmas 1968.

> **"** When I read a good book, it's a habit to pass it on to my dad and discuss it with him, a tradition we've kept since my junior high days. **"**

My mom was a preschool teacher extraordinaire, the kind of teacher all parents want guiding their kids. Even though she's retired from teaching, neighborhood kids still knock on her door asking her to identify the fossils and bugs they find, knowing she'll be excited and eager to help them. She taught me to be curious and always to look at the world with the discovering eyes of a child. These are traits that serve me well as a writer.

I remember thinking of myself as a writer way back in grade school, though I never thought about writing for publication until I graduated from college. Former classmates to this day tease me about the interminable stories I was always writing about horses or bands of stray animals. I have journals dating back to third grade and leading all the way to the present day. Their existence in the world somewhat troubles me, but I don't ever plan to run for public office so I think it's safe to keep them! From the time I was a little girl, we often wrote original stories for each other and it's still a tradition to write a poem for the birthday person. These birthday poems feature such stellar, masterfully rhymed opening stanzas as:

Lauren Reed

> *Once there was a girl named Monica.*
> *She did not celebrate Hanukkah.*
> *She was married to Rick,*
> *who was really quite slick,*
> *'cause he could play the harmonica.*

Or for my father:

> *Once, a man had two lovely daughters,*
> *Time telling them stories was never a bother.*
> *He made up tales outlandish and silly,*
> *Behaving much like a goat, especially a billy.*

I'm embarrassed to admit that those are recent examples and not verses written by an eleven-year-old!

My childhood was full of fuel such as hiking in the woods, camping with Girl Scouts, playing with my pet rabbit Stevie (the Fun Bun of Fairborn), bossing the neighbor kids into huge theatrical productions, and horses. I never outgrew that smitten phase most young girls go through with horses. I took riding lessons at the magical Rocky Point Farm. I worked there in the summers—feeding and mucking stalls and soaping saddles— and boarded the horses I would lease for the summer show season in exchange. It was my second home and the place where many of my fictional animal characters originated.

I'm eternally grateful to my parents for never buying me the horse I pleaded for. Because I had ▶

66 I never outgrew that smitten phase most young girls go through with horses. **99**

With Stevie Bunny, in seventh grade (dig those glasses and feathered hair), February 1982.

Meet Katrina Kittle *(continued)*

to plan, and work, and budget, and save to earn my way to a horse myself, I learned invaluable discipline and the extreme satisfaction of achieving goals, without which I would never have been able to finish a novel.

Thanking Silhouette at my very first horse show ever, 1979.

Originally interested in dance and theater, I studied at the North Carolina School of the Arts and settled at Ohio University, first as a theater major, then accepting an invitation to join the Honors Tutorial Program in English. I led quite the artful undergrad life—I had a double major in English and education, worked in the theater costume shop, rode on the university's equestrian team, kept a theater minor, and moved from one funky apartment to another every single year (bless my poor parents who were there to help each time!). I graduated in 1990 with two undergraduate degrees (practicality has never been my strong suit) and earned the honor of Outstanding Graduating Senior in both of my major departments.

I taught high school AP British Literature and theater for five years, then spent several years freelancing as a children's theater director and creative writing instructor. I covered all ages in my creative writing workshops. I taught a group as young as third grade, and once had an eighty-year-old student in my Fiction Intensive course at the Antioch Writers' Workshop.

During "the freelance years," I also worked in case management support at the AIDS Foundation Miami Valley (now the AIDS Resource Center), cleaned houses (which I found very Zen-like and perfect for the writing life: you get left alone with your hands busy doing mindless work while your brain can simmer story ideas), and worked as a veterinary assistant. I was always seeking the "perfect job" that would allow me more time to write. I discovered that there is no perfect job, and if you want to write, you simply must. If the true desire is there, you will find ways to carve out time

> ❝ I was always seeking the 'perfect job' that would allow me more time to write. I discovered that there is no perfect job, and if you want to write, you simply must. ❞

when there seems to be none. I became very disciplined and ruthless about defending my writing time from other obligations.

I'm now teaching sixth and seventh grade English at the Miami Valley School in Dayton, having learned that my writing thrives on routine. Morning hours are my most productive time, so during the school year, I get up at 5:00 a.m. and write for two hours before going to school. That sounds dismal, but, truly, I get more done in those two fresh hours than I do in an entire free evening after a day of teaching (middle schoolers will wear you out). And I'm a happier, more generous teacher, having accomplished this progress for myself before I face the students.

When grading papers, holding parent conferences, and traveling on overnight school trips threaten to keep me from writing, I remember those nurturing words of Julia Cameron and practice gratitude for my "artful life."

Other loves that provide me with fuel are Latin dancing, gardening and cooking (lately I've been experimenting with Indian and Italian food, and my friends seem very willing guinea pigs), playing with my amazingly smart niece Amy and my adorably happy nephew Nathan, spending time when I can with the horses on my friend Judy's farm, getting onstage to act whenever possible, and traveling. Recent travel highlights include spending the night with a goat under my bed in Ghana, riding horseback through the hills of Sintra in Portugal, and floating on my back in the Mediterranean while looking up at the cliff-cut city of Positano, Italy. I already know I'll return to Italy. My love of the tango may even take me to Brazil. And just mention China, India, or Kenya and I get a certain glint in my eye. . . .

At the Temple des Pythons, Ouida, Benin (West Africa), 2003.

Fuel. It's all fuel. I've never had sympathy for people who claim they are bored.

Oh, another quote on my wall? It's from Tennessee Williams: "I don't believe in dullness. I believe in passion and wonder and excitement." ∽

A Conversation with Katrina Kittle

What inspired you to write Traveling Light?
What led you to write about HIV/AIDS?

I have lost friends to AIDS, and those losses were the seeds of the story. A college friend of mine lost touch after he moved to L.A. to become an actor. I was concerned but didn't pursue it, as I was busy and buried in my first year of full-time teaching. I later learned he had died from AIDS. He was diagnosed shortly after moving to California, and when he told his family, he was telling them that he was gay and sick at the same time. They refused to let him come home, and so he faced his illness in a brand-new place without any support system or close friends. An AIDS service organization helped care for him during his last months. This knowledge horrified me and led me to the AIDS Foundation Miami Valley, which has since been renamed AIDS Resource Center. It was too late for me to do anything for my friend, but I thought if there were others in Dayton like him, I could perhaps do something for them. I wanted to get myself into a Buddy Program, but the good people at AFMV were more interested in the fact that I was an educator. They trained me for their Speaker's Bureau, and I began talking to high school and college groups. Sometimes I led an "AIDS 101" class, and sometimes I led workshops on what it was like to live with chronic illness.

I was teaching high school at the time, and the novel began to take shape out of my desire to put a human face on AIDS for my students.

What challenges did you face in tackling such difficult subject matter?

One challenge was facing the ignorance that exists out there to this day about HIV and AIDS. I know, "ignorance" sounds so harsh, but even very educated people would ask questions such as, "Todd couldn't really get HIV that way, right?" Even the manner in which Todd and Jacob make love came into question

> 66 Sometimes I led an 'AIDS 101' class, and sometimes I led workshops on what it was like to live with chronic illness. 99

with readers ("They can't really do that, right?").
I worked hard to rewrite and revise in a way that
might make fewer readers question these points.
It's always a goal to educate, of course, but you
never want a novel to sound like a lecture or lesson.
Another challenge was the occasional urging from
early readers to "soften" a few of the scenes, but I felt
it was critical not to turn away from the uglier aspects
of this disease.

Traveling Light *is your first novel. How long did it
take to complete? What was the writing process like
for you?*

That's always such a difficult question to answer
because I spend a long time "simmering" a story in
my mind before I ever begin to commit it to paper.
I would say the entire process, from turning on that
initial low flame to the book deal, was just over a
decade.

This was the novel I learned on, so I made quite
a few mistakes along the way. (I still make mistakes,
of course, but I strive to make *new* mistakes with
each novel!) *Traveling Light* actually began as a short
story—the hayloft scene where Summer discovers her
brother is gay. When I shared that story at a writing
conference, half of the readers said the story ended
where it should begin, and the other half said they
wanted to know these people more before they could
care about this event. I took the advice of both "sides"
and started expanding the story in both directions.
It kept growing and I realized that I was working on
a novel. I find it fascinating that the original hayloft
scene ended up right in the middle of the novel.

The writing process was very . . . shall we say,
fraught with U-turns and detours, as I stumbled
along, learning along the way. My very first draft
was a long, self-indulgent, rambling mess, in third-
person, with complete biographies of even the most
minor characters! At the end of that draft, I began
to see the shape of the story, and to make decisions
about whose story it was, but I originally told it from
Todd's point of view. As I immersed myself in all the
AIDS literature I could find—fiction and memoir—
I realized that the gay male perspective had already ▶

> 66 *Traveling
> Light* actually
> began as a short
> story—the
> hayloft scene
> where Summer
> discovers her
> brother is gay. 99

A Conversation with Katrina Kittle
(continued)

been told, and told beautifully and movingly. There was nothing I could add to the heartbreakingly exquisite works that already existed. Then, for a time, I had this absurd idea (but I really believed in it at the time)—no doubt inspired by seeing the NAMES Project AIDS Memorial Quilt—that the story would be told in this "patchwork" of different monologues, all talking about Todd after his death. Ugh. It was awful, and I took one of my strengths—dialogue—away from myself. It didn't work at all, but it was not time wasted. The year I spent on that draft really helped me discover the characters' voices. At long last, I decided to make it Summer's story, and that cracked the story open for me in a whole new way.

How did you eventually decide to write the novel from Summer's point of view?

I realized that what I could offer to fiction was a character who could be a point of entry to an AIDS story for a reader who might find the gay male perspective a barrier. I wanted to create a book that would be accessible to those readers, as well as ones who would be interested in a story that had gay characters and strong gay relationships. That was my goal—to touch both of those audiences. And making it Summer's story also solved some storytelling issues. The outcome of Todd's story is never in doubt—I hope the reader senses that this is not a fantasy where the cure is found and Todd lives to be a ripe old age!—but the outcome of Summer's story is uncertain, giving the plot some much-needed conflict and tension in comparison to my earlier drafts.

Are any of your characters or scenes drawn from real-life individuals or events?

No characters are actually based on real people. Todd is a composite of three different people I knew who died from AIDS—but only portions of those people. For instance, the progression of his illness was based

66 I realized that what I could offer to fiction was a character who could be a point of entry to an AIDS story for a reader who might find the gay male perspective a barrier. 99

on the various experiences I observed in these three people. His grace in facing the end and his forgiveness of Grandma Anna was taken from one of those people. His sending the postcards with the quotes is actually something a wonderful former student of mine did when she traveled across Europe one summer. Writers use everything! I may take one person's name, another's particular quirk or gesture or signature phrase, but I never try to model a fictional character solely on one real person.

My animal characters, on the other hand, are nearly always taken from life. The cat, Cooper, is shamelessly based on my own cat and writing assistant, Montgomery (who passed away in 2004). He had those golden eyes and giant "boxing glove" paws, and he stole the hearts of all who met him. Chaos is based on my own mare, Trilby, who came from the track and who was every bit as fiery and hyper and stunning as Chaos is in the book.

Are any parts of Summer's character autobiographical?

I think we can't help but use parts of our own lives. I don't think of Summer as autobiographical at all, but it is true I filled her life with things I knew well—ballet, teaching, horses. But the actual people and story are completely works of fiction, and even the things that are from my own life are altered. Summer, for instance, got to be a fabulously talented ballerina and I . . . was not. I did study ballet seriously and was wildly in love with it (and still am), but I didn't fit the "body profile" (I'm too tall and far too fond of desserts) . . . not to mention I just wasn't all that good at it! That's the beauty of fiction—you can change those details to your liking! Summer got to be the promising ballerina I never was.

Which scene was the easiest to write? The hardest?

Actually, the scenes that featured Todd's illness were the easiest to write, as I had solid experiences ▶

> " I may take one person's name, another's particular quirk or gesture or signature phrase, but I never try to model a fictional character solely on one real person. "

A Conversation with Katrina Kittle
(continued)

on which to base those descriptions. Something already existed out there in the world for me to latch on to and create a scene around.

The hardest scenes were those involving Grandma Anna and Denny. In early drafts, both of those characters were cardboard, one-dimensional villains. They were the dumping ground for all my own intolerance for those I see as intolerant! Fortunately, some early trusted readers called me on it. I had never before considered what it would take to ask someone like Grandma Anna to change a fundamental belief. I had to increase my own compassion and really consider what this situation was asking of her— here was this grandchild whom she loved, and she sincerely believed he would burn in hell. I learned the most and had to change the most to write her. Those scenes were rewritten more than any others.

Your descriptions of Todd's gradual deterioration suggest a tremendous amount of research. Where did you turn for information about HIV/AIDS?

My training at the AIDS Resource Center also taught me a great deal. To be a part of their Speaker's Bureau required staying up to date on the ever-changing "AIDS 101" facts. Volunteering there—and for a time being employed by them in Case Management Support—I met many clients in various stages of the disease. Knowing them, and learning from their wisdom and different ways of approaching their illness, all helped me with the book.

All of my novels center around social issues, and I always try to immerse myself in the issue before I begin writing. I read everything I can find that remotely relates to the issue—fiction, nonfiction, case studies, memoirs, news articles. Once I had a pretty good base of knowledge, then I felt willing to ask an expert for more help. I'll never be able to thank one expert enough—Dr. Robert Brandt in Dayton was incredibly generous with his time and expertise. A well-known AIDS doctor in the area, he was already familiar to me through my work at the ARC,

> 66 The hardest scenes [to write] were those involving Grandma Anna and Denny. In early drafts, both of those characters were cardboard, one-dimensional villains. They were the dumping ground for all my own intolerance for those I see as intolerant! 99

but I also knew the enormous demands on his time
and his reputation for being a bit of a curmudgeon!
I flagged every page of my manuscript that dealt
with any detail relating to HIV/AIDS, worked up
my courage to approach him, and asked him to read
those sections and check them for accuracy. To my
amazement, Dr. Bob read the entire manuscript and
became a huge supporter. He helped me tweak and
correct some medical details (because Todd's illness
was based on three people I knew, I had inadvertently
piled on poor Todd symptoms and problems that
would rarely all occur in one person!) and also
offered me great objective feedback on the story in
general. I was honored when Dr. Bob attended my
first book signing and am proud to now count him
as a friend.

How can readers learn more about HIV/AIDS?

One way that anyone can help to combat this disease
is to correct misinformation about HIV and AIDS
and to speak up when people don't know the facts
(so it goes without saying, know the facts, right?).
To get the basics, check out www.unaids.org or
www.amfar.org and a fabulous site called
www.thebody.com. A simple Internet search
of "AIDS Facts" will take you to sites devoted
to the worldwide AIDS epidemic, more specific
treatment information, and a host of "what you
can do" suggestions.

AIDS service organizations always need financial
assistance and volunteers. Even if you cannot give
money or supplies, you can probably give your time.
TheBody.com has a great, comprehensive list of
ASOs, divided by state (they also have Canadian
and international listings), so that you can find one
near you.

What advice would you offer to first-time novelists?

To write your book. I don't mean to be flippant, but
there's a great Isaac Asimov quote: "It's the writing ▶

A Conversation with Katrina Kittle
(continued)

that teaches you." Once you have a story actually on paper, you can then begin to edit and revise and learn from it. As long as you're talking about a story as an abstract idea, you've got nothing.

Also, start writing *now*. Don't wait for some ideal day when you're going to have a giant chunk of time fall into your lap. If your life is anything like mine, then that's never going to happen! I wrote the first draft of *Traveling Light* in two-hour slots on Saturdays over the course of two years. It was difficult, and sometimes those two hours were found in the wee, wee hours, but I did it.

Soon, I discovered those two hours a week were not enough, and I became more creative at finding more time. I compare it to being in love. You know when you meet someone new and you're in that breathless, exhilarating, all-consuming stage of a crush? And you will do anything—rearrange schedules, skimp on sleep, overcome impossible logistics—to be with that beloved person? Well, you need to feel that passionate about what you're writing. If you're not (if I'm not, anyway), you shouldn't be writing this particular story.

And if you are writing, and writing regularly, then my advice is to read the great books. Read literature from the past and present and look at how the stories are structured, how the authors use language, how they move through time, how they characterize. I think the very best training for a writer is to read! I highly recommend Francine Prose's wonderful *Reading Like a Writer*. ❧

Have You Read?
More by Katrina Kittle

TWO TRUTHS AND A LIE

Dair Canard has long been a master at weaving
stories out of thin air. A natural actress, she leads a
life that's a minefield of untruths she can never admit
to anyone—especially not to Peyton, her husband of
eight years. But the bizarre death of her best friend
and fellow actor—initially thought a suicide, then
believed to be murder—is forcing Dair to confront
the big lie that led Peyton to fall in love with her in
the first place. Haunted by the terrible events that
are suddenly ripping her life wide open, Dair is
struggling to find answers—taking steps that
could well lead to the destruction of her marriage,
her career . . . even her freedom.

But everyone around her has secrets and
something to hide. Dair's determination to unravel
the decade-old web of her own tightly woven
deceptions is awakening inner demons she has
fought hard to control . . . and revealing that she's
closer to a killer than she ever imagined.

"A chilling, sensitive thriller. . . . Readers will hold
their breath as her tale comes to a suspenseful
conclusion."   —*Publishers Weekly*

"A tale of suspense, lies, and redemption."
                  —*Tacoma News Tribune* (Washington)

"Always surprising. . . . Ms. Kittle follows up *Traveling
Light* with equal aplomb."   —*Cincinnati Enquirer*

"Fiction as it ought to be. . . . A superbly tense and
witty novel that offers a fresh angle on the human
soul. It will leave you craving more from this
deliciously talented writer."
                  —Chris Gilson, author of *Crazy for Cornelia*

THE KINDNESS OF STRANGERS

A young widow raising two boys, Sarah Laden is struggling to keep her family together. But when a shocking revelation rips apart the family of her closest friend, Sarah finds herself welcoming yet another troubled young boy into her already tumultuous life.

Jordan, a quiet, reclusive elementary school classmate of Sarah's son Danny, has survived a terrible ordeal. By agreeing to become Jordan's foster mother, Sarah will be forced to question the things she has long believed. And as the delicate threads that bind their family begin to unravel, all the Ladens will have to face difficult truths about themselves and one another—and discover the power of love necessary to forgive and to heal.

"Katrina Kittle's compulsively readable *The Kindness of Strangers* is a powerful public-service narrative about child abuse and its effects on a family."
—*Chicago Tribune*

Excerpt:
Two Truths and a Lie

DAIR WAS A HABITUAL LIAR. Not pathological or anything, just . . . recreational. As she drove through Cincinnati on her way to Interstate 75, she mulled over the lie she'd tell her husband when she reached the airport. So often the truth needed a little spicing up.

What lie would she tell Peyton today? Traffic crawled on Clifton Avenue, and she cursed, realizing she'd forgotten about the University of Cincinnati's football game. She glanced at her watch; she'd be cutting it close. What could she tell Peyton had made her late?

Dair knew the secret to a good lie was to include as much of the truth as possible. This meant, however, that she had to be sure to remember which part was the truth and which part the lie. Forgetting, or, worse—believing her own lies—was a dangerous line she feared to cross.

Sometimes, though, she lied because the truth was already so amazing that no one believed it. Sometimes the truth needed to be tampered with just so people didn't assume it was a lie.

She checked on the dogs in the rearview mirror. They rode contentedly along in the backseat. The car windows were up, the air-conditioning on, the day unseasonably hot for this late, drought-dry October. Blizzard, their imposing Great Pyrenees, licked Dair's sleeveless shoulder, leaving a string of drool. "Our guy is coming home," she said, reaching back to pet his long white hair. "We gotta share the bed again."

Shodan, their black Doberman, looked out the window and yawned at the Victorian homes passing by, the avenue lined with stately trees and old gas streetlights.

What were the true things she'd actually done today that she could shape into a more interesting story? This morning she'd taught her acting class at the Playhouse in the Park. Then she'd been to the liquor store, but she didn't exactly want to tell Peyton that, because he might ask why she hadn't bought the celebratory champagne at the grocery store. He ▶

> **❝** Dair knew the secret to a good lie was to include as much of the truth as possible. This meant, however, that she had to be sure to remember which part was the truth and which part the lie. **❞**

wouldn't be suspicious, he'd just be curious, and it would make her feel too small to explain to him that she'd also had to buy a bottle of wine to replace the bottle of wine she'd *already* replaced five times since he'd been on tour. Dair worried that the same pink-faced high school boy would be her cashier at the grocery, a boy who'd taken one of her acting classes, who might someday make an innocent reference about her wine purchases in front of Peyton.

Dair drove under I-75 and inched toward the entrance ramp to the notoriously gridlocked highway. Some damn event always snarled up the traffic: a Reds or Bengals game at Riverfront Stadium or some concert at Riverbend . . . Dair wanted to kick herself for not opting to go downtown. In the car ahead of her, some college-age kids passed a beer around. She thought longingly of that replacement bottle of wine.

The bottle was from their party stash—the gifts people brought to gatherings at their house that never got opened before everyone went home. Dair and Peyton kept them in a cupboard with the bread machine they rarely used, and it gave Dair great pleasure every time she drew attention to them, as they left for this cast party or that season opener, announcing, "Hey, there's still wine left from the New Year's party. Let's take a bottle with us." She felt such satisfaction handing Peyton a bottle identical to the bottle that Craig, perhaps, or Marielle had brought to their house. Peyton didn't guess that it was the sixth such bottle that had been there, the original and all its substitutes wrapped in newspaper and tucked into someone else's recycling bin down the street.

So . . . she could tell Peyton she'd been to the grocery store and develop her story from there. What could've happened? An armed robbery? No, too much follow-up. Maybe someone had an epileptic seizure? Hmm . . . that had promise, but why would she have to stay once help arrived? Ooh, the ambulance just happened to park in front of her car. No, something about that scenario wasn't grabbing her. For a lie to work, she had to be committed to it. Could someone have gone into labor in the checkout line?

> ❝ It would make her feel too small to explain to him that she'd also had to buy a bottle of wine to replace the bottle of wine she'd *already* replaced five times since he'd been on tour. ❞

"C'mon," she muttered to a driver studiously ignoring her as she tried to merge. "Let me in, you jerk." He did, and she nosed her red Saturn into the sluggish stream of cars heading south on 75.

Blizzard whined.

"I know, sweetie," she said as traffic came to a complete stop. "What's the deal?" Northbound 75, across a concrete barrier to her left, seemed to be moving without a problem, cars zipping by as if to taunt her. She thought about telling Peyton she'd been stuck in traffic. Ha. Too lame to even utter.

A little girl in the car beside Dair smiled and pointed at Dair's dogs. Maybe . . . maybe Dair's shopping got disrupted by a hysterical mother screaming that her kid was missing. They'd locked the doors to the store, not letting anyone in or out while they searched. She practiced the story, talking aloud: "The mom kept screaming that Katie was a little blond girl. 'She's in a pink dress!' she kept saying. 'She has ponytails.' So, I'm helping look around; none of us know what to do, really, and I step into the corner by the wine racks. You know how it's kinda dark back there? Well, back there, I see a cloth on the ground. I pick it up and it's a dress, and as I lift it all this long blond hair falls to the floor. I run out into an aisle to tell someone, and the first thing I see is this woman with a stroller, and in the stroller is a little blond boy, sleeping, and he's got a buzz-cut, and he's wearing overalls, and I know it's the little girl; it's Katie."

Dair jumped when Blizzard growled behind her head, a sound that never failed to tighten a fist around her heart, even though it wasn't directed at her.

"Hey, hey, what's the matter?" she asked. She put the car in park and twisted around to face him. Shodan growled, too, baring her teeth, her sweet Doberman's face transforming into a werewolf's— lips curled back, ears pinned flat, eyes hard and hateful. Both dogs stood, hackles raised, staring out the side window. Dair turned in time to see a woman in a purple dress burst out of the trees flanking the northbound side of the highway. Dair blinked. ▶

Had the woman come down from the hill from the fancy homes on Clifton Ridge above the highway? The homes, obscured all summer, were now visible through the autumn-thin foliage.

The woman waved her arms at the northbound traffic and stepped out onto the interstate. Dair cringed as cars honked and tires squealed, and a minivan swerved around the woman, almost sideswiping another car. The minivan slowed, but when the woman ran to it and pounded on the window, it peeled away.

Did the woman need help? Or was she drunk? She wore no shoes and weaved in a weak-kneed sort of way toward the concrete divider and the already stopped southbound traffic.

Blizzard and Shodan barked—predatory, savage sounds that dropped ice down Dair's spine. Dair hit the automatic lock as the woman climbed the divider and stumbled between the lanes of cars, yanking on door handles. Dair could see only the woman's torso as the woman came close to the Saturn. The woman's head came into view as she drew back from the snarling dogs hurling themselves against the window, but Dair didn't see her face—the woman looked away, across the highway from where she'd come, her shoulder-length black hair obscuring her profile.

Some northbound traffic had pulled over, and other people crossed the interstate toward the woman. Some got out of cars on the southbound side, too, holding cell phones to their ears. The woman scrambled across the hood of Dair's car. Dair glimpsed hairy legs, bare feet, broad hands with fine black hair on the knuckles. As the woman ran to the guardrail to the right of Dair, Dair saw that the purple dress wasn't zipped up all the way, didn't meet or fit across the back.

That was a man. A man in a dress.

And Dair recognized the dress. She'd worn that dress. ❧

> **"** Dair hit the automatic lock as the woman climbed the divider and stumbled between the lanes of cars, yanking on door handles. **"**

Don't miss the next book by your favorite author. Sign up now for AuthorTracker by visiting www.AuthorTracker.com.